Diamond
Sutra

Diamond Sutra

Colin Hester

COUNTERPOINT WASHINGTON, D.C.

LIBRARY OF CONGRESS CATALOGING-IN-PUBLICATION DATA
Hester, Colin, 1951–
     Diamond sutra / Colin Hester.
     I. Title.
PS3558.E79789D53   1997
813'.54—dc21   96-53360
     ISBN 1-887178-33-3 (clothbound) (alk. paper)

FIRST PRINTING

Printed in the United States of America on acid-free paper that meets the American National Standards Institute Z39-48 Standard

Book design by David Bullen
Typesetting by Wilsted & Taylor

COUNTERPOINT
P.O. Box 65793
Washington, D.C. 20035-5793

Distributed by Publishers Group West

Because it is hard and sharp

cutting off all conceptions

leading to the other shore

prologue

London

He read:

Dear Friend,
The urn you have purchased has been hewn and crafted from the *Fraxinus americana,* the legendary white ash of the Appalachians. The urn's base, also of white ash, is fastened to the hood by four hidden solid-brass screws and can be removed with ease. When filling the urn yourself, remove the base and tenderly transfer the cremated remains from whatever temporary container your crematorium has supplied *without breaking the enclosing sealed plastic bag.* Then refasten the base and hood.

Because of its solid ash construction and additional weight when it is occupied (imagine a large-sized coffee can filled with sand), the urn is best placed on a fixed level surface that can bear its load.

Straight-grained and both strong and resilient, its wood has been darkened slightly in finishing. It requires no care, other than that which you bestow on your beloved.

Bardsman Woodworks & Co.
Ellicottville, NY

◇

He folded and slid the letter underneath the thick autopsy report beside the urn. The urn was on the desk in front of him – he was standing – and the autopsy report was sheathed in the same white number ten envelope, opened across its cuff and soiled by time, in which it had arrived. A ceramic lamp sat on the desk and the white lamplight fell in a drift of illumination not only across urn and envelope but across some other letters and across two postcards. After a moment's hesitation he picked up one of the cards. On it, a vast sea brimmed beneath a gray sky. No land, no liners, no tankers or trawlers. Only the swollen sky and the sea green as concrete beneath. He set it face down atop the urn and picked up the other card. This had come with the room, a watercolor of the stone hotel itself. Blue wind bristled the hoteltop Union Jacks and tilted the clouds so they leaned like white pyramids at quintain. Down in front, Marble Arch stood square-shouldered, its iron gate closed. Soapbox preachers harangued in Hyde Park across the street and red double-decker buses and taxis as tall as top hats streamed past the arch and the glimmering trees. Though large, this hotel postcard was not large enough to contain all he had to say. But it would do for a beginning. As for the one of the concrete sea, it was blank but used, what with its stamp and round cancellation imprint that read, Whitefish, Montana. Had spring risen by now into those mountains? Like the tide when you slide in the tub? He checked his shirt pocket for his fountain pen, set the hotel card with the other on the urn's top and with two hands carried the urn and the autopsy report across the room. Past the beds. Past the dresser. Before he flicked on the bathroom light he hesitated. He turned to look back to the window. The curtains were drawn. He had neglected to look outside to foretell from the departing sky tomorrow's weather: the sheet of lamplight falling on the curtains and desk now bare of the urn, a white topography, hiding and revealing like snow on the moon.

home

They sat calling their sons' names, sat crammed in congregations with their cigarette smoke and beverage steam rolling up from their cupped hands, smoke and steam and their sons' names calling and echoing and calling until the tiny arena rang like a burning church. They were from both sides of the Falls, these mothers and fathers, and the sons whose names they called skated headlong into each other on the rink below, deaf to the calling, blind to their peril. Boards enclosed the rink as high as the players' ten-year-old heads and twin team benches lined one side behind. At the far end of one bench a boy not dressed as a player sat minding the gate. He was nine and despite earmuffs and his father's hooded parka he was shivering. His name was Rudyard – Rud – and he let the gatelatch fall shut to turn and watch his father pace behind the bench, then bend and urge along a blond-haired boy named Troy. A woman leapt from her first-row seat when Troy stood and she cheered and whistled loud as a sailor.

–Go son! she yelled. Kill em!

Rud's father glanced back once at Troy's mother, then again longer. She didn't sit down and in the steaming light her earrings shone, her

eyes shimmered. Her hair was as red as her plump lipstick and she
looked right into Rud's father's eyes. She puffed on her cigarette and
clapped with fully extended arms. Knitted geese adorned her black
sweaterfront and when she took and held a deep lungful of smoke, they
seemed to erupt into flight. The boys on the bench were all hollering
now and stamping their sticks and Troy's mother exhaled and waved her
arms madly, pointing first at Rud's father, then at Rud. His father's eyes
followed her finger.

–The gate! his father bellowed at him. Lad! The gate! Open the bleeding gate!

Rud turned. Troy leered down at him. Troy's skateblade flashed,
kicked up the latch. The gate sprang open. In and out the players
poured. Their skates threw chilling roostertails on Rud, showering him.
The gate slammed shut and the puck bounded past, sliding black and
molten, rolling down the ice. The players chased after it. They clacked
their stickblades. Troy, his blond flag of hair at mast, flattened an oppo-
nent, stole the puck. The stands roared. Troy's mother bounced up and
down.

–All right! she shrieked. Go son!

Troy jitterstepped through the other team. Players collapsed, twirling, strewn across the ice. Troy's mother in her excitement now stood by
the team bench, right beside Rud's father. Troy deked the last de-
fenseman, blistered a shot, scored, and, his stick raised, carved on the
ice a wide circle of exaltation.

The arena rumbled as if it were sliding downhill. Troy's mother
hooted and whistled. Rud's father covered his ears with his gloves and
laughed and she laughed and whistled louder. Rud gaped and a triangle
clanged in the stands and the clear stones on her fingers when she play-
fully shoved his father's chest glittered silent as tiny bells. That was Amherst, New York. Winter 1960. The place Rud's mother died. The season
his father fell in love.

$\Diamond$

She died during the Christmas holidays that year. During a winter storm Russian and malicious. They were out in it – Rud, his mother, and his sister – because his father and mother had rowed horribly. Rud no longer minded the gate at his father's games but on the night of the storm something made him ask to go. When his father said no, the row began.

–I'm not blind, his mother snapped.

His father lay on the bed smoking between mouthfuls of beer.

–I'm not stupid, she added.

–Wha' are you then?

The crack! of his mother slapping his father's face stung the air. Rud and his sister started sobbing. Their mother raised her hand to slap again.

–You do, I'll throw you down those bloody stairs!

Then they three were out in it, bundled hurriedly and impotently against the whittling storm. No buses came. They fought their way across Amherst on foot to a basement apartment where a woman waited in the doorway. The woman hugged them. There they slept. When Rud awoke the storm had left a thick white evenness. But his mother was gone.

The people who came a few days later to their walk-up apartment smelled like a hospital. Some cried and left and some stayed long after the buses stopped running and slept on the livingroom floor. They made the rooms seem as small as appliance crates. Rud's ear was still numb from frostbite and he heard the word *croup* a lot. Turned out of his pull-out cot he was forced to sleep with his sister Bev. She was a year and a half older and only agreed if they slept head to toe like a pair of broken scissors. In the middle of the night the woman from the arena – Troy's mother – came and stood in the hallway with their father. Rud's sister kicked Rud's shoulder until he woke up. The woman left after a few wordless minutes but Rud somehow recognized her. The others that had left returned the next day, in suits and rustling dresses and they stood tall and without much movement. His father drank his beer from a glass. His father's twin sisters arrived and made tea. Cath was a war bride out in Elyria, Ohio, and Iris a war bride up in Toronto. Iris was the last to leave and by the puddle of galosh slush she hugged Bev, hugged Rud. Iris said:

—Wishes he were goin with you, your daddy does.

—Liar, Bev mumbled.

At the Buffalo airport a day later his father, suit and tie under his unbuttoned macintosh, dropped to one knee and embraced his daughter and his son together until Rud gasped for breath. His father's eyes were wet and his breath smelled like leaves you picked up off the ground. He said:

—Daddy has to stay.

—Why?

—You know why, lad, to work. So we have a place to live when you get back, a proper place.

—We're not *coming* back, Bev said.

—Don't say that, love.

—We're not.

—Course you are.

—Never!

She shoved their father so hard he let go to brace his fall. The stewardess snatched at her as she ran through the gate, but missed. His father stood and wiped his eyes and for a long time stared after her. Tight-rolled comics stuck up out of his mac pocket. He knelt and brushed Rud's bangs off his forehead and kissed him and the rolled comics leaned in his pocket like the handle of a sword.

The comics were *Pogo* and *Henry* and tired Rud quickly. Their plane was a turboprop Vanguard and in gunmetal arcs it leapt across the dark top of the world. It stopped in Goose Bay and Iceland and Edinburgh and in Heathrow his mother's coffin was hearsed across London to Saint Mary's Anglican Cathedral where two days later his grandparents buried their daughter. Rud's grandfather had bought him a gray flannel school blazer, kneesocks and shorts and a cap with a round bill barely big enough to grasp. His grandmother squeezed Bev's and his hands. Above him rain curtained down off the grown-ups' umbrellas and greened the grave's fresh spade marks.

—Let's get on with it, his grandfather said hoarsely.

His grandmother's face when Rud looked up swam imprisoned behind her gray veil.

—My pretty ones, my pretty ones, she said.

They sent him when school resumed to live with his other grandparents, the Gillettes, forty-odd miles up the Thames in Reading. Bev they sent to boarding school somewhere in Somerset. His train was maroon red and rain fell on its slate-colored roof. He sat opposite a Royal Navy officer who had a silver roll-your-own cigarette case. At Clapham Junction a man in a bowler hat boarded from one of the platforms arrayed across the landscape like spavined piano keys. He wore a black eye with the aplomb of a monocle and he wrote in a leather-bound diary. Rain splattered the compartment window as the train started up again and council houses and factories with chimneystacks as gray as elephant trunks grazed slowly past.

—Off to school? the naval officer asked.

Rud nodded.

—Miss your mates already?

He nodded again.

—These'll do you then.

The officer uncrossed his knees and leaned sideways and worked from his jacket vent pocket a white paper bag. He underhanded it across the aisle. Rud caught it two-handed.

—Sweets. Licorice All-sorts. Go on, open them.

–I can't.

–Go on, pour them out.

Rud shook his head.

–I should expect he's forbidden, the bowler-hatted man said.

–Here, I'm captain on board this ship, thank you.

–This is a train and you're a petty officer.

The whistle blew. The train shot under a tunnel of bridges. Flashed past a lengthless station.

–Don't mind his nob, the naval officer told Rud. Go on – do you a world of good.

–They're not poisoned?

–Only some. But I'll tell you which'ns is.

Rud tilted the bag open and the train's swift waddle jiggled the licorice bits into his lap. He pointed at a lemon square.

–Poisoned, the officer said. Surely.

Rud ate it. Cor – blimmin sour, but sugary. He smiled again. The naval officer smiled back.

–You American then?

–Don't know.

–Reckon you're English again then?

–A bit.

–Couldn't count the mates I've lost, he said.

The naval officer was silent and Rud listened to the train's running and to the rain drumming on the roof. It fell as heavy as it must have before they'd emigrated, but the rain of earth and stones on his mother's coffin was a heavier.

Perhaps they'd been Tudor minstrels and grooms these Gillettes, or centuries later buccaneers' pipers and press-gang 'seers. The paltry geneal-

ogy divulged to Rud those first months by his father's remaining
brothers and sisters went back only to Rud's great-grandfather, Thom,
and did not include their kin scattered across the world. For instead of
families Gillette men and women spawned something more like small
villages. Gillette bedrooms were barracks choked with siblings. Thus at
first opportunity their sons cleared off for Auckland, New Zealand, and
Portland, Oregon, and for odd places like Wollaston in the Drake Passage and Zurich. The arms of local cabmen and lance corporals on leave
were the nearer-flung destinies of the daughters. As for Thom, the
great-grandfather, his destiny had been the merchant marine. Autumn
of the last year of the nineteenth century Thom fell in love in Lisbon
with a woman with waist-length hair as thick as ore who sold locks of it
to the local Umbanda priestess for philter. First year of the twentieth
century she bought their passage for Ellis Island and Thom bought the
downpayment for a small printing shop in Niagara Falls, New York.
That part of the world because of something he'd read in a book a bosun
had cast away: to hear Niagara's water churn and boil itself white as the
sun then roar down over the cataract. To hear it crystallize and freeze
while you stood under the dawn stars, then crack and explode minutes
or months later like massive slabs of solid sky. The death of water, the
smoky blood of your baby's birth. But in Albany she left him, the
bloody tramp, for God knows who or where and Thom returned to England with their son. To Newbury. He never remarried but his son did.
And Thom's own son had a son and that lad was Rud's father. Each week
Rud's father would bicycle Sunday dinner – the roast carved thin as
pages of a prayer book – to old Thom's hotel room while his own dinner
dried on the stovetop. The old man, Uncle Thom to even his own
grandchildren, staggered one Sunday night after the Three Crowns'
closing into the Kennet River. He drowned. While in the Royal Navy at
the close of WWII Rud's father's turn came and he fell in love with a
WAAF and when Bev and Rud were eight and seven they all tried to

complete old Uncle Thom's trek but made it only as far as Amherst where Rud's father cleaned toilets in U. of Buffalo dorms and at a hockey game fell in love again and the WAAF died.

Came May and a trip from Reading to Nan and Granddad Stirling's in Harrow. Waiting for him was a floppy-ended envelope from his father and his own turn to fall in love. Few in all of England were the ten-year-olds who did and fewer those who did with Mickey Mantle. Rare too, it was a love that would last – as those rare loves that do last – because it could reside in various parts of the body: the brain when he read the back of Mantle's baseball card, the space in his throat when he imagined Mantle vaulting into the emerald shade of Yankee Stadium to backhand a line drive, and, when he returned to his father in Amherst and watched Mantle succumb to injury and lose the '61 home run race to Roger Maris, the smallest part of all, the heart.

He fell in love again the summer he was twelve and a half. Because she was a girl it never occurred to him Mantle might mind. Her name was Caroline and she was his stepsister. His father had remarried – the woman from the arena – and for reasons Rud could only guess at, Memorial Day weekend they U-Hauled up to Toronto, migrating to a brick bungalow in the eastward suburbs. Caroline was two years older than he and two hands taller. In the backseat of his father's baking Plymouth Fury she sat glacially beside him until they arrived. The moment the towels were unpacked she showered. The next morning she showered again. She lined her slippers with kleenex and later in the day hand-washed her own underwear. That night the sun wouldn't set and after yet another shower she flashed by his room like a ghost on fire. The hedge that perimetered their backyard had blossomed and the petals were raining white onto the grass and the white scent drifted through his open window and mixed with hers. That was late May 1963. In June the Buddhist priest Thich Quang Duc sat on a street in Saigon and burned himself alive. Early July Rud read in his stepmother's *Time* how the old priest's heart had supposedly not burned with the rest of his flesh and through July and August this miracle and the image of the priest sitting quiet and aflame in the street stayed in Rud's mind the way the sun stayed in the summer sky.

Summer's end, midmorning of Labor Day to be exact, Rud sat on a streetcurb in shorts, T-shirt, Yankee cap, his baseball glove tucked under his ass. A haze clung to the world where the other kids, in sweat-matted hockey sweaters, hockey gloves, and jeans, hammered up and down the asphalt, slashing at each other like battling urchins locked in a mirage. Road hockey! Shit – that's all they played it seemed. No matter the month, no matter the weather. Even today with the sun climbing and the air at a standstill. Noon neared. A horizon of air conditioners hummed in Rud's ears. Beneath the prickly sky the game roiled on, until it ended as summer road hockey games always end, both gradually and all at once, like ice cubes cast on the hood of a hot black car. Eventually Rud too wandered home, halted at the screen door by shouts from inside.

–It's the heat, his father said.

–The heat didn't get drunk, the heat didn't lose the envelope, his stepmother shot back.

–It was stolen, bloody stolen, I tell you.

–By the heat?

–Good christ, his father muttered. People down south, no wonder.

–No wonder what?

–Nothing.

–No wonder what? Well?

–No wonder they kill each other, his father shouted.

–Each other? his stepmother shouted back. Each other? You're saving *me* the goddamned trouble!

It was too hot to eat anyrate and a measly half-day of summer holiday remained. He walked to the north park of the two narrow parkettes. That was deserted, so he cut through to the south one. The sky and the grass were near white with the sun, and whiter was the far row of new apartment buildings. Maple trees separated the park from the apartments and shade trickled down from their trunks, spreading like dark water. A dozen or so boys lounged in this coolness. Rud knew some of the boys, one in particular, Troy Coltrane, estranged son of Rud's stepmother. The boy lived alone with his own father and so far had never menaced Rud. Rud went over.

–H'llo.

No one answered. Booger Lashman, a high school boy, a goon, looked up.

–Hey, Troy, it's your stepbrother.

Troy rolled onto his stomach, smoothed his blond hair. He plucked a burnt grassblade.

–Hey, Coltrane! Booger snickered.

–Don't be an asshole, Booger's younger brother said.

–Want yours widened?

–Just don't.

–Why? Booger made a fist, thrust his thick body forward onto his knees. Why don't?

–Just don't.

–Suckboy, Booger said.

–Hey, the youngest Lashman brother, breaking through, called to Rud. Decent hat.

–A bit, Rud said.

–A bit, Booger mimicked. And what's it say: N, Y, ny? Ny? What the fuck's ny?

—Says New York, Troy, still on his belly, announced.

—Brotherly love, Booger taunted.

—That's Philadelphia, Rud said, a tremor in his voice.

Booger raised his fist.

—Say that again, he dared.

Rud stared at the parched earth in front of his feet.

—Lay off, Boog, Cort said to his brother.

—Brotherly love, Booger repeated, even louder. Still on his knees he made a sexual motion with his hips. He got no response. Not from Rud, who knew he'd gone far enough. Nor from Troy, who lay still as an assassin. Booger huffed back against the tree trunk.

—S'that why you talk all fucked up? Booger needled Rud. Cause you're from ny?

—He's a fuckin limey, Troy called out.

—I asked *him,* bonelick.

—Quiet! Troy hissed. It's coming.

Troy scrabbled behind a tree trunk.

—What is? Rud asked.

—Finally, Cort Lashman said.

He and the others plastered their bodies into the trees. They all crouched, slithering down the bark; gosling-necked, they reconnoitered. Rud, though, hadn't moved. He worked his baseball in his glove's oiled pocket.

—What's coming? he asked again.

Through the trees the apartment's sticky parking lot was empty. Nothing moved. Beyond, cars cruised by like touring clouds. One of the boys whistled, long and low and slow.

—Wow! Cort Lashman said.

—What d'I tell you, Troy said. Truly? Huh?

—Truly, Cort Lashman said. He fished in his trouser pocket, drew out a quarter, handed it to Troy.

—Now the rest of you, Troy said. And you.

—Me? Rud asked. He raised his eyes, flashed them over the apartment roof. For what?

—That, Troy whispered, pointing.

On the closest second-floor balcony a girl their own age leaned over the railing, book in hand.

—A d-r-fucking-eam, Troy said.

One at a time the boys handed over their quarters. Bright sunlight sliced diagonally across the building and the girl stood on the glare's edge. Rud squinted, shielded his eyes. She moved back into the shadow. There. She wore a blue and white bikini, and as she moved, her shoulders curved under long, softly blond hair. She shook her head and her hair lifted and before it touched her shoulders it revealed her face. She turned their way. *Quiet!* the boys hissed at each other. And her eyes — they were large and a blue green, like when you snapped a spring branch and the bark came away slightly. Rud didn't move. Her lips were a gentle pink and slightly pouted. She chewed gum, granted, but at least she hadn't blown a bubble. She backhanded her hair off her shoulders again and she turned and he could see her bikini profile to her waist.

—That's a dream? Booger snickered.

—Pay up, Troy said.

—She's

—Don't, Troy warned.

—a dream all right, Booger continued.

Troy took his eyes off the girl. So did Rud.

—A fucking carpenter's dream, Booger said, grinning.

—Just gimme the fuckin quarter, Troy said. He stood.

—Flat as a board and

Troy lunged. He crashed into Booger in full flight, fusing their bodies. They rolled over once, twice. Dirt spumed up and the other boys whooped. Booger's size engulfed the smaller Troy and Booger's brothers held each other back. The fighters rolled again and Troy surfaced with his arm locked around Booger's head, his legs scissored across Booger's thighs.

–Take it back, Troy commanded.

–Flat as a

Booger's words were choked off.

–I'll snap your fat fucking neck! Troy seethed.

Rud believed him. Booger's brothers did also. They searched their brother's face for a sign to jump in. None came and they yelled, *Pile on! Pile on!* and dove and the other boys dove on, a fourletter swirl of T-shirts, dirt, and grunts. Only Rud turned back to the girl, to the balcony.

A uniformed man held her by her upper arms. Open-necked, his uniform was a deep blue. The girl set her book on her head like a cap and he took her hands in his and together they spun, slowly, full circle. She became the shade and he breached the brightness at the balcony's edge. He let her go and he turned and stood gripping the balcony railing. He yawned and stretched as if he'd just gotten out of bed and he gazed out over the green trees riffling in the brightness. His cheeks were crimson and the buttons sashing down his shirtfront and across his chest now fired by the sun were so black they were silver.

Rud sat the next morning, the first day of school, in the truncated corridor outside the Principal's office waiting to be assigned to one of the two eighth-grade teachers. Early daylight illuminated the bare wall opposite and he made fingernail furrows in the thighs of his corduroys. Another new boy sat beside him. The boy had clusters of pimples on his cadbury-colored skin and a crew cut as planed and rigid as a tabletop.

Their eyes touched and deflected. The office door opened. The Principal emerged, ducking and frowning and perspiring from his brows to the back of his bald head.

–Gentlemen, he said. Your parents really should have registered you during the weeks previous. We are, as it is, to the limit.

Down the hallway perpendicular, a class filed by. Girls first. Crossing from shadow through the silver trunk of daylight then back into shadow again. Ponytails and pageboys, eyes riveted, skirts swinging. She – the girl on the balcony – was among them. Came the stabbing elbow throwers and pocket-billiard artists, the line of boys. Troy led, his eyes everywhere but meeting Rud's.

–Mr Kito's class, the Principal said.

Rud stood.

–Sit down, young man, the Principal ordered. Such eagerness. A sure sign of stealth, of certain mischief. You will go to Mr Allan's.

◇

Her name was Gale Harmon and Rud managed to glimpse her in library or at recess or on the way back from lunch. The only day he missed her was the Monday after President Kennedy was shot. She was absent but back to school the next day. She wore a black armband and the darkness about her eyes faded quickly after Kennedy's burial, though the armband remained until Christmas holidays. The first day of school after Christmas the mourning band was gone: Rud's class was going in to the library; hers, Mr Kito's, was coming out. A doorshape of light swirled up from the hall floor. She was last in the girls' line, Troy first in the boys'. She'd checked out *Cue for Treason* and she wore a white skirt and a baby-blue cotton sweater that turned her eyes newborn blue. She wore the same white skirt only with a light green sweater on Saint Patrick's Day in March and her eyes turned the color of spring grass. An early morning blizzard a few days later crawled through the city. It closed

Rud's school. He spent most of that morning at the bathroom mirror, combing his hair, changing sweaters, shirts, trying in vain to change the slate color of his own eyes.

$$\diamondsuit$$

Only two boys remained after school so, with its pools of brittle slush left after the janitors shoveled the snow up against the school wall, the playground resembled some desolate tar-and-macadam tundra. That morning Rud had rushed the baseball season and worn running shoes he'd soaked at recess and changed at lunch. Now he wore Wellington boots and a short leather coat his father called a jerkin and a single glove, his left, under his baseball glove. Pivoting and rearing he fired his baseball so that it tailed up high and white into the March sky. The wind caught the ball, blowing it toward the school and Rud skipped sideways through the slush, tracking it through his glove's webbing. Skeddy – short for Skeddington – the boy with the pimples and tabletop crew cut, trailed after him.

–My old lady says they come from broken homes, Skeddy said.

–Who?

–The Beatles.

–Why'd she say that?

–She says if I wore my hair like you she'd get the old man to whale my ass.

The ball landed in Rud's glove with a soft thupp.

–I just washed it, Rud said. There was no Brylcreem.

–'Ats a sack a shit. A sack a – jesus, there they blows.

Around the far corner of the school walked Gale and her best friend, Jennifer Budd. Troy was with them.

–Fuck, man, Skeddy said. That Budd has the buds.

Troy said something to Gale and she nodded. He punched his fists in his windbreaker pockets and the two girls stood talking as he walked toward Rud and Skeddy. Soft as a kiss Gale's pink cashmere beret was set above her blue-green eyes, the only touches of color in a gray world.

—Hey, Skedd, Troy called out.

He stopped. Rud coiled and fired again his ball skyward.

—Look how she never wears her fuckin coat done up, Skeddy groaned. Ooo, her tubes just stickin right out.

—She's all yours, Rud said. His ball peaked.

—Then lend me your glove.

—Why?

—More'n a handful's wasted.

The ball curved down. Rud dodged a slush puddle. He twisted at the waist, his glove open behind his back.

—Skedd, Troy called again, louder. For fuck's sake.

—I'm busy.

—We got hockey practice.

—Told ya, I'm busy, watchin.

The ball flashed white behind Rud's back. He held his glove open, felt the snap of impact, the yield of his wrist. There was soft, woolen applause. Rud looked over. Gale was smiling his way and clapping her pink mittens.

—Quit screwin off, Troy told Skeddy.

—I'm not, yet. I'm gettin a fingernail tattoo.

—You're getting shit.

—Says, *Jennifer's,* on my dick.

Rud pivoted and hurled the ball once more, the wind buffeting it like a tiny cloud closer to the roof's edge.

—You missed last week.

—Rud'll cover for me, Skeddy answered loudly. With his old man.

—You're a stroke-off.

—I know.

—A fucking stroke-off, Troy repeated.

Rud's ball had curved up in a long feather, but it fell like a Stone Age axe. Cold air moved past his ears, and his boots penetrated the shoveled snow by the school wall. The wall here was windowless and he reached out and touched the brick. His ball winged down. He stretched and leaped. The bricks raked the back of his glove hand, but – there! – he had it, and he bounced off the wall, landing on one foot. He slipped, then tumbled back-first into the snow. The ball dribbled out of his webbing. He was up at once though, plucking it up, wringing its hide dry. He heard Gale's soft applause.

–Nice try, she called over. She clapped her hands in the throw-it-here style.

–You've no glove, he said.

–That's okay.

–It's a real one.

–It's a real one, she mimicked, smiling.

She clapped her hands again. Rud moved closer to her. Troy suddenly loomed between. Rud wristed the ball softly, floating it over Troy's head. Gale caught it with two hands. Troy turned to her.

–Monkey in the middle, Skeddy called.

–Don't, Troy said to Gale.

She fired the ball right at Troy's head. He flinched and it whistled by his ear and landed in Rud's glove.

–Hey, Jennifers, Skeddy said. I'm gettin' a tattoo.

Troy charged Rud. Rud shied, and Troy snatched the ball from Rud's glove, bounding sideways. Both boys breathed in lungfuls.

–Give it back, Rud said.

Troy toyed with it, tossing and catching it one-handed.

–Make me.

–Leave him alone, Troy, Gale said.

–Yeah, Skeddy said.

–Butt out, stroke-off.

–Troy!

–Give it! Rud said.

–Make me, I said.

–What about hockey practice? Skeddy said.

–Practice, Gale said. Remember?

–You're lucky, Troy snorted at Rud.

–Just give it.

–Lucky this ain't *your* National fucking Sport.

Holding Rud's ball like a slick fossilized turd, Troy spun and drilled it over the school, and Gale shouted, *No!* and with a metal thwang the ball ricocheted off the flashing, rose in a high loop, then landed on the roof.

–That was miserable, Gale cried. Miserable!

A rage filled Rud – not as though his evil twin had stepped inside him but as though his real self had taken a step away. He wanted to claw open Troy's ribs, the miserable prick, tear out his heart and hurl *it* up on to the roof. The intensity of this rage terrified him and he turned, fleeing from it. Across the schoolyard he raced, slush flying, Troy on his heels. He leapt at the corner drainpipe as though trying to run right up the wall and the pipe was of institutional-grade clay and didn't buckle and he shinnied once and grasped where the pipe boned away from the wall. He swung free, the pipe creaked, and Troy grabbed his ankle. Rud kicked out. His boot sailed off, up on to the roof, and he snagged with his ankle the roof edge above him.

Up he hauled himself, rolling like a high jumper. When he stood, his bootless foot plunged into ice water. He heard Troy climbing, the drainpipe creaking. His boot stood nearby and he thrust in his wet foot. His ball lay by the far flashing and he half-hopped across the frozen roof, Troy pounding behind. His breath was aflame and the tv antennas bobbed in the sky like masts in a harbor and he slid, stooping, touching his baseball with a fingertip before Troy crashed into his legs and knocked him over the edge.

He fell backward to earth like a toppled crucifixion. The gray sky swooped up from behind his head with such alarm he shut his eyes and he heard himself land with a whump! before he felt it. He felt it then, no

more shocking actually than a very firm mattress, a deep wave or vibration passing through his ribs, his organs. Once through him, it passed
out of him, as quickly as – the simple assume – life passes from the
newly dead. He was still. His back was cold and he kept his eyes closed.
Sluggish runoff dripped through a nearby sewer grating with a trickle.
He moved his arms, his legs. His clothing made a rustle in the crystal-
line snow.

He waited for as long as he could bear the wet cold for her to come.
Finally he pushed himself up. He sat, stood, in his soaked boot on his
heel only. A solitary light burned in the long school building. The Principal's. He'd fallen right past his window. That was probably against the
rules and he drove himself through the waist-high cedar hedge onto the
sidewalk that ran parallel to the school front. A pebble tinked metal
above and he swept his eyes down the length of roofline. Gone. He hob-
bled up the sidewalk. Turned through the empty parking lot between
the end of the school and the woods. A general ache gripped his body
now, as pervasive as sadness. He hoped to at least salvage his glove. It too
was gone.

$$\Diamond$$

Pounding in his ears like a galley at ramming speed, the filling bathtub
drummed and foamed. Steam somersaulted through the narrow bathroom and Rud squeegeed the medicine cabinet mirror with his palm,
leaving on the glass a swath of water stitches. He twisted, examining
over his left shoulder the mirrored flesh-and-bone cage of his back.
That his fall had not altered his young being physically led him to sus-
pect it had not altered him at all. A suspicion that nagged at him until a
knocking on the bathroom door penetrated the drumming water, his
groping thoughts.

–Avez un nager?

It was his stepsister.

–Huh?

–Quelle année finishez-vous?

–Just a minute.

He bent and shut off the drumming taps. He hooked a towel around his loins. Tiptoed to the bathroom door.

–Caroline?

–Oui.

Outside, the front storm door shuddered open. They listened for the knock.

–If it's Skeddy, he whispered, I'm

–Alors.

The main door opened.

–Oh shit, his stepsister cried softly. Mom! Quick!

His stepmother pattered out from the kitchen as his stepsister fled.

–Caroli – Good god, not again, his stepmother cried. Look at you. Drunk! Look at you!

–He zhoots

It was Dad. Jesus. Rud backed slowly away from the bathroom door, brushing his shoulder along the wall. He squeezed shut his eyes but that didn't vanquish the voices.

–What are you covered with?

–Lipstick.

–Mud?

–The players' mothers.

–Covered! You're

–Got keep'm happy.

–Quiet, Erik, please. You fell?

–Players' mothers.

–Shut up.

–Like you.

–Shut up, you rotten – Shut up!

–Here, help get, get this off.

–Do it yourself.

–Can't. Who'll – ? Rud, Rud'll help me. Rud!

–He's in the bath.

–Rud?

–He's in the bath, I tell you.

–Lad! Help me get

–Leave him alone!

–S'my son, mine!

–Why you

He heard his father thump against the front door.

–Oh you'd like me to, slap you wouldn't you. Wouldn't you? his step-mother said. Well I won't. I won't.

She sobbed quietly. The soft rip of a seam tearing.

–Washer, his father mumbled. I'll

Unable to stand it any longer Rud cranked hard the faucet cocks. The water burst out in a battering glassy column, exploding into crystal froth. In the silence of this din he said a prayer for his father's protection. Not to God exactly but to whatever portion of his father's self could still endure the self-destructive part. His guardian angel perhaps. The bathtub filled and he climbed in.

He lay in the steaming water for a long time. He felt again and again the arising earth thumping up at his falling back. He arched his spine and his genitals floated and lolled like a drowned puppet. He noted the darkening hair above, a single eyebrow. He winked back and twisted onto his stomach. He hated soaking to where his fingertips pruned and pleated and he flipped over onto his back and wound the plugchain around his right big toe and pulled. The water glugged and he toweled off and wrapped the towel around himself again. He balled up his dank and dirty clothes and dispatched them down the laundry chute under the bathroom sink. They landed with a soft puff in the basket, blooming apart. He saw framed by the square opening of the chutebottom the right half of his father's body. Dad was sitting on the basement floor, his back propped up against the white enameled front of the clothes dryer.

–Piss and jesus, Rud said under his breath.

His father's black forelock lashing forward when the head slumped then stiffened. The sleeves of his white dress shirt rolled to the soapthin elbows. On the floor beside his right hand was a small array of white cigarette butts, stabbed out, almost orderly, as if staking out the passage of time. A castaway, a lone survivor of some suburban equivalent of a shipwreck. Rud shut the trapdoor carefully, quietly. Kneeling, he held it shut for some time. Should he take a second look? He shifted his knee. His back ached a bit now and he stood. Tired, whatever, Dad was okay. Sleeping peacefully – yeah, sure. Now in the mirror Rud brushed back his own hair, made a part, forged the top part sideways so that as it dried it would tumble of its own accord into forbidden bangs. He opened the bathroom door a crack, surveyed the dark hallway leading down to the bedrooms. His stepsister was not in sight. Soft Ray Coniff scat drifted over his shoulders and into his ears from the livingroom Clairtone.

–Hey, cutie.

He turned. His stepmother.

–Wanna dance?

She stood in the tiny front hall by the closet. He clutched his shoulders, covering his bare chest like a pigeon.

–No, he said. I, I can't. Yet.

–Well, we'll have to fix that, won't we?

She smiled gently. Her eyes were red-rimmed from crying and when she smiled they crimpled and her hair was redder than he had ever seen it and short. She wore bright red lipstick and a yellow print blouse with no collar but a lacy frill. Rud felt behind his back for the doorjamb.

–But first we're going to have to get you a body for those arms and legs, she teased.

Smiling she slid open the closet door. She reached up on tiptoes and rummaged the shelf above the coat-hanger pole. One of her heels slid out of her shoe and the back strap of her bra stood out under her yellow blouse like some exquisite desert artifact.

–Here, she said, bringing out a brown paper bag and unsnagging a gauzy kerchief from its center seam. She sniffled, then handed over the parcel.

–Thanks, Rud said. I mean, thank you.

–Well, open it, she said.

–Dad? he blurted.

–Sleeping, she said.

–In the basement, Rud added.

His stepmother nodded. She bit her lipcorner.

–Came home from hockey practice, she explained. Wanted to do the laundry. Honest. Anyway.

She nodded at the yet unopened gift. Books. He slid them out of the bag slowly, like two piggyback kids peeping over a fence, until he could read the front title: *The 5BX Plan.*

–Calisthenics, she said. Exercises.

She made a muscle with her arm and her breasts lifted the frill of her blouse.

–Alley-oop, she said.

Rud let the front book slither back down into the bag so he could read the title behind: *The Year the Yankees Lost the Pennant.*

–What the book companies call remainders, she said. So, so don't be so shy.

–Okay.

–What am I saying – be shy. It's nice.

She touched his shoulder. He started.

–I – can I go? I've got to, to read them.

–Right. But don't forget. This time tomorrow night.

–Huh?

–Dance lessons. Only, *before* your shower.

—Sure.

—And Rud: never change, okay?

The suspicion that he hadn't changed, indeed never would, niggled at him. Niggled at him as in his bedroom he labored through a dozen push-ups, the dangling waiststring of his pajama bottoms coiling and uncoiling white on his brown carpet. He lay in bed listening to Caroline showering and he read intermittently in his other book until the devil came calling on the hero Joe. The house was quiet, cool. The heating ducts clumpfed. Maybe he was the same guy except he accomplished twenty push-ups this time and he measured his chest muscles' growth with his fingerspan and slipped back in bed and read until Joe signed over his soul. The year the Yankees lost. His '61 Mantle card leaned back glassy in its small frame on his night table. In '60 they'd lost the World Series in the last inning of the last game. Rud laid the book beneath his Mantle card, remembering opening the envelope in England. He clicked off his lamp.

Whenever he thought of his mother buried in England he mostly stewed over how rarely he thought of her, wondering, agonizing really, at some deep fault in his being, and now the book spurred tonight in his head this doublethink until he fell asleep. The devil who chased him in his dream just before dawn moved slippery as a troll down the thick-gorsed bank of a ravine. Spires of trees and soiled light. Thoomp! He wakened. Pitch black and silence. Slowly his bedroom furniture, his dresser drawers, his desk and its slanted globe surfaced like water-logged flotsam.

He kept as skimp exorcia against burglars and vampires a pocket-knife and Bible under his pillow and when the floor creaked beyond his bedroom door he crept his hand under to check them. Pricks! They'd spilled down his headboard. He turned onto his side, rigid with vigilance. Perhaps he was still dreaming. Across his room the narrow channel under his door ignited with light pale as smoke. A tap turned in the kitchen, filling the kettle with the sound of hailstones. His father's slippers scupped the linoleum. Rud turned on his side, his back to the door. He made a hood of his bedding. The hinges of his door creaked. Footsteps soft on his carpet. His father's two smells, tobacco and ale. Both bitter, both sweet. From out of his hood of blankets, Rud stared at the dark wall. His father sat on the bed edge. Rud turned in the darkness, his sudden whisper near involuntary:

–Where'd you sleep, Dad?

–I knew you were awake, lad.

–The basement?

–Sshh. What about you, lad, d'you do your studies?

He nodded. Like seafoam, what light there was seemed to gather and climb about his father's profile, flowing soft around his neck and shoulders.

–I love you, Dad.

His father smiled warmly.

–Dad?

–I love you too.

–And, and Etta?

–Why'd you say that? his father asked.

–Why'd I say what?

–Etta?

His father sighed and ran work-callused fingers through Rud's hair, a gentleness Rud could feel as a sharp pain in his heart.

–Course I do, his father said after a moment. People fight. Mums and dads. Girlfriends and boyfriends. Lads and their mates. Right?

–I guess.

–Even you and I, right?

–No!

–Yes. One day you'll want to box my ears.

–No.

–Sure you will. Anyrate

–Dad?

–Son?

–Troy, was he, was he at practice?

–That's kinda why I came to talk to you.

–I didn't start it, honest.

–Start what?

Rud fell quiet.

–Look, his father said. He missed. He never missed before and I called his dad but the housekeep answered, didn't know, and

–Dad?

–What, son?

–I'm sorry I can't play hockey.

–Neither can I. Son, listen. You listening?

–Yes.

–You know he won't talk to his mum, see her. Y'know that?

–Yes.

–Not at all, a word even.

–It's just that my feet get so cold and the skates

–Ssh, his father said. Well after this year – you listening?

Rud nodded in the darkness.

–Well the lad's such a wonderful player, Troy is, wonderful the way he can nip through the whole other team, and I shan't be able to coach him anymore, be his coach.

–Sure, Dad.

–Mark you, I'm not asking you to be his friend like.

–You're not?

–Is all we've got, lad, each other, and those we

His father's voice fell away as quietly as a doused candleflame. In the kitchen the heating water stirred in the kettle. His father cleared his throat, ran again his fingers through his son's hair.

–Gettin long.

–Is that okay?

–I'm proud of you, very. Best keep it spruced off your forehead though, when at school, or the flippin headmaster

–The Principal.

–Right, the Principal. Go back to sleep now. I've got t'make me tea.

–Okay.

His father kissed him on the forehead, tiptoed out of the room, drew shut the door. The kettle's overflow sissled on the burner and the teapot lid tinked. Rud rolled onto his back. Why, if it was not miraculous, was it not even momentous? No more now than a moment: his fall, his survival. His father one moment conked out, the next brewing his morning tea. He thought of his father's plea for help the night before and, with shame, of his own fleeing under cover of the bathtub taps. He spooked a hand out of his bedspread and felt his books on the night table. Inklings, and dim at that. He pulled his arm back under the covers. His father left the kitchen and closed gently the bathroom door. The toilet lid struck the water tank with a knock. Rud buried his head under his covers. And what, as his father's piss poured like heavy coinage into the toilet bowl, of the whereabouts of his baseball glove?

$$\diamondsuit$$

That last mystery was solved when he got to school. It had snowed lightly and a helm of tight cloud sealed off the school grounds. Primary graders shrieked after each other, skidding through the gray and white drabness. A grim morning, save *she* clutched his glove in her arms. She wore a waist length fur jacket and her beret was blue. Her blonde hair was tied back, somehow by itself. Jennifer Budd, her long duffel coat buttoned to her chin, stood not far to one side and a ways beyond her Troy leaned glumly against the corner of a whitewashed portable, erecting with his feet a tall fin of snow. The dickhead.

–Hi, Gale said.

–Hi.

–Did you get your ball?

–No.

–I got my tattoo, Skeddy interjected. Wanna see?

–Well, here. Gale held out his glove.

Rud didn't move.

–Here, she said again. Take it.

–Thanks.

–Ah, so, so where'd you go?

–Go? asked Rud.

–Troy said you jumped off the roof.

–Jumped? He said I jumped?

–Yes. And Jennifer and I

–Don't forget me, Skeddy said.

–and Skeddy here, we waited, then we walked round but couldn't find you.

A warning bell rang, obliterating the sound of the playground.

–I sorta went the other way, I guess.

The scent that emanated out of his glove when Rud slid in his hand was as if tanners now made leather from peaches.

–You've

He paused to savor again her perfume.

–You've got a good arm, he said.

–Really?

–Yeah.

–Thanks, she said. Thanks.

She smiled, turned, and walked to where Jennifer waited. Her plaid skirt curved over her bottom, the hem swaying. She dropped to one knee and spooned up a blue-mitten-full of white snow. She and Jennifer walked over to Troy. He never once looked up. Gale grasped Troy's hand and Rud could see him scowling. She dropped Troy's hand, spun on her

toe, and lobbed her snowball at Rud. Not wanting to spoil his glove's
new fragrance Rud caught the snowball with his bare hand. It disinte-
grated. Gale took Troy's hand again and Rud knew in his heart that her
greatest kindness and cruelty would be to leave them both alone.

$$\Diamond$$

The evening June sky visible through the wedged-open gymnasium
doors was the color of distant bonfires and this pink light bathed the
hoods, the hardos — that is, the half-brazen high school boys, loitering
gate-crashers who jellyrolled their hair, smoked one-eyed, and spat thin
jets from between their clenched teeth. Just inside the doors Gale and
Jennifer Budd swayed in each other's arms. As did the other thirty-odd
girls at the eighth-grade graduation dance. At that end of the gymnasium, a swath of pink and white and crinoline. Perfume and hived
coiffures, their arms sleeved in long gloves. Under the opposite back-
board, its blue helium balloon fatigued, Rud and Skeddy and a crew of
boys in coat-hanger suits gangled about. They saw Troy duck back in
from outside with the high schoolers. He reclipped his tie and propped
himself up against the cinderblock gym wall. He threw impatient
scowls at Gale. When the song ended, chunky Mr Kito, at the turntable
between the two sexes, snatched the microphone from Mr Allan. He
pointed at the boys.

   —Gentlemen, he bellowed. Preen. For this, my favorite song, is a ladies' choice.

   Cliff Richard started singing "It's All in the Game." The girls resumed
swaying with their female partners.

   —The boys, ladies, hollered Mr Kito. With the boys.

   Their shoulders sighing, they dispersed toward the ganglers under
the limping blue balloon. The music ceased with an abrupt cackle.

   —Mr Richard is eternal, Mr Kito said. I am not!

The girls quickened. In the clot of ganglers Rud watched Gale coming right toward him, shadowed along the peripheral wall by Troy. Rud straightened his back.

—Dance? Gale asked Rud.

He looked at Skeddy.

—She aint askin me, dinkus.

Gale held her gloved right palm upward. A few feet away Troy glared like Achilles. Rud hesitated. The song started again and his hand took hers. She put her left hand on Rud's waist, he put his right on hers. She pressed her body against his. Her hair was a single wave of blonde and her light blue earrings swung and followed him like eyes as, though wobbly at first, he led. He couldn't look into her real eyes.

—You're supposed to tell me you like my dress, she said.

—I am. I mean I do. He caught a glimpse of her green-blue eyes. The gloves are dumb though.

She let go of his hand and his heart stopped until she rested her hand on his shoulder and he touched the soft bare skin of hers. She leaned and pressed into him again as Cliff Richard crooned, *All in the wonderful game. . . .* The slight give of her breasts tickled him everywhere except where they touched him and her perfume was the same peach richness that had blessed his baseball glove. God, it was heaven – no, it was fucking hell. Because through shuffling couples Troy still stalked them. Once, twice, Rud spun them away. His hand slid from Gale's waist to where her hips, her bottom began and the only thing anchoring him to the earth was the terrifying lightness weighing in his stomach.

—What were you reading? he croaked.

—Pardon?

—Last summer. You were reading.

—Every day, she said.

Troy now loomed directly behind her and Rud spun them again, nearing where Mr Kito stood.

—A policeman? Rud asked.

–Who is?

–Your dad.

–A fireman.

Troy hooked Rud's shoulder with his hand, twirling him slightly. His face was inches away, his breath oak-smoky, his lips as tight as a boulder's.

–My turn, Troy said.

–So? Rud asked weakly. He still held Gale's waist, her shoulder. With granite hip Troy shoved Rud and turned to Gale.

–Quench your thirst? Gale asked Troy bitterly.

–Not yet.

–Then go back to those little creeps.

–First, let's dance, Troy said.

–She is, Rud said.

–With you? Troy sneered.

–With me, Mr Kito said. He had dipped between Gale and the two boys and now whisked away her hand, her waist. As he swept Gale off into the music Mr Kito flashed at Rud and Troy his wide moon of a smile.

–It's called heartbreak, guys, Mr Kito said. Get used to it.

They stood gaping as Mr Kito and Gale swirled and danced.

–Why'd he say that? Rud asked.

–He's a fuckin chink.

Rud started to laugh.

–What's so funny? What is?

For a moment Troy looked away.

–A lousy fuckin dancer, too, Troy said. You, though

The song ended, fading into soft applause. Mr Kito kept Gale in his arms.

–Jesus, look at that, Troy said. The fucking guy.

–A CHEE-I-fucking-ink, Rud said.

–Smartass. You're a smartass. I still might kill you.

—You won't, Rud said.

—I could you know – like that. Just like fucking that.

—Nah.

—Aw, you're probably fucking right. Anyway, you still owe me a quarter.

◇

And so they became friends they did – became friends as only true enemies can. As for the heartbreak part and the getting used to it, Rud would have plenty of chances. And what about the lovely gravity-less pang of joy he felt just before it broke? Like when he was dancing with Gale. Now that the song was over the girls abandoned the boys, cleaving the dance once again into genders. Rud and Troy watched Mr Kito watch Gale walk back to Jennifer Budd and her other girlfriends. They watched her girlfriends grab and clutch her arms and cocoon her with whispers as they would watch her through the first year of high school, memorizing her class schedule so they could intercept and glimpse her between the classes neither shared with her. At first she said hi. By autumn's end she had adopted the same somnambulant indifference as the rest of the girls in their grade. One even beyond intolerance. Not as if you didn't exist but as if they – the girls – never left the delicate fragrance of their beds but instead summoned into existence through the power of dream the sordid school and the thronging in the halls that fell dead away when the doors closed, dreamed up the domed cafeteria and the Gloria, Gloria again and again on the jukebox, dreamed all this immensity into being but never wretched little you. Thus by June of ninth grade, plotting and scheming – the game of seeing her – almost equaled in thrill the actual sight of her. Almost. Came tenth grade they still shared no classes with her. Nearly three thousand students crammed the school that year and the school board made their school a pilot for a new computerized scheduling system. Troy picked the lock on the chilly computerroom door in late April and thieved from one of the morguelike drawers Gale's punch card so they could select the same options. Rud didn't get the chance. On the first Monday in May he was summoned from trigonometry class to the office. Complicit and alibiless, his throat lumped, he half-staggered through the lockered halls. Maybe it was his father who had once or twice dropped off his lunch when he'd forgotten it. The office was air-conditioned and as clearly lit as water in a glass. The head secretary told him to sit on the bench with the truants. She swiveled her chair.

–That's him.

The vice principal looked up. He stood, baggy-suited, his face lean and solemn. In the last year he'd shed sixty pounds but had not yet acquired the faith to buy new dress shirts.

–Please stand, boy.

Rud stood.

–Your mother phoned.

–My stepmother?

–Oh, yes. Well, your father's in hospital.

Rud swooned with the scalding shame of his relief.

–Did you hear me? Hospital. You two, quiet!

–Yes.

–No, not you.

Rud sat back on the bench.

–You may sign out.

–Sir?

–Suspend your classes for the duration.

He did. Friday his father sat on the bed edge in the hospital's burn unit looking out the window, quiet, smoking. He'd been up an extension ladder bucketing a high-pH agent into the brewery's huge copper kettle when it boiled over, its acid scalding him. He'd lurched away, pitching down the ladder, landing on a drainage cock. Stooped, Dad was now, by the bandage on his back the size and thickness of a sidewalk section. Unshaven. Hair knot-ended around the strap of his eyepatch. On the bed's swivel tray a copy of Michener's *Hawaii* was closed over a handheld magnifying glass.

—So what d'you think, dear? Rud's stepmother asked.

—Wha'?

Their voices echoed. The ceiling lay beyond ribbings of thick conveyance pipes. The room sad, industrial.

—Which job should I take?

—Job?

—Parks and rec? Or the school board? Mind, they're both typing.

—S'fine.

—Which one d'you think? The school board's more money?

A nurse came and stood beside Rud in the doorway.

—You can see flying waterskiers on the lake, she said.

Etta squeezed past the bed to see out.

—It's up to you, duck, his father said.

$$\diamond$$

His father came home in early August and Rud walked with him, his father's shirtsleeved arm across his shoulder, Rud on the outside watching and hearing his father cough and rale and push his left leg forward a step, then bring his right leg even. They jerked thus down their quiet street and out along the main artery. His father's eyepatch was gone but there remained on the knee of his right leg a magma of scab, and with each slow step of that leg, this thick scab would form in the knee of his trouser a small crater of cloth. They headed south. It was warm but the porcelain sky cast no shadows under them. They talked of the great Chicago hockey player Bobby Hull because summer training camp was beginning.

—Reminds me of young Troy, said Rud's father. Skating so smart. Wish the Habs had 'im.

–So do they prob'ly.

–You still doin your push-ups at night?

–Yeah.

–Marvelous.

–What is?

–To think how many you've done since you started.

They struggled by the Salvation Army's new two-story offices. They could see the crabapple orchard, green and gravid, with the north park peeking through the trees and they could smell the apples and hear the leaves rustling like pebbles in a child's sandbucket. Three apartment buildings stood beyond the orchard, Gale's in the middle. The massive white scar on his back his father said looked like, to Rud's surprise, Iberia, and the aqueous white scar in his right eye:

–A hummingbird's egg, what fell out of the fridge.

His father tugged his arm, stopping on the sidewalk.

–Hold on a mo, lad.

–Dad, Rud began.

–What, son?

–The night of your accident – I mean, were you drinking?

His father looked at him.

–Were you? Rud asked again.

–Somewhere else – I was, his father answered. Uncle Thom. Your mum.

–The night she

–As I was fallin, bless her heart. Then when I landed, nothing. He gestured vaguely, weakly, up at the invisible sun. All these friggin dregs I'm missing. You playin hardball?

–I was. Season's over.

A Lincoln slunk by. Its occupants owouga'd and waved.

–Your mates? asked his father.

–Troy. Skeddy.

–You don't mind if they see me like this?

–No.

–You don't, my foot.

They returned. September his dad was back at the brewery, back working, back boozing, his hummingbird flights of poetry a memory not recovered – like an envelope used as a bookmark in a rarely read book – for over two decades. The interims passed with such alarm you wanted to hug on to a lamppost. Back at school that year neither Rud nor Troy were in any of Gale's classes. The punch-card theft went undiscovered and the next summer Mickey Mantle, knees floundering and tendonless, was shifted to first base, hitting so dismally Rud could no longer bear to follow the linescores. The Tuesday after baseball season ended Rud was stretched out on his side on the livingroom carpet, the sports section unfolded and papyrian before him.

–Two forty-five, Rud thought out loud.

–Come gen?

He looked up. His father – recently home from work – sat on the couch, weaving like a buoy from the waist up.

–Mantle, Rud said.

The evening was aztec colored on the window sheers.

–Supper! Etta called from the kitchen. For what it's worth.

–His batting average, Rud said, rising stiffly from the rug. Two forty-five.

Caroline in pajamas sashayed by and into the kitchen.

–Mon dieu! It smells like a brewery in here.

–Whatid you know? his father barked.

–Don't start, Erik, Etta pleaded. And get some clothes on, Caroline. Erik!

His father didn't budge.

–I just showered, Caroline said. Ew – egg and mash

–He should quit, Rud said.

Mantle didn't quit. The following summer Mantle hit .237, sinking his lifetime average below .300. That same summer Rud played the local equivalent of American Legion ball and in June Bobby Kennedy was shot: Thursday morning and he found his stepmother in terrycloth dressing gown weeping at the kitchen sink. The tap running. Not quite half past five, yet light thinned their faces reflected in the kitchen window. Theirs faced the kitchen window next door and a cat trapped in glass napped beside a miniature saguaro on the neighbor's inner sill.

–Mr Kito too, his stepmother said. Dead.

She looked around.

–Anyway, what are you doing up? she asked.

–I heard the tap. Shot? Mr Kito was shot?

–I went to make tea. Thought your father was on the couch. Then I remembered he's on nights. Oh Rud, Mr Kito, he hung himself, Monday. On Monday.

She pressed the back of her wrist against her nose and sniffed. Her wristwatch glass left a small crescent.

–I heard yesterday at work. What next! everyone said. That's what we said: What next!

A lot. For out of Mantle's knees and Kennedy's assassinated vision and ten thousand Mr Kitos the world would forge the twisted irony of nostalgia. And Rud's stepmother? She made tea. She scrambled some eggs. And they ate listening to the all-night DJ's final half-hour, Mike Layne's voice showering down from the fridgetop radio tender as a lawn sprinkler. At six a.m. each went back to bed and Rud lay in his, wondering if Gale would wear an armband in mourning for Kennedy and if she knew of Mr Kito.

Turned out Gale was in Sapporo on an exchange trip – Rud hadn't even noticed. His last year of high school Rud quarterbacked the football team. At the semifinal he noticed Gale arm-entwined with her boyfriend who wore a mohair sportcoat and a tartan scarf around his coatcollar. Leather gloves without salt stains. At the championship Rud

didn't remember to check the stands. Mantle retired the next spring and
Troy won a hockey scholarship to Cornell and at their high school graduation Gale didn't show nor at the dance after.

–Gone to New York, Skeddy said in the parking lot.

Troy had beers in his trunk. Skeddy's foamed up and over. Troy
clenched his unlit cigarette in his teeth.

–It's goin on the fender, tit-stroke, he said.

–Nice talk, Troy's date said.

Skeddy put his mouth over the bottle's top and neck like a circus lion.

–B'oadway, he said.

–What? barked Troy. He frisked his tuxedo pockets.

–She's not going to any Broadway, Troy's date said. She's going to art
college. In Rhode Island.

–The fender, Troy said to Skeddy.

–No. She's going to *teachers* college, Rud's date said. She looked at
Troy's date. Here, she added.

–Will ya get the fuck off the fender Skeddy.

–It's Amahd, Skeddy said.

–I thought it was a Lincoln, Rud said.

–Yukkity fucking yuk, Troy said. Who's gotta match?

–Not since Superman died, Skeddy said.

Summer's end Rud too enrolled in Cornell like Troy, though Rud
without a scholarship. When a sophomore, he made the varsity baseball
team as a walk-on. Second base. Last day of the season Rud went 0 for 7
in a doubleheader against Cornell's archrivals, crosstown Ithaca College. The coach hooked his arm on the way to the showers.

–Son, the coach said like an armed forces lawyer. Others say a second
baseman's but a shortstop with no range, no arm, and no bat. You're
making me a believer.

–Yes sir.

–And I don't wanta be – understand?

Rud never graduated. The tuition alone was bank breaking. He

ended up back in Toronto selling books – textbooks. Gale had evidently
been in teachers college because at two widely separated intervals Rud
saw her at teachers' conventions. He never gathered the nerve to approach her. Troy did graduate and remained in Ithaca. Rumored to be
selling dope, mostly grass. Then the eighties barged in. Rud married.
During the Reagan recession bought an uptown row house. A deal
brokered by Skeddy who since the Iran hostage crisis was no longer
Amahd but Warren P.

   –Value? Sixty cents on the dollar, Skeddy told Rud and his wife. With
the recovery? The sky! And you two?

But before the recovery Rud and his wife divorced. His ex got the
stemware, the flatware, the certificates of deposit. He got the townhouse. Dad and Etta? They separated because Dad wouldn't go to AA.

   –Why not? Rud asked him.

   –Go see for yourself, his father said but eventually relented and thus
reconciled with Etta. A few weeks later at two in the morning Rud's
phone rang.

   –Is Dunc.

   –Who? What?

He sat up. The woman beside him sat up.

   –Dunc'n, the voice slurred.

   –Dad's friend?

   –From Wheat Sheaf. Couldn't take yu dad's keys.

   –Jesus

   –Rud – yu got ta

   –But my car's in the shop, Rud said.

   –Take mine, the woman whispered into his other ear.

   –No, he whispered back. J'you try Etta? he asked Dunc.

   –Aye – sh'ung up on me.

   –Shit! He set the phone blindly into the cradle.

   –Take mine, really, Rina said.

   –No. He – I mean – ah, damn.

—Drop me at home, Rina said as he dressed. She was an editor and slim and lithe as an umbrella. She had a swimteam haircut. A boyfriend. But they'd played squash and then had supper and then – and now she had a TR 6. Its top down, the little car growled as he tracked his father's likely route eastward. Not quite home he came upon a single-car wreck in a deserted intersection. His father's Galaxie. Abandoned. The front fender wrapped around the base of the center island traffic pole. In the red light it looked like a whaler impaled on its own harpoon. Rud turned left. Drove slowly, the engine throbbing. Past the mall parking lot, lit and medieval. Past the Meccano giants of the hydro field. There – up ahead staggering toward the phone booth in the Wendy's lot. Hands ripping his windbreaker pockets. Rud wheeled sharply into the lot. The road screamed under the tires. His father twisted, his face, in the headlamps' white venn, black with blood. Rud leapt out.

—In the car. Quick! he said.

He hurried his father in. Stretched back, hauled the top up and over. Snapped it in place.

—Pone Ett, his father said through split lip.

—She won't come.

—Pone 'er!

—I'll come, Etta said. But this is it – I-T!

Back up the road a patrol beam whirled to the intersection in a blue balletic of light. Rud slid aside the phone booth door. Inside the little car his father lit unsteadily a cigarette. Rud signaled *okay* and *stay put* to him, then began the long walk uphill to the wreck and the police.

—I must've nodded off, he told them.

—And tried to walk it off? one cop asked.

—I had wine at dinner – a glass. I meant to phone a tow truck.

—We already did, the other cop said. He held a clipboard and stood in the middle of the road. He gestured at its white line. Heel to toe, please, he told Rud.

Rud complied. As he did so, he could see a flashing amber bubble set high above two headlights approach from downhill. Behind it a car –

Etta's – turned left into the Wendy's lot, drew up to the phone booth, and stopped.

–Sober'n I am, the cop with the clipboard said. And here's the tow.

A half hour later Rud walked back to the TR 6. He sat for a while in its tight cockpit, looking at the glowing instrumentation. Something small, glinty, was on the passenger's seat. He picked it up. His father's Ronson. Smooth – a forged ingot of rare earth. He flicked its striker and watched the flame's small yellow hood spring into being. Then he headed for Dad and Etta's.

–He'll only feel more sorry for himself, Etta said in the front hall.

His father's wet snoring punctuated the livingroom.

–What am I saying, Etta confessed. You were brave – but you can't keep – She looked away, her face worn pale, her eyes moist as caves. I'm no better, she said, I'm not. If he lasted a year in AA, I'd likely, you know

–Yes.

But now, with his father fucking homeless? He offered to finish his townhouse's basement, have his father move in.

–I'm bloodywell payin rent, his father told him.

–Whatever.

–And you'll raise it every year.

–We can draw up a damn lease if you want.

–And only if we do separate fickin entries.

They got permits and as they worked nightly his father seemed to settle. Traded the car in for a red Chevy half-ton. Talked of quitting the brewery, starting a landscape business. Bought Salvation Army furniture.

–Make Ett feel guilty, he teased. If she ever pops over.

They humped the couch down the concrete zag of stairs. Across the street the afternoon recess bell jammered above the schoolyard dust. They stooped and twisted the couch through the front door. There was an eat-in kitchen, a small livingroom, a smaller bedroom. Another hour, the pickup emptied, the livingroom floor was strewn with liquor-store cartons of dishes yet unpacked. His father hooked up the speakers to the one-piece stereo. He knelt, threading the wires.

–Saw Troy's dad I did, his father said.

–Oh? Rud knelt beside him. Bumped into him, did you?

–Intentional like. Pleasant enough bloke. You'd never guess me and him'd have the same taste in

–That's the negative, Rud pointed out.

–Here, who's the chief stoker? Anyrate, Troy's back.

–Ah

–And lookin for a job. Maybe you could take him on – there.

Finished wiring, his father shtunked in Ed Ames. "Help Me Make It Through the Night."

–Jesus, Dad.

–Still got that Scottish lad then? With the bent nose?

–Rod Stewart?

–Nip up and get him then, will ya?

When he returned with it his father punched it in.

–Lad's a born salesman, he said.

–Señor Stew?

His father cuffed his shoulder with a light backhander.

–Troy – he ever sees the sun doesn't shine out his ass.

His father was right. Troy *was* a natural. In two years he was western regional sales manager. Rud eastern. Years snatched away like some dinner-tablecloth sleight of hand. Except the past, like the place settings, somehow remained when late one morning his office phone rang:

–Rud?

–Yes.

–It's Dunc. Duncan.

–Yes.

–From the keg room, the brewery.

This time his father had caught his hand in the keg bander when it lurched. The bander had chomped the top half of the middle finger and

macerated what was left. The hospital was the same one as with his father's first accident and Rud drove several blocks west beside the rail
yard, then several north through the industrial zone of steel jobbers,
garment wholesalers, and open-air vegetable markets.

—Least I'll get a week or two off, his father told him after completing
the papers for his release.

An East Indian girl, a young candy striper, fetched a wheelchair. She
had faint wispy sideburns and long eyelashes that coursed, when she
blinked, like otters. She and Rud funneled his father into the chair, his
father holding aloft the U of tape and steel that for now fastened the remains of his mashed finger to his hand.

—Please tell me, the candy striper asked Rud. Is this your father?

—He is that.

She smoothed adoringly his father's ever-glistening black hair.

—A saint, she said impishly.

—Nah, his father told her. But the lad here is.

The candy striper smiled.

—Got my glasses? his father asked her.

She pulled them from her hip pocket, threading them gently on his
face. Fine-framed, brass. The hinges worn green.

—See, she said. A saint.

At the car, yeasty air from the brewery clung to them. It was warm,
busy. This sidewalk and the one across the street moved under market
goers, telephone poles. Above the cat's cradle of telephone wires the sky
westward went from silver to blue and back to silver. The pavement
shook. Tandem red streetcars labored north, like iron wagons.

—I won't ask if you were drunk, Rud told his father.

—There's a good lad.

The pavement shook again. A southbound cement truck thundered
past as loud as a derailing, its huge cauldron turning, mixing, slopping
the concrete to fill the monstrous excavation of the new domed stadium.

—What're you going to do? Rud asked.

—Change, his father said, my bloody golf swing.

He helped his father into the car.

—Me too, Rud said.

—You? Golf?

—Yes.

—But I golf Sundays.

—So?

—So what about your hardball?

—Baseball, Rud corrected.

—Come off it, lad, you hate golf.

—I'll caddy.

—Caddy?

—All those push-ups I do, put them to use.

—Nah. You just want to keep an eye on me.

—That too, Rud said. While I've got one to spare.

—Be hell keeping you out of the bar, his father said.

Rud swung closed the passenger door.

—I'll take the wheelchair back, he said.

—Tell her you made me walk again.

$$\diamondsuit$$

One of those leather hoods with which a falconer blinds his bird: that's what the leather splint – his father had replaced the metal splint – resembled. So Rud thought a month later as he helped his father ascend his basement apartment stairs. His father's breath came in heaves, and his good hand snatched and hauled in armlengths of handrailing.

—Minute till closing, his father said. And fickin Dunc, he orders the table covered with draft.

—Sure you're gonna make it, Dad?

—Covered. But I'll tell you, son, we weren't the last to leave.

They crested the stairs, the midmorning heat and sun striking their heads and shoulders. In the dirt schoolyard across the road a solitary kid pitched a softball into the wire screen of the backstop. A neighbor drove by in his '65 Mustang. He beeped, waved. Rud nodded back.

—Been lookin forward to this for weeks, his father said. He sniffed deeply. Do you good too.

$$\diamondsuit$$

Bearing his father's clubs over his shoulder, Rud thought she held a barrette between her teeth as she gathered reeds of her dark hair into a ponytail and with her arms raised and her hands behind her head moons of perspiration darkened her blouse. Rud's father stared across the putting green at her standing and stretching by the pro shop.

—Good christ, lad, he said. If I started shagging that I'd never bloody stop.

His father's voice was wool in Rud's ears. His throat constricted. Blindly he touched his father's navy blue golf shirt, the touch humid, electric, as charged as the dark underbellies of thundercloud that rolled in the suburban sky. Rud unlooped the golfbag strap from his shoulder, dropped the clubs on the green with a thump and clatter. He raked with his fingernails his sweat-thickened hair. He started down the path toward her.

—Where're you off to, then? his father called out.

—Golf lessons, Rud answered, because, since he was still an abject coward in the face of lust, that was his ploy. When he stood in front of her, she slid the barrette from between her teeth.

—Hi, she said.

It wasn't a barrette but the fourth and final finger of a KitKat. Rud didn't utter a sound. She took a last bite and swallowed. She polished her teeth with her tongue. Groomed out with long handfuls her ponytail.

—I can help you? she asked.

Her slight Spanish accent and smile emboldened him.

—Go out with me, he said impulsively.

—No, she said.

—No? he managed.

—That is right, no.

A foursome of dripping golfers tramped past, headed for the parking lot. They twisted to eye her and their wet shirts puckered across their backs. Beyond them, through the haze, Rud's father putted crazily. Get 'em saying yes, that was his father's strategy. And Troy's. Rud looked at her again. She wore almond knee-length shorts. Her skin was the color of a new penny.

—You the pro? he asked.

—Assistant.

A baffle fluttered in his ears. She smelled wonderfully of wet grass. Maybe she was wise to the yes strategy. Maybe he should keep getting her to say no.

—Marry me? he asked.

—Okay.

—What?

—I said, okay.

—I'm serious, Rud said.

—Me too. She didn't flinch.

—Okay, Rud said, okay's not serious.

At the first tee someone drove a ball into the clouds with the sound of a brick hitting concrete. Rud allowed her a moment to break off. She didn't shift her eyes from his. Since he had obviously already obtained in her eyes the status of imbecile he tried one more time.

—You give lessons? he asked.

—Sometimes.

—Sometimes?

—*Some times,* she said.

Rud started to laugh, things were going so badly.

—Caddy lessons? he asked finally.

—Caddy lessons?

–You know, how to carry the clubs, write with those pencils.

–Pencils?

–Yeah, the little ones.

At this she brightened. Her eyes measured him from head to toe. His skin prickled. He was wearing a T-shirt, cutoff denim shorts, white Tretorn clogs with no socks and this antigolf costume seemed arch, ridiculous to him, especially when she said:

–For a man, you have lindas piernas – beautiful legs.

Now he had the heart of a lost sea calf. He could not meet her eyes, nor could he look at his legs. He turned back to the practice green. His father waved, made the thumbs-up sign.

–Well, Rud said, maybe – maybe later.

–Later?

She smiled out of one side of her mouth, a white saber of teeth. She had one eye closed and she squinted with the sunlight flashing across her cheek.

–I'll book a lesson, Rud said. For him, my dad.

He took a steep breath, turned, and slowly headed back up the path through the heat. Her gaze burned across his body and he walked as if on a boiling sea. In the near distance, on the practice green, his father made the thumbs-down sign. She called to him.

–That first time, she said.

He stopped but couldn't turn around.

–If you *asked,* she said, *asked,* perhaps I would say yes.

Her words faded. Seashells of thunder filled his ears. Golf club shafts clicked and his guts moaned sliding down into his groin. What touched him deepest though, above all that, was the soft laughter of his father as at the edge of the hole his putt died.

The next week the weather changed. Toronto's is cyclonic, yet Sunday rose chilly, as heavy as the four days before. Rud made coffee – he usually took tea on Sunday mornings – and waited until eleven when he could safely telephone his father to find out their tee-off time. At ten-thirty Rud's own phone rang.

–How d'you get to the Bluffs? his father asked.

Rud looked out his sliding glass doors at the rain glazing his deck and side privacy fence.

–You okay? he asked.

–Course. How d'you get there?

–Why?

–Because I don't know.

–I don't either. D'you have a map?

–You do.

–They're atlases, Rud explained. Of the world. He could hear music, Rod Stewart. Look, he said, I'll be right down.

He went out the door of his townhouse, splashed down his brick steps, descended the zigzag concrete stairs to his father's. He knocked. Rod Stewart sang through the door: "I Don't Want to Talk About It." Rud knocked again.

–Come in.

–It's locked.

–You've got a key.

He did. He opened the door. Two quick steps and he was at the entrance to the kitchenette. He entered, dragged out a counter stool, perched his backside on its edge.

–What's this stuff about the Bluffs?

The Bluffs were tall chalk cliffs, white carvings of wind that stood in the lake east of Toronto's downtown.

–Well?

–Dunno. Thought it might remind me of the sod.

–England?

The song ended. His father slid off his stool, walked into the dark livingroom, rewound the cassette, fast-forwarded it, rewound it. On the beige kitchen counter beside Rud's elbow a shell-shaped spill from the pepper shaker thinned itself out into isolated grains. Beyond, a buff envelope lay, unopened. Rud turned the envelope a notch to read the return address: *Workmen's Compensation*. The harplike glissando of Rod Stewart's lament began again.

–Good bit a rasp, old Rod, his father called into the kitchen. When he's sad.

Rud turned the envelope back the way it was. His father came back into the small kitchen, bypassed the stools. With the heel of his hand his father punched open the high window then sat at the small table beneath, where he ate and, as now, smoked.

–How'd you know I had a key? Rud asked.

–Same as they know.

–Who's they?

–Well they can kiss my starboard nut, his father muttered, then drifted into the ballad's sentiment, humming.

–Who is they? Rud repeated. Knows what?

His father crooned the song gently.

–Dad? Please?

His father held up the splinted finger.

–That I was drunk, he said. They'll cut me off, off my bloody benefits. Mine. And Etta'll find out.

–How?

–The way she knows everything, the way you do.

–I don't mean Etta. The workmen's comp people. You haven't even opened it.

–No need to.

His father spraddled his elbows on his thighs, clasped his hands, stared at the floor between his feet.

–You know what? his father started.

–What?

–The trouble with living in the past is?

—That it's so damned crowded? Rud suggested.

—Ha! And the weather's the shits, his father said.

Rod Stewart raled on. Rud knew his father didn't want to talk about it either. All these years, they'd never talked about the night his mother had died, never would.

—Your mother, his father began.

A sharpness in Rud's chest, a shortness of breath.

—She — and now Etta. His father squinted up through his cigarette smoke. Never have me back, never.

—Things, you know, change.

—Nah, his father said. He appeared puzzled.

—What?

—Why in God's name, his father asked, are you wearing those ficking shorts?

—These?

—Those. It's cold, rainy.

—I thought we'd, you know, go to the golf course.

—You're that daft.

—I am, Rud said. It's supposed to brighten. We can have a coffee while we wait.

—It's not gonna brighten.

—We'll get a street map, then. We'll buy one. Plot the way to the Bluffs.

—Yeah, his father said. He crushed his cigarette.

—You're positive you don't want me to open it?

—No, his father said. He stood.

—You'll know for sure.

—No such bloody thing, his father said.

They left the city, heading northeast up the river valley. The grim weather followed them. Rain dripped on the hood of Rud's Bonneville and wind moaned in his closed windows. Yet on the golf course people were indeed stalwart. A few argyle tramps swung down the chilly fairways, chipped white arcs onto the soggy greens. One golfer, Rud noted as

he hefted his father's clubs out of the trunk of his car and carried them
to the clubhouse, even dared plus fours. But no one else wore shorts.

–Christ, his father suggested. Let's give it a rest.

–We're here now. Let's stay.

His father squeezed his splinted finger with the thumb and forefinger
of his right hand.

–Know how bad I feel?

–Like when you backed the tractor into that lady's toolshed?

–Her greenhouse. Jesus, is there a sound more fickin wonderful than
glass breaking?

–Wonderful?

–Yeh. When the bloody sky falls, that's what it'll sound like.

–What about the thump, the metally thump telling you it's not a
vampire but the furnace waking you? Rud said.

–Some nights I'd rather himself.

They went up the wooden steps, crossed the staves of the deck. The
patio table umbrellas were shut and battened to their poles. His father
strode past the lockerroom entrance – not a glance – and stopped at the
lounge door.

–I'll nip in here for a bit, his father said.

–Coffee, Rud reminded him. With milk and sugar.

–Tea, his father said. J'you get that map?

–Not yet, Rud said. I'll check the pro shop.

She wasn't there. He went outside, prowled around the shrubbed pe-
rimeters of the cedar clubhouse. His eyes searched the practice green,
the deserted first tee, the flagless dark teardrop of the eighteenth green.
Beyond the green a stand of willow trees hung heavy as wet friars. Rud
hopped a shrub, took cover under the overhang, rubbed the goosebumps off his legs. Did golf pros take Sundays off when it was raining?
Surely even he could pry her name out of whoever was working and he
returned to the pro shop. It was still unmanned. He went to the counter,
by the cash register, seeking her name on the roster that dangled there:
Amaranta Elena Versalles.

She was behind, on one knee, shelving cellophaned pairs of golf balls. She wore a beige cap with an elongated peak that read Links and also a Walkman. She glanced up at him but did not stand and he dipped under the counterflap and stooped beside her and asked with a marked rise in intonation:

–Go out with me?

–Silencio.

–What?

–Shush!

Her hair was braided thick as chestnuts down her spine. He heard a swell of applause in miniature.

–Santana? he whispered.

–The Jays.

–Who?

–The Jays, baseball.

–Really? You like baseball?

–No, she said, waving him quiet.

He duckstepped closer, tilted his head earward.

–Who? he said.

She glared at him.

–Who, I mean, he whispered.

–Guillermo Dedos.

She said the player's name as if she'd not only pronounced it a thousand times but in a thousand and one ways. That one way, that thousand and first, bred in Rud an unquenchable jealousy.

–He's the same age as me, Rud said. From Argentina.

The look she gave him said either, So what? or No shit! She rifled into the shelves a few more packages of balls.

–The only one, he is, Rud said. Ever.

She held up a finger.

–From Argentina that is, Rud said.

She held up two. This close she was as he'd all week imagined her to be: dark complected, yet about her nose, freckles. Their eyes touched,

momentarily. Hers, in a complexion that dark, were startling: a quarrylake blue.

—I played too, he said.

—Wait.

—In college.

—Please!

—At Cornell.

She clamped her hand over his mouth. She blinked, made a loose fist
as if clutching a stopwatch. The pro shop door scraped, opened, and
they turned as one. The door did not close and frigid air slapped the
bare skin of Rud's legs. Through the glass counterfront, like looking out
from inside an enormous aquarium, the golfer's trousered legs were visible, his brown and white tasseled shoes. Rud's father. The shoes shifted
right then left, stumbling slightly. His cleats made a plucking sound on
the rubber. He left.

—I gotta go, Rud mumbled.

She unclamped his mouth.

—Don't, she said.

—Yes.

She shook her head, raised her blue eyes, as if the radio waves entered therein.

—Go out with me? Rud asked.

—When?

—I don't know – tonight?

She waited a minute before answering, listening.

—Tonight? Rud reiterated.

Her face bloomed suddenly into a broad smile. She clapped her
hands.

—Home run, she said loudly. Home run!

—Great, just great. Well?

—Dos y dos, tuk! She clapped again.

—About tonight? he repeated.

—Tonight? I cannot, tonight. Tomorrow?

–Tomorrow, Rud said, disappointed.

She blinked at him, as if calculating.

–Of course, Rud said quickly. Tomorrow. Great.

He went to stand. She snatched his wrist, halting him, laid it with her hand on top on his upper thigh.

–Late, she said.

–Late is okay, fine.

–After midnight. Just a walk or something.

His hand trembled. She snapped hers from his.

–Don't worry, she said. The horny latina lady is not going to fuck you to death.

She swiveled on her toes, her face grim. She pushed golf-ball packs into the display two, three at a time.

–That's not what I meant, Rud said.

She ignored him.

–I was worried it might be cold, rainy.

–You are wearing shorts.

–Yeah, Rud said. I'm daft. Late?

–Yes, she said.

$$\diamondsuit$$

On Buffalo PBS they – Rud and his father – watched *All Creatures Great and Small*. Rud drank a can of Molson's, his father sipped spring water from an emptied rum bottle. Rud sat on the chair from the kitchen; he'd changed his shorts for Levis. His father sat deep in the couch, smoking, in work pants, T-shirt, slippers, emerging from the couch's viscera to flick his ash into the beanbag ashtray on the coffee table. A nearby plate with lumpy mashed potatoes and smears of egg yolk and ketchup gobs lay half eaten. Bits of ash scarred the plate's rim when his father, as now, tapped the barrel of his cigarette on the ashtray edge.

As for the tv show, young country vet James Herriot took fair Helen's hand, led her up the stairway of a ruinous flint-walled castle. The same castle where Mary Queen of Scots had been imprisoned. As they climbed, their shoes clopped and scuffed on the stone.

–Lend me some runners? his father asked.

–Some runners?

–Plimsolls, running shoes.

–Is this for the Bluffs thing?

–I can't wear golf spikes. His father pointed to the egg and mash. You going to eat this? he asked.

–No.

–Off your grub? Too much ketchup?

–Sorry – I'll

Rud collected the plate, carried it into the kitchenette. What was his father going to do at the Bluffs and how could *she* have blue eyes and freckles? On the countertop the pepper spill remained, the envelope gone. Gray sudsless dishwater half-filled the sink. Rud scraped his egg and mash into the garbage bag, slid his red-stained plate into the water. He swept with the blade of his hand the white and gray pepper grains into his other palm, stropped them into the sink. He saw, on the other side of the sink, the envelope sticking out of his father's paperback book like the feet of a too-tall sleeper. With hallucinatory clarity he was walking with his father again.

–The night Mum died? he whispered.

He heard his father's laughter. That was better. He swiped up the paperback, wandered back into the livingroom, studying the title page.

–Reading *Shogun* again, I see, he said.

His father didn't answer. Rud peeked at the envelope's underside. Still unopened. On screen they stood on the castle's topmost battlements, the stone crumbling. Distant, the north English dales, green and gliding, swelled into soft mountain fells of snow, of mist. There was wind, and the two actors looked raw and cold.

–I like the way he proposes to her, Rud said.

—Do what?

His father, the cigarette smoldering in his righthand fingers, blottered his eyes with the back of his wrist.

—James, Rud explained. The way he proposes to Helen.

—Sure, his father said. The weather's the shits.

Maybe what Rud had heard coming from the livingroom wasn't laughter. So he convinced himself when, after the show ended, he left to fetch his father a pair of his Nikes. A lovely summer warmth had arrived, wild, bareback. Rud paused a moment on the grass patch outside his front door. He could smell the grass sweetly, feel the nearby trees warming. The shadows of the playground equipment in the schoolyard across the street drew back into their wood and pipe forms. A block west the lights of uptown store signs were underscored by their darkened windows beneath. Sunday night was rotten with irony and he'd had enough, especially of his own, so when, by his father's door, he handed over the Nikes, he asked:

—Why don't you try AA again? You last a year, Etta'll have you back.

—No.

—Why not? Rud asked.

—I can't pay the rent this month.

—I'm not talking about the rent, Dad.

—Can't pay next month either.

—I don't care about the fucking rent, d'you hear me? Never cared.

—I'm not living here for nothin.

—Fuck the money. Fuck it! Just go to the fucking AA.

—No!

—It's once a bloody week. Once a week.

—That's not it.

—What then? Rud asked.

His father searched his pants pockets, turned, went into the kitchenette. Rud followed as far as the entrance, his back to the hallway that led to the bedroom and bathroom. His father sat on a stool, took out his cigarettes, his lighter, his nail clippers. He clipped off the white filter of a Player's, tapped the tobacco down.

—It's the religion.

—The religion?

—The jumbo mumbo.

—I don't get it, Rud said.

—The born-again horse's ass.

—So?

—I believe in God and all that bull, but theirs's not sincere.

—Sincere? Rud said. Not sincere?

—You asked me, I told you.

—So fake it, Rud said. Fake it.

The irony of his own words would have rotted orchids.

—Sunday, Rud said. He shook his head. I never thought I'd long for fucking Monday morning.

—I never thought I wouldn't, his father said. Old Uncle Thom – and your – anyway

Rud waited. His father didn't finish.

—Look, Dad, he said. Look. I don't care. Stay here forever. Shove the goddamn brewery.

—And live off my kid? No bloody thanks.

—There's our book warehouse. I could get you in there.

—You'd feel responsible. People'd blame you if I ballsed up.

—We'll hire you through Troy, Rud said.

—So bloody what?

—They still don't know he and I, that we're related, sort of.

—But you and me, we've the same last name – and not a Smith or Brown neither.

—Yeah, well, you got him his job.

—No. No, I said. His father's face fell blank, his mouth slightly open. Anyhow, he said, still rainin?

—Warm, Rud answered. Almost muggy. A relief.

—And the lad, Troy, how is he?

—My boss.

—Bloody fear! Since when?

—Since a few weeks from now. I heard a rumor.

—Sorry, his father said.

He finished his cigarette. Rud stepped fully into the kitchenette.

—Dad? That night

—Does he ever talk to his mother? Troy? See her?

—No.

—Not even secretlike?

—Not that I know.

Rud looked into his father's brown eyes. At the scar tissue in the right: the spilled hummingbird egg. He could hear crabapple trees rustling. His stepmother at the sink.

—Dad?

—What, son?

—I gotta go. Can I – give you a hug?

Nodding, eyes swimming, his father stood. They embraced with the slow care of surgery patients. Rud felt the shadow of his father's whiskers, the smooth skin of his cheekbone, the Brylcreem slick of his jet-black hair. Like all men embracing, they began simultaneously to pat each other on the back, on the shoulders.

—I love you.

—I know that, son. I love you too.

They stepped back from each other. Walked to the door.

—And thanks, Rud said, for going to the golf course.

—Ah – anyrate, how'd you do?

—Pretty well.

—She looks nice, kind.

—I don't know yet.

—Well, even if she's not, his father said. Bit of tail, especially a lovely one like that, never hurt a man.

first

Troy, on the hottest day of the year, the next day, had gotten a haircut. Not the barberpole special he usually sported but a fashionable bristle look around the ears and long on top. He had a new tie, kelly green, clipped and collar-pinned. No jacket, just a starched white shirt. He passed Rud's open office door, slapped twice the doorjamb, grinning. He clutched his arms and shivered in an exaggerated manner. He slapped the doorjamb again and vanished into his office adjacent. The turbines that drove the air-conditioning system had not yet been installed and Troy's voice carried all the way over from his office on the other side of the sales reps' tunnel, as, on the telephone, he enlisted workers from the warehouse.

—And that Davis kid, the one who's fuckin blasted all the time, get him up here too.

A brief pause ensued. Rud thumbed through a manuscript proposal: *Shakespeare: A Translation for the Modern Teen.* He reread the yellow sticky-memo:

Cutting title, huh? One of Troy's finds. Still, one never knows, and you are English, aren't you? When's our next squash game?

Rina

He couldn't refrain from finding *King Lear.*

—Let me deal with Jan, Troy said loudly. Just get 'em up here, prontolla.

Rud searched for the suicide-off-the-cliffs-of-Dover scene. Within
minutes the conscripted workers straggled up from the warehouse.
They wheeled about huge freestanding fans. At Troy's direction they
stationed them at strategic points. Yes, there it was: *He kneels. . . . He
falls.* Rud looked up and through his office door. Troy was rolling up his
shirtsleeves, issuing commands. His solid athletic frame was lank but
strident with the purpose of one who knows with certainty the future.

—Contact! he shouted with a laugh.

The fans commenced a howling, almost subterranean whirl. Desk
papers went airborne. The secretaries snatched at them, emitting mock
squeals. Rud stowed the shambles of a manuscript, got up and closed
his office door, leaning his back against it. Beyond his uncluttered desk
his fourth-story window gave out on to the tar and gravel roof of the
three-story warehouse. The roof was long and at its edge treetop cres-
cents wavered and shone like green footprints, leading the eye onward
to the lake. He could not see the sky. He went and sat at his desk, back to
the window. He opened his sales printout. An input error had assigned
the wrong accounts to the wrong sales reps and, as eastern regional
manager, he needed to tally up the commissions by red pen and calculator. As western regional manager, Troy had not had to. He closed the
printout. He dropped the pen and calculator in his top drawer, tugged
over his phone by the cord, dialed his father. No answer. He dialed the
golf course.

—Pro shop?

—Yes? The voice was male.

—Who – who's on today?

—Me, sir.

—Great, but the assistant pro who was on yesterday

—Elena?

–I thought it was Amaranta.

–She likes to be called by her middle name.

–Oh, well, I have a lesson I'd like to move up.

His plan was to cadge her home phone. His door thumped heavily. He stood. Before Rud could speak or move, an electrician barged in, shirtless under bib overalls. He lugged in long veins of power extensions. He nodded to Rud.

–We need your window. Sorry.

He strode past the desk, towing the lines behind him. He rattled the window screen. Troy walked in.

–Cluttered desk, cluttered mind, he said.

Rud turned slightly away.

–My father, he said guardedly into the phone. Erik Gillette. I was wondering if he's been in today.

Now Troy stood right beside him, his aftershave deteriorating in the heat.

–This is a semiprivate club, the golf pro said. They join, they pay, they play – we don't do names.

–Jet-black hair, clean shaven, likely with razor nicks under his chin.

–Not that I remember.

–A leather splint on his middle finger, his left hand.

–No, sorry.

Rud hung up.

–All okay? Troy asked.

–Nothing I can't deal with.

–The bad news is, Troy said, going to the window, they gotta put the fucker outside your window.

–The fucker?

–The air unit.

–What?

–It won't red-tag if they stick it on the roof.

–Pass code, the electrician offered. His legs straddled the sill.

—The good news is, we're going to lunch.

—Wait a second, what's wrong with outside *your* window?

—The man here thinks they should've torn this sucker down, built a new one.

—It's an historic landmark, Rud objected.

—A firetrap, the electrician called in. Even a plumber'd say so.

—Hold on, Rud said, facing Troy by the window. What's Tom say to this?

—He's in New York.

—Steve?

—London.

—They didn't tell me.

—You weren't exactly around.

—Fuck. Who's in charge then?

Troy took a deep breath.

—Ostensibly?

—Ostensibly.

—The bean counter.

—Van Castle?

—For the next month, anyway.

Rud stopped his train of thought.

—This is stupid, he said. Petty. He left his office, determined to phone Workmen's Compensation himself.

—Lunch in thirty, Troy called after him.

He went past the entrance of the long sales-reps' tunnel that separated his office from Troy's. Air hurled by the fans parted his hair at his temple, a lock of it poking him in the eye. He shut Troy's office door, locked it, smoothed his hair back. Troy's desk was covered with memos, some from the parent company in London. Rud denied himself the barest of glances, carried the phone to the side chair. The cord drooped. He called workmen's comp.

—Claim number?

—It's not handy, Rud said.

—Date of birth?

—Twenty-first February.

—Year?

Swiftly Rud calculated.

—Don't you know? the clerk asked.

—I need a minute. It's my father's.

—Then, without the claim number we can't help you. We must protect our claimants.

—Of course.

He hung up. Shit. Again he phoned his father. No answer. The office door handle turned, clicked against the locked tumbler, shook. The door bowed slightly in its frame. Rud walked over, opened it. Troy backed away, waving some teachers' conference brochure.

—You'll never goddamn guess who

—*Rud Gillette,* the intercom announced over the whirring fans. *You've a visitor at reception. Rud Gillette.*

—Who the – ?

—A customer, Troy said loudly.

—It's summer.

—So? Attack mode! Anyway, he continued. He slapped the conference brochure. No shit, it's *her.*

Dian, the sales department secretary, cleared her throat.

—Troy, she said. Sorry, but can I take lunch early?

—Dunc, Rud said to no one.

He brushed past Troy, down the aisle to the elevator. Jabbed the button. Counted to five.

—She broke my heart, he heard Troy tell Dian.

He jabbed the button again.

—I'm serious, Troy said, laughing.

Rud fled down the four flights of stairs.

She wore sunglasses jammed under her long-peaked cap. Her cheeks were puffy and swallowing made crow's-feet out of her neck tendons. She wore shorts and her blouse was V-buttoned across her breasts and tied above her navel and when she swiveled and faced Rud the ties of her blouseknot lifted like small white wings.

—You are late, Amaranta hissed.

—Just a minute?

—Late!

The switchboard trilled. The receptionist stopped her off ear with her forefinger. The cubicle was redolent with the stale smell of potted plants and the window cleaners had not been for weeks and a clam-colored light sullied the air.

—It's Troy, the receptionist said. For you, Rud.

—Late for what? Rud said to Amaranta.

—Rud? the receptionist repeated.

—Our date, Amaranta said.

—It's Troy, the receptionist said.

—Tell him I've, I've gone, Rud said quickly. He took Amaranta's arm.

—Here, he said and he led her down the brief flight of stairs and out the door into the parking lot. Yeasty decaying air blew in from the brewery. There was a painful haze and a sharp glare deflected off the rows of parked cars.

—No, she said.

—No what? asked Rud.

—No that it was for tonight, our date.

—But it was.

Someone whistled and the sound fell onto the pavement between them like a wet stone in the desert. They looked up. Troy stuck out of a third-story window, a blond-haired starched-cotton bust. His green tie end hung over the sill. He was clamped onto the mullion.

—I'll change the reservation to three, he called down.

—Quién es? she asked. Who is that?

—Hungry? Rud asked back. Are you hungry?

She looked at Rud.

–Joe Allen, Troy called. I'll even drive.

–Is that your boss? she asked.

–Not if I can help it. Are you hungry?

–Yes, she said.

Rud gripped her bare upper arm and tugged her tenderly toward his car.

–I'm serious, Troy called out. This is important.

–Did you drive? Rud asked Amaranta.

–Sí. Yes.

–Where?

She pointed across the road to an unpainted Volkswagen Beetle, then looked over her shoulder at Troy.

–Shouldn't we – ?

–He's ragging me, that's all.

She seemed not to comprehend.

–Riding me, he explained. Pulling my leg, he added in his father's accent.

–Leg? Pierna?

–He's my stepbrother.

They stopped momentarily at the curb as a police officer clopped by on a large brown horse with swaying almost-white hindquarters. They crossed.

–Where are we going? she asked as she rolled down her window.

–Just a sec. He hustled smartly around the car's roman nose. He scoped out the building one more time.

–Wait! Troy shouted, waving from the window like a flagman.

Rud stooped and ducked in the car. She had her thumb and forefinger poised on the ignition key.

–The Bluffs, Rud said. Ever been?

–Not yet.

She didn't budge.

–I'm worried about my dad, he explained. My father, and I think he might

–Not yet, she interrupted. Not until you explain why you were late.

–I thought it was tonight, Rud said. Tonight. I mean

–That is the truth?

–Yes, Rud said, I watched tv. With my dad. *All Creatures.* Had egg and mash. A measly beer.

He fell sullen, remembering his father's cry of despair. The VW's engine snapped on behind them.

–I like that show, she said. But what is egg and mash?

Across the road Troy emerged from the front door, chewing gum with vigor and hooking on his aviator sunglasses. Amaranta checked her side mirror and coaxed the wobbly stick shift into first and lurched from the curb. She shot her arm out her window and waved at Troy and without warning swung into a U-turn. Rud seized the dashboard handle and she shifted fiercely and didn't stop driving along the lakeshore until Scratch Daniel's in the Beaches where they bought takeout wings and fries and cole slaw and pilfered each a handful of paper napkins. And he stripped off his tie and unbuttoned his shirt and cuffs and rolled up his sleeves and they ate as she drove one-handed guttering in and out of the streetcar tracks with the wind blasting hot through the little car and the radio on AM. Still the road climbed and the shops whipped past – funeral homes, rentals, blocklong strips of hardwares and bakeries and banks – until they turned right onto a side road that curved plummeting back down through large Tudor-style homes to the Bluffs.

They parked beside some red clay tennis courts swarming with mixed-doubles matches. They stuffed a plastic grocery bag with their lunch refuse. A ways farther in the bright sun some municipal workmen were staking out and framing a long form for concrete where the sidewalk had been ripped up. Through the mesh fencing of the tennis courts they could see how the manicured grass ramped upward to the edge of the cliffs where it became sparse and rocky, the grass yellowish and overhanging like a ruined footbridge.

–What does he look like? Amaranta asked. Your father?

Rud answered without turning from the window, his eyes roving the galvanic lake:

–My height about, my build maybe, though not as, as, you know, and smooth black hair combed straight back kind of, kind of how, like a for-ties matinee idol maybe? Yeah, and handsome as one too and come to think of it as sad, and these red veins, these tiny ones, along the skin of each cheek. And ah – stop me any time now – his thumbnails're always mashed and trenched though he's a great untier of knots in things like shoelaces and the string in Meccano.

He halted abruptly and turned from the window.

–A brief sketch. Brief.

She nodded.

–Funny, he said.

–Why?

–Only, women usually remember exactly what he looks like.

–I do, she said. I just wanted to see you describe him.

–And?

–What is a Meccano?

–Kind of metal Lego. Take your sunglasses off for me?

–No.

He stared at her, at the freckles on her blunt nose.

–I had no sleep all night, she said.

And at her yellow cap and her hair barbed from the heat and the wind and curled on her sweat-damp shoulders like strips of soft copper left on a magnet in the rain.

–What? she asked. You are looking. What?

–Nothing.

—What?

She reached up and twisted down the rearview mirror, aiming it. She inspected her face.

—I like your freckles, he said.

—I do not.

She moved her head ever so slightly from side to side, continuing the inspection.

—You go out with him, don't you, Rud said.

—Who? she said.

—Dedos – last night. That's why you said, late.

She didn't answer immediately. Through the small windshield they watched one of the workmen, a sun-blackened hulk naked from the waist up, hoist and lower behind his neck a longhandled shovel as deftly as a shower brush. He had a huge perfectly spheroid gut that hung above his skinny jeans like a brown skull tethered around his neck and he scratched his lower back with the spade's bootlug.

—Would it bother you if I did? she asked.

—Yes, he answered. He looked at her. No, he said. I don't know. Least he's not a hockey player.

—He cannot skate.

—Neither could my dad.

—That is him? she asked, nodding out Rud's side window.

Near the cliff's edge a tall bony man sporting a long beard and clad in the white robes, leggings, and sandals of some cult maundered along, eating snack chips.

—Very funny, Rud said. I'm wretched, aren't I?

—Wretched?

—Foolish, childish. The way I worry about him.

She swabbed the sweat from under her chin with the back of her wrist.

—His membership card, she said. On it, the In Case of Emergency. This had you and your two numbers.

–Really? He has my number?

–You are surprised?

–A bit. More than a bit. I would have thought – I don't know. Etta maybe. My stepmother.

–I have two brothers, she said. Back home, in Argentina. Real gauchos, cowboys. One saw a movie where Australian cowboys herd cattle on motorbike. The other says we are descendants of Huayna Capac – the last Inca. Talks talks talks, of a lawsuit against the king of Spain.

–So you're a princess. An Inca princess.

–Italiana. As a boy my papa immigrated to Argentina from north of Milan. What I am saying is: both his sons refuse to ride my father's horses.

Rud was dumbfounded by the wealth of what she said. Yet with the brevity of a windvane. He swallowed as discreetly as possible.

–I've got the worst taste in my mouth.

–Me too.

–From the wings.

–The french fries.

The interior of the car was as quiet as it was hot. Save the steady sliding and pok-pokking of the tennis matches. The thud-thud hammering of the workmen.

–When do you have to be back? she asked.

–I don't.

–You are not going back to work?

–No. He looked out the side window. Not today. Hey, maybe never.

The white-robed man turned from the lake and walked eastward. Above him a single gull the same color as the sky seemed to despair of the heat and heaviness of the air before it fluttered and banked right, descending. Other gulls swooped after it, appearing as sudden as if they'd been poured like thickened paint out of the sky.

–He's not here, Rud said.

She didn't respond.

–Jesus, listen to me – now I'm doing whatsitsname, augury. Reading birds in signs.

–Qué?

–Signs in birds, I mean. Would you, would you give me a lift home?

–Yes.

–If it's out of your way

–It is not.

They drove west back to the city, then plugged steadily north through the uptown traffic. There were Chiclets in her glove compartment and when they turned down Rud's street his father's red half-ton pickup was parked across the road from the townhouse. It was just two o'clock.

–He'll get ticketed, Rud said and crossed the road.

He rummaged under the truck's worn floormat for the keys but they weren't there. He slammed the truck door and watched over the bed of the truck some kids on the playground shriek and chase each other's dust trails. No, it was soccer. From not far up the sidewalk the rahazz of a gasoline weedtrimmer. He turned to recross the street and a low-riding sedan blared inches by. Then a furniture van. He made the other side.

–Is the world louder?

–Like your car radio the next morning, she said.

He held out his hand and she took it. Just like that. A single ring she had, and a lovely heaviness to her palm.

–My dad lives down there, he pointed out. And I live up there.

They made love like spiders dropping down from some chapel ceiling onto his livingroom couch – and this image appalled him. Though he remained inside of her fucking her until she came with her temple clamped against his and their cheeks exchanging blood-color medallions, orgasm eluded him. He sat up and back on his heels. His cock pliant along his tanned thigh. She shifted her hips, twisting as she pushed up onto her elbows. She frowned. Her blue eyes steamed. He leaned forward and kissed her.

−Your hat's fallen off, he told her.

She confirmed this with her hand and she swung her arm down, searching the floor for it, and her breasts moved under his chest. Came a heavy foomp from the front door. She froze.

−I say, he mimicked, it's the post.

The letters slid onto the hall floor like palm fronds. Leaves too, fallen ones, were the color of the smooth skin of her throat with its darker sweatscars and she flicked her errant bangs to one side, found her hat, and placed it not on her head but on his.

This pleased him and he thought their going upstairs to his bed would banish the image of the dropping spiders.

−I have to go, she told him. Don't look, please.

She rolled him off her body into the delve of the couch.

−Hey, he said. Our walk tonight, late.

−Close your eyes.

She stood and gathered her clothes.

−Close them.

−Okay, okay.

−Is there one upstairs?

−A bathroom? Rud asked.

−A phone.

−Yes.

He listened to her climb the stairs and he smelled her fragrance and their seaside scent. He had a water and ink print hanging above his fireplace mantel and he reopened his eyes and studied it from across the room. Huddled trees filed out of an arroyo cut by a right-to-left spillage of foothills and mountains, single file like forlorn one-legged warriors. Under an eggshell sky. He leaned back in the couch. The small pillow he rested his elbow on was damp and where it had bunched under her neck it was dark blue and he suddenly wanted her to be here while he checked on his father, or rather, be here when he got back, and he bolted up and stuck his legs in his pants. The mail he swept aside with his bare foot and he zipped his trouserfly just as he opened the front door.

The heat hit him like hot oil. He left his shirttails untucked and barefoot walked down his steps. Cars grumbled by and a large black dog, draped across his neighbor's top step, lifted its head. He turned his back on the dog and descended his father's short zigzag. The temperature dropped. The concrete was cool under his bare feet and he rapped softly. He'd forgotten his keys and he considered going back up to phone but the door was unlocked.

–Dad?

He closed the door. Quiet filled his ears. The curtains were drawn and the place was steeped with a stale darkness. He smelled something like pepper.

–Dad?

A note lay shadowed on the kitchen counter. By the phone. DARLING, it began and feeling the heat off himself knew it was not for his eyes. But by then he'd read it forever: DARLING, FORGIVE ME. I CAN'T BEAR THE CONSEQUENCES OF WHAT I'VE DONE. As for how long he stood at the entrance to that dark funnel of hallway, he would never know. He did scan the coffee table and livingroom floor for broken glasses. Could see none. Now he trod, listening between each step, down the hall. It was longer than he could remember and seemed to narrow and finally he stepped into his father's bedroom. He did not need to turn on the light.

Bunkbeds stood in the corner. The top bunk unmade. The bottom filled only by a naked mattress, its grommets exposed.

–Dad?

He couldn't hear his own voice. Footsteps on the ceiling above – his floor – and he turned to intercept her – to tell her – but was drawn into the woodframe mirror above his father's dresser. A frayed black and white of Rud's mother in the top righthand corner, curling out of the gap between mirror and frame. Out of the left corner a color snap of Etta. Player's Navy Cut butts filled the metal ashtray on the dresser beneath, the filters clipped. His father's Ronson, burned brassy by years of pocket change. The whir outside of Amaranta's Volkswagen. A glimpse at his own reflection, drawn and sunken, making sure it left the bedroom with him. The only room left was the bathroom.

Two days after he found the body he was summoned downtown to the morgue. To identify – after the autopsy – the corpse. Early morning and he sat on the curb outside, the skyline a dark cowl above. The sun came up, came over. He couldn't remember sleeping, though he knew he had.

The sky grew livid. The morgue opened. He rose and drifted inside. In the muscle beneath his left shoulderblade a sharp knot formed. A nick-shaven young man stood behind the reception counter. He asked Rud for ID. He smelled of Old Spice, of breakfast onions. He pointed to the far corner. The knot in Rud's back tightened.

–Watch, the young man told him.

–Watch? Where? Where's the drawer?

–Just watch.

Bolted into the wall by the ceiling was a black and white tv monitor. Rud guided himself across the foyer. Stood beneath. He watched, as instructed. No, he didn't, he stared. And stared. Into this porthole of a grave. And lo! His father's face, now tortured, floated up. Ghoulish. As though buried in water. Only his hair was the same. A jet of black combed straight back. A single curl unruly. But the forehead twisted, twisting. Twisting in agony.

The screen faded.

–Sir?

He could not hear.

–Sir?

He heard in his head a voice at once his own but also not:

–Because of our Etta? Our mum? And why oh bloody why this way?

And he waited for his father's lips to move.

$$\diamondsuit$$

Two evenings later the horror of writing an obituary still gnawed like some vile parasite at his heart. He went for a walk. South past the emptying open-air cafés of uptown. Past the mansions. The prep schools. The blue sky escaping. Near downtown he turned east. Faster through the housing projects lit and profane. Eyes straight ahead crossing the canyon-spanning viaduct. The hot night blew down on him. Traffic here and far below muttered by in gatherings, with headlamps vigilant. To make the other side. The lake a black hump in the south. The railing – the railing – there. Another hour, he was in the Beaches. At Amaranta's apartment. In the tiny foyer. Porcelain buzzers above steel mailboxes. He found hers.

–What on earth do I say? he asked her.

She closed her door with her bottom. She wore jeans with one torn knee and the shirt of a housepainter. He encircled her waist. Pulled her to him.

–You are sweating, she said. And get your shoes off.

She tossed her red and black hair behind one shoulder like a magician his cape. He kissed her. Lips. Freckled cheek. Strands of her hair split past his eyes. Her neck. Buried himself there. Buried. After, he asked her again.

–What do I say?

They sat in her bed. She hesitated, yawned, then flopped back onto the mattress, one wrist behind her pillow.

–My sonso.

Her other hand caressed his shoulder. He shivered and said:

–I need a shower.

–I don't have one. And you must go soon.

–This place only has a tub?

She swung her legs over the bed edge.

–Yes. I have to pee, she said. Close your eyes.

He followed her. She left him in the hall, leaning on the bathroom doorjamb. Listening to her but then not.

–And what do I leave out? he asked.

–Otros – others – what do others? she called.

–Others? What others?

–Others, people – like you – what do they write?

GILBERT, KIKI, 97, died of natural causes, Monday, August 10, at El Manor Nursing . . . services will be 10 A.M. Friday at the Greek Orthodox Church of . . . burial will be at Saint Gregory's

GILLETTE, ERIK, 62, half-naked, climbed into the ?????

– You could almost fucking laugh, he said.

He looked up from the paper. Glanced around his kitchen. He was alone.

He wrote Bev his bloodsister and now a Labour member of Parliament in England: Our father committed suicide by

He tore that up. Began anew: Our father killed himself

That too. He wired her instead: REGRETS BUT MONDAY FORTNIGHT PAST OUR FATHER DIED AT HIS HOME STOP

As if in gruesome retaliation to this lack of detail he received the last

week in August through his door mailslot a thick envelope. Not from
Bev but from the coroner containing a copy of the autopsy report. He
did not open it for two nights and after he did and began to read it with
revulsion – Stab wounds of chest (six) Large circumferential cut almost
amputating the apex and portion of the medial wall of the right ventri-
cle – he awoke later in bed with all his houselights ablaze. He turned
them off from the ground floor up until – his skin so goosebumped he
might have molted – he reached the bathroom light and the next night
he made love to Amaranta in her apartment first kissing and licking her
cunt with the fury of the pentecost then fucking her so long that when
he came he did so like a hot pipe burst.

    –You have to go, she said after they'd made love again.

    He rolled in her bed to gather her even once more.

    –No, she told him. Please.

    –I want to stay.

    –You can not, she said.

    He read obituaries in the public library much of that day – didn't go
to work nor the next – and the following night he awoke in his own bed
and again the houselights were blazing and he phoned her:

    –You have a key, don't you?

    –It is – she paused – three-fifteen.

    –I know, he said. You have one

    –One?

    –A key, Rud said.

    –I don't

    –Don't you.

    –Rud, please.

    –You must.

    –Screw you!

    She hung up. And that night he went to bed *with* the lights all burn-
ing white and when he awoke they burned brown as salt and he stood at
his bathroom door in the bellowing quiet then at the top of his stairs
where it was even quieter and he felt his father drawing near to him.

—What the fuck now? he whimpered.

Breathing, drawing near, borne and unsheeted by the dark horsemen of the beyond and a moment later he was standing in the middle of his street panting, his townhouse windows exploding with light, the cold October night a black tonnage above him. He drove the damp streets until daybreak.

—I need a leave of absence, he told Troy on the phone.

—Hey – sure.

—A week maybe. Two.

—No fucking prob. Anyway – I'm planning a restructure.

And when he phoned the golf course:

—I'm sorry.

—I have a lesson, she replied curtly.

—I'm taking a week off.

—You need more than this.

—I know, I know. Troy's planning a restructure.

—You know what I mean, Amaranta said.

—Help? That I need to see someone?

—I must go, Rud.

—Well I'm fine – fine.

—Adiós.

—Fine! he shouted at the dial tone.

GARNETT, DAVID C., 51, died of cancer, October 31. He was preceded in death by his . . . Survivors include two sons . . .

◇

Dr McLeish was short, plump, with a cropped gray beard, a Scottish brogue somewhere between a Stradivarius and a gatehinge.

—I – I read obituaries, Rud confessed.

—Many people do.

—At my age?

—Well

The office was small and spare as a schoolhouse. Rud sat in a wooden chair facing the doctor at his desk. The office wallpaper cool as fresh linen.

—Do you believe in ghosts? Rud asked.

The doctor pursed his lips thoughtfully.

—Do you? Rud asked again.

—Your father? Dr McLeish asked.

—Maybe. Maybe *his* grandfather – Uncle Thom.

—I'm not sure I

—I guess what I need to know is

He hesitated.

—What, Mr Gillette?

—Did I – am I going crazy?

—No, Mr Gillette.

—No – that easy.

—That easy, the doctor said. Now, would you like a prescription?

—What about ghosts – the ghost. Do you believe?

The doctor raised an eyebrow.

—Do you? Rud persisted.

—I believe – what do I believe?

The doctor bootstrapped his chair back from his desk.

—Have you read Julian Jaynes? the doctor asked.

—Who's she?

—Juli*an*, the doctor smiled, picking up from his desk blotter his fountain pen. Julian and ghosts – well, he mentions somewhere a study, the only one actually, scientific that is, on people who'd seen ghosts. It was in England.

—Where else, Rud said.

—Precisely, the doctor agreed. Where ghosts are prized gossip. Even for the Royals, hmm? With his capped pen the doctor scratched his graying temple.

—But you, Rud insisted. What do you believe?

–Hmm – I believe that *if* I believed, I'd see one.

–That's an evasion.

–Perhaps. Would you like a prescription?

–To keep the ghosts away?

–To sleep.

–Titles, Troy told him a week later, are for snots. District Manager this, Regional fucking Manager that.

    –What's wrong with Regional fucking Manager that?

    –Even mine – right? General – what d'you call it?

    –Generalissimo.

    –Generalissimo – yeah. Well, fact: this is a textbook company. Fact: we sell textbooks. Fact: we're all fucking salesmen – right?

    –What is this?

    –All Willy Loman, right?

    –Wait a second – you're demoting me.

    –Restructuring.

    –I'm getting demoted.

    –Running lean, Troy said.

    –By the guy *I* hired.

    –I'm saving your job, Rud. It's a blackboard jungle out there. He tilted back his chair and blew a pillar of smoke.

    –You can have your pick of territories. Your pick. Except Nash's.

    –Nash?

    –Starts after Christmas. Wait until you see her.

She – Amaranta – skated like a skydiver. And Rud caught her and they sat on the low bench bordering the ice rink with the music and lights whizzing under the other skaters with City Hall lit and towering like a forty-story ribcage.

—You are worse than I am, she said.

—You rented me two left ones.

She had a small steel thermos that he unscrewed. The aroma and steam fleeing up like time past. He poured some in the thermos lid. Handed it to her.

—He is asking me to Florida, she said.

A policeman greatcoated and earmuffed slid in his jackboots in front of them. Shone his flashlight on her. Into her thermos lid. Back on her.

—Coffee, she said holding it up. Smell yourself.

—Just checking.

The policeman shuffled away flatfooted. Rud began to untie his skates.

—To Dunedin, she said. For spring trainings.

—The funeral home – they sent me a letter. About my dad's ashes.

He shivered, plying first one skate then the other free. He could feel her studying him.

—My feet're English, he said. They get cold easy. But Florida – hey – sun. Disney World. He rubbed each stockinged foot with the other. He sighed.

—Give us a sip, he said to her.

She refilled and handed over the thermos lid.

Came a March Monday – with Amaranta gone – and the librarian at the Beaches branch was beautiful: white hair, a white Mennonite beard, a parolee's suit.

—I can help you over here, he said to Rud.

Behind the checkout desk, two-story atrium windows looked onto a parkload of oak and chestnut trunks waxen with snowmelt. Onto a slat bench enseating a young black woman and bundled infant. Rud reread his book's title: James Hillman's *Suicide and the Soul*. The black woman on the parkbench wiped her nose with a tissue. Her fingers supple as bicycle chains.

–Sir?

–Ah, not just yet, Rud answered.

In the readingroom he sat at a long blond table under a swag lamp with several bums trembling over newspapers. Cars splashed by the library's far window. He opened the suicide book at his thumb: Children, some as young as ten.

◇

–Some as young as ten, he told Dr McLeish.

It was August. Overcast. He'd been that long stewing about what he'd read.

–I mean, how? Why? As if it were in them, in their – I don't know – from the day they were

Rud shifted in his chair. Rain splatted the office window with the mass and intermittence of highway insects.

–What am I saying, why? he continued. Everyone asks that, you know. Imagine. He shook his head. Though Amaranta didn't. Or Troy. Everyone else though: why? Why?

–And what do *you* say?

–Why, I say – why? Read the freaking autopsy!

The doctor jotted on the yellow legalpad in his lap.

–No I don't, Rud said. I mean jesus – the way he did it – good god! Rud shook his head. You know for a while, that day, I thought he'd jumped.

The doctor was silent. Rud examined his wingtip pocks.

—Any thoughts why he did not? Dr McLeish finally asked.

—He had a basement apartment.

Rud looked up at the doctor.

—I'm sorry, Rud said. An old joke.

—It's just your anger – and that's good.

—Sure.

—What about his note? He did leave a note?

Rud raised his eyes to the ceiling.

—Darling forgive me, he recited. I

He stopped. He squeezed shut his eyes and swallowed. He exhaled, then sat erect in his chair. He looked at the doctor. Who smiled kindly and asked, after a moment:

—Your stepmother? The darling?

—That's what I took it for.

—Your mother, perhaps? You know: as well?

—I expect.

They were silent for a short while.

—What *about* your mother, Mr Gillette?

—Where she fits in, you mean?

—I suppose that's what I mean, yes.

—You know, when I was a kid, when I thought of her at all, I, I worried how rarely I *did* think of her. I mean, Etta my stepmother was wonderful, other than hounding my father about his boozing I guess. And my stepsister about how she dressed.

A moment passed quietly. The doctor checked his watch.

—It's like, Rud continued, like can you remember at that age your hand or your foot or your face in the mirror?

—They say pigeons can.

—Pigeons? I

The doctor gestured.

—Sorry, he said. Foolish – go on, please.

–Or do you just imagine you can? I mean, jeez, I was nine. I slipped down the bank of this ravine and got all muddied, you know, caked, really caked, in Amherst, in the spring, and she spanked me when she came home from work.

Rud looked at the doctor.

–She worked in a bank.

–Ah.

–As a teller. Another time, just before she died – she came home and I asked her who'd won the World Series – our teacher wouldn't let us listen on the radio, and one or two bigger kids I asked only laughed at my English accent. But she knew. The last person I'd've imagined knowing, and she knew. Anyway.

Dr McLeish checked his watch again, placed his hands on his thighs then stood. Rud stood. They shook hands.

–Tuesday, Rud said.

–Pardon?

–The first anniversary – Tuesday. Still haven't written his obituary.

–You have picked up his ashes though.

–No.

–But I thought

–They sent me another letter – the funeral home.

–And?

–I will.

He did. The parcel was brownwrapped and crosstwined and pen-addressed like an overseas Christmas parcel. Big as a bootbox. Heavy as a fieldstone.

–Have you considered an urn? the ascotted assistant asked.

–No.

In his car he wedged the parcel into the seatjoint.

–Had a busy year? he said to it. Well this time I *will* keep an eye on you.

GONZALES, NAOMI, 67, died Christmas Day following a lengthy illness at
. . . Cremation will follow the services and committal of the urn at Trinity
Cemetery.

Christmas that year Amaranta spent in Argentina. She returned and on
his birthday in late January handed him a long giftwrapped cylinder.

—A rolling pin? he joked.

—Qué?

—Nothing.

He tore off the wrapping.

—Great! An empty roll of paper towel.

She shoved his shoulder.

—Mirá adentro – look inside.

Some sort of paper thing – rolled. He picked a corner, tugged. It
coned out and he unrolled it.

—Bachelor of Arts, he read. The Matchbox Correspondence School.
He looked up. Thanks.

Her eyes were glittering blue. Caribbean.

—Are you going? he asked.

—To the school?

—To Florida again – with Dedos.

She put a finger to her lips to silence him.

—In March? he persisted.

—Por favor.

—Are you?

—No, she said.

He smiled. Until he saw tears form under her eyes. His heart fell and
he entwined her fingers in his like ten rains.

◇

And then summer – outside the doctor's window – was standing on the university rooftops, bright as brass and gigantic.

–He could've bought a gun, Rud said. Though I don't think he ever fired one. Even in the war, seeing as he was in the Royal Navy. Which is a little, I suppose, like saying he did it that way because he was rereading *Shogun*.

The doctor said nothing.

–The second anniversary, Rud said. Wednesday. He laughed nervously. Perhaps I should celebrate.

–I might think it hard not to.

–Really?

–Last year you picked up his ashes.

–And this year? Bury him? Write an obit?

–Let's take one step at a time.

–You know, when I was at Cornell – I was thinking about this the other night at Amaranta's – we had to read in Psych a book by R. D. Laing.

–And? The doctor inked his legalpad with codings.

–Laing says a son's freedom can only come about when he admits to wanting to perform, ah, fellatio on his father.

Dr McLeish ceased writing.

–Fellatio? he asked.

–Yes.

–On his father.

–That's what he said.

–You know, I never much liked R. D. Laing. Now I know why.

They laughed together. And the next week on the second anniversary Rud used up his floating holiday and bought a Weber barbecue red as Amaranta's toenail polish and with her help assembled it. Then they sat on his deck smelling the mesquite coals whiten. They watched his neighbor wash his '65 Mustang as the blue window of sky thinned downward.

—My father kept my grandfather's ashes until my abuela – my grand-mother – until she died, Amaranta said. She sipped her wine. Then he mixed them and scattered them.

—I'm thinking of keeping my father's, Rud said.

Smoke toweled up out of the kettle's lidhole.

—Smells good, she said.

—I miss poking at the meat.

She kicked his bare leg gently with her toes.

—You've got a lovely mind, he told her.

—What are we having?

He got up out of his deckchair. Lifted the kettle lid. The smoke rose in a dense flock.

—Inca food, he answered.

—Huanaco?

He turned, brandishing the lid like a red shield.

—Wah what?

—Llama.

—No! No one could eat llama – no one.

—My brother.

◇

—So you *did* observe the day, Dr McLeish pointed out.

—We barbecued. Veal chops. Then she had to leave.

He was silent for a while.

—What is in your mind, Mr Gillette?

—Her. Uncle Thom – my father's grandfather. And if I had one – my father's grandson.

—Go on.

—That suicide is hereditary.

—You mean passed through genes.

—I suppose.

–Like shortness. Or baldness.

–Somewhat.

–Intriguing, the doctor said. But fanciful. Closer to home, may I ask if you've thought about his ashes? To perhaps bury them?

–I'm looking at alternatives.

GIGNOUX, MARIE K., 71, died of cancer, Sunday, September . . .

It was a month later. His eye then caught the obit that followed.

–Good god! he blurted.

HARMON, GABRIEL ALOYSIUS, 59, died Monday, September . . .

– You? Impossible.

He read on:

Survivors include his wife, Nora, daughter Gale

– Gale, he said. You.

He looked around his kitchen. As if checking for eavesdroppers. Which in a way he was. He reread:

daughter Gale. Cremation has taken place. A memorial service will be held at a later date.

Rud stared at it. No details. No rites. He cut it out. Taped it to his kitchen cupboard doorbottom.

–No sacred ground, he said to himself.

He studied it at erratic intervals. Taped there like some wavering and aghast mnemonic. Through his early fall visits to schools – trembling at times that he might chance into her. He did not. A Monday morning in mid October he typed and mailed a query on company letterhead to the council of English teachers. A Sunday morning in late October the light fell through his kitchen sliding doors quiet as stars onto his day-old

newspaper and his letter's response. The World Series was over. A fea-
ture article told him his Mantle card was worth thousands. And near
the headwaters of the Saint Lawrence River Gale taught at Our Lady of
Grace Catholic High School.

–Does he dare? he asked her father's obit.

Through his glass doors he could see his barbecue covered and standing on his deck like a droid and beyond his fence the mayan cliff of
apartment balconies and he phoned Amaranta and got her machine
and after he left a simple *Hi, it's me,* he drove, late morning, north to
the golf course, sadly driving both his car now and the shade and echo
of the car he'd driven that Sunday with his father in the rain. The emptiness of the seat beside him palpable. He was not wearing shorts this
time but jeans and sweatshirt and idling the car in the course's parking
lot he secretly watched her sweep her nine iron back and forth, warming
up in the smoky autumn air, her smile white as a rose as Dedos came
out of the pro shop with his sunglasses reared and glaring atop his head
and his nine iron under his arm like a ruling colonel and two packages
of golf balls.

She phoned that night and by then his bitterness over Dedos had
subsided.

–Yes, he told Amaranta when she asked him over.

–No, he told Gale's father's obit and he unpeeled it from his cupboard doorbottom and put it in a drawer.

Christmas he unearthed a poem written to a lady with Amaranta's
name, by Richard Lovelace, a Jacobean Englishman 350 years earlier,
and he translated it painfully and inaccurately into Spanish and copied
both versions out by hand

> *Pero menea la cabeza y desparrama el día*
> *But shake your head and scatter day*

and rolled them up sliding them inside a paper-towel bole and gave it to
her. A month later on his birthday she gave him a book of poems.

–Lorca, he said.

They were in bed, hers, facing each other on their sides. He read aloud her inscription:

–Siempre, siempre, siempre.

–Always – always, always, she said. Here.

She reached across his chest and flipped to her inscription's source.

–"Gacela of Unforeseen Love," he read. It's beautiful.

–Rud.

–Beautiful.

–Rud, por favor, please.

–Yes?

–He asked me to Florida.

Rud fixed his eyes on the page.

–For spring training, she added.

–Your body elusive always, Rud recited from Lorca.

–There is no good time to tell you.

–No. He rolled onto his stomach. I picked out an urn, he told her.

At home he lay in bed for an hour with the light on and then rose and went down to the kitchen. Before switching on the light he stood at the entrance. Across the kitchen the sliding glass doors were dark but clear. A meniscus of snow at their bottom. He flicked on the light, blackening the glass, vanquishing the snow, and in the kitchen drawers he searched for Gale's father's obituary.

She was bald. Either that or she wore a skin-colored bathing cap. Rud's view from the staffroom window tunneled south between twin wings of classrooms and she ran out from the end of the east. She carried a bundle of field hockey sticks like she was toting kindling and a trail of teenaged girls – some dragging sticks, others not – lagged behind her. Bald or bathing-capped though – christ, she was lovely – still slender, dressed unfashionably in a stretchy sweats top and a short khaki skort that buffeted as she ran. Ran? She could've outrun the sun! She certainly, as stiff-legged as foals they followed her down a slight incline, outran the girls. Crossing the cinder track she veered under the goalposts and sprinted for the middle of the field. There she scattered the sticks onto the yellowed grass, and while she blew her whistle and waved the girls toward her the sticks lay like cumbersome sortilege.

Finally the girls arrived and in nests they gathered around the sticks to hug their arms and exhale white breath tunes and bounce up and down in their aerobic shoes. Behind the field were the headwaters of the Saint Lawrence – the Thousand Islands a dense archipelago moored against the water's whorling green force – and the late-March sun on the keels of cloud above was a smoky pink. Again Gale blew her whistle and laughed and Rud smiled and someone tapped him on the arm and asked:

–The Academy Press?

Rud turned. A teacher – a huge man – well over six feet with a great barbered face and vandyke beard. He had his arms folded over the barrel of his chest and instead of a necktie he wore under his open-collared shirt a paisley cravat.

–Sorry?

–Or are you supply?

–Supply? No, no – the book rep.

–As I thought. I got your letter.

–Good.

–A copy.

–Good.

The man shot out a hand.

–Monsieur Michel, he said. Head of Moderns.

–Rud Gillette.

–It said you have something nouveau.

Rud nodded his head in the direction of his samples, fanned out on the coffee table beside the lounge entrance.

—*Français vivant,* Rud said.

—That's awful, M. Michel said. An awful book.

—Second edition, Rud added.

M. Michel pondered this. Rud turned back to the window. Gale had divided the girls who carried sticks into sides. Those girls without stood queued as, on one knee, she doled out the remaining sticks. Idly, Rud combed his fingers through his own hair.

—The teacher out there, he said over his shoulder.

—Oui?

He glanced back. With a foomp the lounge door swung open and Rud and M. Michel turned to see a black-gowned priest, in his early sixties, sweep in.

—Mitch, the priest said.

—Father?

The priest had a vaselined widow's peak of silver hair above a complexion fair as moonrise.

—It's happened again, he said.

—It is her head, M. Michel replied.

—You're telling me there's no cause for alarm?

Behind the priest the door swung closed then shot open again, bumping him forward. A younger priest, in trousers and habit, entered with a sheepish grimace.

—Sorry, Father, the younger said.

—Penitence, Father, the elder answered. Los Hermanos Penitentes.

—Coffee? the younger asked.

He was dark – almost handsome – with eyes stitched together by his eyebrows.

—You go ahead, the elder said.

At the far end of the lounge was a kitchen table where several lay teachers in lab coats sat reading and chatting. A coffee urn, battered as space debris, stood on the counter by the window. The younger priest acknowledged M. Michel and Rud and went to sit with his fellows.

—Comme ci, M. Michel said.

—Comme ça? the elder priest asked. I thought we were across that Rubicon.

—What if she did it for Lent?

—Really? She said that?

—Non – no.

The elder sighed and with his finger buffed his lips. He smiled at Rud.

—Busy morning?

—Not so far.

—It'll pick up.

He left to join the others. Out on the playing field the girls kept their arms pinned at their sides and when they budged at all they moved stiff as clothespegs, and cautiously, as though fearing they might step on their classmates' shadows. One girl with her stick's phoenician prow maintained effortless dominion over the ball. She was bigsisterish taller than the others and she moved with a floating grace and Gale, her head smooth, sidestepped and backpedaled a few yards from her, keeping up. Her whistle she held constantly to her mouth while with her free hand she made shoveling motions of encouragement to the others.

—Silly, n'est-ce pas? M. Michel said.

He towered beside Rud at the window.

—Field hockey?

—Non – that there's so short a time.

—Sorry?

—The class periods.

—Oh, right.

—Oui – they change – they play – then rrring. D'accord – *Français vivant* – let's have a look, eh?

—The teacher out there, Rud asked as he and M. Michel crossed the room to his display.

—You asked that before, monsieur.

—Gale Harmon.

They stood at the coffee table's edge. A worn yard-sale couch was behind, an armchair at one end.

−Where? M. Michel mused. *Living with Living Things* − ? *Modern Stories in English?* Shakespeare?

−The other side of the atlases, Rud said.

−Voilà.

When he bent at the waist to pick the book up M. Michel's pipe and tobacco slid out of his shirt pocket and he quickly halted them with one hand, nabbed the book with the other, and straightened.

−Well, I am out for a smoke.

−She *is* the English head, Rud persisted, Miss Harmon.

−She's no budget.

−That's not why I asked.

−None of us does.

−It's just that

−What, monsieur? You addressed your letter that way?

−The English Department − yes, Rud said.

−Well, she's a spare next period. Sometimes she comes in.

Thus did he spend the next eventless quarter hour on the couch waiting for the bell to ring. He fiddled with his display, then sat back on the couch and tugged free from under his backside the vents of his Harris tweed. He tightened the knot of his wool tie. He drew from his vent pocket a thin stack of business cards and bent them into a bevel and thrummed their ends with the clicking sound of a bicycle-spoke fillip. He slipped the cards back in his jacket and leaned forward and looked through the new *World Atlas*. He replaced it, opening it slightly and standing it upright on the table to allow more room so that if she came in, Gale would see readily the fanned-out English titles.

Finally the bell rang. Out in the hallway feet churned. At the kitchen table the younger priest and lab-coat teachers scorched their chairlegs back across the wooden floor and stood. The elder priest shook his head no and remained seated. The lounge door swung open and M. Michel cruised in, the French book tucked under his arm. Rud stood. His knee bumped the coffee table and the atlas teetered and fell onto another book. The lab-coat teachers and the priest allowed M. Michel leeway and the door swung closed. The younger priest reached for the handle. The door swung open and he recoiled from its arc and dipped his head politely as, about to crunch into an apple, Gale walked in.

—I'm sorry, Father, she said.

She *was* bald. She stepped aside, her back to Rud, inches from him. She smelled like peaches and talcum. He could see she hadn't *lost* her hair but had shaved it. As for M. Michel, he was somewhere nearby but as vague to Rud as a banished djinn. Without a sidelong glance Gale crossed the lounge to the window. She took a deep breath, as if recuperating from some vast journey, and with a soft crunch she bit into her apple. She was still dressed in zippered sweats top and skort. She even had her whistle around her neck. Sun and shadow streamed in the window and when she turned, both clamored across her face. She wagged her apple at M. Michel and smiled and took another bite of it and looked directly into Rud's eyes. He went rigid. Her eyes were the same blue green but starker somehow. She looked down at his textbook display and glancing up at him again strode right up to the coffee table. M. Michel stepped back and Gale stood between table and armchair, reading the titles.

—Hamlet, she said. *A Translation for the Modern Teen.*

Rud said nothing. The lounge door swung open again and some other lay teachers carrying coffee mugs passed in and, talking, headed for the lounge's far end.

—Macbeth, she said.

She looked up from the books, her eyes meeting his. She had no eyebrows. Except for lipstick, her face clean of makeup.

—We're doing *Lear,* she said. I am.

He pointed at that edition.

—Though I don't think my students would call themselves modern teens, she said, smiling. She turned to M. Michel. Yours, Mitch? she asked. Postmodern?

—Post-mourant, he replied, adding quickly, or post-dormant – some of them. Anyway, monsieur – ?

He handed the French text to Rud.

—Merci, he said to Rud, I have class. Bonjour. Gale?

—Bye, she said.

M. Michel squeezed Gale's arm gently and she watched as he walked around the table to the lounge door. He allowed still more teachers in and was gone. Gale turned to Rud.

—So, I'm the English head, she said.

—I know, Rud said, his voice hoarse.

He cleared his throat.

—And phys ed head. And —

She pointed to the smooth skin of her skull.

—Except you don't have the right accent, he said.

—Hmm? Oh, right. London — cockney. Nice, she told him smiling. You remember me, don't you.

He nodded.

—And I — when I got your letter.

—It's not a Smith or a Jones, he told her.

—No.

They were silent. She took another bite of her apple.

—You remember Troy? he asked.

—Another unforgettable name.

She waited.

—Well? she asked.

—Oh, he said laughing at his clumsiness. Right. Ah, I work for him.

—He's your boss?

—Yeah — yes.

—As well as being your stepbrother.

—Yes, Rud said swiftly. Though I didn't plan it that way.

—I wouldn't have either, she said. Well

She looked down at the display. Pointed with her apple.

—And that? she asked.

—That? That's an atlas.

—No, she said. Beneath.

By its thin spine he plucked up the atlas and it butterflied open.

–*Modern Stories in English*, she read aloud the title now revealed.

–An anthology.

She picked up the grain-colored book.

–As is an atlas, she said.

–Now that I think of it

–Imagine if the earth, you know – its surface – really was that way.

–Smooth?

–Yes – and tidy, with dots instead of cities.

–And place names.

–The capitals in red. Of course, she said, imagine, then, what the atlases would look like.

–Ugh, he said. Don't – my job's bad enough already.

She looked again at the anthology she held.

–Not very powerful, she observed. The cover I mean.

–Troy calls it a bowser.

She compared it to the atlas. Its cover had a conical projection of the Eastern Hemisphere – from Asia Minor to Mongolia – and onto the blue seas and oceans the continent, hued brilliant as polished copper, cast a dark blue shadow.

–As though it's hovering, she said.

He examined it.

–Or can't swim, he said.

She hadn't heard. To someone at the lounge's far end she was smiling slightly and lifting a still hand of greeting. She looked behind her at the armchair, then sat in it. She held up the anthology.

–A bowser, hm? she said.

Rud sat on the couch. Gale bit her apple and set it on the coffee table and when she did her whistle swung down and clunked the table's edge. She dabbed a droplet of juice from her lipcorner and sat back, setting the anthology open on her bare knees. She slid both ankles to one side – Rud's side – and he noticed how her slender legs still seemed cold from being outdoors. She fiddled with her whistle as though it was a chrome charm while she thumbed the book.

–"Ivy Day," she said, "A Rose for Emily" – maybe Troy's right.

–Right?

–I know, she said, looking up and smiling. I hated it when he was right, too. But it's just that, I don't know – it's just that these anthologies all have the same –

She paused. Her fingertip, the nail split, bounced on the open page.

–Now this, she said.

Rud snaked his neck to see.

–Which?

–Here.

–Hemingway?

–"A Very Short Story." That, that's different. Usually it's "A Clean Well-Lighted Place."

She ran the bitten quick of her finger down the editor's introduction. Her lips moving faintly. Halfway down her finger stopped. She made a loose fist and thumped with disappointment the anthology's page.

–Damn, she said under her breath.

–What? Rud asked.

–God damn, she said.

She kept her eyes on the page.

–What? he repeated.

She shook her head.

–Not this one too.

–Tell me.

–They all say this.

–Say what?

–It would be better if they said nothing at all.

–Who?

She chewed at her lower lip. Rud shifted to the couch's very edge.

–What? he asked.

—Don't you see, she said. It's a lie.

—What is? he asked.

—The author, she read aloud flatly, died in Ketchum, Idaho, in 1961 from gunshot wounds. *Gunshot* wounds?

There was a nearby rustling of gowns.

—Gale?

On the other side of the coffee table the elder priest stood. Slowly as a sunflower, Gale looked up, her face white.

—Father Bergeron, she said.

Rud stood. Gale began to, but Father Bergeron held up his hand.

—No, please, he said. Sit – both of you. I just stopped by – for a word. That is, if I'm not interrupting.

—We were just talking about Hemingway, Gale said.

—The Monsignor's favorite.

—About the way he died.

—Ah. And?

Gale looked down at the anthology's introduction.

—And about old friends, Rud said.

Father Bergeron looked at Rud and pointed his finger at him and Gale.

—Old friends?

—Yes.

—Really?

—Yes.

—How far back then?

—Years, Rud said, glancing at Gale, remembering her body leaning into his as they danced, twirled. Then the anonymity of high school.

—We went, he told Father Bergeron, to different schools together.

Father Bergeron took a moment, then said with a grin:

—Very ecumenical – yes. But Gale, the game. Its outcome.

—There was none, she replied.

—No one scored?

–No.

–Not even – ?

He held his hand in measure several inches above his head. Gale shook her head no.

–She's too kind, Gale explained.

–A tender heart. Which is the quick word I, ah

He smiled at Rud. Collected his thoughts.

–Have you started the Merton? he asked Gale.

–I will, Father, Gale said. It's just that

–Because there's a retreat, he told her. A lay one, at a skete across the river. Weekend after next.

–Thank you, Father, really, but

–Now don't – don't say no, he said smiling. Or yes, at least right now.

–Certainly.

She lowered her eyes.

–Good, good.

He scratched the silver hair behind his ear. Pointed to the book in Gale's lap.

–Have you talked her into it? he asked Rud.

Gale closed the anthology and, stretching forward, replaced it on the table.

–I think she prefers the atlas, Rud replied.

–Just as well, the Father said and, nodding at both, with a black drape of his cassock he left.

–Thank you, Gale said after a moment.

–I'm not sure I

–Yes you do, she said.

Holding her whistle to her chest she stood. He looked up at her.

–You know, don't you, she said.

–Know?

–Don't you.

He nodded.

–About my father.

–Yes.

–The way you steered me clear – of – of Hemingway.

–Yes.

–Did Mitch tell you?

–Of course not.

She looked around the lounge, contemplating rather than seeking.

–Father wouldn't, she whispered.

–No.

–But how?

He shrugged. Still she gazed off. They were quiet. The voices of the other teachers came in murmuring bursts, with a sound fallen leaves might make returning in clusters to their branches.

–I have a small office, she said. Upstairs.

She looked down at Rud. She blinked. The pain in her expression so clear in her uncluttered face, even when she smiled and said:

–I'll make tea – if you have time.

–I've plenty, he said, standing and sidling around the coffee table.

–Are – aren't you going to bring your books? she asked.

–Only this.

–The atlas?

–It's yours.

–Mine?

–A gift, he explained. Gratis.

–No, she said. By its stem she picked her apple core from the coffee table. No, you mustn't.

–It's no big deal.

She stepped around the coffee table.

–Well, she said, only if you let me give you one in return.

–Lovely, he said.

She dropped her apple core in the wastebasket and pulled open the lounge door.

–You might not think so, she said.

◇

Our Lady of Grace High School was a seventy-year-old stone and brick two-story, a building the Catholic school board had purchased from the public one when the government funded the upper parochial grades. Its stairwells were narrow as real wells and the one Rud followed Gale up creaked, giving out into a long hallway of shadow. A floor-to-ceiling window they walked away from was the sole light and this wan windowlight fell like a wimple across her freshly shaved head, her shoulders. The floors were wood and smelled like pinecone and her sneakers squinched and though he tried to walk softly his wingtips clomped. His heart thunked in his chest: from the climb, he told himself.

    –Do you believe in omens? she asked over her shoulder. I try not to but

    –Me too.

    They neared the hallway's end.

    –Your letter, then coming – here we are.

    She took her keys out from the muffler of her sweats top and unlocked the office door.

    –In you go, she said.

    The ceiling light already burned. He entered, sidestepped her desk. Bookshelves ran behind her desk and down the far wall perpendicular and he quickly weighed up the atlas's dimensions with the height of each shelf, reading from habit the bookspines within: *Fowler's; The Oxford Companion*. Behind him Gale closed the door. He meant to turn and ask where he should shelve the atlas when he saw, on the shelf just above eye level and separated like an oasis from the other texts and curricula, a small canon bookended by two chunks of flesh-red feldspar: *The Gospel According to Zen* by Ernest Wood; *Zen in the Art of Archery* by Eugen Herrigel; and *Zen Seeds, Zen Diamonds* by Bernard Klearmann.

    –It's green, Gale said.

    He turned. From around her neck she unveiled her whistle's string, looping it over her smooth head and tossing it onto her desk blotter.

–Green? Rud asked.

–The tea.

–Oh – ah maybe I

–Irish Breakfast, she said with a slight smile.

She unzipped her sweats top and pared it over either shoulder and down her bare arms. Rud looked away, at the side wall nearest the door. There, a series of stark pencil sketches – unframed, just maskingtaped to the bare wall – ran in a gallery row from doorjamb to the end corner. Gale's chair squeaked as she hung her jacket by its shoulders. Rud stepped closer to the sketches.

There were eight portraits – eight faces. Men's faces. Rendered, lean as coins, in three or four pencil strokes: nose and chin; the eyes; the head from prow to spine. The middle was Hemingway. To its right, Jack London. Then a bearded sage.

–Homer, she said.

Whose portrait – the eyes – looked out at Rud from across a vast sea of Ilium and wandering and home. The next, of a large-eyed boy, from some sort of orphaned make-believe.

–Chatterton, she said.

But the next? The one closest to the door? That one had no portrait. It was blank. Just a crane-colored depth of strokeless silence. He looked again at Chatterton.

–I must've drawn him a thousand times, she said.

He turned. She wore a white poloneck and her shoulders cringed, pushing her breasts together.

–A thousand times, she repeated quietly.

–Chatterton?

–On our phone book – funny ones. On birthday cards, romantic ones – god. She laughed sadly and shook her head. By Etch-a-Sketch even, she said. Grumpy ones when he'd make Mom – She paused. A thousand times, she said. But not a thousand and one.

Rud looked back at the large-eyed boy. At the blank sheet of paper.

–Tell me something? Gale asked softly.

–If I can.

–Who told you?

–No one.

–How then?

–Just – I don't know – I – look, I shouldn't have come.

He faced her.

–The drawings are beautiful, he said. His cheeks flushed. And you're – but I – I shouldn't have come.

–Why?

–I had no right.

–No right?

–No – to find out where you taught. To send you the letter.

–Wait, she said.

She came from around her desk, not really frowning but struggling somehow. On impulse, he held out the atlas. She took it and without turning set it on her desk behind her.

–What you told the Father, she said.

–What?

–About you and me.

–Being at different schools together?

–Yes. And even now – what with my father – we still are, aren't we?

He didn't respond.

–Aren't we?

He nodded. She was an arm's length away. Less. A moment passed. She reached back and gripped her desk's edge and half-sat.

–Can I ask who?

He put his hands in his pockets. She waved her hands in the air as if dispersing smoke.

–I'm sorry, she said. You don't have to tell me. She looked down at the floor. Good god, I'm doing exactly what others – what I

–My father, Rud said.

He turned and looked again at the portraits. Homer. Chatterton. The one of her father, awaiting. With a finger he touched the crane-colored paper. Both soft and hard, like callus.

—Three years ago, he told her. Then, when I

He paused. She said:

—Mine seven months.

He turned to find her staring past him, her eyes cold, clear. Her fingers she ran across her head as if she still had hair. She was perspiring, like rain falling underground.

—I'd come home from my run, she said and she pushed herself off the desk edge and stepped behind it. Longer than usual, she said. She opened a side drawer, fiddled absently with its contents. She closed her eyes. Opened them. Took from the drawer a dark green box of tea.

—But not much, only a moment, she continued. I – I'd stopped to talk, to talk

She kept her eyes on the box of tea. It was still in its cellophane. With her bare thigh she closed the drawer. She looked up at Rud.

—The firetruck was green too, she said. The one in the driveway, but I thought that's okay I thought, that's okay, Dad's a fireman, why wouldn't it be? But then

She took a deep breath. The tea box she turned on end and she plicked with her quickened thumb the glued fold. Rud stood now by her desk.

—My shrink, she said lifting her eyes to her shaved head. She's not going to like this.

—Tell her it's head lice, he suggested.

—Twice in two months? No – *Continence, Gale,* she'll say.

—Continence?

She didn't answer. Finally she split the cellophane and skinned its wrap.

—To live with our ailments, she explained. With the circle of firemen, standing, kneeling, by Dad's car. Gale crinched the wrap. Mom propped

against the garage wall, she said – and here Gale looked, with eyes ei-
detic, still seeing, directly at Rud – looking at me like I'd

Her voice broke. Rud reached to soothe her but she drew away.
Moved her empty hand as if secreted there in the essence were words
that, might she yet seize them, would alter what she could not stop
seeing. She looked at the tea box. Strove her thumb through the lid's
perforations and opened it.

–This tea, she said, it's – I, I was there for the week, she said. Visiting.
The week before Labor Day. And now look.

She sobbed. Masked her nose with her fingers and thumb, tossing the
tea box onto her desk by the atlas.

–It's leaves, she said.

Without even realizing, he'd stepped beside her and with his hands
Rud cupped her shoulders, drew her close. She laid one hand palm-flat
on his chest. Then seized his shoulders. They held each other, trembling
like culprits.

–Do people ask you why? she asked him.

–It's better than when they ask me how.

Her breasts nudged against his chest and being that tall she only had
to raise her head a little to look into his eyes. Wet, her eyes were green
more than blue and to allow her to daub them dry with her wrist he let
go of her. She sniffled.

–I've no strainer, she said.

–That's okay. My country still denies the existence of tea bags.

Gale smiled and from the deep desk drawer took out a single hotplate. Beside her desk wedged in the corner was a shoulder-height filing
cabinet and on top was a motorcycle helmet. A phone book was beside
the helmet and she swung the book up and set it on her desk. It was the
New York 1970 White Pages. Atop the phone book she stacked the hotplate and, shifting aside some textbooks in the side shelves, plugged it
into a wall socket.

–Skeddy said you went to Broadway, Rud said.

–Skeddy?

–Yes.

–Is he the one that became a Muslim?

–Now he's a real estate agent.

She took a copper kettle and a jug thermos from the lowest drawer of the filing cabinet, bending in her skort with such grace and naturalness – like someone who believes she is utterly alone – that Rud had to look away.

–Rhode Island, she said, filling the kettle with water. The School of Design. But the day I was to leave

She placed the kettle on the burner.

–I just couldn't, she said.

Cups and saucers – white china ones on robin-blue saucers – she took from the side bookshelf, and when the kettle whistled she spooned the tea – rich and green as its patronal isle – into the teapot, which was white with a single robin-blue streaking. It was like a pastel ballet of silence, the way she moved each item with utmost care. While the tea steeped, she unpacked from a well-worn lunchpail two lettuce-and-tomato sandwiches and a rhubarb bran muffin.

–I can't eat your lunch, he protested.

She put a finger to her lips. He hushed. She cut the sandwiches and muffin and arranged each of the two small meals on a white napkin. A card-table chair was tucked beside the filing cabinet and she tipped it out and passed it to Rud and gestured him around to the other side of her desk. There he unfolded it and she turned and faced the bookshelf behind her desk. He could see how she placed her palms together with her fingertips just under her eyes and when she bowed, slow as a laurel, was revealed in the bookshelf a small Buddha. Rud clasped his hands in front of his hips. Once more she bowed before turning and bowing to Rud. He didn't move. She sat. He sat. She poured the tea. And in silence they ate.

After they'd finished she wiped clean the cups and saucers. Rud pointed to the line drawings.

–May I?

She nodded. Beginning at the door, he stopped to examine each with his hands clasped behind his back as he might a row of epitaphs. Chatterton, Homer, Jack London, Hemingway, then a rugged, boyish face, like that of a handsome village lad.

–Sergei Alexandrovich Esenin, Gale revealed. A poet, a Russian. He loved Isadora Duncan.

–Vanessa Redgrave?

–Yes. He wrote a final poem in his own blood

–As ink?

Gale nodded.

–Then hanged himself.

She paused.

–The rest are the same, she continued. My mustard seeds. Hart Crane. De Nerval. Writers who committed suicide.

–This one again? Rud asked of a face with a pasteur beard.

–De Nerval, she told him. He wrote *Daughters of Fire*. Walked the streets of Paris with a lobster on a leash.

–You're kidding me.

–Honest, she said.

–A lobster.

–Yes – what was it he said – ?

–He actually

–I remember, she said. Because it does not bark and knows the secrets of the sea.

–When it will give up its dead?

–Perhaps. He hanged himself, she said. From a lamppost, with the apronstring of an actress, his great and unrequited love. He – he was the last I drew.

–Not that one? Rud asked pointing to the final one in the row.

He turned. She was behind her desk, standing, holding the telephone book. She shook her head no and looked down at the hotplate on her desk. She twisted at the waist and returned the phone book to its place atop the filing cabinet.

–Daughters of fire, she said, barely loud enough for Rud to hear.

She shook her head and with her cupped hand trailed the electrical cord to the wall socket in amongst the books. Her canon of three books was on the shelf above, and Rud reread the spines. Wood's *Gospel*. Herrigel's *Archery*. Klearmann's *Seeds . . . Diamonds*. Rud looked again at the haunting gallery of portraits.

–One more, he said, you'd have a ball team.

He looked at her.

–Sorry, he said.

–You needn't be.

–It's just, well, Chatterton here, he could be the batboy. Hemingway – Rud puffed up his chest. Gale grinned.

–The bullpen, she suggested. What about Homer?

–The catcher.

–He was blind.

–The umpire then.

She laughed.

–Jack London though, he puzzled.

–The skipper? she suggested.

–And –

He bent closer to the one nearest the corner. An oval face, with Asian eyes that didn't seem right somehow – donor's eyes perhaps.

–Hiraoka Himitake, she said.

–Who?

–Mishima, she said. He

–I know, Rud said.

She'd come around from her desk. There was a burning sensation in

his chest and a horrid wave of vibration in his ears. He inhaled a deep
ballast of air and forced himself to say:

—How my father did.

She didn't seem to catch on. Then she asked:

—Seppuku?

He nodded. He wanted to look away but again he willed himself to
keep her glance.

—In the bathtub, he said and fearing for her sake she might laugh
he camouflaged any embarrassment with his own. But she wasn't
laughing. She was crying, barely but crying, quiet gems on her cheekbones. Quietude that now spoke to Rud with precision and certainty
of the half-cry half-laugh his father had unleashed their last night together.

—Rud

—It's okay, he told her. I found him.

He winced slightly and she swam toward him and they held each
other and then were at arm's length – all, it seemed, within a breath.
And she said:

—The parable of the mustard seed. With her fingers she wiped her
cheeks' teargems. D'you know it?

—Jesus?

—The Buddha.

She looked at her small statue in the bookshelf. She said in a near-
recital voice:

—Fetch a seed, a mustard seed, from each house where no one has
died, where no one has grieved, the Buddha told her, and I will make
you medicine for the dead.

She paused.

—I think sometimes, she said, that even if you picked up that statue
and hurled it into the wall and it broke into ten thousand grains of
dust – She looked at Rud. Sorry, she said. Anyway, from house to house
the woman went, her dead son on her hip. Asking for mustard seeds.

Gale waved her hand at her line drawings.

—I thought these might be mine, she said.

He looked at them too.

—They're someone's, he said.

—Because when you think of it, in books, no one ever dies. You pick up *Anna* again and

A short bell rang.

—Three-minute bell, she said. I have to get my stuff.

She slipped behind her desk to the filing cabinet.

—*Lear?* he asked.

—Sorry?

—D'you have *King Lear* next period?

She shook her head and opened the cabinet's top drawer.

—The one after, she said.

She closed the drawer and from over her white polo-collared shoulder looked at him.

—I'm glad you came, she said.

—Are you?

—Very.

She tilted the motorcycle helmet on top of the filing cabinet and slid from beneath it a sheaf of paperclipped papers. Then gently let the helmet down, with its visor dark and lucid, a scarab from some future Nile.

—Last I heard, you and Troy'd won scholarships to Cornell, she said, counting the paper clips.

—Sort of.

—Sort of?

—Troy played hockey.

—You baseball?

—A walk-on.

—The boy with the glove, she said.

—Yes.

–Jumping off school roofs.

–And catching snowballs.

Another bell rang. Babble and feet exploded down the hallways. She stood inches from him.

–You didn't answer me, she said.

–About what?

–Whether you believe in omens.

–Can I sleep on it?

–Yes.

She opened the door to a thundering train of students.

–I was unsure about something, she said. But now, your being here, our fathers – She paused. Anyhow, here.

To his surprise she pressed at him her sheaf of papers.

–In return for the atlas, she said.

–A manuscript?

–I warned you, she said.

–Yes, you did.

They plunged into the throbbing train. Descended the narrow stairs – few students noticing her shaved head. In the front foyer they said goodbye.

–I'll be in touch, he told her. About the manuscript.

–Gale!

It was M. Michel, piloting through the crowd his baronial girth.

–Miss Harmon, a kid called, waving a Signet *Lear*. Nice cone!

She responded to neither. Nor to Rud when he said:

–I'm glad too – very.

What she did was point her palms up under her chin and bow. Then, with her eyes green and smiling, she was gone. And Rud, after sweeping his display into his barrister's bag, walked up the front path to where he'd parked his car. He could smell the damp reek of the Saint Lawrence, like fish thawing, and the grass on either side of the walk was matted and puddled with neapolitan dog turds. But the sky – the sky was an angel's wing of cloud. From it snow spittled down and while his car idled, warming, he opened Gale's manuscript. *Mustard Seeds: An Anthology of Literary Suicides.* There was an epigraph. In Latin. By the time he'd surged west back to the city, he'd memorized it.

second

They stood on the roof in the rain. Rud and Rina Kucharski – now the editor in chief. Stood watching, from under the bat-wing lip of the umbrella they shared, Troy. Who stood solo under his umbrella, facing them, smoking.

–These fucking Brits, Troy said. It's bad enough they're coming, they have to send their weather ahead.

–Misters Peale and Davis-Carmedie, Rina on tiptoes whispered to Rud.

She clutched Gale's manuscript. Gloves of fog reached around the air-conditioner turbines, deepening beyond the roof's edge. A foghorn bleated: the island ferry.

–Why can't it fucking snow?

–It's spring.

–Snow – snow you can fucking shovel. Is this a social call?

–We're getting married, Rud said.

Rina elbowed him.

–Ho fucking ho.

Troy dropped his meg end sizzling on the wet tar and gravel.

—A week they give me, Troy fumed. Less than a fucking week. Scuse the language.

He went inside. They watched him wrench open the firedoor, lash his umbrella closed, whip the rain off.

—I'll keep trying, Rina said.

Rud could see the light burning warm through the windowsquare of his former office.

He sat at his desk at the far end of the sales reps' tunnel. Ostensibly sorting his mail. In truth he was doodling into his briefcase leather with his thumbnail. Nose. Chin. Hair. Two postcards over the week past from Amaranta in Dunedin: *Spring Home of the Blue Jays!* Sun. Sea. Sand. Dedos. He looked up at his Matchbox Cover Correspondence School Degree. In his *Far Side* desk calendar D. B. Cooper parachuted into a kennel where teeming rottweilers lapped their chops hungrily. February 21? His father's birthday, for christsake. He tore off the near month and a half. In his directory of schools he looked up Our Lady of Grace.

—Gale Harmon, please.

—Just a minute.

With the postcard edges he swept away the doodle in his briefcase leather. He reread one postcard back.

weather is here, wish you were wearing shorts
I have my own room – a phone call? a letter?

—Ms Harmon's left early, I'm afraid.

—Will she be in tomorrow?

No answer. The other was postmarked a fortnight later:

This is it! Don't call us? We won't call you.

—Hello? Will she be in tomorrow? he repeated.

—Sorry. Yes. Father Bergeron thinks so.

◇

—Three or four lines? Dr McLeish asked Rud.

—Yes.

—And all of them suicides.

—All of them.

—But no drawing of *her* father.

—No.

—I don't know, Mr Gillette. Is she married?

—She wasn't wearing a ring.

—And you were in love with her.

—My first.

—Unrequited?

—I don't know. She was Troy's girl in grade school. Troy's girl. Sounds funny now, doesn't it? Troy's girl. Anyway we danced once, at our graduation.

—Once.

—She asked me.

—Ah.

—"All in the Game."

—Cliff Richard.

—You know it?

—Glasgow *is* on this planet.

—Thas nut whu the see in Edinbarra.

Dr McLeish laughed.

—*That*'s not what they say either.

The doctor's brogue was tart as rhubarb. Rud laughed – for a moment.

—And then, he said, in her office, we – he leaned forward – we had tea. And made up a baseball team.

—It's not up to us who we love, who we lust after.

—Who our parents are, Rud added.

—Who our children are, Dr McLeish said.

Elbows on knees now, Rud held his face in his hands.

–She'll be home Monday, he said. Amaranta.

–There's no suicide gene, Mr Gillette. We had agreed. And our time is

–She went because she wanted.

–And?

The doctor spread his hands flat on his trouser thighs.

–I couldn't have made any difference, Rud said.

–Let's end on that thought, shall we.

He stood, held out his hand. Rud shook it.

–Next Friday?

–Yes.

–It'll be in my head all day, the doctor said.

–What will?

–Cliff Richard. My wife saved Jeana's poster of him when she graduated to Pink Floyd. I've always wondered if they feel it somehow.

–Pop stars?

–Yes, celebrities. When they lose a fan.

That was the Friday after he'd seen Gale. Monday Amaranta returned. She did not call. He did not either. Opening Day passed but Rud
didn't even read the linescore. When finally he did phone he got her answering machine. He hung up. He was sitting at his desk in the tunnel.
His phone rang. Troy.

–Okay, Rudmeister, come take your best shot.

–Gale's manuscript?

–Yeah. Then maybe you'll go back to *selling* books.

The elevator stopped automatically one floor down – Troy's floor –
the third. Troy'd had it programmed that way to monitor comings and
goings. His office door was open and as Rud walked between the Apples
and IBM clones he could see Troy sitting at his oak veneer desk in
rolled-up shirtsleeves jotting notes.

He went in when Rina arrived walking on the toes of her low-heeled
pumps. Troy shook a cigarette out of a softpack.

–Close the door.

He lit it. Tossed the match in his large glass ashtray. There was a day and a half out his window. Blue jigsaw pieces of sky above the warehouse roofs and the trees in the small park. Cloud pups. Troy peered lordly over the pages of Gale's manuscript. He exhaled, coughed, flicked back his hair. He read aloud:

–Homer hanged himself because he could not solve the fishermen's riddle.

He eyed Rud. He eyed Rina.

–Okay. First question, what's the fishermen's riddle?

Rud looked at Rina.

–Their feet sought the earth, she said. Twitched a little, and were done.

–That's it? That's not a goddamned riddle.

–It's the *Odyssey.*

–Christ.

–When Telemachus hangs the suitors' harlots.

–Doublechrist. See what I mean?

Rud objected:

–One little

–One? One? They're all men. They'd kill us.

–Who?

–Who the fuck else.

–Aa! Rina objected.

–The Brits don't come until tomorrow, Troy countered.

–You said.

–All right all right – *whom* the fuck else.

–Troy's worried about the manuscript's gender balance, Rina said, shaking her head.

–The fems'll hang us. What'm I saying, hang us – have our cajollies: it's got a Latin epigram.

–Epi*graph*, Rina pointed out.

–Latin – more dead white male sh – Troy stopped himself.

–I'm not sponsoring it as a textbook, Rud said.

Troy leaned back. His leatherette chair creaked.

–Oh?

–A trade book, Rud suggested.

–Nada.

–Who'd buy it? Rina asked Rud.

–Nobody, Troy answered.

–Psychiatrists? Rud thought out loud.

–Psychiatrists, my ass. Troy lifted his hands in exasperation and the chair ptwanged to rights. Come on, Rud. So what if it's Gale Harmon. You and I know her but to everyone else, especially Herr Doktor Blurred Fist

   –Aa!

–That's not swearing.

Rina rolled her eyes.

–to Herr Doktor or even Frau Doktor it's just a bunch a stories put together by some high school English teacher with a blah-blah intro about fishermen. Nothing you can't get from the *Norton*. Or the *Oxford*. Even our old bowser. Right, Rina?

–Certainly Hemingway and Jack London. As for

Troy waved her quiet.

–Two against one, he announced to Rud. Now go sell some books. Post-Brits, I'll come out with you.

–Still, Rina said as she slid the filefolder with the manuscript off Troy's desk, I would like to see those line drawings.

–So would I, Troy said. He crushed his cigarette. But we're a book company, not an art gallery.

Rud stood. Rina unrolled her sweater sleeves down the white of her lean arms. She took off her glasses, pushed back her chair.

–I wasn't much help, she said to Rud, was I?

—Lots, actually.

Outside a police officer on horseback rode down the street. Hoofs klop-k-klopping on the pavement.

—Stay a minute will you, Rud? Troy asked.

Rud sat. Rina closed the door behind her. Troy stood and circled his desk. Hands thrust deep in his pants pockets. He jingled his change.

—Pocket pool, Rud said.

—Ha ha.

Troy's laugh was too loud. Wary, Rud watched him drop hard into Rina's chair.

—Still warm, Troy said.

The horse hoofs klopped faintly now. Troy lit another cigarette.

—Tomorrow. Tomorrow. A new fucking regime, Rud.

—The wretched English, Rud said.

—Limeys. They arrive tonight.

Troy rubbed his eyes. He yawned.

—I been up all night all week pounding out the goddamned numbers. I think they're going t'make me president. Imagine? El presidente. Holy shit! Unless I go fucking stare first.

—Or call them tit-strokers.

—Right.

Troy appraised the gray shimmy of his smoking cigarette end.

—So. He took a deep breath. I'd like it if you could stick around to-morrow.

—Why?

—I don't know exactly – to translate. Unless you've got calls hard-wired.

—None wired, exactly.

—Well, bee eff and ee then.

—Let me guess.

—Bright and fucking early, Troy said. Before eight.

Rud could no longer hear the horse's klop.

—Is it a deal? Troy asked.

Rud had turned his attention to the window.

—Bee eff and ee?

—I'll be there, Rud said.

He shifted his gaze from the window to the bare wall opposite.

—You okay? Troy asked.

—Hm? Never better.

—I just don't want the suicide thing, you know, your dad, starting up again.

—Dad? Not a chance.

—Excelcius, Troy said. He carved his loafers' heels into the rug and tipped back onto the hind chairlegs.

—So what'd she look like? Troy asked.

—Gale?

—Who the fuck else?

He tilted back his head and blew. A perfect smoke ring ascended.

—Still a looker?

—She was bald, Rud answered.

—She was what?

—Bald.

Pissed as a rat – that was his intention anyway as he left the office. He ended up eastward in the lakeshore traffic. Past the concrete gort of SkyDome. Battling through the construction like infighters. Past the Olympic pool, past Scratch Daniel's. To the south the lake was awrithe with waves and he turned northeast. The wind had shepherded the clouds into dense flocks in the sky and he reached his old neighborhood before five.

—That's from the Requiem, Etta said.

She poured tea. Her hands chubby now.

—We never had drink in the house when your dad was here.

She finished pouring. Her hair was strawberry.

—You're looking tired, she said.

—Catholic? The Catholic requiem?

—And more and more like him.

He poured in milk, spooned in sugar, took a sip.

—Ahh!

—Confutatis maledictis, Etta began. The choirboys would always snicker at that. Flammis something – us addictis, wait now, voca me cum benedictis.

—Beautiful.

—Terrifying, Etta said. When I was a girl.

She sipped her tea.

—I didn't even know what it meant. We've Harvey's Cream?

—No, thanks.

—Voca me cum benedictis, another line, then your two.

—Cor contritum quasi cinis, Rud recited, gere curam mei finis.

—A natural. Your dad used to tell me, when I'd suggest I convert, an Anglican's just a Catholic with six wives. To think I laughed.

—It's funny.

—I guess it was.

They both looked across at the kitchen window. A small trumpet plant stood in a Styrofoam cup. A squirt dispenser of Neutrogena hand-soap. The window held the sky's reflection adrift.

—How's your Aztec lady friend?

—Tanned. And it's an Inca she's supposedly.

—Where from?

—Argentina.

Etta stretched and cuffed Rud's hand across the table.

—You know what I meant.

—Sorry. Florida.

—But she's not the same one with the Requiem thing.

—No. I would've thought it would be in Japanese. She, Gale, had these books on Zen.

—You know, Etta said, I was thinking about him, Mr Kito.

—Yeah?

—Mm – the other day. Now I can't remember why.

—Is it in the Bible?

—I don't think so. I should know. When I saw Ingrid Bergman in *The Bells of Saint Mary's* I fancied myself being a nun. Like Patsy.

She pushed back her kitchen chair and stood.

—Well, I'm going to have one.

She shucked open the fridge and took the black-labeled bottle from the door. By their stems between the fingers of one hand she plucked two crystal sherry glasses from the cupboard. Filled them. They drank quietly. The oven clock clicked at one-minute intervals. They talked about his stepsister Caroline. She was pregnant again.

—Out to here, Etta said – like a bulldozer.

They were silent for a short time.

—It was in that Mozart movie, Etta suddenly said.

—The Requiem?

—Yes. With the cute little actor. The Lacrimosa. Or maybe the Rex part.

She started to hum.

—It's out on video now.

She refilled her glass, topped up his.

—You're awful quiet.

—Sorry, he said. I want to tell you something.

—Well?

—About Troy.

He waited.

—I was thinking what we should do with your father's ashes, she said.

—He's going to be president.

—His being in the Royal Navy – your dad – we might, you might, scatter them at sea.

Rud waited.

—In England.

—I've thought about that, Rud told her.

—Near where he was stationed, she said.

They held hands across the table.

—D'you get the if-onlys? she asked.

—If only I did.

—Bugger, she said. A smile lit her eyes like a firefly. You know, us moving up here, your dad moving me here to be close to – to Troy.

She said nothing for a while. Refilled their glasses. The neighbor's kitchen door snapped open and shut. They turned to the window. A voice singing:

—The summer wind

The top of the neighbor's head scurried by just above the sill like a dark blue rabbit. The voice baritone:

—And the winter wind

—Sinatra, Rud observed.

—They're Vietnamese, Etta said. He demonstrates some sort of electronic organ.

—In malls?

She didn't answer.

—Etta?

—Oh? Somewhere near Plymouth.

—Plymouth?

—No, near there. Where your dad was stationed. Iris will know.

She reached across the table and pinched Rud's wrist affectionately.

—My other son, she said. I'll write him, Troy, about Caroline. Does he read them? My letters?

—I think so, Rud lied.

There was a Record World in the mall on the way home where the clerk implored him to get the Academy of Ancient Music version and two stores down from that a liquor store whose glass doors he snaked through with a minute till closing. In the absurd English-style pub he had two Budweisers to fortify his sherry buzz. The 7-ELEVEN at the end of his street had Coke in the sentimental six-and-a-half-ounce bottles that he bought and in his townhouse kitchen fizzed and frothed up from the ice cubes and black rum in his glass. Sipping, he sat on a stool at the counter. Requiem. It was night. Dark. Chilly. Way too fucking quiet. He punched up the thermostat and in the livingroom put on Santana. When he flicked on the kitchen counterlights they billowed like white laundry in the wind. Santana was louder then hell over the kitchen speakers. He went in and notched it down.

He was hungry. There were Cheerios: With rum and Coke? he asked himself. Fickin vile. He fetched from the front door the mail he'd earlier shuffled aside. Bills and a Pizza Pizza coupon. He sat astool with the phone on the kitchen counter and mulled about toppings. He peeled the cellophane wrap off the CD cover: the Virgin adored by a conflagration of Saints and Hosts.

—What did Dad have with his rum and Coke? More rum and Coke. Rud followed suit. Santana played again. He had another. Looked at his watch. Past eleven. Pissed as a rat?

—The fucking gerbil stage, he shouted over the music.

"Jingo" came on. Chi-boomboom chi-boom. Chi-boomboom chi-boom.

—Fuck her! He phoned Amaranta. Listened to her voice message. Beep! He phoned her again. Her voice pawed at his throat. Beep! Nothing. He despaired of air guitar. He swam unsteadily into the frontroom.

Jettisoned Santana. Dropped in the Requiem. Turned toward his fireplace and half-saluted his father's urn.

—So, he said, back in the kitchen. He reread the pizza flyer, examining
it from a variety of armlengths.

—Should've eaden earlier, he scolded himself, slurring. There was a
notes booklet in the CD cover and he pried it from under the cover's
plastic toenails. He paged through. He sipped his drink: Blech! Still
reading he shucked open the fridge: A cold ber, I command ye. He bent
and looked inside. Shit! He fired shut the fridge door. Turned another
page in the CD booklet. There was Gale's epigraph. Was the word:

cor contritum quasi cinis / my heart as though ground to ashes

He called directory information for Gale's home number.
—I have no listing under the name Harmon, sir.
He tried the towns east and west along the Saint Lawrence.
—None there either, sir, under the initial G.

gere curam mei finis / help me in my last hour.

Good christ! You are a sorry sentimental fuck, Rudyard Stirling Gillette, but you are not prepared for what will happen next. For, son! the
Lacrimosa begins. And he was on his feet, swooning. The music showering painfully down. The violins were cold and suffering as steel and
the chorale lifted and fell: a beautiful howling genesis that, rising and
forming, shaped and moved slowly through his body like a dark planet.
He was crying. Crying. He didn't *that* night but now his teeth ached
with it all, ached. Without shame he conducted the music. Without
shame he mouthed the words:

Lacrimosa dies illa	Oh, this day full of tears
qua resurget ex favilla	when from the ashes arises
judicandus homo reus;	guilty man to be judged;
Pie Jesu, Domine	
dona eis requiem.	

Gentle Lord Jesus, grant them rest. He was. He slept. He woke on the couch. Dragged himself upstairs. Sat on his bedside.

—Still drunk, he mumbled. He tipped back and fell asleep again. This time when he woke up he pushed himself into the bathroom. He flicked the lightswitch.

—Ahhh!

He clutched his eyes. He clawed the light off.

—Light, he said steadying himself. Light.

With light from the bedroom he washed at the bathroom sink head to toe. He brushed his teeth. Pink on the toothbrush.

—Fucking Coke. Surely there was an ice pick suspending him from the ceiling by the eyes. In the mirror his ears were bigger. His hair defiant. His nose plugged. He swallowed Tylenol and in the kitchen downstairs extra C and E and beta-carotene.

—Who the hell cleaned up? He pulled open the fridge. Pizza? He plied up and lifted the boxlid. Leftovers – you're saved. He wolfed the two slices while he phoned the office for Rina's voice mail.

—Hi. Did you order me pizza? Anyway, could you tell Troy – tell him I've gone to see a man about a dog.

East through the dawn and the lowlands he drove, his radio mute. Rising gnomons of sunlight stood on the drumlins and moraines where hunkered cows rigid as plinths watched his wheeling to Our Lady of Grace, to Gale.

$\Diamond$

Except she was gone. Everyone was. The parking lot was empty. The sun stood partially behind the school building though a sliver of yellow vibrated the tile along the roof's edge emphasizing the darkened classroom windows beneath. He parked at the lefthand curb and grabbed his briefcase and walked up the sidewalk. The lawn had been rid of dog turds and seeded where winter salt had eaten the fringe. He rattled the

front doors. Locked. Pricks. He crossed the lawn, making for the west
doors. The earth was soft and sucked at his heels. The mud he scraped
off on the doorslab edge.

These doors did open. A long hallway runneled back the way he came
and he stopped in front of the main office, waggling his case on his
thigh, brooding because it was dark and shut.

—All for nothing, he muttered. He checked his watch. Ten past ten.

—Coffee time!

Our Lady of Grace's head secretary, a tall woman with a narrow but
kind face beneath a country singer's hairdo, opened the teachers'
lounge door and the smell of coffee and tobacco smoke escaped.

—Yes? she said, smiling at Rud. She looked at his jacket and tie. Down
at his briefcase. Her smile fled. Quickly she stepped out into the hallway
dragging shut behind her the lounge door.

—The school board? she asked.

—The Academy Press.

She pressed her palm against her blousefront.

—Thank heavens.

She smiled at him again.

—I'm here to see Gale Harmon.

—Oh. Ohh. Did you, did you have an appointment?

—No. I was here last week. About this time.

—To see Gale?

—Yes.

—Well, I don't know what to say.

—That's all right.

—Father and the teachers are all at the Red Lion. It's teachers day.
But Gale

—I'm a friend.

—Then you don't know?

She paused, her eyes darting to either side.

—I left so early, he said, I couldn't phone.

—The phone – my gosh – I've forgotten to – come on!

She ran in her skirt and high heels from the knees down only. At the main office she jabbed some console buttons and waved Rud around and through the counterflap. Memos were pinned in vertical columns to a bulletin board outside the principal's office and, as she finished programming the phone, she pointed Rud to it. One memo listed statutory holidays. Another beckoned lay teachers to the retreat. A third announced the resignation of Gale Harmon, effective immediately.

He turned. The secretary already stood out in the hallway, holding the door open.

—I've only a few minutes left for break, she said.

He scanned the memo again: Gale did not disclose her plans in her letter . . .

—But

She fiddled with the doorhandle anxiously. Back around the counter he hurried. She closed the door behind him.

—You were here last week?

—Yes.

—Which?

—The day she

He pointed to his head.

—That was the second time too, she told him.

They reached the front double doors. Rud could see his car by the curb, gray as a nickel in the shade. Sun skipped atop the low houses across the street. The secretary edged backward down the hall. She spoke in a near whisper.

—Poor Father Bergeron. He'd hoped that would be the end of it.

—But it wasn't.

—No. The day before yesterday – you are a friend?

—We grew up together. Then I heard about her dad.

He tucked his hip against the long door rail. The doorglass chilled his shoulder.

—She came – the day before yesterday – not saying a word. Not a word. Even in class.

—She didn't say anything? About what she was doing?

—No – not even to Monsieur Michel.

—The French head?

The secretary nodded, crossed herself.

—Please – I've said enough.

—Yes, and I'm grateful.

Backward, the secretary increased the length of floorspace between them.

—Father is praying for her eternal soul, she said. We all are.

M. Michel wasn't at the Red Lion. He was in the phone book and his address was on the street map and at his bungalow a De Soto as derelict and low slung as a lab cadaver sat in the driveway bottom. Halfway up the driveway M. Michel was slapshooting pucks the rest of the way, firing them in long black gashes into the carport to hammer off a sheet of heavy ply fixed to the rear wall. A block from the school, the backyard swarming down into a lionpride of weeds at the river's edge. A goalie was painted lifesize onto the ply. When Rud slammed his car door M. Michel ceased shooting and turned.

—Bonjour.

—Bonjour, Rud said. Hello.

Scythes of sweat darkened M. Michel's gray T-shirt untucked and skirted over his jeans. Sweatbeads bloodied his vandyke. His bare forearms, as thick as a minotaur's, were gauntleted in hockey gloves.

—Monsieur, my name's Rud Gillette. I met you a week back.

–Oui?

–At your school.

–Ah yes.

–I'm the textbook salesman

–And you make house calls?

–No, no. This isn't – I came to

–I know why you came, and I will tell you what I told everyone else: rien – nothing. Bonjour.

He bent, reaching into a plastic gallon pail, tossed a few pucks on the asphalt, then slapped one up the driveway, hammering into the board.

–It's business, Rud said, appealing.

–Ha!

He slapped another puck, lashing it like the end of a whip.

–She gave me her suicide notes.

M. Michel turned on Rud, glaring.

–Her mustard seeds, Rud explained.

There was swift wind from the river.

–Pardon?

–Her manuscript.

–You intend to publish it?

–Perhaps.

–Your company?

Rud walked up the driveway, past the De Soto.

–If we had the line drawings, he said.

–No, monsieur, M. Michel said.

He picked his pail up and walked in vast strides into the carport. Rud followed slightly. There was an almost-chrome color to the sky above the river and a Harley-Davidson, its torso bared, was hunched back on its kickstand on the other side of the brown porchposts. The porchposts desperately needed painting. M. Michel scooped the pucks into the pail.

–Jacques Plante, Rud said, indicating the goalie.

–Ah, a Habs fan.

–No – my dad – you'd think it was him, Plante.

–Gale's work, M. Michel said. For this, my aerobics.

He strode back past Rud, picked up his stick, dished out some pucks.

–You'll have to move.

He slapped a shot, cannonading it off the thick ply. He commandeered another puck. He looked over at Rud.

–I am being a grouch, he said. But whatever it is you want you are too late – she left this morning.

–For where?

A horn beebeeped. They turned. A blue Saab, brand new, slipped in front of Rud's sedan like a cobalt jet fighter and braked noiselessly at the driveway bottom. Father Bergeron waved from its cockpit like a dignitary.

–Playing hockey? he called out the driver's window.

–Hooky.

–Ha, yes. He examined Rud.

–I haven't told him anything either, M. Michel said.

–I'm merely here to ask your attendance this afternoon. At the conference. The Monsignor

–Conspicuous by my absence, am I?

–We all are, at first. Good morning, he said to Rud.

He touched up the engine revs.

–Good for the heart, he said to Rud, hooky is.

Rud glanced at M. Michel, who smiled.

–New car, Father?

–That's what I was saying. The Monsignor's a chum of Desmarais. He's letting us each test-drive this ticker.

–It's two wheels too many for me, M. Michel replied.

–Gale would have agreed.

They listened to the wind's tumult, the river's.

–This bonhomme, M. Michel said loudly to the priest, is going to publish Gale's manuscript.

–Well

–Wonderful, the priest interrupted. Wondrous.

–It's more complicated than that, Rud said.

–Of course – wondrous – she'll be Gale again. At least in print.

–Now wait.

–You're giving him second thoughts, Father.

–That's my job. My job. Well, I have to – you know – he gassed the engine again – or they'll think I've made off with it. Wondrous!

The driver's window darkened. The car slid away.

–So you were at the Red Lion?

–Yes, Rud admitted.

–He doesn't miss a thing.

–The Father?

–Bien. And now I will have to –

M. Michel fished with the puck.

–She's okay then, Rud said. Gale?

M. Michel unleashed a wicked wrist shot.

–Okay? No.

–What then?

–She found me with this book, Herrigel's little book on archery and – just after her father's

He swept his stickblade across the pucks, deliberating.

–after his death. I thought it might improve my shot.

He batted a puck with his stickblade, twisted and fired another shot keening into the plyboard goalie, puck and board tolling like some enormous Luddite bell. With his stick he slapped the asphalt.

–Okay? Is she okay?

He paddled his stickblade on the driveway.

–How I loved her hair. Her voice in the afternoon, even after teaching all day. Her name

–Gale Harmon, Rud said slowly.

—Oui – imagine.

—She changed it, Rud thought aloud.

M. Michel looked directly down into Rud's eyes.

—Didn't she? Rud asked.

—Leave her her secret, monsieur, her name, her désespoir. Let the Father – let God – worry about her Zen.

—This much, this much you know, he said aloud to himself while driving back to the office. Some Zen thing. Some retreat or commune or monastery.

He stopped talking to himself when an old Ford Galaxie convertible boated past. His own speeding car seemed as fixed as a pier. The freeway dipped and a steel guardrail replaced the median. A new Dodge Ram towing a mobile home cruised past. Long as a neighborhood. Arizona plates. The hills began again. Ungreen.

—Sheep, he said to himself.

Motionless sheep, as rooted to the stream of hills as the bare fleshless trees throughout which they were pastured.

—God, you're hung over, he told himself. Ah! Atop an enormous pole were McDonald's arches. He slowed.

The Big Mac he wolfed in the parking lot; the fries as he banked round the cloverleaf back onto the freeway. He sipped his coffee until the city's outskirts where he usually swung down to take the lakeshore route in. Except now he was in the express lanes instead of the collector lanes and he couldn't get over.

—You don't know a flipping thing, he said.

He plugged westward. He might keep on going until he caught up with Gale. Unless she'd gone east. He took the parkway south.

—You do know one thing, he muttered when he reached the office late afternoon. He slowed past the parking lot, peering. Standing room only in Troy's office: the Brits.

—You're fucked, mate.

$$\diamondsuit$$

There was a U-Parkit lot behind the offices and he circled the block. He was up to stealth. His office building still retained its original fire escape – a zigzag of iron riveted to the sandblasted brick – and as he climbed the city rose. The dome of the stadium. The long-stemmed concrete toadstool of the C.N. Tower behind. He toted his briefcase, his macintosh over his forearm like a waiter's cloth. By the fourth and last zag he was panting. At its summit, a sign on the fire door announced the door was AT ALL TIMES LOCKED. Troy had the key. Rud took out his secret duplicate. Nash – Troy's first hire – was in the second-to-last cubicle, filling out call reports. He let the fire door close softly. She didn't look up.

He hooked his mac on the coatstand, sat at his desk, took out a call report. Blank as his mind. His phone rang.

—Where've you been?

—Rina?

—Yes! Lord! Troy's going ape.

—Didn't you get my message?

—One of the Brits saw you sneaking up the fire escape.

—No chance.

—Perhaps both.

—Impossible.

—Not from the window of the men's.

—The john?

—I could hear Troy swearing from here – despite my coaching. He's on his way up.

Rud stood, looking up-tunnel over the partition tops. Troy filled the

square of the entranceway – a pinstripe gunslinger backlit by fluorescence. Rud hung up his phone.

–For a hundred I'll get you off the hook, Nash teased him over her
shoulder.

–Too dear.

In the next cubicle Kruger was on the phone:

–I told them both

So in the next was Taliferrano:

–Who both?

In the last cubicle Mace hummed the intro to Beethoven's Fifth but
gave the thumbs-up behind his back.

–This better be good. Troy wasn't laughing. He jerked his thumb ele-
vatorward. Rud followed.

–I got fucking Marley and Scrooge crawling all over me I can't take a
fucking leak and you're skulking fucking around like, like

–Bob Cratchit?

Troy pressed the button.

–Actually, I was thinking of the little lame kid.

–Tiny Troy?

–I might be at that – if you keep this up.

The elevator doors opened. Rud held his nose high.

–I say, he mimicked, that chap's not using the lift.

–Exacto. Ah shit.

They stepped inside.

–You're here now – what the hell.

The doors closed, encasing them in the cube.

–At least tell me you were out selling fucking books.

The elevator shuddered downward.

–Well?

Rud stared at the numerals rowed above the door. Like profiles.

–I went to see Gale.

Troy stabbed the red elevator button. A bell shrilled. The elevator kept descending.

–Fuck! Troy said.

He scanned the panel, stabbed another. The elevator jerked like a strappado. Hard against the back wall they were heaved. Rud snatched at the handrail. The floor shivered. He searched for his feet and stood.

–What the christ? he shouted.

Troy found his feet. The elevator stilled.

–I knew it, Troy snarled.

–You coulda snapped the cable.

–Wasting time.

–The fucking cable.

Troy aimed his finger at Rud.

–On that suicide shit, right?

Fear simmered through the elevator.

–It's gotta be fifty, maybe a hundred years old!

–Right? Troy demanded.

–Screw you!

–Look, Troy said, still pointing.

–Your fingernail's broken, Rud said.

–What?

–When you stabbed the button.

Troy looked.

–Oh shit. He shook his wrist. To the fucking quick.

–It's your own fault.

–Mine.

–Yes.

–Look – fuck. He shook his wrist again. Shit – it's gonna keep catching on my clothes and shit.

–Just don't press any more buttons, Rud said.

He pressed the down button.

–Anyway, Rud said. The elevator bottomed on down. She's gone.

–Gone?

–Japan. California.

–Japan, Troy repeated. No shit – well, at least you won't be fucking off to see her every day.

–I just might, Rud said as the elevator braked. Besides, what the fuck do you care?

–I don't. Except about you.

–Well don't. The anthology's as good as dead.

The doors opened.

–All right! Troy said.

He blocked the doors open with a pennied loafer. He grinned, touching each finger with his thumb like closing a sale.

–All right – that's the Rud I need. Cause I'll tell you, we got some real hitters coming out for fall. And Rina

–What about her?

–You poking her? he whispered.

–Piss off.

–I knew it. Well, wingy or not, she's found us some great authors. And the Brits

–Did they make you the honcho?

–Not yet. That's where you come in.

–Me?

He steered Rud through the elevator doors onto the third floor. Across the way his office door was closed.

–Yeah, tonight – put in a good word.

–Tonight?

–Just leave alone this suicide thing.

Rud stopped and reeled Troy's arm.

–What about tonight?

–The nobility

–Me? No – uh-uh. Nee-fucking-yet. I've been up since

–This's my fault? Troy said. Mine? I mean, you

−All right all right − what?

−They're cricket fans, Troy said. And they want to see a ballgame.

−The Ploo Chayzay?

−The Blow Js.

−Impossible. I mean, this late − tickets. You'll never get tickets.

−I won't.

−We agree!

−Your connection will.

Rud shook his head.

−No.

−Oh yes.

−We're no longer connected.

Troy drew close.

−Yes you are. He smiled devilishly. I already called her.

$$\diamondsuit$$

−You couldn't have.

−Pardon?

Rud looked up at Mr Geoffrey Peale. Back down at the tickets he'd slid out of the sealed white envelope.

−Nothing, Rud said.

−Got them? Alan Davis-Carmedie asked.

They stood crushed together outside SkyDome's will-call booth. Someone jostled Rud's arm.

−Scuse me. Jack − hey! Jacko!

He read. *For A. E. V. courtesy G. D.* Handwritten on the envelope in flourishes of blue fountain ink.

−Lovely hand, Mr Geoffrey Peale said. Have a look, Alan.

−Mm? Oh. He unlooped partially his eyeglasses. A Mont Blanc I should expect. A friend? he asked Rud.

−Billy Martin, the next person at the window said.

Rud turned. Someone pushed by. He thumbed into a fan the three tickets. Fucking Troy.

–What did he say? Davis-Carmedie asked Geoffrey Peale.

–Well, Rud said. Mr Peale? Mr Davis-Carmedie? Shall we?

They entered the gate, moving slowly within the caravan of people: a bearded man holding his three children's hands, a woman with her Jays jacket caped on her shoulders, two men with pint whiskey bottles in their jacketsleeves.

–You got clipped last time, the short man said to his taller friend.

–Only cause I was fucking wavin the prick when Gonzales homered.

An Asian kid in a black Raiders cap was fighting his way back against the flow.

–They do serve beer? Alan Davis-Carmedie asked.

–It's cold, Rud observed.

–As long as it pours, Geoffrey Peale said.

–Fabulous, Mr Davis-Carmedie said when finally Rud ushered them down the section aisle and to their seats.

–Good god! Geoffrey Peale said.

They *were* fabulous: jutting rail seats perched high, like an opera balcony, third base sailing beneath their feet.

–Ale or lager, gentlemen?

–Both.

–You have to fetch them?

–It'll only be a minute.

Back out and into the keg line. He bought two beers, drained one, wiped his lips on his sleeve, bought a replacement, then sat, when he returned, between the two Englishmen. Their suitjackets armholed inside their macs flung over the seatbacks. They already were munching.

–Toad in a blanket, Geoffrey Peale said, his mouth full.

–Hot dogs, Geoffrey, Davis-Carmedie corrected. When in Rome.

–Alan gets vexed at touristisms.

Applause clattered around the stadium swift as wind through a ghost town as the Blue Jays ran out onto the field. Geoffrey Peale held his hot dog in his mouth like a lightbulb and applauded. Mustard goobed yellow onto his starched shirtfront.

—Swine, he said.

Dedos was the DH – designated hitter. He would only bat. Alan Davis-Carmedie plied the plastic lid off his beer and looked inside.

—Here! It's only half full.

—They pour a full head, Rud said.

The first Yankee batter was announced.

—Fucking cheek, Davis-Carmedie proclaimed. He poured it down his throat. Rud stood.

—No no, wait until the inning's end, Geoffrey Peale said.

—I'll go, Alan Davis-Carmedie said.

Before Davis-Carmedie moved Rud skipped quickly by, and back at the keg stand bought two, guzzled one, replaced it, and carried them back. The Blue Jays were at bat.

—Do any players not spit? Geoffrey Peale asked.

—Only in bed, Rud answered.

—Ha ha.

He stood to buy more beers.

—Sid-own! someone yelled.

He stooped. His knees were sore. The inning ended.

—This is ridiculous, Geoffrey Peale said. He laughed.

—You're only permitted two at a time, Rud explained.

—Bloody hell!

In the bottom of the second inning the Yankee centerfielder hawking a deep fly ball ran then backpedaled toward the wall, backing, groping behind him, eyes raised tracking the ball against the great girdered aperture of the stadium roof and – the crowd ahhhing – jumped, wall-climbing like a statue come to life, and stabbed it – the crowd ohhhing – and ran in. When Rud returned with more beers the two Englishmen were glued to the replay coursing across the huge vein of the outfield video scoreboard.

—All right! Rud cheered.

—Not a home-team supporter? Geoffrey Peale asked.

—No, the Yankees, I'm afraid.

—That's letting down the side, Davis-Carmedie said.

—He also claims to be English, Geoffrey Peale quipped. Oh look!

A Blue Jay hat helicoptered like a magpie corpse from the dugout onto the field and Guillermo Dedos poked his curly head out, pranced out onto the field to retrieve it, pausing in his return to prowl the chants of the crowd. He looked up and straight through Rud like something smack in front of your binoculars. He vanished, not to return until the next inning when on three pitches he struck out swinging.

The crowd booed, then forgot as the Jays scored four runs, batting around so that with the score tied and the bases loaded, Dedos made his second at bat of the inning.

—May we keep the stubs? Geoffrey Peale asked Rud.

—The tickets?

—As souvenir.

—And for if we go to the gents', Alan.

—If?

Rud dug the tickets out of his back pocket, passed them over. Glad in a way to be rid of the damn things.

—Now watch the pitcher, he told them.

Dedos's name filled the vaulted basilica of the stadium. The crowd grumbled, its collective memory stoked.

—They fidget an awful lot, Geoffrey Peale said. The players too.

Dedos swung and missed. A metronome of clapping. Geoffrey Peale placed his beer cup between his feet and joined in. Alan Davis-Carmedie swallowed his, turned it bottom up, stepped on it. Moosh. Dedos missed again. The clapping built. He pulled the next pitch foul, chopping it down the first-base line; slashed a liner howling foul, fissuring the third-base crowd. Whistles pierced.

–It's Syracuse for you!

–Or softball!

He foultipped the next off the catcher's mitt.

–Yeah – slow-pitch!

Dedos stepped out of the batter's box.

–A real manager, the man behind Geoffrey Peale began to dictate to one of his party.

Dedos read his bat label. Tugged his jersey sleeve.

–Would spend time teaching diversity. Brokers today

Dedos stretched and puffed, distorting his patrician frame. He adjusted his batting helmet, his gloves, his cup, stepped into the batter's box and ripped at a knuckleball two feet out of the strike zone.

A terrible hail of booing covered him. He remained in twisted isolation. The Yankee catcher underhanded the ball to the umpire. Rud, Davis-Carmedie, Geoffrey Peale found themselves at the railing, standing, open-mouthed.

–I'd not change places with that poor chap, Davis-Carmedie shouted.

–I would, Geoffrey Peale said.

He found a payphone outside the men's and stabbed in Amaranta's number. People crowded quick and garish past him in the spectral light, rushing like electrons through the concrete tube of the concession area. Swerving out of that rush and hurrying past him was a pressing stream of male humanity – tall, short, young, old – all grimacing on their way into the john. Then on their way back out as though strolling out of a revival tent. A busy signal.

–Shit.

He hung up. He queued for beers. A half-inning later he tried again.

–Come on –

It rang through.

And rang. Until her machine answered. He left no message. Delivered more beers. Waiting out another half-inning.

–Why do they wear their trousers tucked in their socks? Geoffrey Peale asked.

Davis-Carmedie answered:

–Forgot their bicycle clips.

Even Rud laughed – while yet again stabbing her number into the phone. He turned. A man in a brown jacket with the yellow Shell insignia on its breast pocket dashed by, bobbing through the others entering.

–Scuse.

–Hey!

–Sorry.

The telephone rang through. A woman answered.

–Hello?

–Hello.

–Yes?

–Sorry – I must have the wrong number.

–How would you know? the woman asked.

–Good point. Amaranta?

–You were right, the woman said.

This time delivering the beers he didn't even wait out the half-inning.

–But you're missing the match, Geoffrey Peale said.

–He's down th' pub, Davis-Carmedie said with a slight slur.

Her phone was busy – he'd dialed carefully. He kept dialing. Beside him a tall, thin man in a Blue Jays visor steadied himself like a deckhand as, pizza box at chin-level, he wolfed the slices. Rud turned his back on the man. Dialed again. The fourth time got through.

–Hello? she said.

It took a minute. Fans streamed past. A roar from the stadium.

–Rud?

–How'd you know?

–You are still at your party.

–Party?

–The one last night.

–Last night? God! Santana.

–Sí. "Jingo," big – loud. We decided you were having fun.

–He was there?

–You don't write.

–Dedos was there?

–Or call.

–Who then?

–I had my own room.

–Ah, not quite your own.

–I was hurt.

–Hurt? What about me?

–You? You were not hurt. You were melancólico.

–What?

–Sulking, all the time brooding. Reading obituaries.

–Your idea, remember?

–Feeling sorry for yourself.

–This is bullshit.

–That is not hurt.

–Bullshit.

–No, not bullshit.

–Yes it is. It's

Rud glanced up to find the pizza-eating guy poised, listening.

–Tell her it's bullshit, Rud snapped at the guy.

The guy shrugged.

–Tell who? Amaranta asked.

Rud kept his eyes on the guy. Who looked away and opened his mouth, folding the poised slice inside.

—Who? Amaranta repeated.

—I don't know – Dedos.

—Gio?

—Your brother, christ.

—My brother?

—Just some guy for all

—Rud?

—Yes?

—Adiós.

—Don't you dare hang up

When he heard the dial tone, he slammed the receiver onto its chrome forceps. It bounced off and he grabbed at it, missing, obtaining only a handful of steel-armored cord.

—Shit! he seethed. I shoulda gone for beers, he told the pizza-eating guy.

—Fuckin-A, the guy said.

Rud glared at the pay phone.

—I'm at work, he told it. Work!

He dug out from his pocket another quarter. Dialed. Got her machine. Said:

—Amaranta? Amaranta, pick up the phone – please. Amaranta? All right all right, Elena, then. Elena, pick up the phone. I know one of you is listening, Amaranta Elena Versalles? Amaranta Elena Versalles, please come to the information kiosk – we have found your child. Ama

Click. Rud shook his head. Turned to the pizza-eating guy. Said:

—She's Argen

The guy was gone. Rud hung up. Thumbed in a quarter. Took a breath.

—This is it –

Her machine.

—Hey, so don't answer, he said into it. Your brother? I was just wondering about his Inca lawsuit. I'm entertaining these two Brits. C'mon love – answer the goddamned phone. All right then, don't. Please? We're at the ball game. Course *you* should know that.

She picked up the phone.

–It was nothing to do with my brother, she said.

–I know.

–Okay?

–Yes. Who were you calling? he asked gently. Your line was busy.

–He is worried.

–Who?

–It was a very bad spring, Gio's.

–Yours too.

–Sí.

–Were you calling *me*?

–It doesn't matter.

–To come over?

–It doesn't

–Because I've changed.

–Ha!

–Shaved my head, Rud said.

–What?

–My head – I shaved it, he repeated.

–You? You? I don't think so.

–In solidarity – for your brother.

–You are pulling at my leg.

A deep warmth – like a body smile – spread through him.

–Your linda pierna? Yes, he told her.

–Gracias a dios. Shaved heads look horrible.

–Not on some.

–On you.

–Thanks a lot.

–Your ears would stick out.

–D'you mind!

–Sorry. She laughed.

–Anyway, I've got to get back to my charges.

–The English?

–Yes. They won't last much longer. I can't believe they've lasted this long. And after, I could be there in a couple of hours?

–No, she said.

–The Jays are flying out, after the game.

–So? That is not why not.

–Boston – I checked.

–No. Nen-Oh.

–Why then?

She didn't say anything. He said:

–Maybe I was sulking – okay not maybe – but I missed you. I can be there by midanotch.

–Midnight?

–Yes.

–Rud?

–We can talk about all this.

–Talk?

–Yes.

She was thinking. He waited.

–You cannot stay, she told him.

–I don't mind, he lied.

When he returned the Brits weren't in their seats.

–Damn, he said. First Gale

And for two innings he legged it around the huge concession tunnel. Finally he found them. In a keg line. Both standing at attention in heel-deep beer puddles.

—'Ere, Davis-Carmedie said, pointing to Rud.

—Dinner, Geoffrey Peale said sternly.

—Toad in bangit, wah-ery af-binds, Davis-Carmedie slurred. Nough.

—Dinner, Geoffrey Peale reiterated. Or I'll have you sacked.

He was grinning.

—I've made you a reservation, Rud said.

—Zack 'im anyrade.

Davis-Carmedie stood stiff as a stalagmite. Rud stewarded him and Geoffrey Peale out of the concession area, then through the glass artery of the Skywalk.

—The Underground! Geoffrey Peale shouted at the station.

A subway train rumbled and shot screeching into the station's hilt. Geoffrey Peale tugged Davis-Carmedie barging through the turnstile.

—Fares, the collector said.

Rud fumbled in his pockets.

—Wait! he yelled.

The two men raced three-legged across the platform.

—Wait!

Rud stuffed a fiver under the collector's sill and bolted. The train doors closed on his coattail. Three stops north, on the edge of China-town, the restaurant stood in a small village of cafés and boutiques.

—Here you go, Rud said.

The wind-paled aurora of the skyline above them. They squinted three-eyed at the sign.

—Lee pet it gas tun, Geoffrey Peale read slowly. French grub to boot! He ruffled Davis-Carmedie's hair. Come along, Alan, he quipped. Our Rudyard's pressing for advancement.

Rud held open the door. He'd made the reservation for ten. Not quarter of eleven yet. Lots of time to get to Amaranta's. Geoffrey Peale steered Davis-Carmedie inside. Rud held out his hand to shake.

—It's been a

—You're not going anywhere.

—But

—You heard me.

—Mr Peale

—Close the door close the door, Geoffrey Peale implored.

Rud did so and followed into the tight foyer. In the restaurant's apricot light the gruel of his long day swept past him and out the door in a great rush. Replaced by ladles of warmth. Copper pots dangled pink by long handles from the kitchen's potrack, turning.

—Christ yes.

—Beg pardon? Geoffrey Peale said.

They propped Davis-Carmedie against the hall wallpaper.

—A quick dinner, Rud conceded.

They shed their macs, tugging Davis-Carmedie's off his shoulders, and hung all three on the same wallpeg. They rubbed their hands hungrily.

—Yes, Rud said.

—Lovely, said Geoffrey Peale.

Each took a Davis-Carmedie arm and they stepped into the restaurant. With a crannied mask of hauteur, the maître d' barred their way.

—Oui?

Geoffrey Peale reached across and clasped Rud by the elbow. Beaming into that mask of hauteur:

—*This* finest of fellows has a reservation.

—Monsieur, the kitchen closes in twenty minutes.

—Yes, well we're quite hungry, so if you don't mind.

He swept past the maître d'. From a stack on an uncleared table he snatched a menu and a wine list. The maître d' chased after them. Mr Peale claimed a table already set, deigned Rud a chair, and both poured nodding-off Davis-Carmedie into his. Mr Peale did not look up from the menu.

—Gin-and-Its all round; oysters bienville; foie gras; soup? oui, potage: vichyssoise, veal bouillon

—But, monsieur

—Then the game course: bécasse – that's grilled woodcock, Rudyard; salade verte for palate cleansing; finally dinner: two tournedos à la crème and rack of lamb Dijon.

—But, monsieur, the kitchen

—If it closes soon as you say, well, bring it all at once then – or just the liver paste, the beef, and the sheep.

He grinned at Rud.

—As for wine

He bestowed the wine list unopened on the maître d' and pronounced to Rud's amazement in near-perfect Parisian French: Pouilly-Fumé maintenant. Et à dîner pour monsieur et monsieur Châteauneuf du Pape et pour moi Château Mouton Rothschild.

The hauteur faded. The maître d' beamed out of his crannied mask.

—Soixante-et-un?

—Please, Geoffrey Peale answered.

Rud couldn't help but clap his hands.

—What was it Shakespeare said, Geoffrey Peale sighed. God save Berlitz?

A waiter brought bread, pâté, uncorked the white wine. Geoffrey Peale pointed to sleeping Davis-Carmedie, touched a finger to his lips.

—We'll get him a proper English breakfast.

—In the morning, Rud added.

—Before our flight out: gammon rashers, sausages, grilled tomatoes. The lot.

Rud spread a slice of bread with butter white as ice.

—Fried bread? he suggested.

—Ha – of course. Fried bread. You *are* English. But will you be hungry in the morrow?

Rud's mouth was full.

—Pay me no mind. By all means finish.

Rud shook his head and hurried chewing.

–Then tell me, your people, are they all over here?

Rud swallowed all but a corner.

–Both my mother and father are dead. He finished swallowing. My father two and a half years ago.

–And your mother?

–Pardon?

The waiter's tuxedoed arm snaked in and replenished their wine.

–Your mother – I'm sorry – it's awfully forward of me – but when?

–That's okay – I was a boy. He actually shivered calculating backward his age. Nine.

–Ah – here? England?

–Amherst, New York – near Buffalo – where we, where my father – there were no buses, you see. And winter, real winter – like something out of Tolstoy.

–Or Pasternak? Geoffrey Peale interjected.

–God yes, exactly, and we were out – out in it – my mother, Bev my sister – me – and

He shivered again. He looked away. Across the tables a party of four in the front hall was frisking their coats for the armholes. Laughing to themselves. The door floomped open. A draft raced under the tables, burning across Rud's feet and ankles.

–And? Geoffrey Peale asked.

–And, Rud said sitting up straight, and my father, he

–Mine also, Geoffrey Peale said gently.

–*Your* father?

–My mother. This year past. In her sleep. Geoffrey Peale filled his entire body with breath. My father could not waken her, I'm afraid. Age – herself aged – you see. Her age, he sighed. Broke her own heart – well.

Rud rolled his wineglass stem between his fingers. Coughed. Geoffrey Peale's thumb fidgeted on the rim of his glass.

–Unnerving, he suggested. This grieving.

–Yes, Rud agreed.

—I used to think, Geoffrey Peale said, you know, as one got older one was less prone to it, especially when they're not – when your parents aren't snatched away – fancy. He sipped his wine, pursed his lips.

—But it's not? Rud asked. It's not easier?

—No, Geoffrey Peale answered. He nodded across at Davis-Carmedie, sleeping perfectly erect. Alan's mother too, he said. But also not his father. Anyhoo, tuck in.

They ate the goose-colored slices of pâté with tarnished silver forks from the white china plate. Swallowed bread floes. Their white wine.

—Strange, I suppose, Geoffrey Peale said.

—Strange?

—Mm. It's usually the men who go down with the ship, eh?

—I never

—Then again perhaps not so strange. Proves he can't be charmed you know.

—Who?

—Hmpf?

Geoffrey Peale drank off the rest of his Pouilly-Fumé.

—Who can't be charmed? Rud asked.

—The Reaper, Geoffrey Peale answered. Dreadful chap. Must be English.

—You must be English too, he said.

He was naked. In Amaranta's bathroom. Holding himself in front of the vanity mirror. Behind him he could see her claw-footed bathtub. He looked down at his groin. Like a fireman's helmet. With a fish's mouth.

—Dreadful chap, he told it.

For after the pink steak and frequent refills of what Geoffrey Peale called claret – after the narrow restaurant emptied around you with the diners smiling at Davis-Carmedie's windsor-knotted statue while you

and Mr Peale drank coffee and brandy and then again – you cabbed up
to Amaranta's, made it by half-past fickin midnight.

   –And you couldn't get it up, Rud said.

   Now in the mirror he examined himself. His fine, sandy hair. With a
hand he drew it back off his forehead. Stretched forward his neck to see
his red and bleary eyes.

   –A shower, shit, and a shave, he said softly. A dick transplant.

   In the mirror he appraised the bathtub. It still had no shower. The
apartment was quiet. He stepped to the bathroom door and out into the
small hallway. The floor creaked. He froze. From the bedroom he could
hear her breathing, rhythmically. Sleeping.

   (–Go, she had commanded. You need a bath.)

   He stepped back into the bathroom.

   –Not tonight, he said and closed the door.

   At the bathtub he fully opened the coldwater tap. He left the plug on
its chain though, hanging over the faucet, the water drumming and
curling down the plughole. He returned to the sink, listening to the
water chanting buddudududu into the tub. Beside the sink was a
cake of Ivory and – enjoying its lovely scent – he washed himself. Body
part by body part. Feet first, then standing on the pink bathmat, the
rest, rinsing with the washcloth. When finished he wrung the washcloth
into a rope and yanked a towel off the rack, shivering, wrapping his
waist, tucking its end. He brushed his teeth with his forefinger, popped
open the medicine cabinet in search of a comb. Chanel, nail-polish re-
mover, two airline vodka bottles – Dedos? – Ortho-Gynol. But came up
with only a six-pronged trident thing that hardly coiffed. He closed the
cabinet, turned, bent and shut off the cold water.

   The water coughed and glugged in a final swirling return to earth.
Water that had splashed up above the tub's chipped edge crawled down
the wall now like crystal-tailed ants.

   –What on earth did he look like? Rud whispered.

   The officer who, after they'd gurneyed his father's body up the basement stairs into the disintegrating sunset, had stayed. Rud could not remember. He gripped the tub edge. His gut ached with the need to remember that face. Or Gale's father on the balcony. He drew brow, nose, lips, chin in the film of moisture on the wall. His finger trembled.

The likeness struck him the same moment her perfume did. He turned. She stood in the door. Her camisole wrinkled with sleep. Eyes lidded with blurred mascara. Hair like a blackberry thicket afire in a windstorm.

–Leave please, she said.

–What?

He stood. Took a breath, tightened the towel around his waist. He was moments from her.

–Andáte.

–This is stupid. Why?

–Somergido en llanto, she said.

She rubbed her bare arms.

–Brooding, she said.

–I know what llanto is.

–Feeling sorry for yourself.

–From Lorca.

–I heard the tub, she said.

–It wasn't brooding.

–Heard you, she said.

–It was drawing.

–It will be this – feeling sorry – always, she said. You will never be cured.

–Cured?

–I am crazy.

–Bacon, he said. Fucking bacon is cured.

–Jokes. You, Gio – I am crazy. Leave.

–Fine! he said. He threw up his hands like casting rice. Put his hand
on her shoulder to shift by her in the doorway. She didn't budge.

–Wait, she said.

–What?

–Who were you drawing?

–You wouldn't believe me.

–A woman?

–No.

–Your father?

–No.

He still had his hand on her shoulder. She seized it.

–Why do I want that it should be a woman?

–Mickey Mantle, he said.

She flexed her thumb. Her nail bit into his flesh.

–Mentiroso, she said. Jokes.

He ripped his hand away.

–Mickey fucking Mantle. He sucked at the small nail wound. And the
cop, the young cop who stayed, who – and the father of this girl I knew.

–A girl?

–Ages ago, he said. He licked at the crescent gouge in his flesh. Burning like a papercut.

–Goddamn you! he said and caught both her wrists in his left hand.
What is your problem?

–*Your* problem.

–Mine?

–Yes.

She tugged either way, trying to wrench free from his grip.

–No, he said. I make you laugh.

–So?

–I ask no questions.

–Sí.

He held firm, his muscles roping down his forearm.

–I leave you alone.

She no longer fought him.

–Yes! she said. You leave me alone.

–I make love to you.

–You used to.

He let go of her wrists.

–Is that it?

–No.

–One night – one night of

–No, she repeated.

–Not fucking you, and

–No, she insisted. Not fucking. Or yes. You – you

–I what?

–You used to know how to love, she said. And, sí, hacer el amor – how to fuck – but also how to both, at once.

–And now? he demanded.

She said nothing.

–And now there's someone else. Right?

She remained silent.

–Right?

–There has always been someone else. Even the first time. And for you too.

He drew away from her, his reflection shifting in the mirror. Hers straightened. Then relaxed, leaning her hip against the counter's edge.

–Tell me? she asked.

–About what?

–Him.

–Dad?

–The cop, she said.

He looked away from her reflection and at her.

–The cop?

–Sí.

He looked back at her reflection. He could see, from how she stood, how one of the back straps of her camisole noosed out, like a shoelace.

–You have freckles there too, he said.

–Please?

He took a breath. In the mirror behind him was the toilet, and he sat.

–Good thing I put the seat down, he said. He was younger than I.

She fiddled absently with a dark reed of her hair. Her fingernails were vermilion. As were her toenails.

–And I – *I* should have cleaned up the blood. Dad's blood. But – but the wall. The wall. I mean jesus.

He looked up at her. She blinked.

–He used a spatula, Rud said. The cop did.

Rud set his elbows on his thighs.

–It was not *his* father, Amaranta said. She stepped close. He left you enough to do.

She combed her fingers through his hair. After a moment she said:

–I am glad you did not get your head shaved. My sonso who can take baths in a teacup.

–Want to have one?

–A birdbath?

–Sort of.

He stood. With the back of his hands he brushed back her hair. At the same time palming slowly her camisole straps over her shoulders. He stopped. Looked into her eyes. They were quarrylake blue.

–Do you?

She nodded and he tugged her camisole over her breasts and it fell like a child falling backward into a snowbank and she stepped out of it. She scrunched up her shoulders.

–Here, he said.

He pulled the ear of his towel from its tuck at his waist and, joining it
and its opposite behind his back, brought it back around, folded it, and
set it on the vanity counter.

—There, he said. One person is naked. Two are nude.

Then he began to wash her. Filling first the sink. Using washcloths
full of warm water. Clouds of soap raining small squalls across her neck,
her freckled shoulders, under her raised arms.

—Your boobs are getting smaller.

—Don't.

—Maybe just this one.

—Rud!

—No, this.

Washing down to the navel where our insides are knotted to our
outsides.

—Oh well, she said.

He looked up. She was looking down, sizing up her breasts. A dark
bramble of her hair fell over her shoulder, getting in her way, and she
reached behind her neck and pulled it back and said:

—Un clavo saca otro clavo.

—Lorca?

—An old saying.

—What?

She shrugged her shoulders, taking her time.

—It means many things, she said.

He lathered up his hands again and knelt to wash, from her ankles
up, her legs.

—One grief cures another, she said.

He stopped. And with the same lovely heaviness of her hand she
smoothed Rud's hair. And said:

—Don't.

So he continued, soaping, rinsing, and when he reached her thighs
she gripped the counter behind her and half-sat on its edge and opened

her legs slightly more and then he was there, kissing in that darkness.
She was wild cherries and the English seaside and he stood and asked
once more:

   —Who were you calling?

And she slid onto him and said:

   —Who else?

On the fourth ring her answering machine kicked on. He did not hear
the tenor, marginally drunk, who left a message or if he did he heard it
as he heard the sky battling itself aloft the night they locked his father's
punctured body behind the silent doors of the ambulance.

Blackstone was wearing a top hat and talked a spiral of airbubbles Rud
Rud! in his dream and he woke stretched out on the bathroom floor his
hands folded on his chest Amaranta shaking them.

   —Fuck! she said.

He sat up. His shoulder bumped the bathtub edge. She cast aside the
huge bathtowel that sheeted them and swiveled on her heels into a tight
crouch. She yanked her hair back.

   —Him, she said.

The front doorlock jiggled.

   —Him?

He got to one knee. But they're gone, he said. The Jays.

She looked at him.

   —Your brother?

She shook her head and he grabbed her arm. The front door opened.

   —Who then?

She tore her arm free and still in her crouch snatched the other towel from the rack.

—Who? he demanded.

She stood and, clothing herself in the towel, fled out the bathroom door, slamming it. In an instant he whipped up and wrapped around his waist the bathtowel and stood. A fist thumped the hallway wall and the medicine cabinet door swung ajar. A voice growled:

—Released!

—Dedos? Rud whispered.

—Gio, Amaranta said.

—Desatar!

The hallway wall thumped again, jarring open the medicine cabinet even more. With a hand Rud steadied it. His mind cartwheeled. Barely hearing Amaranta's voice:

—No Gio.

Or Dedos's:

—Desatar!

He went to close the medicine cabinet. Didn't. Listened.

—Adentro.

—Qué?

Stay calm, Rud told himself, their speech as rapid as one person: Dónde! Quién? Dónde! Qué? El Inglés. No. Dime la verdad! Andáte. La verdad!

Calm, he repeated silently. A weapon? He looked around. Nothing.

—Go, Amaranta said. Vete.

—No.

He opened the medicine cabinet. Silently shuffled aside the clutter.

—Por favor.

—No.

Her Light Days. The trident comb.

—Sí.

—No, no, no.

He picked up the comb.

–I'm not asking, she said loudly. Andáte de una vez!

–No esta noche.

–Fuck it, Rud said. He put back the comb, half paying attention. It tipped. He snatched at it. Knocked one of the vodka miniatures off the shelf. Read the tumbling label: Finlandia. It smashed in the sink.

–Perfecto! Dedos snapped.

Rud turned his head to the door. It swung, heavily. Whomped the doorstopper. Rebounded. Dedos filled the doorway. His face hawked, dazzling in the light.

–Want to talk? he asked Rud.

–Not really.

–Fight?

–Uh-uh.

–I neither.

Dedos smiled. He crossed the threshold. He wore tinted driving glasses, a powder-blue shirt, sleeves rolled to the elbows. His hands he dallied in his jean pockets. He took a halfstep forward.

–Okay, he said. Cool. I know about you.

–I – you.

With his eyes Dedos measured Rud's torso.

–This does not bother me, Dedos said.

–Hey. Rud sighed heavily.

–Pero la toalla.

–La what?

–The towel!

Rud looked down.

–Get it off.

Rud read the towel's pattern, its print. LAS PAMPAS – Jesus, he said under his breath. There was a map.

–Look, he began.

–Wait, Dedos said, holding his hands up and open. We are – grown men.

–Adults, Rud agreed.

Dedos clicked his fingers like castanets.

—Jingo – he sang.

He stopped. Swallowed an enormous breath.

—Qué día, qué día – Shit! He pounded the vanity counter with his hand. Amaranta! Amar

He turned. She was already in the doorway.

—His clothes.

She held them up, wadded. Dedos faced Rud again.

—You take the towel off. You leave. No problem.

—You both go, Amaranta said.

She flung Rud his clothes. Dedos knocked them out of the air. Heaped on the counter by the sink. Rud reached for them. Dedos stood his fist on them.

—La toalla! he shouted at Rud.

—Me promiste! Amaranta shouted.

With a fist of fingers she slapped Dedos on the temple.

—This is bullshit, Rud declared.

Dedos shook his head to clear it. Before she swung again Dedos one-armed her out the door. Again he pointed to the towel. He swiped. Rud knocked Dedos's hand away, his feet slipping. Dedos swiped again.

—Off! he yelled.

Again Rud knocked away Dedos's hand, twisting. Then he lost his balance.

When Rud landed on the counter the piece of bottleglass crooked by the basin's edge sliced across his shoulder flesh like an invisible flame. He rolled off it, unsure what had happened, pushed himself up. He stood and Dedos raised his paw to swipe again but held it poised as a lantern.

—Oh shit, Amaranta cried.

Rud looked at his shoulder now. The gash was thin, long. Someone pounded THUMP THUMP on the apartment door and blood bubbled up across the gash's envelope in tiny fingertips, then ran thickly down

his upper arm like the fingers' hand and forearm of some dark and liquid creature that he gathered up smearing with his own hand trying to
sequester back into his body. The thumping ceased. The blood kept
flowing.

–Oh man, Dedos said.

–What'n hell's going on – ah jaysis!

Amaranta's building superintendent stood behind her in the bathroom doorway.

She said, when he had asked to come up:

–It is too late.

She stood in the pall of light yellowing out from the tiny foyer of her
apartment building. A taxi waited, idling. Damp wind from the lake
gusted through the cedars and they could see the red and blue neon
signs of the Beaches cafés and diners beyond the taxicab's roof.

–Don't sulk.

–I'm not.

He was.

–I would say the same to him, she said.

The night sky above them twisted impenetrable, castellated and
awhirl with journeying stars.

–He's a fucking maniac.

–He stopped your bleeding.

That was true. With a pantyhose tourniquet. Mollified the super.
Drove them to the clinic in his Lexus. Six stitches.

–It was not just me, Amaranta said.

–Surely not me.

–Don't joke. You are English.

–I know, I know – he fought. The fucking Falklands.

She nodded.

–Las Fuerzas Especiales, she said.

For a moment neither of them spoke.

–Come to England with me? Rud asked out of nowhere.

The taxicab's engine ticked and sputtered, nearly stalling.

–No jokes, she said. It was a gift – the bathtowel.

–And you think I should've taken it off?

–No – but

She bundled herself in her trenchcoat, warmed each ear on her shoulders.

–I am going in, she said.

She turned to the doorway. Rud touched her arm.

–I was serious.

–When?

–England.

Her freckled nose was runny. His own was as cold as a setter's. The cabdriver pumped the gas pedal.

–Like that?

She snapped her fingers.

–Yes.

–No.

–Why not?

–Because.

–That's no reason why.

–He wants to marry me, she said.

–He wants what?

–To marry me.

–He's already goddamned married.

–So?

–*So?*

–Divorcio, you have heard of it?

–What if his wife hasn't?

–Aiee, she said.

She looked up at the heavens. At the blackness with its imploded chandelier of stars. She looked at him, thinking. He, his mac and Harris tweed unbuttoned, shivered.

–All this happened while I was getting my stitches?

She nodded. Then asked:

–How are they?

–Itchy. Look, come on Amaranta, he's not

–What?

–He had a bad day, and

–A bad day?

–We all did.

–I hit him.

–You know what I mean.

She laughed bitterly. Brought herself within inches of him.

–I *hit* him.

–He shoved you.

–When I went to again.

–Jesus.

–You know what he is to me.

–And does *he* know what I am to you?

–Sí, both of you, both of you know. You are no different, Rud – you, Gio.

–Don't lump me in with him.

–You both – both

She clenched her fists.

–What?

–Both use each other.

–Oh come off it.

–Yes, she said pointing at him. Yes. So you can brood and llorar and and he can – can have his cake and me too.

–So why'd he ask you tonight?

–Same as you.

—What?

—His is different than your asking me to England?

—Of course it is.

—To do what?

—We'll scatter my father's ashes.

—In England?

—At sea. I'll get a job.

—And that will bury him?

—I'm supposed to answer that?

—It won't, she told him. It is only once. She touched with fingers trembling the breast pocket of her coat. And for in here, my sonso, one time is nothing. Nothing.

She reached behind her for the foyer door handle.

—I am tired, she said.

—It's tomorrow, he said.

—No, she said dredging open the foyer door. Tired of having both of you.

—Don't.

Shooting an arm above her head with one hand, he halted the door. With the other tugged her arm.

—Wait, he said. Tomorrow

—No, she interrupted. Tomorrow is yesterday.

He let go of her arm.

—I'll call you, he said.

She spun away and into the foyer, saying loudly behind her:

—Try una postal.

The door phoomped closed. Through the doorglass he watched her pass under the foyer light – her hair enflamed for a brief instant then extinguished then lifting as, hurrying now, she turned down the corridor to her apartment.

◇

At home, a ten-minute cab ride later, he had mail. His front door when he opened it swept over several envelopes and flyers, the lighter ones swirling in the gusting air. He flicked on the hall light, flicked off the outdoor light, and shut and bolted the door. He unyoked his mac, wriggling it over his shoulders and down his arms. There were coathooks on the wall behind the door and he hung it on one and stooped to pick up his mail: bills, pizza coupons, a folded flyer. His bandage pulled at his shoulder as he gathered it all and he straightened. He plied off his wing-tips. Checked his wristwatch.

–Four, he muttered. Tomorrow better *not* be yesterday. He entered the living room, glancing at the fireplace mantel and his father's urn. And he sighed sadly and thought for more than a moment, hearing her voice, *Clavo otro clavo,* and his eyes burned and with the wrist of his empty hand he rubbed first one eye then the other. He crossed into the dining room, shuffling through the bills and coupons. The flyer was not taped closed and he unfolded it. The paper crane-colored. He yawned entering the kitchen, yawned so entirely his jaw clicked and his eyes watered and that delayed for a moment his shock of recognition.

His own profile. A line drawing. Wearing a baseball cap.

–Gale, he said quietly. He smiled. It was wonderful and flattering, the portrait, and he brought it close to his face to see if her perfume was upon it. It was not. But it occurred to him that she might have dropped this off minutes before he arrived home. That she still might linger outside.

Up the hallway he hurried, sliding in his stockinged feet, the portrait flapping like an unlashed sail. He unbolted and opened the door like fleeing a housefire and he stepped out into the chill of the night.

His heart thrummed. His blood charged through his body. To the east zodiacal light outlined the chimneytops like a city plateaued on some high and distant elevation and across the street the school wall was floodlit as though by a prowler. Westward the street was quiet. He ventured off his stoop, descending his three steps on the balls of his feet, the bricks cold and spiky beneath his socks. There were no motorcycles parked. None of the cars' rear windows were steamed. Stepping farther out, he reached the grass patch where the pavement stones turned down to the basement.

He stopped. The light from the streetlamp lay about his feet like some terrestrial cloud and when he unfolded and again examined Gale's drawing it rose and spread itself across the paper. Revealing in black ink – almost brushstrokes – an inscription beneath. He read it softly and aloud:

–Gere curam mei finis. Help me in my final hour.

He lowered the paper. The cloud of light did not illumine anything beyond the first basement step and into that trench of darkness he now stared. He touched the railing. Took one step down. He filled his body with chilling air and forced himself to check his jacket then his pants pockets for his keys. In his mac (–Thank god) and he shook his head and again on the balls of his feet climbed his steps and reentered his townhouse. His furnace was howling and with his good shoulder he shut the door then bolted it. Tapped with the portrait the back of his hand. The mark between his thumb and forefinger where Amaranta had nailed him was now a blood blister and he went into his living room and sat deeply into his couch. Beyond the coffee table above the fireplace was his father's urn and above that the watercolor of the trees filing down the mountains. He could see Gale on her balcony, lifetimes ago, her book on her head, twirling with her father. His own father's face twisting with agony on the monitor screen at the morgue and he shut his eyes.

–No goddamned way, he groaned.

He hefted his legs up onto the couch. The day fell off him like the clothes off a drowned man and he moaned with fatigue and was immediately asleep. The living room blinds when he awoke were cream with midmorning and Gale's drawing was half-unfolded face up on the floor between the couch and the coffee table. He retrieved it and carried it upstairs and, draping his jacket across the bottom of the bed, crawled still dressed under his top bedcover and after he turned off the bedroom phone's ringer he slept again. His kitchen phone rang at dusk, waking him like some distant armada, but he merely rolled over and reentered another hold of sleep. He dreamed his father came knocking at his kitchen sliding doors and he let him in and then his father said I have to go lad. He woke saddened beyond even grief and he lay awake on his back listening to the occasional car whoosh by outside with his father's voice echoing in his head.

–Fucking Dad.

Gale's drawing was on the nightstand and he sat on the bed edge and and examined his face as Gale imagined it. Pondered the inscription. Asking softly:

–Do I dare?

He put on his jacket and, downstairs at the closet by the front door, staved his feet not into his wingtips but into the workboots he'd bought when he and his father had finished the basement. In the false dawn he descended the basement stairs. He had Gale's drawing and his keys and, first holding an ear to the door, he entered and at once flicked on the light. The apartment smelled like old books but it was clean and bare of furniture. The hallway was ten thousand steps shorter than he remembered and the bathroom door was open and he turned on the light. The shower curtain was gone, though the steel hooks still hung on the rod like some tribe's shrunken display. White streaks were on the tub and on the tile and he stepped and with a fingertip – his hand shaking, a lump in his throat he couldn't swallow – brushed at them but they remained.

Scratches, he realized, and he stepped back from them. Now he could swallow and he chewed at his lip and heard once more Amaranta's words:

—One grief cures another.

And after several moments replied:

—Not always.

If it was a trial by fire it was a pale one, and a half-hour later – twenty-four hours since he'd first seen Gale's drawing – he was sitting on his couch eating Cheerios. The drawing on his coffee table – the paper partially folded in a triangle, a long prism. Its top and bottom thirds touching like palms. Like Gale's when she bowed to her Buddha statue. Or when, at the main doors of Our Lady of Grace, she bowed to him.

$$\Diamond$$

He shampooed and showered with a plastic Safeway bag looped over his stitched shoulder. He dressed in his thin-waled black corduroy suit, white shirt, knotted his red wool tie, then went back down to the kitchen, scoffed two more bowls of Cheerios, and drove in his father's pickup down to the office. By the time he'd parked in a metered space across the road it was seven-thirty just and he examined the four stories of windows for life. Rina's only. Above the building drifty cloud scored the morning sky. He crossed the road and went inside. His timing was perfect. For he had decided – or rather admitted finally to himself what he'd known all along.

—And after you find her? Rina asked.

She was scrolling through her Balaam box – her cardboard box of rejected manuscripts, looking for Gale's.

—I don't know, he confessed. Move to England. Become a diarist.

—Become Mr Peale, she suggested.

—I could do worse.

—Davis-Carmedie?

—You should've seen him: one hundred sixty-five pounds of stiff upper lip – lovely actually.

—He – Mr Peale – was once the Dalai Lama's editor, Rina said.

—Yeah? I saw him on Buckley – years ago.

—And Jonah

—Your ex?

—A disciple of Ram Dass.

—Never-pay-retail Jonah? No shit.

—His god – until he read that book by

She paused.

—Oh piss, she said.

She replaced the manuscript pile in the box.

—No luck?

—None. What next? she asked.

—I don't know.

—I'll bet Christopher mailed it back. The little fink's always damned
efficient when I want him not to be.

Rud walked to the window. Troy's parking space was still empty.

—Would Christopher've mailed it to her school?

—He'll be in in a half hour or so.

—No – I

—You want to make your getaway before His Excellencia gets in.

—A coward, Rud confessed.

The light outside was soft, as if the earth, not the sun, radiated. He
could see in that soft brilliance northeast across the patchwork of warehouse and row-house roofs, see the great hotels white and clustered
around the nearest tower of City Hall.

—Did you ever get to ask her about the fishermen's riddle?

Rina was miles away, right beside him.

—Sorry? he asked.

—Homer, she said. Troy!

Rud startled.

—Troy?

—Come on!

He followed her across and into Troy's office where she poked through the redspined dossiers on his bookshelf.

—Ah, she said. Here – damn.

It was empty.

—What now?

—Doesn't make any difference, he said.

He opened Troy's desk drawer, searching for a Spee-D-Memo. Then his top-right drawer. None. Troy's pen lay precise on a clean pad of notepaper on Troy's immaculate blotter. With it Rud wrote his resignation:

I quit.

—There's still her line drawings, he said.

He tore the sheet from the pad and slid it into Gale's folder and tossed in his company car keys. He set the folder on Troy's desk. Then on impulse he turned over Troy's large glass ashtray and plunked it back down, bottom up. As they walked out Troy's office door Rina stopped him.

—Don't change your mind, she said.

She arched onto her tiptoes and kissed his cheek.

—And do me a favor? she asked.

Across the office the elevator thumped to a stop and the doors parted. They held their breath. Christopher. Looking badgered.

—You gave me the willies, Rina called over to him.

—He's going right back out for coffees.

—Jesus.

Troy had followed Christopher out of the elevator. He smiled at them and waggled his briefcase.

◇

Now Rud was glad – for he realized if he did not break cleanly he might not break away at all. He watched Troy lope across the carpet.

–What a day what a day.

Rud and Rina parted as Troy walked between them.

–I hear you boys did the big French food numbrero the other night. And Mr Peale tabbed up. Good work.

He slapped his Samsonite on his desktop. Punched the locks with his fingertips.

–Had a manicure last night, he said. You

He glanced up at Rina.

–Goodbye, she said.

–This is a harmless story.

–Right.

–Listen, Troy, Rud began.

–No more Generalissimo, Troy said. A new regime. He took from his briefcase a white number ten envelope. Called you last night, Rud, he said. You iced it. Here.

He waved the envelope at Rud, taking a puzzled head-to-toe look. Rina tiptoed past.

–The *Whole Earth Catalog*, she whispered.

–Job hunting? Troy asked.

–Huh?

–I just thought, Rina said.

She was gone.

–Here, Troy repeated.

Rud took the envelope. His name written in ink.

–Got the snappy interview suit on. After two straight years of Misters Harris and Tweed.

–This has been opened, Rud complained.

–Hey – company letterhead. It's from the Poob.

–Who?

Rud drew out the note inside.

–The Poo-bah. Mr Peale.

Troy laughed. Glanced at his watch. The folder on his desk. While Rud read:

> *You are under sentence of death*
> *when next you visit London*
> *for cricket and dinner.*
> *The Reaper.*

–What's this? Troy asked Rud.

He looked up. Troy had flipped Gale's folder open. With his finger he poled up Rud's car keys. He lifted the folder. The note page flew, pendu-luming down.

–Holy shit, Rud – I was right.

–Right?

–The interview suit. Who stole you? Macmillion? Scott, Foreskin?

Troy read the heading on the file folder.

–Harmon, G. *Mustard* – no, he said.

–Yes.

–I don't believe it.

–Believe it.

Troy sniffed, frisked his jacket pockets.

–Close the door, he commanded.

Rud didn't move. Troy whipped out his cigarettes, lit one, waved out the match. When he tossed it at his ashtray it ricocheted onto the floor. He eyed Rud suspiciously.

–Same old Rude-yard, he said, grinning.

–Not this time.

Troy flipped the ashtray over. He slid Rud's car keys across the desk.

–Here, he said. Take the day off. Go home. Tomorrow we'll

–There is no tomorrow.

Troy snatched up his desk calendar, waved it at Rud, thrummed its pages.

–That's not what I meant.

–Oh?

–Tomorrow, I'll be gone.

–After Gale?

Troy stepped out from behind his desk.

–All right, I admit, I'm worried too.

A white smokecone escaped his mouth.

–But that's no reason to screw off after her. She may be anywhere in the world. You said yourself: Japan

–By motorcycle?

–Huh?

–She wouldn't have strayed that far, Rud said.

–More reason to stick around then, Troy said. Right? Go back over your territory. The schools. Especially the dogans. We don't call enough on the parochials.

–Forget it.

–Look, Troy said. You and I – we, we go way fucking back. He paused here, fidgeting with his cigarette. She's gotta work, he said. And so do you. You'll need money.

–No.

–Oh really? He waved his arms as though ushering in a chorusline. What? You gonna fast? Beg? Piss in your gas tank?

–I'll rent out the townhouse. Dad's basement apartment too.

–The market's soft.

–The market.

–Yeah, the rental market. I was reading.

–Look, Troy, she took my coming as an omen.

–Jesus fucking christ.

–I – I'm not asking you to understand.

—Oh I understand all right. You think you'll get laid.

—Fuck off.

—No wait – I know, it's midlife city.

—Not at

—Your big heroic quest, right? Right?

—That's hardly the point.

—The fuck it is, Troy shouted. Running away.

Rud could see he was wounded.

—Troy, he said.

—Fucking running away.

—Come on, you can replace me in a second.

—Just fucking hopeless. When the fuck're you going to grow up?

—You got what you wanted, Rud said. The big cheese.

—Can the crap.

—You open my fucking mail.

Troy snorted through his nose. He crushed his cigarette. Flexed the pulpy muscle in his jawhinge.

—Fuck you, he said. I've a book business to run. I'm through helping you.

—Helping me?

—Anyone else, anyone else, woulda been let go.

—I hired you!

—No second chance. No third, Troy muttered.

—If it wasn't for me hiring you, you'd still be

Rud lowered his voice.

—Running dope.

Troy slashed the air with Gale's empty filefolder.

—We're talking now, this!

—What the hell do you know?

—Plenty: you're crazy, and she's fucking worse – mustard seeds – half-assed Latin and Zen dumped in among a bunch of writers' suicide notes. She even made some up.

–Then why'd you take it home to read?

–To show you I was fair. That it was nothing to do

–With Gale? Rud interrupted.

–Yes.

–The school roof? My father?

–Now don't start that shit.

–Etta?

–I'm warning you.

–Warn all you want, Rud shot back. You fucking lecture me to grow up. Me? Jesus! Goddamn forty years old you are – over forty – and you can't even talk to your own

–That's *enough*!

–Or even read her letters.

Troy tightened his hands into fists. Rud stepped back, ready before he knew he had moved. Outside the office Troy's assistant clicked on her clone. It beeped. Troy lowered his fists.

–Wait a second, he said. What am I saying?

He picked up Rud's resignation, mangled it, dropped it into the wastebasket.

–You'll be back.

–No.

–A week – maybe two.

–No chance.

–Yes – oh fucking yes – and d'you know something?

Rud started for the door.

–You can have your job back – ha ha.

Rud was out Troy's office door. He heard Troy follow, rubbing his hands.

–It'll be here waiting for you – morning, Dian – waiting for you, he called across the carpet.

–Hold your breath, Rud called back.

He took the stairs.

– You've not much time, Mr Gillette.

Dr McLeish stood by his window, hands folded in front of his belt buckle. Rud stood in his office doorway.

–Will it not keep? the doctor asked. Till next Friday?

–No, Rud answered, his mind thick.

Lodged in his father's pickup and now here, he felt not the slightest sense of liberation.

–Come along then, Dr McLeish said.

They sat facing each other. The doctor leaned over his desk. His jacketsleeve shone from pressings. He swept a legal pad across and into his lap. Set a box of tissues beside Rud. Drew his fountain pen from his breast pocket. Unscrewed the cap.

–What is in your mind, Mr Gillette?

–I quit. My job.

The doctor crossed his thumbs. Averted his glance. Rud relaxed back against the chair spindles. The doctor scratched some notes on the pad, stopped. The two men looked at each other. Dr McLeish at his watch. Rud at his.

–Troy said it was a midlife crisis.

–And what do you say?

–I say, so what?

–Well, you cannot be having a midlife crisis.

–I can't?

–Technically.

Dr McLeish set his pen beside his pad.

–For midlife is thirty-six years of age and you are past that.

–Not by much.

The doctor smiled.

–The point is, a midlife crisis is just a vulgarism, a way of marking and dismissing something precious.

He pinched his nosewings with his thumb and forefinger. Rud waited.

–A religious waking up.

–Religious?

–I'm not supposed to use that term – I know.

–It doesn't bother me.

–Yes. The doctor thought for a moment. A waking up, he said with care. To, to that part of ourselves and others that isn't going to change. That doesn't need to change.

Rud shifted in his chair.

–Death?

–Perhaps. It visits the great and not-so-great, this crisis.

–Did it visit you?

–Me?

–Yes. Did you have this, this crisis?

Slivers of light glinted in the doctor's eyes.

–If I told you, he said, I'd be breaking my oath of secrecy.

–Me then?

The doctor tilted his body sideways, closed one eye.

–What I'm saying is that since your midlife you have been walking into your father's bathroom.

–But not finding the body.

–That's

The doctor paused.

–What? Rud asked.

–I'm not sure. A little too easily put, perhaps. In any case, we're out of time. Next Friday?

Dr McLeish stood. Rud stood.

–Well?

Rud said nothing.

–Ah, is that a no then? the doctor asked.

He held out his hand to shake. Rud took it.

–That woman I told you about.

–The one with the drawings?

–Yes. She's gone.

–Gone.

–Yes.

–And that's why you quit.

–I would've quit anyway.

–Quit your job.

–Yes, so I can

The doctor waited for him to finish.

–find her.

–And you wish me to dissuade you.

–I suppose.

–And of course fail.

Out the window the sun was quiet on the university buildings across the street. They stood in the small office like two men on an easily swamped raft.

–Look, the doctor began as he guided Rud to the door, why not let

–Troy said I'd be back in a week, Rud said suddenly.

–Let me know about Friday in a few days.

–Maybe two – two weeks.

–He might be right, Dr McLeish said gently. He opened the door to his secretary's outer sanctum. On her blond desk a spearmint plant grew. Her pink sweater folded over the deskchair back. Scent like a child's garden hideaway.

–She could be anywhere, Dr McLeish observed.

–Yes.

–And you'll be alone.

–That's okay.

–Though perhaps not.

–Perhaps – ?

–Your father's ashes, the doctor said. Take them along.

third

And so he journeyed east. Left a few days later in his father's truck. With no companion save his father's urn. No guide save a road atlas. And no plan, save the telephone book. At a mall in Kingston – where Lake Ontario vented into the Saint Lawrence and hence mere miles from Gale's school – he bought a Slumberjack sleeping bag and by a dry cleaners found a payphone and lo! There in the White Pages under Z.

It was called the Zen Institute and it was in a small fieldstone house atop a high moraine overlooking the military academy, the lake.

–I was wondering, he told the man who answered the door, if you had a member by the name of Gale Harmon.

The man wore hospital greens, only white ones, and he shook his head no and smiled serenely.

–Well actually, Rud said, she's changed her name.

The man waited. Nudged with his fingertip his glasses up his nose.

–I don't know to what, Rud continued. A teacher. Formerly. Newly joined?

The man shook his head. Said:

—We have a small affiliate sangha across the river. In Alexandria Bay. Perhaps?

She was not there either. There was a KOA upriver near Ogdensburg but it was offseason so, finding a turnout, Rud parked and decided to sleep in the truck. He'd packed only two other pairs of jeans, several pairs of underwear and socks, a half-dozen T-shirts and a sweatshirt, and this lean wardrobe fit nicely into a single duffel bag that had as its underlay his papers – the autopsy report, the workmen's compensation envelope, Gale's line drawing, his joke Matchbox Correspondence School Degree – and on this his first night he set the duffel bag in the passenger footwell and then beside it the urn. He untied his workboots and tucked them behind the seatback, then squirmed out of his jean jacket. Jacket went atop the urn. Across the truck's bench seat his Slumberjack unrolled like an upholstered lizardtongue.

—Not bad, he pronounced.

It was a tight fit though. He had to sleep Swiss-army-knifed: bent at the waist and knees. But the bag was warm as a greenhouse and in the morning the windshield wore a gorgeous frosting of privacy that when he scraped a portal revealed under a blue sky a small forest of jade. He climbed out, peed, and found a gas station wherein he washed and brushed his teeth. The station was so close to the Saint Lawrence he could hear and see it pour and plunge against itself, spitting color in the morning light like an unquenchable grassfire. A phone booth stood beyond the pumps and he jogged over and called Warren – Skeddy – who was to arrange and manage the rentals in Rud's townhouse.

—Any bites? Rud asked.

—You've been gone a day.

—I'm worried.

—Don't. Prime real estate like that? You'll have money to burn.

—Troy said the market was soft.

—Troy's got his head up his ass. By the way, he phoned.

—Had he taken his head out?

–This is Troy we're talking about. Though you know, if it had been anyone else I'd have said he envied you.

–But it isn't anyone else.

–How about you? Skeddy asked him.

–Hmm?

–How goes it?

–Great actually. Like being on sabbatical.

–But the big quest part?

–Hey, there can't be that many Zen places – right?

–Yeah, but it's finding where they are, bud.

And in trying to find them he drifted over the next days northeast through Quebec checking the phone books in futility, then south in late April through Maine's jutting shield of forest and rock. Sleeping in the truck. In Bangor he gifted himself, staying in a long white motel just off I-95, toting his father's urn in and standing it by the tv. On the floor by the bed he did a hundred sit-ups, a hundred push-ups. Repeated them. He checked the phone book under B and Z. Nothing. Washing his hair in the shower with his eyes tightly shut he told himself, You might as well try numbering the stars in the sky. Still in his towel he stretched out on the bed and watched a Braves game. He drank beer. Being April there was a rain delay. He phoned Skeddy.

–Hey, Rud. Where've you been?

–There's a rain delay.

–There always is. Where the hell are you?

–In bed.

–That's the place. Lotsa good news, my friend. A lease signed on your upper.

–And?

–With key money, fucking key money.

–Great. I'm thinking of taking the basement myself, Rud said.

–Nice one.

–I'm serious.

—Right.

—I am.

—Well you're too late.

—Really?

—A six-monther.

—Shit.

—What's this? You sound ready to give up. Thought you felt like being on sabbatical.

—Now I just feel unemployed.

—As you said, how many Zen places can there be?

—As *you* said, it's finding them.

—Bud.

—Huh?

—Nothing. Hey, maybe there's a list or something.

—A list?

—These places are places, right? Real estate, right?

—*Un*real estate. A fucking MLS of Zen places?

Skeddy's phone beeped.

—Incoming, he said. Oh, speaking of the unemployed, one of the players in your triangle

—Dedos?

—Yeah. Signed with Seattle – a week back.

—Where she'll rot, Rud said after he hung up. Explaining to the urn and his father inside:

—My ex-Inca princess – the weather's the shits.

He slept a pitiful sleep. In the dawn light he admitted the enormity of his task, deciding he needed either some overall strategy or the courage to turn back.

—Turn back to what? he asked his father.

He cleaved the blinds. Out the window the inn's back acreage slid like some roughhewn magic carpet into view under the retreating stars.

−Hell, maybe there *is* a listing, he said to himself. Or a catalog. A catalog?

He turned from the window.

−What d'you think, Dad? Visit the seaside?

He made Bar Harbor by the time the shops opened. He found a bookstore with rain falling against the Atlantic and the storewindow on the main street. The owner was spry and gray-eyed with a trumpet player's sagging cheeks. He was worming a key into the lapel of the cash register. Rud bought a burlap-colored packet of lozenges and studied the postcard carousel. Lots of the ferry. Of Acadia National Park. Of the sea. Rud eased a seacard out of its slot.

−I'll be with you in a moment, the owner said. His sweatshirt depicted two tyrannosaurs holding books.

−Avoid extinction, Rud read aloud.

−Now, said the owner.

−Do you have the *Whole Earth Catalog*?

−Out of print.

−Oh.

−Has been for a while.

−Is there something else like it?

−*Like* it?

−Yes − *like* it.

−Think about what you're asking, son.

−Right − right. Rud ran his fingers through his hair. Great sweatshirt, he said.

−Twenty-six ninety-five.

−Ah, d'you think the library might have it? The *Whole Earth* book?

−What exactly do you need out of it?

−I'm − what am I doing? − Looking for someone. Who's joined a Zen commune.

−Zen Buddhists.

–Right.

–And you're lost.

–I thought they might list them. A catalog of Zen.

–A Yellow Pages of karma?

–That would be sort of the zenith, yeah.

–Come, the owner said.

And he led Rud through the stooped floor of bookstacks to Religion/Philosophy where the man stepped one-legged onto a wheeled stool and glissandoed his fingers down the spine row and pulled out and handed Rud a flame-colored paperback.

–*Buddhist America*, Rud read aloud. Holy shit – sorry.

–Not a problem. I consider it apt.

Walking back to the cash register he found under Maine the address of the Seaspring Zen Hermitage and he bought the lozenges and the postcard along with the book. A sinewy woman Rud's own age with her head shaved but stubbled met him when he knocked that night at the cedar and pine hermitage door. She wore a floorlength brown gown and she bowed slightly to him. Rud pondered his tack. Then simply told her the truth. Of Gale's father's suicide. Of his own father's. Of Gale's manuscript and her shaved head and leaving her teaching job and changing her name to whoknowswhat. Of her line drawings, her mustard seeds.

–Medicine for the dead, he said.

He unfolded the one of himself. The woman studied it. She looked up and studied Rud's face. Then the drawing again.

–It's almost more you than you, she said.

–She took my meeting her, after so many years, as an omen to leave.

–And the inscription – ?

–A hope that I might find her.

–Perhaps, the woman said. I'm afraid she's not a member here. May I make a suggestion?

–Please.

—Your search for her, though admirable —

The woman paused. Gestured at the grounds. At the sky.

—Your search is not out here, she said. It's

—I know, Rud said gently and touched his heart.

—Your hara, she said as gently and touched her gown slightly below her wide black belt. Sit with us.

—In zazen?

—You'd be doing what she is.

—No — no thank you, Rud said. I should get going.

The woman bowed to him. He dipped his head in return.

—One last thing? she asked.

—Of course.

—Remember, to capture the tiger's cubs, you must enter the tiger's cave.

There were just over 140 caves — Zen sites — and come morning of the next day he'd transposed them from *Buddhist America* to his road atlas.

—Now, Dad, he said heading out of Bar Harbor for Surry, sooner or later we have to find her, right?

—Probably later, he said, leaving Surry the next morning for Montpelier, Vermont. The next day for Albany. And so on to Boston and Cambridge for three days — he took in a ballgame at Fenway. Thus did his summer unfold. Filtering down the great decaying cities of the Atlantic coast. One center a day. (—Would you care to sit with us? —Thanks, but no.) Traveling south as the warmth traveled north. Through May. June. The robe-wringing humidity of Germantown, Maryland. The placid Piedmont coolness of Pittsboro, North Carolina. To Atlanta, city of smoke. And a Braves game.

It was in Gainesville, Florida, though, that he first sat in zazen. Not at the center, which had disbanded (—When the teacher is ready, the short curly-haired man told Rud with a grin, the students will disappear), but in Rud's room in the Holiday Inn. He'd done his push-ups and sit-ups and gone to bed. Before dawn he awakened from dreams without incident, dreams beyond narration. As must be those of the unborn. Grasping through the darkness for the bedside light, he knocked over a beer can, empty and contorted from the night before, its rim striking the night table with an echoless tink. In the lamplight he sat for some time on the bed edge. On the dresser's top was the television's dark glass abdomen. Beside it, his father's urn.

—To capture the tiger's cub, he muttered. Why not.

Standing, he took a bed pillow, contemplated its shape, then lengthwise bent it over within its slip. He extinguished the bedside lamp and with only the bathroom light granting stark outlines to the room he knelt and faced the stippled wall. Reaching behind him he shimmed his makeshift zafu – the bent pillow – between his ankles and sat. He cupped his hands as the Zennists did during his visits and he touched his thumbtips lightly and propped his cupped hands fingers down in his lap. He breathed in. He breathed out. He lowered his gaze.

A minute passed. As did another. He was calm, centered. He shifted. An urge to check what was behind him gripped him. He ignored it. His knees irritated sharply like sand in your swimsuit. He rocked slightly on them. Across his shoulders a warm flush spread. The urge revisited. He succumbed and looked. Over his right shoulder, only the bathroom door partly ajar. Over his left, the tv and urn. He resettled himself. Lowered his gaze. The burning in his shoulders again.

—Shit, he cursed, and backward slid off the pillow and stood. Next door a toilet flushed. His knees were stiff and he gimped to the window. Light lifted the night sky like the lid of a pirate chest. In the half-empty lot under a light tower was the truck. He considered it for a moment, then allowed the curtains to sweep closed.

—Not here, he said touching his heart, but here. He touched that place a few inches below his navel, took a deep breath, and walked back around the bed to his bedpillow zafu.

—Quit watching me, Dad, he said softly over his shoulder, or I'll scatter you here in the parking lot.

He endured five minutes. As he did on most occasions, he stayed in motels, occasions more frequent during his blaze across the plateau of the continent, through Texas to San Diego and north to L.A., which was a knot of Zen Centers. Unlike in Gainesville, though, he would first carry his father's urn out to the truck. (—When the student is sitting, the father will disappear.) But it was not until he was plowing back east across the oxen land that he asked to sit at a center.

It was in Taos, New Mexico. On the Fourth of July. The *Buddhist America* listing said the temple was called Yamaji but listed no other address than RR 2. With the holiday the Taos bookstore was closed so he asked at the Kachina Lodge, its adobe walls violet in the sun and heat. They directed him north.

Into the Sangre de Cristo Mountains he drove, ascending. Columns of firs and aspen boles guarded the oval clearing wherein the temple itself knelt. He parked and climbed down. There was a long lawn clipped like a golf green split by a footpath. The path led through a trellised pea and vegetable garden that partially obscured the temple members who spread tablecloths over several picnic tables in front of the temple and cabins. Cabins of cedar, of mud. Two or three dozen women and men in gray gowns and in her gown carrying a bowl of steaming vegetables and rice like a smoking offering to a volcanic deity Gale was among them.

She bent, setting the bowl on the table. Only the wind sounding stroking the tree leaves and their gray gowns rustling. He took a stumblestep back as if he might bolt in terror for the truck and she turned her back and dissolved into the gray-gowned crowd like a raindrop in a bucket. Gathering his breath in his belly he walked up the footpath that continued through the garden preparing his, his what? He didn't know what. He wandered around the periphery, his eyes roving, scouring the faces, receiving sundry bows, greetings.

—Hello.

—Hello.

—Hi.

—Welcome: zazen's been canceled, hurray.

But not Gale. A bell tingalinged, echoing like a small bird migrating.

Gone into the sky above that was cloudless. The mountain peaks red as heated razors. The members gathered into three rows, set palms under their chins. Quills of steam feathered up from the food bowls nearby. They chanted:

All Sentient Beings I Vow to Liberate,

Chanted in unison – in plainsong – like a coin spinning slowly, turning slowly, between your ears:

The Way of the Buddha, I Vow to Attain.

It faded, turning so so slowly, then fell. Silence. Row by row the members filed to the tables. Stiffbacked they sat with poised hands under chins again. A smile washed over their faces and they dug in, passing bowls and plates, forking and spooning food. A tall shaven-headed man stood and unthreaded his legs from under the table and without hurry walked straight at Rud.

–Join us? he asked.

–Actually – I

Rud paused, then released his spiel. He finished.

–No, the man said. No, I don't think so.

–But I'm sure I saw

–No – really.

–But

–Do you sit?

–Yes – somewhat.

–Well sometimes, in sitting, we see things.

–This was no mirage.

–Neither is the dinner. Please, join us? I'm Pete.

–Pete?

–Usually I'm Peter but today we're having fireworks after. And there's punch, punches actually.

He stopped for a moment.

—And I spiked tequila in one of them and Peter wouldn't do that so hey – I'm Pete.

—Pete, Rud said.

—This punch! the members proclaimed after dinner.

—Earn your keep, Pete said to Rud and he and Pete filled then steered wheelbarrows of sand across the grass, tipping them up and pouring the sand into a GI horse trough. As he worked, Rud checked the faces for Gale. The trough finally filled. Then came the fireworks – sparkling up from the sand like neon war.

—It *was* her, he muttered in the dark of Pete's porch.

He splayed his cold bedroll on a straw tatami. He fell asleep at once. And at once, Bong! the gong tolled, rousing the members. Somehow he found the zendo door. The members filed by. But not Gale. Peter was the last. He looked rough. He grinned at Rud and bowed.

—I'll kill Pete for this, Peter whispered.

Rud bowed back.

—I was wondering, he said, if I might sit with you?

—Now? This morning?

—One of the first centers I searched, Rud said, a woman

—The roshi? The master? Peter asked.

—I'm not sure, but she suggested I should sit zazen along my way, the way – to capture the tiger's cub.

—And have you? Peter asked. Entered the cave?

—At the centers, no, but in my motel room.

The sky was a bowl of black and crystal. From out of the zendo, a tingaling. Peter took Rud's hand.

—I tell you, keep searching, but keep sitting in your motels. Remember, what we find is rarely what we start out looking for.

By the anniversary of his father's death a month later Rud had doubled his motel sitting endurance. That – the third anniversary – Rud planned on spending in Niagara Falls and Amherst, where his mother had died. After Ouray and Denver; Kearney, Nebraska; Lawrence, Kansas. Laboring erratically across the cauldron of the Midwest and from St. Louis rumbling up the Ohio River Valley, slowing in Lexington, Kentucky, for truck maintenance and to ensure the coincidence of anniversary and place. It unfolded precisely.

–The only spot on Uncle Thom's atlas, Rud said when he parked by the Falls.

The day's heat was Aegean. On foot he crossed the boulevard to Prospect Park, feeling the needles of spray. There he shed his Nikes. The grass under his now bare feet a bluish sponge. This close to the Falls the sun and the mist above the great hoofprint of water and rock clashed like armlocked gods. It was the earth's thunder, and past the telescopes he walked, set in their swivels like cannons. In his shorts, his Nikes shoelaced around his neck. Most of the other men and boys were barechested and he peeled off his own T-shirt. When he looked down at his chest and upper arms he couldn't help grinning.

–Pale as a potato, he said.

And in his T-shirt of white skin strolled on. The world was water and sunshine and booming. Anniversaries and bridges of flags crackling. Then it was early evening, the softening light somehow softening the waters' roar, and back in the truck he asked his father:

–Want to go over in your barrel?

East along Niagara Boulevard he drove. Into Amherst. Past the brick and grass university, craning out the window. He coasted by a small public library. By a narrow Lutheran church, white and wooden with a single black steeple and windows like bishops' miters. The truck drifted of its own accord. Past a park with slat benches. Perhaps it was gone.

–There, he said.

He pulled up at the curb.

–Where we lived, Dad – remember?

The house where their walk-up had been was white as the church and had black shutters. He had both the truck's windows rolled down and this allowed a lovely breeze to spill through the cab. Birdsong drifted in

the window as though some passerby toted a sackful of budgies. He sat
for a bit.

–What did you write in *her* obituary? he wondered aloud.

A human shape in the house crossed behind the frontroom baywin-
dow and Rud waved, saying:

–Shall we find out?

He U-turned and drove back to the public library and asked if they
held back issues of the *Buffalo Evening News*.

–Only for thirty days, the reference librarian said.

–Not from 1960? On microfilm maybe?

–Try the U. B. library, tomorrow.

Back in the truck he asked quietly his father:

–Did you even fucking write one?

$$\diamond$$

The next days he searched the rusting south shores of the Great Lakes.
Zen Centers in Euclid and Cleveland. Cincinnati, Toledo, Ann Arbor. A
week and a half before Labor Day – the anniversary of Gale's father's
suicide – he was in Chicago. Approaching the city from the south like
walking toward a graveyard. Gravestones of steel. Of glass. Three Zen
Centers, three days. A brilliant afternoon Cubs game at Wrigley and on
to Wisconsin, Minnesota, then pushing across the Dakota badlands.
The badlands a gathering of asteroids. A chalk landscape so ruined by
history that history seemed never to have touched it save the Wall Drug
signs he counted then lost count of when a B-52 pawed bawling inches
overhead like some escaping paleontology exhibit. Yet on, knifing
across Wyoming's corner and west, climbing through wheaty Montana
from plain to steppe to divides of sky, of rock. Driving north from I-90
at Missoula to circle through the mountains that banked a turquoise sea
that was Flathead Lake and beyond toward Whitefish. It was the Thursday before Labor Day weekend and the highway was an uninterrupted

RV and mobile home processional. Whitefish was on its own smaller
lake and of this Zen Center the *Buddhist America* listing contained no
more than a post office box. No street address. Nor was it under B or Z
in the phone book that he checked in a booth at the town's southern
crossroads. The booth was next to a natural foods store and he entered
and asked a clerk who said:

−Try the man who runs the bookstore.

The bookstore was at the north end of town.

−It *was* on 487 − a mile above the lake, said the bookstore owner.

−Was?

−It disbanded − ooh − a few weeks ago maybe.

−Everyone?

−Internal wrangling or such.

−When the teacher is ready

−Beg pardon?

−Nothing. What about the roshi? The director?

−What about him?

−Is he still there? Did he leave?

−The woman who runs the fitness club, the one on Central, ask her.
She was involved.

Pastel-colored Jeeps and Blazers glutted the street and everyone wore
sunglasses with idiot strings. The gym was called Peak Physique and a
workman in overalls, standing inside by the door and holding a putty
knife glaired with spackle, held open the door and dipped his head. Rud
was through, nodding thanks, and the workman left. Black and chrome
weight machines lined one mirrored wall. Music pulsed as subdued as
the air-conditioner and along the other wall people sweated on stair-
climbers and stationary bicycles. Only the rowing machine was vacant.
The reception kiosk was right there and a poster on the tinted front
window held a mountain sweeping up in Himalayan mystery and snow
only to have its peak vanish beyond the poster's upper edge.

On the kiosk counter an opened book, tomelike and white, lay face-down and Rud read partially the upside-down title, *The Origin of*, before a woman walked toward him and asked:

–How may I help you?

Her muscles robbed him of speech. She wore a powder-blue leotard cut at the elbows and knees to reveal her worn skin. With each step her leotard moved across her body with the rapidity of shallow water across stone.

–Directions, he said. Please?

She was sixty and sixteen. Grayish hair pearled with sweat. A bump on her nose as from a breaking.

–Far end of the club, she told him. On the right.

She smiled and snapped a registration card onto the counter. Sweat stood on her forearms.

–Day pass is seven, she said. Eight with a towel.

A man in hightop sneakers and shorts approached. He had a towel around his drenched neck that he uncollared and held out, panting.

–Another please, Victoria?

–Still at base camp?

–Hardly: 24,580 feet. Thanks.

–You bet.

Rud filled out the card.

–Also, Burning Moon Ranch, he said.

He looked up at her. Impassive, she took his money. Gave him a white towel.

–The man in the bookstore said you were involved.

–Well he was wrong, she said coldly. Have a good one.

As it'd been months since his last workout – not counting his hotel-room regimen – he did. He showered and dressed and in the Yellow Pages found a laundromat, then pointed the truck south back to the interstate. He stopped first at the Whitefish Safeway and bought rolls and Black Forest ham and Edam and made supper that he washed down with a bottle of Kirin. In the directory he read his future, telling his father:

—Seattle. Maybe she's there with the new Mrs Dedos.

In front of the truck a pickup bulletholed by rust curved past.

—After that, he said swallowing, there's not many left. British Columbia. Alaska. Hawaii. You can navigate, he suggested. The canoe.

He looked at his road atlas. He was a full day's drive from Seattle. He looked up. Out of the Safeway jogged the man from the bookstore, cradling a watermelon like a thieved pig. Rud, in the directory, reread the Burning Moon listing. Masao Tsuruoka: Roshi. Bernard Klearmann: Sensei.

—What if she'd been there? he mused aloud. What if the roshi still is?

He set his roll on the seat by the urn and he hurried back into the Safeway, bought a Whitefish map, unfolded it back in the truck across his steering wheel. The town was bridged to the southernmost tip of the lake over a rail yard wide as a canyon that he crossed and 487 wound north. He drove along a steep landbelt between the lake and Big Mountain. The mountains here were rainforest green, full-bellied as sultans and dripping with evening sun. He drove past wrought-fenced villas and mansions, past condos stacked like cardhouses, past strewn trailer homes with snarling dogs on rigid chains. A sharp cliff of forest on either side. Where the road hairpinned he swooped the pickup through tightened curves, the lake erupting blue and hyaline before it abated to flicker in the forest gaps. Then the lake vanished and he checked his odometer.

The wide wooden gate he stopped at a mile later had BURNING MOON RANCH carved into its top stringer. But it was chained and padlocked and after he yanked unsuccessfully at it he stood. Westward the earth flattened and saucered into a gnarlish valley, yet east behind the gate the hills rose sharp with trees above, which the sky descended with dusk.

His truck changed hue.

—The tiger's cave, he called over his shoulder.

In three steps he climbed the gate, perched then jumped. He thumped onto the grass of the two-track, stood and slapped dust ghosts off his jeans knees, then started up the path that twisted climbing through the dense woods. Waning daylight lit the trunks with totem faces. Once he heard – between steps – a twig snap. He shivered. Picked up his pace. Then the path billowed out green and mauve-shadowed into a steep clearing.

Several buildings stood at the top of the clearing near where the forest resumed. Up he scrambled in stages, following the two-track that switchbacked up from terrace to terrace. He kept his ears peeled for snakes and the centerline grasstops brushed his knees and in twenty minutes he beheld the house – a three-story frame job, airy and white. A smaller replica flanked it to the right – the bottom story a garage – and four cabin-sized versions flanked the garage. Two more terraces mounded up behind the main house and towering over all was a windmill – its blades motionless – perched like a one-legged crane against the green trees, the blueblood sky, the arriving stars.

Fifty yards from the house he stopped. He rubbed his arms, chilled by the wind. Chilled by the fact that no curtains hung in the windows. That no tools leaned against the exterior walls. There was a graded patch of concrete in front of the garage unstained by crankcase oil and he said:

—Get the fuck out of here.

And he would have, save he noticed on the far side of the garage propped up on cinderblocks a cement mixer.

—The last fucking thing you'd

A soft patter broke the silence, then a shadow fluttered in the corridor between house and garage and an unmuffled engine roared from within and thundering out of the corridor as if pursued by the roar and the hungry souls of all its ancestors came a horse. It was purple in the dusk and its eyes stared back horrified. Its nostrils streamed, and even above the engine its chest bellowed. Rud crouched to jump straight up to escape its path but in a purple knot of muscle it veered suddenly and was gone.

He turned to curse after it but, nagged by the still-closed garage door ensealing the engine's roar and exhaust fumes, he broke into a run. He had no reason to think Gale was in the garage attempting suicide. That anyone was. He didn't think at all. He just ran for the garage, highstepping through the grass, crossing the concrete. He grabbed the T-shaped handle, twisted it either way. Still the engine roared. He took a step back, reconsidering, then a dread rose up in his heart, compelling him to find out the truth: a window.

Deciding on the south side – the sun side – he charged around the corner and slammed nearly head first into the cement mixer. He jerked his body aside but caught the barrel arm just above one eye. The world exploded, his eye blazed, and he reeled back onto the concrete. He weaved and shook his head and pressed his forehead with the heel of his palm. His sight cleared. He stood. The engine hammering had never left and now the visual world reentered his mind and he focused his eyes.

Where moments before he stood, a blurred figure was now stabbing at the garage handle with a key, then another from the keyring. Gale. Rud closed his eyes and reopened them to see her try yet another. Gale. The engine clamored horribly and she tried a third and this one worked and she seized the handle, twisting and yanking it. Then she was dredging up the door and quickly Rud helped and they looked once at each other once – just once – with their arms upraised and

–Who? he shouted. Who?

She didn't answer – the engine still clamored and the door yawned up and up like pushing a long wide board up onto a roof until it settled. A thick wall of exhaust smoke confronted them, almost rearing before, dense and roaring like some iron stampede, it boiled and swarmed over them. They coughed and waved their arms, trying to duck under it, and sideways edged into the sleepsick varnish of its smell. There was some kind of vehicle, or what seemed the fenderless remains of one, but its occupant was still obscured and must've collapsed across the passenger seat. Rud ducking, groping forward, felt Gale stiffen with horror. He could no longer hear her coughing. He could see now the steering wheel and stooping he nearly dove into the front seat. Up and down the steering column he groped until he found the ignition key. He switched it off and the engine's noise and its fumes settled like light snow swept off a porch step.

The driver's seat was empty. He stood and Gale was there beside him. He looked at her. She had a light bristle of hair, like a recruit's, and the same bristle growth of her eyebrows above her eyes that were raw from the smoke. She was staring at Rud, as though in disbelief. The contraption they stood in front of was a dune buggy and with the smoke waning they both looked into the passenger's seat. That too was empty and Rud pointed into the footwell beneath the steering wheel. A paving stone was wedged vertically atop the half-floored gas pedal, and a voice behind them, the accent Japanese but articulate, said:

–You see, Kisa, though you did not stop to talk

They turned. A man stood in the garage doorway.

–As with your father, he continued, you did not come in time.

Gale nodded yes.

–No, the man said. I crawled out the window.

He glanced quickly at Rud. He was in his late fifties with a slim oval face and he wore a rumpled tan one-piece overall. He had workboots on and he stepped toward Gale.

–No, Kisa, he said.

Yes, she nodded to the man.

Framed in the garage door, the earth was the sky's rippling blue shadow and the man took another step closer. Gale stepped aside. On her feet were a pair of pale Chinese slippers and above her white cotton pants she wore a collarless shirt.

–No, the man said emphatically, I just did not want to die.

He took his eyes off her and looked first at Rud and then at the vehicle.

–The brick! he said.

–What?

Dodging past Rud, he retrieved the brick from the gas pedal. A BMW motorcycle, glistening on its center stand like some black tungsten mantis, was in the twin bay of the garage and the man nimbly circled the rear of the machine. There was a shelf on the side wall and with a heavy knock he set the brick amongst the tools and hat stacks of white buckets arranged thereon.

–You are the one she draws, the man said turning to Rud.

–I am?

Gale nodded.

–Yes, the man said.

–And you? Rud asked. The roshi?

The man glanced at him, came back around the motorcycle. He shook his head no. Gale nodded yes.

–You're not

–I, the man said, am an unwanted suicide.

–But a Zen master, Rud added.

–There is no such thing, the man said.

Rud looked at Gale. She nodded yes.

–Right, Rud said to the man. You're not a Zen master, you just talk like one.

Gale laughed. The man neither smiled nor showed offense.

–Perhaps, he said to Gale, he will also get you to talk.

Gale didn't move. The man stopped in front of Rud.

–Your eye, he said suddenly and clamped a hand onto Rud's elbow.

And Rud, remembering now, felt a surge of heat and pain and he raised his free hand to touch his wound. Gale stopped him.

–Thank you, Kisa, the man said.

Coupled thus, the three stood for a moment. The man was not much taller than Gale, and she held his eyes for a moment. When the man swallowed, the cartilage plum of his throat bobbed like a burnt cork.

–Here, he said, taking a breath, and he swatted at the wall and a lightswitch clicked. No light came on. So firmly he towed Rud out into the dusk. His grip was both heavy and loose – and indisputable as a steamfitter's – and he released Rud's arm and took from the breast pocket of his overalls a pair of rimless spectacles and threaded them around each ear.

–How? he asked Rud.

–The cement mixer.

–Ah.

Reaching up, the man gently cupped Rud's head and cocked it sideways.

–Ngha, he said. Stitches perhaps.

–Stitches?

Again Rud motioned to explore his wound but again Gale stopped him.

–Perhaps. Come into the house, he said, tugging Rud's elbow. I have needle and thread.

–Needle and thread.

–Yes.

–You're crazy, Rud said.

–Please, the man said.

They crossed from the concrete onto the packed earth of the corridor between the garage and the ranch house.

–There is fresh water, Kisa? the man asked.

She nodded yes. They followed the two-track to the path that led to the front door.

–Are you okay? Rud asked softly of Gale.

She nodded.

–Of course, the man answered.

They reached the ranch house. The man opened the door.

—Kisa? he said.

She stepped inside the dark house and slid out of her slippers.

—She is lucky, the man said. He guided Rud inside and pointed to his Nikes. You too please, he said.

—Lucky? Rud asked.

He dropped to one knee to untie his laces.

—A believer, the man said.

Rud looked up at the man as he closed the door.

—Why is that lucky? Rud persisted.

—Nyūmetsu no gi, the man said. He raised his eyes, as if remembering, and said:

—For they do not die clutching at the earth.

Rud looked at Gale. Her eyes were closed. He looked at the man. The man pointed at Rud's feet.

—What? Rud asked.

—Socks too, the man said.

He felt a hand on his shoulder. Gale's. She also touched the man's shoulder and when he turned to her she hugged her arms and mimed a shiver. The man plucked at his thin lower lip. Asked Rud:

—They are clean? Your socks?

—As a whistle, Rud said.

—So, the man said and to Gale asked, you will practice, Kisa?

Gale put her palms together under her chin.

—Practice? Rud asked.

She bowed to the man. The man bowed back.

—Zazen, he explained to Rud.

Gale bowed quickly to Rud. Still kneeling, he bowed slightly in return. He stood.

—But not for you, Rud said to the man.

Banistered stairs climbed one side of the hallway and Gale turned now, like someone pursuing her child, and made for them. When she began to climb them – her footsteps a soft calligraphy – the man said quietly:

–For you and I, iodine. And whiskey. Come.

At the other end of the hall stood a dark doorway and starting toward it their footsteps thupped on the hardwood floor.

–You are Rudyard, the man said.

–Yes.

–I – Masao Tsuruoka.

–Tsuruoka – the roshi.

–No, Tsuruoka said. Tsuruoka, your nurse.

Rud made no reply. At the doorway Tsuruoka added:

–You were supposed to laugh.

The room smelled of soap and smelly feet. It was the kitchen and at the counter Tsuruoka lit several candles with the first. With each candle the light leapt further across the floor until at the back door it brindled over the hulk of a sleeping dog. The dog snuffled.

–Cletis, Tsuruoka said. Out!

He lit another candle. The dog stood. Half the door disappeared.

–Jesus, Rud said. What kind of a dog is that?

–A ripe one. But most harmless. Like me. Here. Sit.

The dog sat. With his foot Tsuruoka hooked and dragged over a high wooden stool. He shunted Rud onto its seat.

–Okay, Rud said, so you're not the roshi – fine, but *were* you?

–I was a player, Tsuruoka said as he studied Rud's wound.

–A player?

–Yes. Like you – besuboru.

–Baseball?

–In Japan major leagues. That is why Kisa came here.

–Here?

–And not somewhere else.

–Ouch.

—Sorry.

—It's okay. So because you were a player.

—And because you were.

—Me?

—Yes.

Tsuruoka braced his hand under Rud's neck.

—Lean back please.

Rud tilted his head back until his skull touched the countertop and Tsuruoka spread the candles in a semicircle about Rud's head.

—How do you know all this? Rud asked him.

Tsuruoka peered down at him. The candles' light, like tiny effigies, swayed across his spectacle lenses.

—Her blackboard, he said. He stopped to rub the back of his neck. Good I am not a dentist, he moaned.

—Her blackboard, Rud said. Is that another joke?

Tsuruoka rotated Rud's head a notch, examining the wound.

—You will find out, he said. One stitch?

—Goodbye, Rud said, lifting his head.

—Perhaps not, Tsuruoka said, soothing him.

—So – so when did you play?

—For Hanshin Tigers, he told Rud. Thirty – forty years ago.

—Hanshin.

—Yes.

—That a city? A province?

—It is a railroad.

Rud laughed.

—I do not joke, Tsuruoka said.

—You played for a railroad.

—Yes.

He let go of Rud's head. A cleanup, he announced. That is all.

—How long? Rud asked.

—A few minutes.

—No no. Rud twisted his head. How long did you play? For this railroad.

Tsuruoka stepped to the sink. Two galvanized buckets stood, their rims inches above the sink edge. Tsuruoka squirted dishsoap on his hands. Scrubbed them in one bucket.

—In Japan, Tsuruoka said over his shoulder, major league teams are named after their owner.

In the other bucket he rinsed his hands, then toweled them dry.

—And you played for a few minutes?

—A few minutes – in the Emperor's game. A lifetime.

Rud sat up.

—What's the Emperor's

—Lay back, Tsuruoka said smartly.

Rud did so. And from the cupboard above Rud's head Tsuruoka slid out and, with his fingers squidding underneath, lowered to the countertop a large coffee can. He plied off its lid and shook from a vial found inside some pills into his hand.

—Aspirin, he told Rud.

Tsuruoka poked again at the can's inside. Drew out and set on the counter a small eyedropper-stopped bottle, its glass once amber but now stained to ochre.

—Iodine, Rud said.

—And Cutty, Tsuruoka said.

Tall and green as an island was this bottle Tsuruoka took from the cupboard. A rigged ship sailing out of its label.

—Whiskey.

—And two cups.

Which were two handleless teacups. White ones. Tsuruoka pondered the pills, the iodine, the whiskey.

—So, he said. Here.

And he helped Rud sit up. Then splashed into each cup a measure of liquid, gold as an alchemy.

–Put your hand out.

Rud did. The three pills rolled across Tsuruoka's lifeline and tumbled into Rud's palm. Rud popped them into his mouth. They raised their cups.

–For the aspirin, Rud said.

–For the iodine.

The kitchen ceiling creaked. They lifted their eyes.

–Gale, Rud said.

–Sitting.

–Cheers then.

–Kan pai, Tsuruoka said.

The iodine, after Tsuruoka swabbed the wound clean with peroxide, was a small fiery brand with its pain, and Rud emitted at its singeing a parceled nightmare from his throat. But then it was gone and Tsuruoka, refilling twice their cups, taped over the wound a gauze bandage.

–The outhouse is past the garden, Tsuruoka said. And tomorrow – if you make it – you can help

–I should leave.

–Ha! You must have my room.

–I can sleep in my truck. I have this bedroll

–My room. It is custom – *the* custom.

–Where will you? Sleep?

–Not down here, Tsuruoka said, grinning. He fanned the air under his nose.

–But my things?

–I will get them. Have a nightcap. Make yourself a home.

–But *I* should go.

–You will get lost.

–I'll take the – the thing, in the garage.

–No rear gear. You can ride Penny?

–The horse? No.

The dog, until now still as a discarded carpet, bristled against the door, rattling its collar chains.

–They do not get along, Tsuruoka explained.

–You're right then, Rud said. You go. Thanks.

–So, Tsuruoka said and he drank off his whiskey and set the teacup on the counter. He turned to the dog and chanted:

–Rettsu go, Cretis.

Cletis, with a rippling tremor of fur and muscle, stood.

–My truck, Rud said. Where it's parked

–I know, Tsuruoka interrupted.

–But how? – Unless you knew of my coming.

–A friend, Tsuruoka said.

–The bookstore?

–Uguisu, Tsuruoka said.

–Oo-what?

–A little bird, as you say. So simple. Penny and I wait. Then we follow you through the woods.

The skirl of the joists within the kitchen ceiling above him beckoned him, after a while, up off the stool. To drain his nightcap and set the cup on the counter and, carrying a candle, follow. Back down the hall to the front stairs. He thought he heard his name and he aimed the candle up at the landing and its light flew upward like a sudden bird snared in a white veil. In that veil Gale stood. On the landing. Waiting. He climbed the stairs to meet her.

She wore the same loosefitting pants. The same buttonless shirt. In one hand she held a square chalkboard and a stick of chalk in her other and she looked at Rud and then at the chalkboard and chalk and she wrote:

RUD

and showed it to him.

–Hi, he said.

She looked again at her chalkboard. At him. At the board.

–You will stay, she said.

–You're –

–You must, she said.

He stopped climbing. A whiskey dizziness wafted through him. He gripped the banister.

–Did you hear me?

She cleared her throat and tapped with her fingers her collarbone.

–You're talking, he said.

–I know why you're here.

–Talking, he repeated.

–In the garage, she said. The roshi

–He said you'd talk, and –

–I wanted it all along, she said.

He climbed the last two stairs, gaining the landing. Entering her jasmine scent.

–Wanted your coming. I just didn't –

She stopped. Looked at him, as though pondering some diagnosis.

–What's wrong? he asked her.

–The roshi? she asked.

–What?

–He's been drinking too?

Her face was thinner, more determined. Still, though, exquisite.

–Between cashmere, he said.

–Has he?

–Your hair, he said.

–Is he still?

–Between cashmere and snow.

–Please! she said. Damn.

–Gale, nothing s'wrong.

She closed her eyes. Their shadow from the candlelight a vibrant host on the landing's wall.

–Yes there is. He's – anyway, I thought wonderful, your coming was wonderful –

–I thought so too – except for –

Here Rud mimed whapping into the cement mixer.

–But now you're making things worse, Gale said.

–No one's getting drunk.

–How can you stay if

–Stay?

–Be his student.

–His student?

–Yes.

–I didn't come to be his student.

–Why else would you've then?

He looked at her.

–Well?

–Lots of reasons.

–Such as?

–To find you.

–To find me.

–Yes.

–And do what?

–I don't know –

–You don't know.

–Ask you about your manuscript.

–My manuscript?

–The anthology – there was a question we couldn't answer.

–You didn't come all the way here to ask me about my manuscript.

–About the fishermen's riddle, Rud said, grinning.

–Rud, please. Be serious.

–I am.

–No, she said, no. I wanted – willed you to come – the drawing I did of your father –

—My father?

They heard a dog's bark and downstairs the front door foomped open and Cletis, despite Tsuruoka shouting, *No!*, barreled down the hallway, clawing the floor loud as a horde. Gale looked at Rud. They heard the front door close.

—Here, she whispered, reaching up to touch his bandage.

—What?

—One of the things's come loose.

She tamped the adhesive back across his forehead, smoothing it. They heard Tsuruoka stump off his workboots.

—Rud-san, he called up. Come. Please. A nightcap.

She put her finger to her lips.

—Kisa! Come down. You too.

—If you don't, Gale whispered, he won't.

—I heard that, Tsuruoka said.

He was at the bottom of the stairs. He had Rud's bedroll and duffel bag and his father's urn. Gale cleared her throat.

—Roshi? she called down. May I talk to you later?

—Talk?

—Please?

—I have wished so, Kisa, since the day you arrived.

Gale took Rud's hand lightly in hers. Hers with a workaday roughness. She smiled, her green eyes crinkling between her cheekbones and the fresh down of her brows.

—You are staying in his room? she asked softly.

He nodded.

Palms together under her chin, she bowed and was gone into the hallway's darkness. Rud descended the stairs. Tsuruoka set the duffel bag on the floor, the bedroll on top, and with his second hand now free, set on the next-to-last step, the urn.

—I did not know what to get, he told Rud. What to leave.

—She wants me to stay.

–So I get everything.

–For more than one night.

Rud looked over his shoulder, back upstairs.

–Here, Tsuruoka said.

–What we find, Rud said aloud to himself, is rarely what we start out looking for.

–Wise, Tsuruoka said.

Rud turned. Tsuruoka was holding out the *Buddhist America* directory, the postcard of the sea bookmarked inside.

–Here, Tsuruoka repeated.

Rud took them.

–Advice I gathered on the way, he explained.

–Which makes it all the wiser, Tsuruoka said.

He turned, his bare feet pattering, and walked down the hall toward the kitchen. Rud followed.

–She still says you are, he told Tsuruoka.

–I will help you upstairs, Tsuruoka said.

–A Zen master.

–After our nightcap.

They entered the kitchen. On the counter awaiting: the green bottle; on either side flanked, like a scales, by the two white cups.

–First, you make Kisa laugh, Tsuruoka said.

He picked up the bottle of Cutty. When he slid the two white cups together Rud shook his head no.

–Now you make her talk. He looked at Rud. What is next?

Expecting Gale, he battled to stay awake. But within minutes of sinking into his bedroll in Tsuruoka's room he succumbed. Into that blackened depth beyond stillness where only the heart stirs. How long before he dreamed? Dreamed his father's pickup, shorn of its tires, that he drove lumbering like some primitive steam conveyance across the cliffs of Tierra del Fuego. The sea all-surrounding. The horizon a thin genesis of diamond. He opened his eyes.

She was sitting beside his bedroll. On a round brown cushion. Her legs crossed in full lotus. On her other side a candle burned, spiriting upward a gray taper, and casting over him and up the wall and across the ceiling a huge origami of shadow.

–I can save him, she said.

–Tsuruoka?

She set her chalkboard on the floor beside the candle and unthreaded her legs, emitting a soft groan. She renestled them like a tailor's, spun on her cushion, and said:

–But only with your help.

–By staying.

–Yes. I told you, it's why you're here.

Tugging his bedroll's corner with him to swathe his bare chest Rud sat fully up.

–For you are why *I* am here, she told him.

–I know.

–He told you?

–Yes.

–And that my coming – ? She hesitated. He told you about his loss of faith?

–Faith?

–That he's not the roshi anymore.

–Because of you?

–Because of that, she said, pointing beyond Rud's shoulder.

In the corner near his pillow was a steamer trunk and on it, standing between two large seashells, was a book, slabshaped and white as a tablet of the testimony.

–This?

He twisted, stretched out an arm. With his finger he poked at the nearest seashell to nudge it aside. He could barely move it. He grabbed it with his hand and wristed it over. Its earshaped chamber was solid. A pewter gray.

–Concrete, he guessed.

He replaced the seashell and tilted his head to read the book's spine.

–*The Origin of Consciousness*, he read aloud, *in the Breakdown of the Bicameral Mind.*

He slid it from between its shells.

–A book? he wondered aloud. One that could make a Zen master – ?

–Bernard-sensei still refuses to believe.

–Who's Bernard-sensei? Rud asked, flipping the book over.

–How I found out about here.

–Startling as Darwin's dissolution of species, Rud read from the jacket, as Einstein's – sorry?

–Roshi's first student.

–And I'm to be the last, Rud said.

–No, she said. That's the whole point.

He examined the back cover again.

–As Einstein's reigning of light. He slid the book back between the seashells. You're sure it's the book?

–No, she said, I don't know – it's what he claims.

–Tsuruoka.

She nodded.

–The visions of the saints, she said. The insights of the masters – I still can't believe

–You've read it?

She shook her head no.

–It's what the roshi claimed – that even the awakening of the Buddha himself was – was just a mirage, a hallucination.

She pinched her eyes with pain. Composed herself with a deep breath.

–But how will my staying – ?

–Help?

–Yes.

–He likes you. He knows about you.

–About my father.

–As about mine. And when you stay

–If.

–Then I will ask him to start zazen again.

–He'd do that? For me?

–For me, she said. Only he wouldn't be forced to admit so. The point is, he would do it.

–You know that.

–Yes.

–Because he loves you.

–All that matters

–Doesn't he?

–Is that he might be the roshi again.

They sat quietly, the candle sissling. Rud rubbed the goosebumps off his upper arms.

–Rud, you and I, we lost our fathers.

–Yes.

–Both horribly.

–Yes.

–Well he, the roshi, in a way lost his.

–Our father who art in heaven.

–Yes – though Zen doesn't really have a God.

She looked away, her eyes lighting at the foot of his bedroll on his duffel bag, on his father's urn.

–Your dad? she asked.

–He almost didn't make it, Rud said smiling. On more than one occasion. But he was someone to talk to.

–Good company?

–Except when I was sitting.

–In zazen?

–Yes.

–So you've already been

–Occasionally –

–Rud, that's perfect.

–In motel rooms.

She made two fists and her eyes brightened and she repeated quietly:

–Perfect!

She half-covered his hand with hers.

–The day you left, he said with great effort.

–Your father's portrait?

–I thought it was of me.

–I drew you all summer, she said.

–On your chalkboard?

–Messages in a bottle, she told him and reached behind her back and picked her chalkboard up. Like tonight.

She showed it to him. Not quite full face. His eyes closed. The mouth open.

–I look like I swallowed a fly, he said.

–You were snoring.

–No –

–Gently, she said.

–Dreaming, he explained. Driving my father's pickup. In Tierra del Fuego.

–Chile or Argentina? she asked.

He pondered.

–Seattle, he said finally.

She waited, smiling slightly. He nodded at her chalkboard.

–I'm going to stay, aren't I.

She did not answer. Chalk and board she put on the floor and in a single movement swung her legs to one side and then under herself so that she now sat on her heels.

–Rud, she said, there is no mustard seed – no medicine for the dead. But the living –

–The roshi?

–Yes – imagine if he had his faith back.

–I can't believe he lost it.

–Neither can he. What he said – at the front door

–About believers?

–Yes – I mean –

–But what about that? Rud asked.

–That?

–Yes, he said twisting and nodding at the book on the steamer trunk.

–I don't know.

–Could it happen twice? he asked.

–I'll say I'll read it.

–In return for his sitting again?

–Yes.

–A swop.

She laughed and nodded.

–All right, he said. For how long?

–It's so beautiful here, she said looking across the room to the window. And after sitting, to go for a walk with the valley so far below, and the air all – it's

He waited.

–What? he asked.

–Like taking a walk in the sky, she said.

–For how long? he asked again.

She looked right at him. Her eyes in the candlelight the color of evening.

–It's up to you, she told him.

–A week? he suggested. Two?

–For as long as you want, she said.

–Three weeks, he said. A month maybe – okay?

She took both his hands in hers.

–A day at a time, she told him.

–I can hack a month.

She nodded and, again groaning quietly, stood. She tucked her chalk in the pocket of her pants and wedged her board under her arm. Then she dropped to one knee to gather her zafu and candle.

–Different schools together, she said softly.

–Once again, he said.

She smiled and nodded and stood. She bowed. And with the candle-light leaping in a great splash of yellow across the room, she turned and left.

–Now what have you done? Rud asked his father.

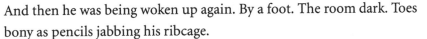

And then he was being woken up again. By a foot. The room dark. Toes bony as pencils jabbing his ribcage.

–What? What now?

–Okite kudasai.

Rud propped himself up. Blinked awake. Tsuruoka.

–What time is it?

–Time for torture. Come on.

He stood and shivering dressed in jeans and sweatshirt. Followed Tsuruoka out of the room. Along the hall. Down the stairs.

–Where's Gale? he asked.

–She told me you have sat zazen before.

–Some.

Tsuruoka said nothing. He wore not a Zen robe but a lumberjack shirt under bib overalls and his wide pantlegs when he walked wobbled like stovepipes against each other. They entered and crossed the kitchen. Its window and the back-door window were squares of cathode blue. Forming a corner with the back door was a woodslat pantry door. It raked across the floor when Tsuruoka pushed it open, held it open with one stiff arm.

—Hole is in the far corner. Urinate only, he said.

—Into a hole?

—A cistern. They wanted it authentic.

—Like in Japan?

—Pour water from the bucket when you are done. Spoon of ash.

The zendo was in the rectangular front room. It had hardwood floors smooth as ivory. Along each side wall a single round cushion – a thick brown disc – was tilted up by a small pillow wedged under its back half.

—What about Gale? Rud asked again.

The light was absent here and at the far end wall Tsuruoka plucked from a tall dark vase a long wooden match and, striking it, lit a candle. On the shelf beside it was revealed a Buddha that seemed hewn from a block of frozen sea.

—Will it always be this early? Rud asked.

—Ha! Tsuruoka said. We sleeped in. Watch.

Tsuruoka stood slightly behind his zafu. Palms under chin, he bowed.

—Gasshō, he said and his body dropped supple as a leaf into the lotus position – right foot on left thigh, left foot on right thigh.

—Now you, he said.

—I – I've been kinda sitting Japanese style, Rud said.

—Seiza – so.

Rud took this for an okay and, at his cushion opposite, mimed Tsuruoka's bow. He straddled the cushion – knees bent, shins flat on the floor – and sat. Cupped his hands in his lap. Thumbtips touching. Satisfied, he twisted to look over his shoulder at Tsuruoka facing his own wall.

—Back straight, Tsuruoka said. Your concentration in your belly. Your breath in your belly.

–Yes.

–Not your stomach, your belly. And count, to yourself, each out breath. Ichi, ni, san, then back to one. Twenty-five minutes. Do not move.

He bowed. Rud bowed. Tsuruoka rang a small bell. For the first five minutes Rud sat still. At ten – his motel limit – he was squirming. His thoughts wandered, then raced. The tops of his feet were numb. He shifted them.

–Do not move! Tsuruoka hissed.

–Sorry.

–Just count your breaths.

He began: ichi, ni, san. Ichi, ni. In his motel sittings he hadn't counted his breaths but followed them. Counting was easier. Where was he? Ichi, ni. He needed to shift his numb feet again. Perhaps if he did it really slowly Tsuruoka wouldn't

–No!

Back to counting. To losing count. Until finally Tsuruoka struck two pieces of wood together clack-clack. Rud heard Tsuruoka stand, rustling. With no little difficulty Rud managed to. His jeans were scrunched behind his knees. He shook each leg out.

–Kinhin, Tsuruoka ordered.

Eyes downcast, hands clasped and held like a tenor at the breast, Rud followed Tsuruoka around and around the periphery of the zendo for five minutes. When they sat on the pillows again Rud's daydreams rose like a cobra from under a rock. Gale was with him in Tsuruoka's bedroom. A kiss goodbye. Then the woman from Peak Physique. In his bedroll. He had a hard-on. He couldn't remember her name. Victoria? Her knees rubbing his hips. He moaned as he slid inside her.

–Count your breaths! Tsuruoka snapped.

–Ichi. Dawn crawled across the wood floor. Ni. Yet somehow he endured. Clack-clack.

–Whew.

–Kinhin.

Then back to the grind.

–Congratulations, Tsuruoka said after the third and final round of zazen. They were in the kitchen. The window fresh and open. Tsuruoka unfolded on the counter beneath it the green wings of a Coleman stove. He inhaled a booming chestful of morning air.

–Ahh, Tsuruoka beamed, I forgot about this part.

Tsuruoka ruminated for a moment, then squatted on his heels and with much clanging rummaged from the undercupboard a kettle and a percolator.

–Coffee? he asked.

–Please.

–Or tea?

–You mean like *tea*-tea?

–Nihon-cha – green tea.

–I think coffee, Rud said. Please.

Tsuruoka stowed the kettle and with difficulty stood.

–Ooow, he moaned. If only I had forgot about this part too.

He rubbed his knees. Rud, sitting atop a kitchen stool, had not ceased rubbing his.

–Does it ever go away? Rud asked.

–The soreness?

–The pain.

–Not really.

Tsuruoka filled the percolator with water cold from a bucket. He added coffee grainy as sand. A pinch of salt.

–What then? Rud asked.

–Like grief, Tsuruoka said. It goes somewhere, just never away.

Tsuruoka struck a safety match, touched a burner, summoning a ring of blue flame. Refusing any help, he made Rudyard-san breakfast. A cheese and bacon omelet. And perched astool, Rud drank through his nostrils the mountain blowing clean and bright through the window.

–You're right, Rud said. He smiled and rubbed his face and stretched his arms out wingy. This *is* pretty good.

Tsuruoka lifted off the omelet pan and lowered the gas jet and warmed the plates and the mugs.

–What do you know about windmills? he asked.

He meant the one they later hauled the extension ladder upmountain to fix. The replacement bearing was the size of a jezebel's earring and, climbing from blond terrace to blond terrace, the midmorning sun wheeled down over their backs and shoulders and when they reached the windmill's thick stem they were drenched and panting. The ladder's weathered feet Tsuruoka stubbed into the coarse ground, then thrusting at Rud his tool apron and telling him, *Steady the ladder,* he scooted like a steeplejack up the wonky rungs.

Rud set his boot soles against the ladder's feet. He hooked the tool apron to a rung and with his hands steadied the uprights. Tsuruoka clamped his screwdriver in his teeth and ransacked his pocket for the bearing. Still gripping the uprights, Rud looked over his shoulder. Downhill was the garden's black loam. Then the wellpump standing like an iron parson and the house and the garage side by side, each white as the sun. The roofshingles were bright and black as the garden loam and to the west the far mountains lay in a dark blue film. In the narrow corridor between garage and house Gale was up the tall stepladder, scraping the garage underhang. She wore a pair of Tsuruoka's dun work overalls. Baggy-assed. With her fingers she skimmed rapidly the paint flecks out of her short hair and slid the scraper into her back pocket. She waved to Rud. He waved back.

–Steady *my* ladder, Tsuruoka shouted down. Not hers.

In the afternoon Rud, on hands and knees, washed the hardwood floors (–What gives them that shine? –Your eyes.) in the main floor, then in the long apex of the attic. There were small windows at either end Rud opened but the heat still beat at him like a kiln's. Tsuruoka came creaking up the narrow stairs laden with Rud's bedroll, duffel bag, the urn, and stacked them by the pony wall. Kneeling, Rud straightened his back.

–My room? Rud asked.

–Is it?

Rud mopped his brow. Nodded. Said:

–A/C? Picture windows?

–And a shower, Tsuruoka added. Come.

It was down two flights. Behind the slat door in the kitchen's corner. The same uninsulated wooden cubicle that housed the pisshole. In the center of the room by the hole was what looked like a miniature clay baker – the soapdish – and two buckets brimming.

–Hot and cold standing water, Rud quipped.

–If you stand one bucket in sunlight, perhaps.

And while Rud had his shivering splash bath – soaping with the haste of a Channel swimmer – Tsuruoka, with the windmill repaired, cooked supper on a plug-in rangetop: a chicken stirfry he poured from a large plastic freezer bag into the fry pan and doled out with a wooden spoon onto two Tupperware plates.

–No Gale? Rud asked.

–She is a vegetarian.

–I'm quickly learning not to ask questions.

Tsuruoka set Rud's plate on the countertop in front of his stool. He smiled and dipped his head at Rud.

–And I, Rud, am learning to not answer them.

But in the zendo before sitting that evening she visited. Rud was limbering up, stretching before Tsuruoka arrived.

–Like infield practice, he said softly and looked up to find her standing in the doorway.

–Hi, he said.

–Yoga? she asked.

—Well to tell the truth, I don't know. I learned them from a girl, a woman, at Cornell.

In the hallway burned a low-wattage electric light and the light was soft on Gale's face.

—She was in dance, Rud continued. I figured they were, you know, ballet or something. So I'd always do them in secret.

He waved a thumb at the zafu awaiting.

—Are you? he asked.

—No, she said.

—Oh.

He straightened his legs, creaking like rails.

—It would only complicate things, she said.

—I suppose.

—How was day one? she asked.

—Sitting. Eating.

—Chores?

—Tilting at windmills.

She smiled.

—Mine are the laundry, the post office.

—Your bike?

—And groceries. In my saddlebags.

—Trade you?

—And painting.

—The garage?

She nodded.

—I loved your Jacques Plante, Rud said. At Monsieur Michel's.

A moment passed.

—My father hated the Canadiens, she told him.

—A Leafs fan?

She was motionless. Rud waited.

—They're red here, she said absently. The firetrucks are.

–Red?

She nodded.

–I pass the station each day I ride into town. You have to. Except on the anniversary I

She made a swimming motion with her hand. She took a breath. Smiled ever so slightly.

–Detoured? Rud asked.

–Stayed home, she said. I mean here. Even though the ones my father drove were green.

–Like the tea, Rud said.

–Yes, Gale said.

They smiled at each other.

–Laundry day tomorrow, she said.

–Perfect.

–And Rud, thank you. And

–And what?

–The hamper is under the stairs, she said.

She bowed and left. He thought for a moment, then whispered to himself:

–You're doing the right thing.

–Perhaps, a voice answered.

Tsuruoka's. He bowed to Rud. To the Buddha at the zendo's far end. And for Rud the next two hours – five rounds of sitting zazen, four thankful intermissions of walking kinhin – were a rack. What of him was once fluid, froze. What was still, raced. His legs were calcified. His back muscles bunched and rolled into knots. His sole hope: to wriggle – just a

–Do not move!

In the attic he slept the sleep of the newly rescued. Furnacing away in his Slumberjack. Came dawn and Tsuruoka's breath when he nudged Rud awake lifted white into the rafters. Pale light on the windows. Rud's own breath as he dressed with haste escaped in small kites. Tsuruoka sniffed. Clenched his overalls' bib straps.

–It is here already, he said solemnly.

Rud looked at him.

–We must chop wood after sitting, Tsuruoka explained. Clean the woodstove and chimney.

He left Rud scrambling into socks.

–Day two, Rud said to his father. Care to join me?

He waited.

–Good.

That morning Rud's back caught fire. A point of flesh under his right shoulderblade. Subsequent days a different part did so, caught fire at each sitting until the pain became so vast it formed a lurid sea. One brilliant morning as the sun touched the zendo's windowtops he *was* the monk who in the busy Saigon street had set himself ablaze.

–*Was* him, he emphasized to Gale that night before zazen while he limbered.

She nodded. A noise on the stairs, like the timbers creaking on some Homeric vessel. She was gone.

–So vivid.

Vividness even in the cedar-plank outhouse where, several mornings later, he swabbed with sponge and Comet the seat. The lid. A tin camper's mug he filled from a gallon of kerosene. Poured it – a long ebony spider – down the hole. The outhouse walls' cracks ignited by fuzes of light the color of burning copper.

Or while priming the wellpump's dew-blackened handle several mornings after that. The pumphandle's cold squeal. The dawn sky slate, vermilion. A flock of birds migrating, passing in a single silent wing.

–Neither in the sky or my mind, he told Gale that night. As though

They stood close in the hallway by the zendo's door. As if discerning two weights Rud held up his hands.

—As though they were that close, Gale told him softly.

—Yes —

He massaged the back of his neck.

—It's worth the stiffness, she said.

Rud shook his head no. Then smiled and nodded yes.

—And in only three weeks, she told him.

—And a day, he corrected.

Tenderly she covered with hers his hand – the one kneading his neck. As though to beckon him closer. Until the stairs creaked. She pulled her hand away. But she did not flee. With the scup-scup of Tsuruoka's bare footsteps in his ears and a blush smoldering his cheeks Rud bowed at the zendo's entrance and entered. She cleared her throat and he turned to see her relinquish a share of the doorway's space for Tsuruoka. Hands set palm to palm under her chin, she bowed. He likewise.

—Roshi? she asked.

—Why are you not upstairs sitting? he asked.

—I was wondering –

—Yes?

—If I might sit with you tonight?

Tsuruoka looked at her, deeply. She lowered her eyes.

—It is best, he said, if you move out.

—What? Rud blurted.

—We are a distraction, each one of us

—You can't, Rud began.

With a hand gesture Tsuruoka insisted on silence.

—A distraction to each other. To your practice, Tsuruoka said to Gale firmly. Your reading.

—My reading.

—Yes.

—Wait a second, Rud began.

Gale put her finger against her lips. Asked:

—When?

–To Bernard-sensei's. Now. Go.

She obeyed. Tsuruoka bowed and entered the zendo.

–Where have you sent her? Rud demanded.

–You will see her again.

Tsuruoka walked past Rud to the zendo's altar. Plucked from the vase's dark neck a long match.

–We were talking about my back, that's all, the pain.

–After sitting, Tsuruoka said, I will do something about that also.

–A bathtub, Rud said.

They were in the kitchen. Twin saucepans of water on the plug-in's burners, simmering. The kettle on the woodstove emitting a boy's first whistle. And on the floor in front: a homesteader's bathtub.

–An honor saved for the end of sesshin – weeklong retreats, Tsuruoka told him. But now?

–A bathtub, Rud said.

–This is not about your father, Tsuruoka said.

–Is a bathtub, Rud continued.

–So, Tsuruoka said.

He gripped its handles. Pointed to the slat door.

–Here. Open please.

It was glorious. Soaking in it like a hillbilly with his legs from the knees down dangling out. Glorious at first under the shed's bare lightbulb. It was metal though and the heat sapped through and the water grew tepid, then cool, then chilly.

He climbed out and, naked, incrementally tipped the bathtub up onto its corner, sending down the drainhole a long sucking guidon of water. He slooshed out the tub with what was left in the cold bucket and, shivering, spun to retrieve his towel that periwigged the clothespeg. He dried and wrapped his towel around his waist, listening to the silence of the house. The quietness increased its presence until he felt it on the cold bare skin of his forearms and shoulders and he longed to hum but told himself:

—It's not going to get to you.

And cleared his throat and whisked his clothes off their peg and appraised the bathtub. Its emptiness. He grasped one tub handle and dragged it across the floor to the door. He went to push the door open but the gesture was so much the one with which he had pushed open his father's bathroom door that a voice inside him said, Stop. He shut his eyes. Exhaled. Opened them and straightened his backbone.

—Besides, it's a pull, he said softly and grabbed the dummy knob and yanked it open.

—How was it? Tsuruoka asked, perched on a stool by the counter.

He was threading a needle. A hill of brown cloth in front of him.

—An experience.

—So.

—Thank you. Sewing?

Tsuruoka licked the thread's end. Aimed it at the needlehole.

—May I ask you something?

—She is in the garage, Tsuruoka said.

—Gale?

—In the apartment above. Bernard-sensei's.

—The loft?

—Your bath, you have used up all the water?

—Yes. Actually I was going to ask something about Zen.

—You must get more for the morning.

—May I?

Tsuruoka looked at him. Said:

—Your question.

Rud stalled. Asked:

—Will you answer?

—If I have one.

—Does – does Zen believe in – in the soul?

—Ghosts?

Rud nodded. Tsuruoka returned his attention to threading his needle.

—That depends, he said.

—On?

—Here, Tsuruoka barked. Quick!

Rud leapt over.

—What?

—My glasses, please. Take them off?

Rud unhooked them from Tsuruoka's ears. Put them on the counter.

—Depends on what? Rud persisted.

—If you believe in Zen or not.

—Do you?

—The water, Tsuruoka said re-aiming the thread, and ghosts, can wait until morning.

Nevertheless, as Rud zipped up his sleeping bag in the loft, he said to his father's urn:

—Tomorrow, Dad, you're going back in the truck.

And he repeated that to himself as, the next morning before zazen, he climbed the path through an ankle-deep mist to the outhouse. He'd borrowed Tsuruoka's workboots and they were two sizes too small but unlaced they did the job. The outhouse door was papered with frost and frost was on the seat inside and the floor like a sunken ruin. He drew down his trousers only as far as necessary.

—At least there's no bathtub, he said to himself and he wondered about his truck. There was a noise outside. Cletis or Penny. He finished his business and did up his pants and shut the lid. The noise again – a fluty murmur. He shivered. He pushed open the door and stepped outside. Neither Cletis nor Penny was in sight. Only, in the west sky, a few vagrant stars. A silence clung to him. He heard a whisper:

—Rud.

–Enough, he said and he started briskly back down the path. Across the back of his neck and shoulders his skin crawled. He picked up his pace and by the time he reached the wellpump he was running. His heart pummeled his chest and he ripped open the screen door and burst through the back door into the kitchen, hurling it shut behind him.

His heart pounded. Tsuruoka was standing by the sink. Dressed, to Rud's surprise, in his robes, brown and flowing, with a wide black belt and tunneling sleeves.

–You called me, Rud said, catching his breath.

–No, Tsuruoka said.

–Someone – Gale then.

–We are late, Tsuruoka told him.

He washed his hands at the sink. He was starving and his mind crackled as though filled with static. He walked down the hall and at the zendo door bowed.

There were slices of sun in the zendo's southern windowtops and during the first sittings those slices seeped downward. By the third sitting they filled the window. And it was during that sitting that someone knelt behind Rud and rested a hand on his shoulder: light, firm, callused. His father.

Rud shifted. Held his breath.

–Illusion, he whispered.

–Quiet.

Seeking sanctuary, he forced his breath deeper into his belly. The hand did not depart. He blinked. His mind was a crushing void; his father's beautiful air – Brylcreem, tobacco, and beer – floated over him. He gagged. With his legs he clove to his cushion. The hand tightened. His terror deepened.

Next thing he knew he was standing. His breath came in clumps. A few feet away the sun burned a white rectangle into the floor past which Tsuruoka perched on his cushion.

–Time is not up, Tsuruoka said.

Rud did not move. He felt his father, now not just the hand but his entire being flowing over him in wreaths. His chest heaved. He groaned.

–Sit! Tsuruoka said sharply.

In two strides Rud was out of the room. He walked down the hall, past the stairs, out the front door, crossed the grass to the garage. He did not run. The blue wind cascaded through him and the sky crackled like ten thousand banners arrayed.

–Rud! a voice spoke clearly in his ear.

He spun around.

–Forget it – I'm out of

He went dumb. He was alone. He clamped his ears with his hands. From the ranch-house door Tsuruoka emerged. Hands clasped at his robe's belt. He walked over.

–What? Rud demanded, dropping his arms.

–I did not say anything, Tsuruoka said.

–You called to me.

–No.

–You did – oh yes you did – some fucking trick – a, a

–Not me.

–Who then? Who? Wait, don't answer. Cause I'm leaving. I mean I've had it, man, fucking had it. I hate this shit, hate it. I'm fucking dying. My back, my ankles. Rud tapped his temple. My fucking head.

–Fucking torture, Tsuruoka said.

–And then this – this – I mean my father, he, he was there covering me like – like

–Like what?

–Wait a minute, Rud said. You swore.

Tsuruoka shrugged. Grinned.

–Well big deal, Rud continued. Look, I want my keys, my truck.

–So get them.

—And I want out.

—You were the one who wanted to stay.

Rud held his tongue.

—Wise, Tsuruoka said. He gazed across the valley floor. The trees on the western wall of mountains were green as bottles.

—Ahh, Tsuruoka sniffed, smiling. It is a fine day.

—For what? An exorcism?

—Yes, Tsuruoka beamed.

—On who?

—We will cast out Zen. Invoke a holiday.

—And do what? Sit around?

—You do not quit, do you?

—No, Rud said.

—Aha.

—Well sometimes.

—Too late, Tsuruoka told him.

—No it isn't.

—It must be – you are still here.

—I'm not so sure.

—I am, Tsuruoka said. He laid a hand on Rud's shoulder. Look, he said, I have errands in town all day. So you – take a holiday. Maybe hike. Sleep if you want.

—In the house? In the attic?

—Write a letter, Tsuruoka suggested after a moment. Your father will not bother you anymore today.

—No?

—No, Rud-san.

—You know about ghosts?

—Yes, Tsuruoka said. I know about ghosts. Trust me – write a letter home.

And – to Etta – that's what he did. The postcard. To tell her about his father's ghost. Though he only got as far as addressing it. He set the postcard aside and read, browsing in *Buddhist America*. For ghosts. He did push-ups. Lunchtime he walked swiftly by the zendo on his way to and from the kitchen. His ears hummed. Suppertime Tsuruoka had not returned and Rud plugged in the range and peeled and boiled some potatoes, mashed them, cooked in butter two peppery eggs. He washed up. The hallway was dark. This time at the zendo he stopped. He looked inside. Across the floor, brown as a spider, sat his zafu.

—Anyone home? he called softly.

He did not step inside. Upstairs he sat in bed, thinking of it all. His heart thumped against the half wall behind him when outside Cletis barked. Horse hooves gaited up to the house. More barking. A slap on the rump. A whistle. The front door opened. Tsuruoka. No longer alone in the house, he slid into his bedroll and into sleep.

The next morning he tried to open the urn. Tsuruoka had not awakened him for zazen and after a solitary breakfast of cold Muesli and milk he tackled the postcard again. The attic window at his shoulder, he sat with his legs crossed like a tailor, the urn set on the floor in front of him. He stared at Etta's name handwritten on the postcard. At her address. That first summer in Toronto. Out the window they were playing road hockey. White trees swept across the sky. A priest in robes of saffron sat within a huge tulip of flames, waiting. Rud shook his head.

—His heart survived, Rud said. Perhaps yours did.

The urn was heavy as a bucket of sand but he lifted it and with a sudden cross of his forearms he upended it and with no little strain set it back down. The underside was blond as bone and as smooth, and in each corner was sunk a screw. He looked at them, thinking.

—Solid brass, he said. My keys?

And on all fours he paddled tenderly the few feet to his bedroll and duffel bag. Yet after searching found only at the bag's bottom his papers, including, in the sheath of its envelope, the autopsy report.

He zipped up his duffel bag and returned to the attic window and the urn. Sun gushed west over the ranch-house roof and washed down the steep camel-colored humps of the mountainside to the fence of trees beneath. Many of the evergreens were feathered with yellow and between their picketgaps something moved red as a bear. Penny? He looked down at the postcard of the sea. Picked it up.

–Try una postal, he said. Or a screwdriver.

There'd be one in the garage of course and, picking up the urn, he stood. Downstairs by the front door were his workboots and he stabbed a foot in one, wriggling it on. The doorhandle turned. The door opened, bumping his shoulder.

–Roshi?

–Me.

He leaned to one side and plucked the door open with his booted toe. Gale stood on the step. Her head freshly shaven. Her motorcycle saddlebags – white and silver – were slung like formal-dress ammo over her shoulder.

–Your truck, she said.

–My truck?

He waggled his other foot in his boot and, still bearing urn and postcard, stepped outside. Gale looked at the urn. Rud looked down the hill. Love a duck if but up over the first rise didn't come huffing and laboring his father's pickup. Red, it slewed sideways across the hill like a fridge and a bathtub on a surfboard, the engine revving.

With a little jitterstep he nipped past Gale.

–Everything's okay – isn't it? she asked. With the two of you.

The truck chugged across the first switchback.

–Will you have a butcher's at that, Rud said admiringly.

–A what?

–A butcher's hook – a look.

Gale took Rud's hand.

–He's riding the clutch, Rud complained.

The truck cornered tightly and headed back across the next switch-back, the engine loud, gravelly.

–Rud? Is it? she asked him again. All right?

–Yes, Rud said. Unless I'm getting sacked.

He let go her hand and, shifting urn and postcard to his left side, moved down the front path. With his right hand he fashioned half a megaphone.

–You're riding the flipping clutch, he bellowed down the mountain. The truck roared.

–I've the laundry to do, Gale said loudly. Come see me later?

–Yes, he said back. Of course.

The truck dipped out of sight. He stood waiting for it. Listening to it. Waiting as the sky whooshed across the valley. Up over the next rise the truck bobbed. Sunshine exploded off the windshield and Rud squinted and averted his eyes. To the south he could see the north loop of the lake, minted and blue as a shilling.

–The lake, Rud called over his shoulder. You can see

He followed his voice. She was gone.

–Gale?

His truck engine revved and he turned back. One last time the truck tacked across the mountainside, snouting down into the tall grass then with a blare reemerging. Tsuruoka bounced on the driver's seat like a crash dummy on holiday. He was grinning. Casting blankets of dust from the spinning tires he rumbled past Rud. He waved. Beeped the horn.

–More torture, he shouted at Rud through the window.

In front of the garage he steered it hood out into the beyond. He stopped, backed up to the garage door. Parked. Rud hurried over.

–Torture? Rud asked.

Tsuruoka vaulted out of the cab and strode around to the tailgate. Rud followed.

–Torture?

Back of the truck Tsuruoka stood, one hand on hip, the other plucking his bottom lip. He had one workboot resting on the bumper's rusted
trailer hitch.

—That, Tsuruoka said, will have to do.

—Do what?

The ranch-house door opened. Tsuruoka looked past Rud's shoulder.

—What will have to do? Rud asked.

—You are now a hod.

—A hod.

—Yes – a helper. Gale, he called. He waved at her.

 I know what a hod is, Rud said.

—Good. The mixer you met, first night.

Tsuruoka gestured vaguely to the garage's south side.

—The cement mixer? Rud asked.

Rud fingered the hard marrow of scar above his eye.

—I was going to wait until next week, Tsuruoka said. But as of today I
am – renga shokunin – a bricklayer. Again. So.

—We're not sitting today?

—No. I need a hod. With a truck. With a trailer hitch.

Tsuruoka nudged the trailer hitch with his boot and the truck chassis
rocked, then settled.

—Gale, Tsuruoka called.

—Yes, Roshi.

Tsuruoka held up to Gale a finger of intermittence.

—Jiinzu? he asked Rud. Jeans. How many do you have?

—As in – ?

—Changes.

—Two others. Why?

Tsuruoka shifted his finger in Rud's direction.

—The laundry, he said to Gale. It can wait a day?

She nodded. She dipped her shoulder out from under the saddlebags
and shifted them to her other side.

–For our things from today, Tsuruoka said. Our bricklaying clothes, he said to Rud.

–It can wait, Gale said. Rud?

She stroked the bare skin of her temple as though threading her hair behind her ear. He nodded.

–Later? she asked.

He glanced at Tsuruoka. Back at her.

–Yes, he said. Yes.

Gale bowed and vanished around the garage corner. Tsuruoka looked after her, lost and vacant.

–This bricklaying, Rud asked. Is it instead of sitting?

–Sorry?

–Laying bricks, Rud repeated. Is it to practice Zen?

–To pay the bills, Tsuruoka said, adding softly. In case Gale does not.

–You mean Gale's been

–Yes, Tsuruoka said. Quiet.

He bent back slightly and called up to the small window tucked under the garage roofpeak:

–Gale.

They waited.

–I got you some Wells Lamonts, Tsuruoka said in an aside to Rud. You can owe me.

Gale's face appeared in the window under the roofpeak.

–Gale, Tsuruoka called up. Can you hear me?

She nodded.

–And I will get the mail, okay?

She nodded again, her face lingering. Tsuruoka gazed up at her. Then bowed.

–What're Wells Lamonts? asked Rud.

–Workgloves.

–Then you're offering me a job, Rud stated.

–No – work, Tsuruoka said. You drive.

Rud stiffened.

Go on, Tsuruoka said.

Waving Rud around the driver's side he marched around to the passenger's side. Rud obeyed.

—Job, work – what's the difference? Rud asked.

—The pay.

—The pay – ah – there is none – right?

—You have done this before, Tsuruoka said. He climbed in. Gestured Rud in. Come on.

—But, Rud said, holding up the urn.

—Bring him, Tsuruoka said. You can scatter him later.

$$\diamondsuit$$

With parking-lot semaphore Tsuruoka guided Rud as Rud backed truck and mixer downhill toward their work site – the grounds of a lakeshore estate. The drive was narrow and of crushed gravel, and fir and pine trees crowded either side. There was a carriage house and immediately downhill from that the mansion and the driveway squeezed between them to then twist and flow beside a stone boundary wall to the lake. It was a stocky house, the mansion, gray with cranberry trim, and a broad cedar deck corbeled to the foundation had once taken it even closer to the water. However the present owner – an actress who never left Beverly Hills – wished the deck bricked and she'd had the cedar torn out and carted off and concrete footings and a pad poured.

Thus several pallets of stacked red brick, a pallet of Portland and lime sacks, and a dune of sand draped by tarpaulin waited for them at the bottom near the shore. That is if Rud, backing up, could thread the mixer down there. On its two black tires the mixer – crusted white with years of dried mortar – waddled between carriage house and mansion like a blind penguin inching backward. Each turn of its axle twisted it

closer and closer to the mansion wall. Finally Tsuruoka yelled *Stop!* and
Rud drove back up the slope. They stood by the truck's open door.

–Your turn? Rud asked.

–No.

–It's your mixer, Rud mentioned.

–It is your truck.

–My father's actually.

–Then let him drive.

They turned and eyed the urn set in the seat middle.

–All right all right, Tsuruoka said and climbed in. Rud loped behind,
backpedaling, glancing over each shoulder for his footing as the engine
revved and Tsuruoka backed down. Rud waved him left then right then
right again.

–Right! Rud hollered.

–I am!

Tsuruoka poked his head out the side window. The mixer drifted
blindly left.

–Right! Rud yelled, waving madly.

The engine howled. The mixer wobbled helplessly toward the wall.
Tsuruoka threw his arm along the seatback, twisting as the mixer
lunged at the mansion wall.

–Stop! Rud screamed.

Tsuruoka did. He flew out of the cab.

–What the hell you doing? he shouted. You say right, I go right.

–I meant the mixer.

–I was not driving the mixer.

–So?

–So – So, he says. Bah.

Tsuruoka drove back up. Left the truck at the crest.

–That leaves one choice, Tsuruoka said.

–What?

—Us.

At the pickup's tailgate Tsuruoka knelt and unhooked the safety chain.

—But how'd they get the other stuff down? Rud asked.

—A hod who could drive, Tsuruoka said.

The two hoisted and unhitched the mixer, then by the long pipe of its tongue swung it around. The tongue they used as a rudder and they braced their backs against the flat front end of the mixing barrel, bearing thus its iron tonnage. They dug their heels through the gravel, seeking solid ground, and with much grunting lowered the mixer a few feet at a time.

—At least there is no smell, Tsuruoka wheezed.

—Or Romans with whips, Rud added.

At the base of the hill they set the mixer's two wheels and single iron pegleg up on cinderblocks. A shore breeze fluttered their shirts. Rud was dispatched back up to the truck to fetch the wheelbarrow. In it he carted down the buckets of trowels, the hoses and hammers, the levels, the shovels, the picks.

—Find an outlet and a tap, Tsuruoka said.

Rud did so, then coupled the hoses and played out the extension cord and plugged in the mixer. Tsuruoka whisked the tarps off the cement, the sand.

—Will we be sitting after work? Rud asked. In zazen?

Tsuruoka seemed not to hear. He snaked a hand inside the mixer's housing and flicked a switch. The flywheel screeched like a teacher's chalk. Rud cringed. Plugged his fingers in his ears. Tsuruoka howled with laughter.

—Moment, he yelled, holding up a single finger.

The screech faded. What remained was a loud oompahoompah — oompahoompah.

—Now, bag of Portland, Tsuruoka shouted over the din.

Rud nodded his head in time to the mixer.

–Cement! From the pallet!

–All right, Rud said. Easy enough.

The bags were stacked waist high on the pallet and though each was but the size of a bedroom pillow, when Rud tried hefting one off the pallet it wouldn't budge.

–Net weight ninety-four pounds, he read. Holy shit!

His back still throbbed from bearing then hoisting the mixer. He spread his arms, gathering his strength. The lake wasn't wide here and a chop cleaved the water so it looked like crushed ice. Beneath the sky the far shore mountains, cave-wall green and orange, sat right in it.

–Get moving! Tsuruoka shouted.

Rud embraced the Portland sack. It buckled slightly. He stood and after a gasp lugged it over. He dropped it with a smoky thud at Tsuruoka's feet.

–Lime, Tsuruoka said. Now the lime.

Rud struggled back with that sack, spitting and blinking from the white powder that floured out. He dropped it. Tsuruoka took a shovel and slashed open each to peel back the sacking.

–Now, he said to Rud. The mud, the mortar, is all.

With graceful longhandled arcs over his shoulder Tsuruoka hooked into the mixer several shovel loads of sand, calling out, *Five!* – then of Portland, *Two!* – and of lime, *A half!* He paused. The load swirled. The paddles turned. Tsuruoka squirted in water from the hose. He presented Rud with the shovel.

–Your turn, he said over the steady suck and oomp.

–Already?

–Already. Keep the batches small so it does not set up in the wheelbarrow.

–Set up?

–The specs say not to retemp. So, five sand, two Portland, half lime.

–How much water?

–You said you knew what a hod was.

–I knew what one *was* – but that doesn't mean

–Well, Tsuruoka said, soon or late, you will catch on.

Unfortunately Rud didn't. This first batch when Rud wheelbarrowed it over Tsuruoka dubbed:

–Soup! Dump it.

Rud's second?

–Too thick!

And Tsuruoka cast atop the wheelbarrow load a wave of water sloshing from a bucket. Then he gardened through it with a hoe that had two silverdollar-sized eyes punched out of its blade. Softening, kneading the mortar.

–There, he said. Halfway between ooze and crumb.

–So it holds everything together, Rud observed.

–Nothing in the universe, Tsuruoka said, will do that.

–Not even Zen?

–Zen, Tsuruoka said. Yesterday you were ready to quit.

–I was spooked.

Tsuruoka's trowel was a pie-slice shape of clean steel and after he dampened his mortarboard he pointed his trowel at the wheelbarrow of mortar.

–Mud, he said. And fetch brick.

Rud shucked a shovel load of mortar out of the barrow and plopped it with a slight splatter onto the square board. Then he carried the brick tong to one of the pallets of pavers. The bricks were as red as salmon and the tong, by hefting up its top arm the way you operate a car's hand-brake, picked up a loaf of ten bricks sandwiched between the steel finger and thumb at either end of the lower arm.

–What I asked you that night after my bath, Rud said as he humped over the bricks.

He set the bricks down on the white concrete close to where Tsuruoka kneeled.

–Other side please, Tsuruoka said.

—About ghosts.

—And bring more.

Tsuruoka had felt-lined pads under each knee. Sitting back on his calves he would, with two slow swipes of his trowel, butter a side and end of a brick with the seagreen mortar. Set it with a flip into place. Butter and set another. Then another.

—Like dealing cards, Rud said an hour later.

Tsuruoka buttered another brick. Set it.

—More mud, he said. And is the mixer clean?

His level was a long articulated shin of walnut and maple locked along its edges and ends by flawless strips of brass and he slid it tingling back and forth across the bricks, tapping it with the trowelhandle's rubber heel. Rud shoehorned the last shovel load from the barrow's corner.

—You didn't answer *my* question, Rud said. About ghosts.

—Is that it? For the too-thick mud?

—For the mud, yes.

—Well, Rudyard, I will bargain. Mix great mud – top-notch – then ask.

—Deal.

—But beware, in case the answer is not one you want.

Tsuruoka crooked his neck around, first eyeing Rud, then looking past at the sky beyond.

—So, maybe one more batch before lunch.

Straightening his back, he rested his hands on his thighs. He uncrooked his spine, rubbed his neck.

—Maybe not, he said. Here, give an old man a hand.

Rud grasped Tsuruoka's wrist and hauled him up.

—Lunch, Tsuruoka proclaimed. But first, the bills.

They drove into town. Flying along the belt of land that girted the mountain, with the lake like a reflection of itself flickering in the trees and the rigid dogs snapping and snarling on chains. This was 487, what he'd driven:

–Three weeks ago, he said.

He geared down into third.

–Three weeks, Tsuruoka said. And three days.

The bridge lifted them up over the railroad tracks and set them down onto the street to turn into town.

–Go straight, Tsuruoka said.

They zipped through the traffic light. Fallen leaves spilled like peach skins from piles raked along either curb.

–Post office, Tsuruoka said, pointing ahead to a one-story building faced with gray tile.

–Rud turned into the lot and parked. Tsuruoka had his left hand palm-down on the urn and he picked up the postcard of the sea. Rud allowed the truck to idle.

–Could you mail that for me please? Rud asked.

–Mrs Rud?

–Mrs Rud – no, not Mrs Rud – Etta, my stepmother.

–Ah. Tsuruoka turned it over. But it is blank.

–I'm telling her only the good stuff, Rud joked.

The engine grumbled in their laps. Tsuruoka fished out from his overalls pouch his flat contractor's pencil.

–Too bad Gale is not here, Tsuruoka said. To do a drawing of you – but

Tsuruoka penciled a tiny smile on the card. Out his window a Cadillac splendid as a coronation brougham slid into the parking spot beside them.

–Dear Etta, Rud said in a mock jolly voice. I am fine, though a slave

–A willing one, Tsuruoka interjected.

–Dad's ghost is fine, Rud continued. No grave yet.

Across the street a small park sloped uphill through varicose-barked trees to a landscape-tie climbing frame. Two little boys, cross as puppies, chased each other in and out of the frame's plastic tunnel. Rud heard Tsuruoka's pencil.

–The way of the world, Tsuruoka said.

He'd drawn, beside the tiny smile, a moonslice of sadness. A young man in a ski jacket got out of the Cadillac. Tsuruoka waited, then climbed out of the truck. He wasn't gone long and when he came back with the mail he sprang onto the seat and slammed the door. Rud backed out.

–So – McDonald's?

–For lunch? Rud asked, the gears growling.

–Or Pizza Hut, Tsuruoka said.

–Pizza – definitely.

The truck lurched across the lot.

–Go right then. To the highway.

They drove south across a blue iron bridge. Beneath, in a gully thin with switches of vegetation, a river streamed, moving in its bed like a drawerful of spoons.

–Your postcard, Tsuruoka said.

–What about it?

–It will tell rest of the world you are here.

–No it won't, Rud said. Etta *has* no one to tell.

The road dipped. They curved by an aquamarine quarry.

–How long will it take?

–The card?

–To get there.

–A week.

–A week?

–No more. Why?

Tsuruoka waved at Rud a letter.

–This took four, he said. For you.

Rud glanced over.

–Stop sign, Tsuruoka warned, pointing up ahead.

Rud braked, downshifted. The engine whinnied. He stole another glance. At the letterhead.

—Shit, he said.

The truck halted. On the four-lane cars and trucks whipped and whistled by. Tsuruoka handed Rud the letter.

Shit shit shit, Rud said, reading now with care the company name:

THE ACADEMY PRESS

T. EAMON-COLTRANE, PRESIDENT AND CEO

— My boss, Rud answered. My stepbrother.

Okuraretsu
okuritsu hate wa
Kiso no aki

Now being seen off
Now seeing off – the outcome
Autumn in Kiso

BASHŌ, "Autumn in Kiso,"
translated by Robert Aitken in *A Zen Wave*

果は

hate wa

Rud did not open Troy's letter. Turning south onto the four-lane he quickly slid the envelope between the seatback and his father's urn. There it remained. For after takeout lunch Rud's sole intent was to mix good mud.

–Too grainy, Tsuruoka pronounced, jabbing at the load.

The letter was still unopened when, having worked until nightfall, they followed the headlamp cones that bobbed and swirled frantic as faeries up the mountainside to the ranch.

–Are we going to sit? Rud asked, parking outside the garage.

–We are going to unload the tools.

–And then?

–Wash up. Eat.

–Then?

Tsuruoka took a moment.

–That *then*, he said, is for you to decide.

Rud yawned, a long baying shudder of escape. Tsuruoka opened the passenger door. The truck cab filled with pale light from the overhead. Rud opened his own door to climb out.

–Your letter?

–Fuck it, Rud said.

◇

—What if it is important? Tsuruoka asked the next morning as they returned to the truck.

It was barely dawn. Rud stopped, jacket collar turned up, by the driver's-side door. The ground was hard and antlered. A mossy layer of frost. He stamped at the earth, dislodging the mold of dried mortar from his boots.

—Can't be, Rud answered.

—A matter of life or death?

—Impossible.

—Why impossible? Tsuruoka asked, opening the passenger-side door. Rud opened his door.

—No one knows I'm here.

He went to haul himself in. But only got halfway. On the seat, propped up against the urn, was Gale's chalkboard. On it the first-night drawing of his profile.

—Shit, Rud said softly.

He climbed the rest of the way in and shut the door.

—For someone who is not here, Tsuruoka said, you get much mail.

Rud looked again at the drawing. At Tsuruoka. Finally revealing it to him. Tsuruoka thought for a moment.

—You were tired, he pointed out. As in the picture.

—No, Rud said.

—From being hoddu-san.

—I forgot.

—She is Kisa.

—Forgot.

—She will understand.

With his fingertip Rud thrice tapped the chalkboard. Tsuruoka raised his eyebrows and sighed. He stood an elbow atop the seatback and turned and looked out the truck cab's rear window, lifting his eyes.

—So, he said. She is awake.

Rud turned. Peered out and up. The light in the garage apex window a dim yellow fluttering, like a hatchling's.

—Candlelight, Rud said.

—Sitting, Tsuruoka said. It happens.

—What does?

—Forgetting.

—Not to me, Rud said. He wedged the chalkboard face-up into the seat's crook and started the truck, pensive. Well, once, he said. Kind of. He revved the engine, letting it warm. Shifted into gear. I'll see her tonight, he told himself aloud. If we don't sit.

—And if *she* does not, Tsuruoka said.

Tsuruoka fell quiet. Remained so all the way to the job site, staring out the passenger-side window. Quiet too as they set up in the puce light – Rud plugging in the mixer, hefting the tools down; Tsuruoka chiseling from in front of the terminal row of bricks the long scab of excess mortar. By the time Rud had mixed his first batch, the sky above the eastern mountains held a glowing fan of pink.

—Sailor's warning, Rud said.

—Too grainy, Tsuruoka said of the mud. Use less sand.

Midmorning it had warmed slightly and Rud was mixing his second batch. He had doffed his jacket. The mixer, propped on its tripod of blocks, rocked rhythmically. Oompah-oompah. Across the lake clouds approached over the mountain peaks, gradual and relentless as a legion. He waggled and wedged the wheelbarrow under the belly of the mixer's tub, then stepped up onto its tongue and lifted up and back the iron grille. Flipping up the steel flange and throwing his weight backward he hauled counterclockwise the mixer's arm as though setting back the minute hand of some Steam Age timepiece. This rolled the tub, and its still-turning paddles disgorged the mortar into the wheelbarrow. That was when, shrugging up the barrow's quarter-ton load, he heard the car.

It was a sedan – he could glimpse it way uphill beyond the mansion's

far corner – and it was dark as a bullet. He set the wheelbarrow down
and to the hillbottom strode to investigate. Tsuruoka got there first. The
car's horn beeped.

—You wait here, Tsuruoka told him.

Like a slugger Tsuruoka jogged up the hill between mansion and carriage house.

—Who is it? Rud called after him.

Tsuruoka reached the hilltop. The car was a BMW and slow as a bul-
lion vault the driver's door swung open. Tsuruoka gripped the door-
frame and leaned forward talking to whoever was inside. The person's
legs dangled out and they were a woman's. Very high heels. Tsuruoka
bobbed his head boyishly like an uncracked egg in a teacup and the visitor crossed her ankles with extreme grace and a hemcorner of her apricot skirt belled below the door. Rud stood riveted. A riot of butterflies in
his belly.

—Well? he asked when Tsuruoka returned.

—How is the mud?

—Fine. Who was it?

—Hm?

—The car – in the car.

—The boss.

—The movie star?

—No, not the movie star. Now back to work.

They worked until lunch. Teetering sandwiches, on fresh rye, built
carefully from the Safeway deli. (—Dagwoods. —Dagawoods? —What my
father called them.) And after the post office (—What did your father
call bills? —He didn't call them, but they came anyway. He just wouldn't
open them. —Ah.) they worked into and past the afternoon as, like some
passing naval convoy, the sky shifted and rumbled.

—Rain, Rud announced as he hustled a tongload of pavers across to
Tsuruoka, tilting to counter the weight of the bricks, his free arm stiff as
an oar. Beyond Tsuruoka's dun and mantic figure the lake was corru-
gated with waves.

–What? Tsuruoka asked.

His brass-edged level as he slid it atop the bricks plect them, producing a sound as distilled as a mandolin's. Rud pointed west. Tsuruoka allowed himself a quick look at the sky.

–That is clouds, he said. Not rain.

An hour later the first drop of rain struck Rud's bentover back like a frozen doubloon. Tsuruoka had instructed him to concoct a small batch but now Rud stooped and gathered the open mortar and lime bags and waddled them over to the pallet. Another drop hit him on his head.

–Did you make mud? Tsuruoka called over.

–It's started, Rud called back.

–What?

Rud chugged over to where Tsuruoka knelt.

–Rain, I felt a drop of – good god! he exclaimed.

The bricks Tsuruoka had laid in just two days swirled and curved in seven stunning rows around the outside rim of the deck – dusky red and canaled.

–Like a city, Rud said.

–On Mars, Tsuruoka added. He stood, creaking. You felt rain? he asked.

–How many, Rud asked, did you do today?

–We, Tsuruoka corrected. Not only me. He lateraled his trowel into the nearby waterbucket. I feel no rain, he said. But tarp the materials.

Like chambermaids they cast the tarps over the Portland and lime and the sand and with cinderblocks battened the corners. Rud snatched the wheelbarrow by its handles and flipped it upside down and by its undercarriage hefted it and stacked it atop the tarp as further ballast.

–You have put in a lifetime today, Rudyard, Tsuruoka said as they drove up the gravel road and left the estate. He pointed out Rud's side window. Here it comes, he said.

Over the far mountains and across the water the rain came in gray toppling windows. When Rud backed up and parked, the rain was black and detonating on the cab's roof. In the colorless dank he hesitated opening his door. Lightning pealed and crackled across the gothic sky. Rud glanced down first at Gale's chalkboard. At Troy's letter, pressed and creased like a prom carnation, behind his father's urn. Tsuruoka studied him.

—You have no – no

Tsuruoka turned to the windshield. As if in the rain bucketing down the right word might be written.

—Curiosity? Rud asked.

—Curiosity, yes.

—About the letter?

—Yes.

—No, Rud answered. None.

—As father, so son.

—This is different, Rud protested.

—How?

He looked at Tsuruoka.

—It just is. I thought somehow my coming here, my – my staying here He didn't finish.

—Cutting off your past?

—There was a lot to cut off.

Through the dense rain yet another pulse of lightning branched across the night. A few seconds later the thunder rumbled like a rock slide.

—Come on, Tsuruoka hollered.

And thrusting open the doors, the two men hurled themselves out into the rain. Their jackets umbrellaed over their heads were soon heavy as chainmail as with bootsteps sucking the soft lawn they sprinted to the house.

—The tools! Rud shouted by the front door. We forgot to unload them.

Tsuruoka put a finger to his lips and burst through the door. Rud obeyed, and followed.

◇

It was a storm without easement. With the ranch house so empty of furniture, the rain sounded on the attic roof like whale bones, then – letting up slightly – like trees running. Rud and Tsuruoka scoffed a stirfry, endured an icewater scrub.

–You first, Rudyard.

–The laundry's not back, Rud said.

–No jiinzu?

Rud nodded and Tsuruoka held up a finger, then left, returning back downstairs with a pair of his overalls. They were worn to buttercup softness and were nearly that color too. But three inches too short.

–Pants've had a row with your shoes then, lad? Rud said.

–How?

–A row – a fight. What my dad would say.

–Ah.

And while Tsuruoka scrubbed himself in the shower room, Rud dragged over a kitchen stool and muttoned up against the throbbing Franklin, thinking about it all.

–An old man, Tsuruoka said.

Rud looked up at him closing with shoves of his shoulder the shower room door.

–Sorry? Rud asked.

Tsuruoka wore an old terrycloth bathrobe – washingmachine drab – and flamingo-pink plastic thongs. He wriggled his toes in them, bending his head to inspect.

–An old man. With mizumushi – athlete's foot, he added.

–From the workboots?

–Yes.

–Least it's not jock itch.

–True.

–Desenex? Rud suggested.

—We had, Tsuruoka said and went to the sink and opened the cupboard above. He shunted some things aside, stopped for a moment as though weighing the gravity of his next move, then noosed out the green Cutty Sark Scotch bottle and set it with a thump on the countertop.

—Nightcap? he said, glancing back at Rud.

—Not for me, thanks.

Tsuruoka tilted the bottle.

—None left anyway, he said and reaching the bottle back into the cupboard took down instead the large coffee can that held the ranch's medicinals.

—Anyway, we do not sit in zazen tonight, he said.

—Sure.

—So you are free.

Tsuruoka peeled off the can's plastic lid. Pausing, he rotated his shoulders and rubbed the back of his neck.

—Free to sit on your own, he said, examining the can's contents. Ozonol. Hydrogen peroxide. He studied the Ozonol label, unscrewed the tube's lid. Sniffed at it.

—Phew – and Rud?

—Roshi?

—About forgetting Kisa. It is my fault. I remembered. Last night. In the truck. But I said nothing. He paused. Tomorrow, if it still rains and we cannot work: we will sit.

And, passing the zendo on his way upstairs to the attic, Rud wondered. Slowing, he stepped in. He stood in the zendo's jade darkness, a darkness so flagrant his bodyhairs ran burning down the back of his arms and forearms to his wrists. He sensed rather than saw the statue of the Buddha on the shelf by the far wall.

—What about you? he asked it in a whisper. Did you believe? Does anything but our ash survive?

He breathed deeply. The black rain sputtered down the two large zendo windows. Beyond the garage roof Gale's window cast a dim light. She would be sitting, and he considered his own zafu on the floor nearby.

–The turtle returns for his shell, he said softly and fetched it up and bowing as he left went upstairs and impelled himself to sit in zazen. He lasted five minutes and then was assaulted not by waves from the beyond but by ones of fatigue. He yawned. Recovered. Opened wide his eyes. Stiffened his back. When the next yawn fibrillated through him he palms-under-chin bowed, stood groaning, bowed to his zafu and walked to the window. Gale's was still barely lit, if at all.

–Just a nap, he decided, and ducked out of Tsuruoka's overalls. And crawled in.

His sleep was gliding slow and deep, stirring only once: upon hearing footsteps. And then again, hearing his own voice as he sat up:

–Gale?

He was naked to the waist and he flicked on the socketlight. Piled atop his zafu was his laundry, crisply folded. Reaching his jeans was such a stretch only his feet were still in bed. In the cold light he stood to dress, his shadow springing up the wall and ceiling sudden as a jackinabox.

He pulled on his T-shirt on the second floor as he hesitated just before Tsuruoka's bedroom. He stood, listening. Tsuruoka was snoring, softly. He crept on past. Outside was still dark and though he had the flashlight he did not use it. The rain had eased even more – as fine on his face as spiderwebs – and he sponged sockless in his boots across the front lawn. In the harbored night Gale's light was on in the garage's apex window. This light faintly sheeted the truck and he hustled to the cab, retrieved Gale's chalkboard and, holding it portrait-down above his head, closed with his knee the truck door. Down the corridor he splashed, turning on the flashlight, following as its yellowish parabola swam ahead along the path. Gale's apartment doorhandle was no more than a peg on a rope you pulled. When he did, a narrow bit of the garage wall swung open. He stepped inside. The door boompt shut behind

him. He was hemmed on either side by walls so he flipped up the flashlight beam and it climbed a narrow set of jackpine stairs and, where the
landing gave into the loft, blended in the room's light.

–Gale? he called in a loud whisper.

There was no answer.

–Gale.

He retracted the light pouring like a yellow rapids down the stairs.
He groped behind his back for the door. Pushed it open. A voice behind
him whispered:

–Rud?

When he spun around Gale ducked under the flashlight's parrying
beam.

–Gale.

She wore her parka undone and she held an umbrella. He aimed the
torch at their feet. Felt her step very close to him. She smelled lovely,
soapy, like Ivory, and shivery, as when a summer's sun shower stops.
The door closed.

–I woke you, she said.

–No – yes. But that's okay.

–I'm sorry. She smiled and leaned a little to allow herself room to col-
lapse her umbrella, eyeing him. You seem – ?

–What?

–You seem okay.

–Cause I am.

–It's just – I thought last night when you didn't come.

–Tired, he said. It's no nine-to-five.

–Five-to-nine?

They were quiet. She hooked her umbrella on a coatpeg and shed her
parka, hanging it beside. Rud held her chalkboard at the side of his
head.

–*My* umbrella, he said.

–Then it did the job.

–Partially.

–Of getting you here.

She turned, her body grazing his. And he asked her:

–That's what it was supposed to do? He handed her the chalkboard.

–You're drenched, she said. Partially. Come on, I'll get you a towel.

He stood his flashlight on the last stair and toenailed off his boots and followed her up. Her loft was a scale version of his own. Bare, the rafters meeting only a foot or so above their heads. Against the righthand pony wall a small Morso woodstove quivered out cedary warmth. There was a drysink next to it and Gale lifted its lid and took out a towel. He accepted it and patted dry his neck.

–I liked where you piled my clothes, he said.

–Your zafu?

–Second base.

She smiled and, stepping forward, kissed him on the lips. Hers were dry, slightly chapped. Her impulse startled him so that all he could do was keep his one arm, the hand still holding the towel, behind his neck. Then it was over and she stepped back.

–Sorry, she said. I shouldn't have.

–No. Not at all. It's just – he licked his teeth with his tongue – I'd have – I'd have brushed my teeth.

She smiled, took both his hands in hers. She took a deep breath. I've a confession, she said.

–So've I.

–But mine

–Last night, he told her. Wasn't that I was tired.

–I knew it. You were angry.

–I forgot, he said.

–Forgot?

He nodded. And this time kissed her. Her hands on his shoulders.

His on her waist. She broke off the kiss and looked at him – her eyes like
the earrings she'd worn when they'd danced – and he kissed her again,
and again she broke it off and asked:
  –It's okay, isn't it?
  –This?
  –Yes.
  –I think so too.
  Once more they kissed. His hands were blind from trembling but
somehow they led his arms around her. The back of her head when with
his hands he cupped it was smooth, tender. He slid his hands down her
back and rested them on her waist. He bit gently the sweet rind of her lip
and she bit as gently back. His hands slid down over her hips, her bottom, and he said:
  –If I start humming Cliff Richard.
  And she said:
  –Shush.
  And dug her body into his, sharp and startling to him. They dropped
to their knees on her bedroll.
  –Here, she said and by his elbows lifted his arms above his head and
with a tug emptied him out of his T-shirt. He brushed his hair back
with his fingers and kissed her again and untucked her cotton shirt
from the drawstring of her pants – pausing – until she raised her arms
with his, then helping. Her white shirt slid up her arms like a truce and
she smiled and her small breasts when she brought down her arms
creased and moved and stilled. Her hands were workaday soft, running
across the peens of his shoulders, and they kissed again and in a sort of
sporadic unbuckling, devoid of order – a belt a drawstring a pantleg a
jeanleg a pantleg – their clothes fell off them – his underwear hers, brief
as a string, over her hips.
  –You're shaking, she said.
  –I'm terrified.
  Terrified he would come the moment he started fucking her. And it

was fucking. She was nettles, not just petals. And sticky and warm – not cool – like a warm pearl, and near the end with the palate of her palm she pressed down on the small of his back and after they lay side by side, as bare and briny and pale – even his arms now – as off-season holidayers.

–Don't say *Don't say anything,* she told him.

–I wouldn't dream of.

And he laughed.

–You were going to, weren't you?

–No!

–Yes you were, she said.

She was on the inside closest to the wall, where her sleeping bag's zipper was. And she slid even closer to the wall, off the sleeping bag, and she unzipped it and unflapped it.

–Scout's honor? she asked.

–They wouldn't have me.

She made a face and tucked the bag's flapcorner under Rud's pec. She touched his shoulder, urging him to roll onto his front, and then they were side by side again with her somehow zipping the bag up. Inside. She curled into him. He lifted his head and looked at hers on his chest.

–You know, he said, I never thought until now that I had a hairy chest.

Something tiny and molten and cold burned the skin of his chest and runneled down his ribcage, tickling him.

–You're crying, he said softly. Don't.

She nodded yes against him.

–Everything'll work out.

She shook her head no against him.

–Why? Why won't it?

–Troy's letter, she said. My confession. What I need to tell you.

It dawned on him.

–That you kept it from me?

–You knew?

–I just figured it out.

–It got here right after Labor Day – right after.

–And you thought I might leave, he said.

–I'd sent you my drawings, she told him.

–The anthology ones?

She nodded.

–To me?

–To your office, a few weeks before you got here.

–But why? Why would that make me leave?

–Because it was from Troy.

He laughed bitterly.

–That'd make me even more likely to stay, he said.

–Horrible.

–Nah.

–Unforgivable.

–No it wasn't, he told her.

They lay quiet and bundled and close.

–Horrible, she said. Knowing it was there. Seeing it there every day.

–It doesn't matter. I haven't even opened the damn thing.

She stiffened with surprise.

–But what if it's important?

–It's not, he assured her.

–But

–Really – trust me.

They were quiet for a while. Just their breathing orchestrated by the rain.

–So – what now? Gale asked.

–Nothing, he said, rippling his hand across the back of her shoulder. Just lie here, with the rain.

They listened.

–It's shivery, she said.

It was.

—It sounds like, Gale whispered, when boys would throw pebbles at my bedroom window.

He lay thinking about what she'd said.

—I never did, he told her.

—My father would go mental, she said. They lay quietly.

—At the window, he then repeated to himself and wriggled up into a sitting position.

—What amazed me most, she began.

—What?

He looked over his shoulder at the attic window.

—It never broke. You okay? she asked.

On the floor their clothes lay in a garble in front of the Morso. They were, he found out as he pulled them over, soaked with warmth. He ran his fingers through his hair, delaying, then knew he had to look. Dispensing with his underwear he swung bent-kneed out of the sleeping bag and pulled on his jeans and stood. He was still sticky so he didn't zip the fly and besides that would let her know he intended on getting back in. She was watching him.

—Just going t'see what it's doing out there.

—You did that wonderfully.

He shrugged self-consciously and smiled. He turned and took a single step to the window. Gale's zafu sat on the floor directly beneath and he parted the cotton curtains, darting aside in stealth.

—What is it doing? she asked.

—I can't see. His heel kicked against something on the floor and he looked down over his shoulder.

—Books, she said. Well?

—Rain.

The only light outside came from the grainy jaundice of the very window he stood to one side of. The light eked across a bit of the bed of the pickup, so that it looked like a lost remnant of some airplane fuselage. He eased back the small curtain another inch: nothing. Just the light. The inky rain.

–No pebbles, he said.

He let the curtains flutter back together. By his bare foot sat her zafu: an oval eikon. On the floor, leaning against the rough laths of the corner wall, four books. He leaned sideways a little to see if they were the same from Our Lady of Grace – *Gospel, Archery, Seeds . . . Diamonds* – which they were. And the fourth, closest to the corner and stark white, Tsuruoka's Julian Jaynes book.

–What's it like? he asked. The Jaynes.

–Weird, she said.

–Any ghosts?

–Voices. In our heads.

–Like Saint Joan's?

–All religions. Except

She paused.

–Except what?

–The Buddha – he didn't hear any voices.

–Unless they signed.

–Hm? Oh – right.

–So it *isn't* the book – why he's not the roshi anymore?

–But he *is* again, isn't he, she suggested.

–Sometimes I think so, he replied. Other times?

He turned and looked down at her. Her eyes, dark green, aimed up at his.

–I should go, he said.

–I know.

–Do you want me to? he asked.

–No, she answered.

She propped herself onto one elbow, punching up the sleeping bag to shawl her bare shoulder.

–But I have to get up too, she said.

—I wonder if it'll be raining tomorrow.

—I think it is tomorrow, she said flipping onto her stomach.

A dark leather bag, fat as a pumpkin, sat on the floor an arm's length from the pillow. She stretched and reached inside, taking out her watch to read it.

—Not quite, she said.

There was a lightness in his head and a sliding feeling in his guts as he fought with himself not to look upon her nakedness until she covered her breasts with her upper arm in a gesture of modesty that – because it evoked the memory of Amaranta asking him to close his eyes that day so far away now on the couch in his livingroom – suddenly chilled him with despair. He snatched up his T-shirt and underwear and stuffed his underwear in his jeans pocket. He pulled his T-shirt over his head, zipped and buttoned and buckled his jeans and belt. He dropped to his knees beside her. They did not speak. The heat from the Morso beat against his back. After a moment he took her hand.

—Can I ask you something? she said.

—Anything.

—How – no, *why* did you find me? she asked. At my school, I mean. How did you know – about my dad?

—The newspaper, he told her. The obituaries department. I couldn't write one for my father and a woman I knew – that I was seeing – suggested I read how others wrote theirs. And then I saw yours, your father's.

—The lack of detail?

—Yes.

—And no sacred ground.

—Yes, he admitted.

—And, and what happened to her?

—Amaranta?

—The woman who told you to read obituaries?

He nodded.

—She was an Inca.

—She wasn't, Gale said with a laugh.

—She was in love with this ballplayer, for the Jays. From Argentina too. Married him, probably.

Gale sat up, covering herself with the dark blue corner of her sleeping bag. She smiled sadly at him.

—I'm sorry.

—Don't be, he told her after a bit. What isn't meant to be, sometimes is.

—Like your ending up here.

—With you.

—And the roshi.

—Yes, Rud said. The roshi.

Neither of them spoke. Then Rud said, to reassure her:

—He says we'll sit if we can't work because it's raining tomorrow.

—Then I'll pray for rain, she said.

But it didn't rain. The morning sky out Rud's window was an arctic blue and a brilliant white mantilla of snow draped the western mountain ridges. Tsuruoka was solemn as he bowed to Rud before they breakfasted on chilled boiled eggs that they mashed with forks and spread on hot buttered toast.

—I made the eggs last night, he told Rud.

—Great.

Rud yawned repeatedly as by the front door they dressed in layers and left the house and crossed the crinkling grass. At the truck Tsuruoka stopped by the rear wheel.

—Tool buckets are swimming, he said, tipping one slightly to peer in.

The job site in the climbing sun was blinding. At the hillbottom they squinted and, removing the turtleshelled wheelbarrow, flung the blue tarps off the sand and mortar mixings. The rainwater, gathered in the tarp's crevices and skeined with ice, flew across the beach like lucite bats and shattered into air. Rud carted down the buckets, the ones with tools

sloshing, while Tsuruoka pushbroomed the rain puddles off the laid
bricks and the concrete pad. Rud played out the mixer's cord, dodging
the broom's leaping tides.

—What if I added the water first? he suggested to Tsuruoka.

—Then added the dry?

—Yes.

—That is how Bernard-sensei mixed mud.

Rud stopped uncoiling the extension cord.

—Bernard-sensei?

—Water first. Top-notch mud. Smooth as cake icing.

—And did you tell him about ghosts? Rud quipped.

—I did not have to, Tsuruoka said, escorting the broom over to stand
it against the mansion wall. He turned, the pantcuffs of his overalls
darkened from his sweeping the rain, and looked square into Rud's eyes.
Until the end, he said. So.

Tsuruoka shrugged and returned to the courses of bricks. He dealt
out his kneepads and dropped into them.

—The water-first method, Rud told himself. Back at the mixer he half-
filled one of the buckets — each of white plastic and each as big as a ten-
gallon hat — filled it with water that kettled in out of the hose with a
whooz. Up he slung the bucket and tipped its contents into the mixer's
iron barrel. Once he'd flicked on the motor and the paddles were chug-
ging around and around he added the dry stuff. The tongloads of bricks
he stacked, at Tsuruoka's direction, in pyramids every six or so feet and
an arm's length inside the last-laid course.

—Not as bad as yesterday, Tsuruoka pronounced when he swiped up a
trowel load from Rud's wheelbarrow.

With the shovel Rud shucked up a seagreen loaf of mud to plop on
the mortarboard.

—Is the mixer clean? Tsuruoka asked.

Rud returned to the mixer and with the hose blasted the mud off the
mixer paddles. Wielding the hose's jet like a spatula he next sliced off

from the inside of the barrel the thick residue, forming, as it peeled off, a gorgeous moist nautilus.

–The courage to clean up, he said out of nowhere.

The sun hackled his shoulders. He shivered and strode over to where Tsuruoka, kneeling, buttered and flipped the salmon-colored bricks into place.

–What next? he asked.

–Clean out the mixer.

–Done.

–How done?

–What'll come off with the hose.

–Chip off the rest. With a hammer.

–The dried crud?

–The dried crud.

–But it's caked – it'll take freaking hours.

–All we have, freaking hours. And unplug it.

The hammer was a squareheaded Estwing – a sabertooth of glistening steel with a blue rubber handle that was pocked with gripholes. To get at the caked-on crud inside the mixer barrel he had to by the barrel's arm tilt it as when dumping a load. Then, like a sideshow Houdini, he contorted himself, head shoulders and arms, inside. And until lunch he hammered. He chipped. He pounded. With each hammer strike the deep U of the mixer's barrel bonged and clanged like a nightmarish foundry. When it did loosen, the gray crust flew off in small sharp landscapes. By lunchtime his forearm had seized tight as an axe handle. He shook it, as they trudged up the hill and reached the truck, to no avail.

–I can barely open the fucking door, Rud announced.

–Can you steer? Tsuruoka chided him.

They climbed in.

–No, Rud answered, turning the ignition key.

They headed into town and the Bulldog.

–Your turn to buy? Tsuruoka asked.

–I'll need to hit a bank machine.

–Then drop me off.

He did, then at the drive-thru ready-teller blipped up a hundred dollars. The machine spat out five twenties. When he read his receipt his balance astonished him.

–From not spending any, he said, driving back up Central, crawling north past the Bulldog until he spotted a diagonal parking space. He shot the truck in and parked, got out and crossed the road. To the north, towering above the worn brown-brick railway station, Big Mountain was a heaven-high green and white dome. Gaining the far sidewalk he could see, through the plate glass of the bookstore, Tsuruoka standing by the cashier talking to the owner. Rud went to go in but, grasping the door-pull, hesitated. Tsuruoka had his hands behind his back with his fingers entwined and he stiffened his arms and lifted them back as high as he could. Then dropped them. While the bookstore owner searched in his computer screen. Rud let go of the door. There was a clothing store next door south in the direction of the Bulldog and he entered. A clerk, his dress shirt collarbuttoned, nodded hello. Rud nodded back and wandered through the racks of hunters' orange and rugby shirts and mountaineer jackets. He couldn't ever have guessed the two stores were connected but they were – by an opening in the wall he now stood in front of. Tsuruoka was still by the cash register and Rud lifted a hand of greeting, but at that moment Tsuruoka turned his back to Rud and marched out. The bookstore's doorbell tinked and, as though floating, he was then ambling south past the clothing store window.

–Need any help?

It was the clerk.

–Oh – actually, yes.

Five minutes later he was walking, his purchase under his arm, down to the Bulldog. Inside there was a charbroiler and small counter, then a long bar. Tsuruoka was astool at the charbroiler counter, knife and fork papoosed in a white napkin. A tall Coors, brown and drenched from the neck down, stood in front of him like a lighthouse.

–Best burgers in town, Rudyard-san.

At the charbroiler the young waitress cheffing flipped Tsuruoka's burger and twisted to get Rud's order.

–Same as his, Rud said pointing to Tsuruoka's burger and beer. And put them both on my tab.

–So you found the bank machine.

Rud set his shopping bag on the counter.

–And this shirt.

Again they worked until the black avalanche of night came crashing down through the trees. At the ranch Gale's window as they rumbled up to the garage was dark as sleep.

–Leave the tools in the truck, Tsuruoka instructed.

And after they ate and scrubbed, Rud, freshly toweled off, pulled on clean jeans and stripped the cellophane off his new shirt and plucked all the pins out. It was white-and-violet-striped and stiffer than the shirt board he took out of it. He put it on, buttoning up to the neck then, re-considering, leaving the top undone.

–Spruced, he said.

And in the kitchen window's spectral reflection combed his hair.

–You look like you were mailed, Tsuruoka said.

He'd just emerged from the shower room. Grinning, Rud turned and said:

–You know how long it's been since I wore a shirt? A real one?

–With parcel creases? Tsuruoka said. You have a date?

–Am I wearing a string tie?

Tsuruoka laughed. After a moment said:

–I envy you, Rud-san.

–Envy?

–Yes. Your faith.

—In what?

Tsuruoka inspected his toes, wriggling them in his thongs, and said:

—That in the end, nothing works out.

—You said we'd sit.

—If it rained.

—And we didn't lay brick.

—Yes.

—So, how're the feet?

—The mizumushi? We forgot the Desenex.

—I could nip in and get some?

—No. Stay here. Sit. He looked at Rud. Laughed again. It is a nice shirt to be mailed in, he said. Good night.

He stood for some time in the kitchen after Tsuruoka went upstairs. Studying his reflection, wavering in the window.

And up in the attic a few minutes later considered his zafu. Considered his shadow poised up the wall and rafters like an ambusher. He took a breath of courage and picked up his zafu and like a league bowler carried it downstairs. At the zendo door he bowed and scolded himself for chickening out in wanting to sit close to the doorway. He set his zafu down against the far wall and walked purposely to the altar and bowed to the Buddha jade and quivering and he lit with one of the long wooden matches two candles.

—If you're here, he said wordlessly as he bowed to his zafu, come and get me.

He knelt, straddling his zafu, and sat. He folded his hands in his lap. He counted his breaths: ichi, ni, san. In a bit there was a glorious sexual fantasy – with first Gale then Amaranta then Gale again – vivid as a tent burning on an iceberg. He tried to look away from it, but that offered only futility. Finally he did look directly into it – a softly tangled thing with her one leg bent and the other only slightly so – and it consumed itself leaving only the wall where in the candlelight it fluted into the hardwood floor. He concentrated. There was a ticklish sensation just under his navel. He aimed his breath at it and it too vanished. Ichi, ni. Footsteps, rustling soft as pouring rice, summoned his senses. They faded. The back door opened and closed. Tsuruoka? The jakes? Yes. San. Still on his cushion, he too stepped into a bathroom: his father's. He flicked on the light. Above the bathtub the white tiles were gorged not by scratches but by a glistening black gout of blood. The shower curtain was tied and knotted around the rod. Another breath. Ichi. Another step. He stood looking down into the tub. The tub a dark and bottomless green. Standing there like a gravedigger stripped of his spade, breathing. Ni. He sat there, breathing. San. Rocking on his buttocks. Almost imperceptibly but undeniably he was doing so. He reined himself in. How much time passed he hadn't a clue. Time perished. He focused his breath in his belly. And then – and then he didn't know quite what.

It was as if the zendo wall had collapsed as in a house of cards yet without the other cards collapsing with it. There was no sound. There was no terror. Shimmering like a heat mirage, the wall rearose and composed itself. He blinked. He continued to breathe. Grace? Illusion? Insight? He'd seen into something. He bristled, sitting there in the fluted solitude, bristled with a soft joy. He longed to tell someone. To ask someone. He could contain himself no longer and he stood and bowed to his zafu, grinning like Christmas. He fairly ran from the zendo out into the front hall, returning once he'd seized at the bottom of the stair banister the newel and remembered he hadn't bowed to the Buddha. In the zendo the altar candles on either side of the Buddha still pulsed yellow. The Buddha was stone-still, like a small newly birthed moon. And in the immensity of the statue's gravity Rud felt his own utter exhaustion. He blew each candle out. Turned to the zendo's far window where, with no light from Gale's, there was only darkness. She was sleeping.

In the morning he tested his insight. The ranch house when he awoke was cold, quiet. He lay in his bedroll in the loft watching his breath laddering. Watching, out the loft's window, the early sky spreading. It was a lavender color. Had something really happened to him in the zendo? Absolutely. Was he changed? Different? Without getting out of his bed-roll he wriggled like a rasher close to his clothes that he'd folded and stowed in his duffel bag. He dressed, pulling on two pairs of socks and a sweatshirt. He found and removed from its bulging envelope the autopsy report. Found the spot where he'd stopped reading the day of its arrival. Read on, aloud:

–Wound number three: Downwards, through seventh costal cartilage and diaphragm into duodenum, mesentery, and omentum

His voice choked.

–Insight or no insight, the horror, he muttered and resleeved the report and went down the narrow attic stairs. He'd get the woodstove humming, he decided, then wake Tsuruoka. He peed, and at the kitchen sink washed his face and brushed his teeth. He noticed he wasn't thinking. That *was* different. He fetched his boots from the front door and went out the back to work the pump. The grass running up the mountain was crisp as gold. The windmill arms turned slowly, like those of a Vedic goddess. While he pumped away he warmed alternately his ears on his shoulders. Cletis padded uncertainly around the corner of the ranch house as though suffering a hangover. Rud whistled. The water clamored into the galvanized buckets and he lugged them back down to the house. Cletis followed him inside the kitchen. When Rud closed the door Cletis sat looking at him, rheumy-eyed.

–What're you so sad for? he asked.

Cletis mummered his chops.

–Hungry? Go wake your master then.

Cletis looked up at Rud, puzzled.

–Go on.

Rud knew then with near certainty that he was alone. He shivered as though someone had poured a bucket of live fish on him. He shooed the dog back out, and upstairs knocked on Tsuruoka's door, calling, *Roshi?*, the door yawing open. The room: the gray futon rolled and tied precise as a hospital bedcorner on the tatami. Where Gale had convinced him to stay that first night. The window to one side of the futon. Tsuruoka's steamer trunk to the other.

He rushed out the front door downstairs without bothering about boots. The ground was sharp as coral and Cletis loped into step with him. And now Rud feared the worst. Gale's loft, when he stutterstepped up her stairs, was bare of her belongings.

–Gone too, he announced to Cletis back outside. Everything. Everyone. But then you already knew.

He hurried around to the back door and collected his boots and with the untied lace ends whipping was back at the truck in seconds. He hurled down the tailgate. Cletis, with a clawing launch, scrabbled up and, dodging tool buckets, skidded in.

–Keys, keys, he said frisking himself.

He retrieved his denim jacket from the front door peg. The truck started after a few sluggish grumblings. A beautiful lid of autumnal fog, flat as a frozen pond, stretched across the valley floor to the mountains and he shifted into gear and plunged the truck down into it.

With the engine hammering and Cletis's massive skull outside the driver's window Rud shot along 487 into town. This early the streets were deserted. He steered south down Central. Past the bookstore, the Bulldog, Peak Physique. He prowled south down the four-lane past the mall, the lavender sky overhead deepening, until the buildings on either side of the highway ended. Slowing, he swung the truck around and looped back into town. His being settled. To what purpose did he scour the streets thus? Preposterous. And he hadn't a clue of the time. A group of men in Adventist suits huddled under the alpine overhang of a low building on Third. Rud slowed.

–Shan't be long, he told Cletis after he'd parked.

The place was called the Buffalo Café. The waitresses wore cross-country ski clothing and hiking boots and chattered with each other.

Rud sat at the counter. Beside a brass pendulum wallclock on the near wall hung a cricket bat as weathered as driftwood. A waitress poured him coffee and slid between his elbows the menu sheet. The saloon doors leading into the kitchen swung busily.

–Any eggs Benny? one waitress hollered as she barged in.

–You have eggs Benedict? Rud asked his waitress.

–Eighty-six the eggs Benny, the other waitress hollered as she barged back out.

–Sunday, Rud's waitress explained.

–Then – poached with hash browns.

An hour later he was at the job site. Calmly he parked and unloaded, Cletis barreling down the incline between carriage house and mansion to the edgewater. Rud followed. He untarped the mortar mixings and lugged and stacked tongloads of bricks in the small pyramids Tsuruoka fancied. Low clouds swept across the white hoods of the far mountains and a damp wind ushered the air. Cletis stood as still as a gargoyle by the water's edge, worrying some unknown marine life. To keep his own blood moving Rud mixed a batch of mud. Also with vague ambitions of calling forth Tsuruoka's presence. The mixer paddles chugged and slopped through the mixture. That meant it was too wet so he hooked in another shovel load of sand and a quarter of Portland. Now he could hear a sifting sound faint as a nighttime seaside. His mind held the chill clarity of the night before when the zendo wall had sheered away and re-emanated. When Cletis barked the sound sailed clear through him. Cletis barked again and Rud followed the sound this time with his eyes chasing up the hill where at the top Tsuruoka, astride Penny, looked down at him.

Tsuruoka dismounted as Rud walked to the base of the hill. Penny tossed her head and swung the pigeon-colored python of her neck and snorted. With half-sideways steps, as though the grade were steeper than it was, Tsuruoka clumped downhill, wincing each time.

–How is the mud? Tsuruoka called down, panting.

–Gale's gone.

–Yes.

–I didn't pose it as a question.

Cletis lumbered up past Rud to greet his master and at the hilltop Penny backed up, hunkering.

–Herro, Cretis, Tsuruoka said, grabbing a fistful of dogears.

–Where? Rud asked.

–Where what?

–Where's she gone?

–Not now, Tsuruoka replied, please?

He was unshaven. His breath had a boozy sting. He wrestled Cletis aside and straightened.

–What did you say to her? Rud asked.

–I told her two weeks, Tsuruoka said softly. To get this done.

He scuffed by Rud. Rud followed.

–A promise? To Gale?

–The boss.

–All right, Rud said, slapping his hands against the side of his thighs, I've all day.

–You must learn how to strike, Rud-san.

–Strike?

–Strike bricks, Tsuruoka explained. He took his spectacles from his breast pocket and threaded them, one side at a time, onto his flat nose. If, he said to Rud, we are to meet our deadline.

He shuffled, listing like a tire with a slow leak, around the laid courses to where Rud had stacked the white tool buckets. He bent and rifled through the bucket containing the miscellany: the spools of yellow string, the reel of duct tape, the WD-40, the tape measure.

–I had extra kneepads, Tsuruoka grumbled.

–But before the day's out, Rud said, walking over.

–Before the day is out you will need them: your knees will

Tsuruoka stopped and looked at Rud square on. Unshaven, unkempt, his eyes milky. On the far side of the Portland pallet and the barchan dune of sand the mixer still chugged away.

–Did you at least eat? Rud asked Tsuruoka. Breakfast?

Tsuruoka blinked rapidly his tired eyes.

–No, he said.

Rud could bear to look at him no longer. The morning-after whiskers, unkempt like he'd spent a week sleeping on the couch. His breath overly sweet from tobacco.

–I'll get some mud, Rud said.

He shook the stiffness out of his legs. He sighed. Shook too his head to clear his mind of all the memories this episode had unleashed. He found Tsuruoka studying him intently. He looked away. At the tufted ground. The shifting heavens.

–You know, he began, for years – years – I did this horseshit with my father and it, it ended – where did it end up?

He shook his head again. And said:

–*Did* it end up?

Neither spoke to the other for a long time. After Rud dumped the mortar in thick green gobbets into the wheelbarrow and with the delivered mud Tsuruoka had laid a long curling course of brick, Tsuruoka mimed to Rud how to strike the joints of mortar. The striking tool was a long flue of steel, wide as his finger and three times as long and bent, at each fingerlength in an opposite direction, so that it resembled, as Rud noted to himself:

–A bolt of lightning.

And until lunch Rud knelt – he fashioned kneepads out of his balled-up jacket – and ran the convex underside of the tool along the half-set mortar that separated the bricks. Compacting and smoothing the mortar as it dried from its nascent green to a soft slush color and settled into beveled canyons between the red pavers.

–Well? Rud asked when Tsuruoka with creaking back stood. You going to tell me?

–Burgers and beers, Tsuruoka said. Best cure for a hangover.

Rud's own back crackled like twigs burning. He stood with no little anguish.

—Is it that bad? Rud asked as they climbed to the truck.

—Worse, Tsuruoka said.

At the Bulldog Tsuruoka devoured his lunch – two cheeseburgers, fries, two drafts – like a mute trencherman. This near-total silence prevailed all afternoon as they laid three more curving red and canaled courses of pavers. Day's end Rud was trying to clean the most recently struck bricks with a damp yellow sponge but each swipe he took unearthed from the joints tiny flints of mortar.

—Here, Tsuruoka said. He was overseeing, crouched. He pivoted on his toes.

Rud yielded the sponge and Tsuruoka brushed it diagonally across the mortar joints, polishing the bricks clean as apples. Having demonstrated, Tsuruoka proffered the sponge. Rud did not take it. In the west the sun entered the white horizon of mountains like some sort of hovering interstellar craft.

—No, he told Tsuruoka. I don't do another thing until you tell me.

Tsuruoka said not a word. He resumed cleaning the bricks. Rud stood.

—I've been waiting all day. Patiently. Now no longer.

Tsuruoka finished wiping the bricks. He stood and underhanded the sponge into his white tool bucket and snatched the bucket's wire handle and lifted it.

—What did you do to make her leave? Rud asked quietly.

—What did you?

Rud said nothing. Tsuruoka looked down.

—I need water, he said.

With the bucket grazing the leg of his overalls Tsuruoka headed off across the concrete, across the job site. Rud stayed right beside him.

—Tell me – please?

They reached the mixer. Tsuruoka fished his tools from his water bucket, fed them into an empty one, and dumped the ditchy tool water. He unnotched the hose nozzle and whooshed in a jet of water, swirled the bucket, and tipped out the silty residue. Rud stayed on him like they were bilboed. Tsuruoka peered up at him. His cheeks were nubbed with sparse whiskers. The lenses of his spectacles were spotted with pinhead marks of gray.

–I lent her a book, Tsuruoka said.

–No, Rud countered.

–And I asked for it back.

–No, Rud repeated. No chance. This isn't about some book, he said. She – she's why you lost your faith. Gale is.

They looked at each other.

–And she is why you found yours, Tsuruoka countered.

–At first.

–Thank you.

–But then, last night

Tsuruoka, waiting for Rud to finish, tipped slightly the bucket and, squeezing the nozzle trigger, refilled it, the water jet striking the plastic bucketbottom like miniature thunder. With the bucket half-filled he released the nozzle trigger and the water settled in glassy coils.

–What last night, he asked Rud.

–I don't know – nothing. Something – perhaps.

–While you were sitting?

–A glimpse – a glimpse – the barest of ones, granted. But enough to know that no book could disprove it.

–That is what *I* believed until

–I don't want to hear about any book, Rud interjected with a wave of his hand. He headed across the site to fetch the wheelbarrow.

–Until the day Gale came, Tsuruoka called out to him.

Rud stopped and turned.

–She sent a letter to Bernard-sensei, saying she had read his book again and wanted to come, because she had an omen.

—Me?

Tsuruoka did not answer. With his longhandled brush in the bucket of clear water he began to scrub his trowelblade.

—Me? Rud asked again, returning halfway.

—You. Bah, I thought at the time. Omens. Still, Bernard-sensei would always go into town to meet the unsui, new students. But for Gale I did.

He stopped abruptly. With his sleevecuff he dabbed a splash off his cheek. And continued:

—She, Gale, was late. So. I waited in the Bookworks. To pass the time.

—And you bought the book?

—Julian Jaynes?

—Yes.

—No, Tsuruoka answered with a laugh. I was looking through *My Favorite Summer.*

—Mickey Mantle?

—Yes. When I was high school student my father took me to see him.

—When the Yankees toured Japan?

—He had the swing, Tsuruoka said dreamily, of a lion's tail.

—He struck out every time, Rud pointed out.

—He was hung over, Tsuruoka said back. All were.

—But the Jaynes book, Rud inquired.

Tsuruoka bent and groped in the icy water for the striking tool.

—It *was* in the bookstore that day, he said.

—But you're a roshi. How could a book make you doubt what you have seen?

—This book, Rud-san, makes you doubt everything you have seen: insight, God

—God?

Tsuruoka lifted the striking tool out of the water.

—Jehova, satori, Tsuruoka said. He let the striking tool drop back into the water with a plop. He stood. Name it what you want, he insisted. It does not exist. Has never existed.

The two men stood face to face.

—But it's not a question of faith, Rud pointed out. You have *seen* it.

—No.

—And I did, last night.

—You saw a trick of the mind.

—I touched emptiness.

—You touched a hole – a blank spot – in the right hemisphere.

—No! Rud said, refusing to yield. I know what I saw. And you, a roshi

—A bricklayer.

—would've seen it a thousand times.

—No! Tsuruoka shouted. With iron strength he seized Rud by the shoulders. I was never a roshi, he said. The Buddha never a Buddha.

Tsuruoka, almost shaking him, said:

—Even the Buddha's enlightenment – a hallucination. Like yours. Like your father's ghost.

Tsuruoka released Rud's shoulders. Looked at him sadly, kindly.

—And without Buddha's enlightenment, he told Rud, no Buddhism. No Zen.

He turned away. Exhaled deeply.

—If only it *was* Gale, Tsuruoka said, looking now at the ground. A heart. A small thing. But eternity. He shoved his hands in his overalls pockets and gazed uphill. So, he said, you are on your own, Rudyard.

—Why should I be swayed by something I haven't even

—Read? Tsuruoka interrupted. Hai! – I meant loading tools. It is late. I must ride Penny home.

He began the slow climb to the hilltop.

—She won't follow? Rud asked.

Tsuruoka stopped and turned around.

—Not with Cletis in back. I am sorry, Rudyard. Buddha was right about one thing: there is no life after – no mustard seed.

—There never was.

—Yes. But it gets worse. For now, with Jaynes, even the dead have died.

–Clutching at the earth?

–See for yourself – desu ne?

–I will, he vowed.

And he gave himself two weeks – their bricklaying deadline – to read Tsuruoka's copy of Jaynes's book, though he began it as an act of defiance.

–Fuck him, Rud mumbled as, after eating and showering, he sat in his bed on the loft floor. He read the introduction. He was cold. Read it again. He was drained. He shut the ice-white tome and slept.

–Well? Tsuruoka inquired the next morning as they flung the tarps off the materials.

–It's too cold to read.

–The book?

–The loft.

–Yes. With money from this job I will renovate. No more authentic. Central heat. Join to Montana Power.

–Indoor plumbing?

–Ha! Until then, Tsuruoka suggested, you must move into Gale's.

He thought all day about it.

–Where's Bernard-sensei's? he asked Tsuruoka as they drove out the gates and the headlamps seesawed up through the black cage of trees. That's where Gale's gone – isn't it?

–Yes. Sangaiji. Coos Bay.

–And she's not coming back?

–No. Tsuruoka cleared his throat. So, I will need a new hoddu-san? Rud thought for a moment.

–No, he said. I'm new enough.

Thus down the ranch-house stairs and out across the nightgrass to the garage and up to the loft he hauled his measly belongings. Once the Morso was stoked and radiant he unrolled and situated his sleeping bag exactly where Gale's had been. Her line drawing of his father – or what she imagined was his father but was only a romantic version of his own profile – he pushpinned to the pony wall. He looked at Jaynes's book in the corner. Out the window the night was starry and quiet as a battleground the day after.

–Like taking a walk in the sky, he said, and fetching the Jaynes book, well into the night he read. As in Sunday school he read not linearly but in and amongst Jaynes's profane and profound testament. And as with all testaments its onslaught was biblical, its voice terrible, possessed.

–Like schizophrenics? he raw-eyed wondered aloud to Tsuruoka.

It was several days later. A damp and drizzling penetrating ache of a day – the lake bottled up with fog – and they'd taken refuge for the countless time since untarping under the mansion eaves until the drizzle abated.

–Yes, Tsuruoka answered finally.

He stretched his arm out into the rain's veil. Poked his head out to confirm.

–My mother, he said and ducked back under, had voices. In her head.

–Of gods?

–At first. Tsuruoka became quiet, thinking. She was a translator, he said after a bit.

–English?

–Roshia-go – Russian. He spat into the ragged grass. Have you ever chewed? he asked Rud.

–Tobacco?

–It would be something to do.

–Gives you wicked breath.

–And tumors.

–We could do laundry?

Nights as he switched off the lights in the pulsing warmth of the garage loft he half-wished he'd have nightmares of bicameral theocrats and prophets and priests – Inca or Hammurabi, Moses or Israel or the emperors of Shang – governing their unconscious brethren by what they and their thralls believed to be divine utterances. Hallucinated ut-

terances that for millennia after would still command obeisance and
awe. That still do. That yet will. For Rud, though, no dreams of antiq-
uity visited. Instead, on the seventh night, he suffered a wet dream of
such ferocity and longing – on his couch that day molding her breasts
together to kiss and lick them she was whispering truants in his ear
about his owing her owing her as he sank his cock inside her – longing
and fierce that he came in a violent boil of semen so copious it wakened
him with shame.

The dream, at least its guilt and longing, dismayed him. Sopping up
his loins with his underwear, he dressed. In the zendo, after he'd with
icewater lashed his shivering genitals like a penitent, he bowed to the
Buddha, saying quietly:

–Voices? You did not hear any voices. And he sat struggling like a
fiend to will once again the annihilation and reemanation of the wall.
His failure fanned both his dismay and his determination. When Tsuruoka surfaced he was in the zendo still. Tsuruoka made no comment
one way or the other. Either at breakfast. Or at the mansion.

–Our last week, Rud-san, Tsuruoka mentioned during morning
break.

They sat in the truck. Coffee vapors made steam mesas on the windshield above the thermos lids. In an unwrapped sack of waxed paper
two date squares lay on the urn between them.

–Who said that? Rud asked Tsuruoka absently.

–What?

–Even the dead have died.

–I do not know. A friend told me.

They sipped their coffee.

–Eat, Tsuruoka counseled.

With his eyes Rud picked over the date squares.

–Perhaps she read it somewhere, Tsuruoka said. So – please – choose.

Rud chose one and with his other hand slid from behind the urn
Troy's letter. He bit into the date square and set it back onto the urn.

He studied the back of the envelope. The yellowed V. With his thumbnail he chiseled open the envelope flapcorner and slit it neckwise and
with a *fwuh* blew it open. He knew Tsuruoka was deliberately not
watching. He looked inside. There was a letter all right. He looked out
the truckcab windshield. The mansion and the carriage house blocked
his view of the lake but he could see across the levitating mist the far
mountains that were green and slashed with yellow. Their crests fringed
with snow.

–The Buddha heard no voices, he said to Tsuruoka.

–I will leave you, Tsuruoka answered, bowing his head, clamping the
rest of his date square in his mouth, and with his finger hooking his
thermos lid.

–The morning of his enlightenment, Rud demanded, did he?

Tsuruoka removed the date square.

–He heard their absence, he answered.

He opened his door and slid fluidly out.

–Take your time, my friend, he said.

Time? Troy's letter required little: *Roodyard!* Rud's eyes raced over the
sole page, tripping on the names like someone fleeing blind at night
through a graveyard: *Davis-Carmedie Your Stepmother; Gale Poo-bah
Your Ex & I.* His mind yammered. He got out of the truck and, with the
letter fluttering and twisting in his hand, he walked to the top of the
hill. He stood there studying the lake, gelid and skippingstone flat.

Someone somewhere was burning leaves and the air was sweet with
the smell of it. Downhill at the deck Tsuruoka folded back the green
garbage bag that covered the wheelbarrow mortar and dug out for himself a spadeload. The pavers Frenchcurved around the mansion corner
like a school of goldfish teeming through a chalk shallows. The mixer
on the shore abandoned and solitary as an art school exhibit. Troy's
voice in the letter had the clarity of a voice in a cave as Rud reread it –
*knew you'd make it, old Davis-Carmedie has died and I've been promoted
yet afuckingain* – a voice even clearer when, after driving himself

through two hours of fruitless zazen in the garage loft that night, Rud read it once more˙ – *your stepmother's skipped south to condo with all the other atrics.* He could hear him. *Call me – pronto – even collect!* Could hear him in the bitter light next morning. Rud and Tsuruoka loaded the bricksaw, struggling it out of the garage like pallbearers and huffing and thunking it onto the tailgate, then waddling it on the back two corners of its whaler-shaped tray down the length of the truckbed to snug up against the outer back of the cab. When at the job site the hollow steel stilts that were the saw's legs were thrust up into the gudgeon at each corner of the tray its orange bladecover stood chest high. Because they did not reach the final course they did not cut any brick that day. In the late afternoon, snow spits flew across the water as though cast up from the lake itself. Breaktime Rud forsook the warmth of the truck. With the lake sloshing at his boot tips he read Troy's letter one final time. *Phone me prontolla the Poob has big plans you and Gale an item yet? Did you check out the letterhead? Nyuh? Remember?*

He scrutinized once more the embossed letterhead.

–Booger, he said softly. New York, New York.

And reading again: *your ex and I big news so big can only tell in person so fone or phax.*

On one of the estates back nearer the tip of the lake someone was burning leaves again. The smoke curled up from the treetops in a thin sarong of blue and orange and its sweet scent falling, here with the snow ticking on his face and the realization that Amaranta had ended up with Troy, only deepened the bitterness of that realization. Knowing them now by heart he said Troy's words aloud: *Your ex and I big news so big,* and he scrunched Troy's letter up in a ball. He reared back to fire it across the lake. It was the certainty that the weightless wad would flub from his hand if he did so that caused him to drop his arm and jam the wad into his jeans pocket.

–I want to get very drunk, he told Tsuruoka at day's end as they draped with five-mil poly the bricksaw.

–What about your sitting? Tsuruoka said. Here.

Tsuruoka hug-armed to Rud the end of the yellow string with which they were tying the poly – dark as a friar's habit – around the saw's legtops.

–I've declared a holiday, Rud answered. And from Julian fucking Jaynes. Well?

–World Series is on, Tsuruoka pointed out.

–I'll take that as a yes then.

Rud tightened and tied the string like a belt and when they'd climbed the top of the hill stopped Tsuruoka.

–You're not worried about the saw?

–No one steals tools – then they would have to work.

They turned to look down at it.

–Besides, looks like the Elephant Man, Tsuruoka said.

Rud laughed.

–You know, he said as the truck winged down 487 into town, I never got drunk with my father, ever, not once.

Dusk pressed the last spine of dark blue sky into the western ridge. The snow thickened and Rud flicked on the wipers. The truck's heater blasted away. The speed limit dropped.

–Now I'd settle for a measly beer. He glanced down at the urn. A few fickin answers.

They soared up and into the snowflurry, crossing the rail yard. The town spread below, Welsh and twinkling.

–To ask why? Tsuruoka inquired.

–Why he did it that way. And about my mother.

They approached the intersection. A Sinclair gas station with its green brontosaurus emblem occupied this corner and in the Conoco station catercorner a man in an elegant Aquascutum bent broadbacked over the gasflap of a stretched BMW – one much like the woman's that second afternoon on the brick job. The man tapped the pump nozzle, milking the fuel into his tank.

—Red light, Tsuruoka said, pointing at the signal.

—I saw, Rud said.

He braked.

Through the distortion of the swirling snow and the filling-station island's white fluorescence Rud could just see into the yellow light of the convenience store. The clerk, her back to the window, was settling up with someone in the full black leathers of a motorcyclist. A Jim Palmer Trucking semi surged throbbing through the intersection, obliterating Rud's view. It passed. The person in leathers had exited the store and now walked along in front of the window, a white helmet tubered under one arm. Her head was smoothly shaven.

—Gale, Rud said softly and involuntarily.

Tsuruoka did not respond. He was staring vacantly out his side window. At the corner of the convenience store Gale counted the money in her wallet. She tucked her wallet inside her jacket and zipped and snapped it closed to her neck and lifted her white helmet above her head two-handed as though performing her own investiture. One of the cars stacked behind Rud beeped its horn. The light was green. Rud checked over his right shoulder for traffic – he intended to pull over to the curb.

—What are you doing? Tsuruoka asked.

He too cranked his head around. From up on the bridge headlamps streamed down toward them through the snow. The car behind Rud beeped again. Rud floored the gas pedal and popped the clutch and whipped the truck into a violent righthand turn. In the truckbed a bucket tipped and spilled. Tsuruoka threw his arms out, swimming for the dashboard. The car Rud had cut off burst forth a prolonged and angry honnnk! and, once Rud had fishtailed around the corner, it skated through the intersection.

—Where you going? Tsuruoka asked.

Rud pulled over. He wrenched the rearview mirror to see back to the gas station. Traffic maneuvered by. Gale was gone. Rud slapped the turn indicator down and shifted and swung the truck left into a U-turn.

–Where now? Tsuruoka complained. You are acting very crazy, Rudyard.

Across the intersection, but this time on their side of the road, waited the Conoco. The BMW driver had gone in to pay. Rud turned right again.

–I will not ask, Tsuruoka said drolly.

In the parking spaces at the side of the convenience store a single headlamp, almost purple with brilliance, flared on, twisting and bobbing. Rud guided the truck to righthand the curb. He stopped. Came the tight European yee of an engine starting that launched forward the light with Gale's helmeted and glistening figure clamped to its dark and chrome thorax.

South onto the road that was oily and shining in her headlamp she banked her machine. Accelerating slowly.

–Ah, this is why you drive like a taxi, Tsuruoka said.

–You said she wouldn't be back.

–You are losing your faith.

Rud glanced at Tsuruoka.

–That nothing works out? he asked.

Tsuruoka nodded at the windshield. Rud touched up the gas. The pickup's wipers continued to lurch across the windshield, leaving on the driver's side only arcs of streaks, like the rings of a quartered treetrunk.

–So, Tsuruoka said. *This* time you will follow?

They watched the red ladybug of Gale's rear fender flicker southward into the dark colander of snow. Listened as her atonal engine fainted away. Her red taillight was almost gone.

–You are losing her, Tsuruoka said.

A sedan motored past, southbound. A pickup towing a horse trailer followed.

–You know, Rud said, the first time I saw her she was dancing.

Gale's taillight was lost in the night.

—Different schools together. Still. Rud looked across at his mentor and asked: You up for that beer?

—Only if it is not just one.

Rud checked his sideview mirror again and with caution this time guided the truck through yet another U-turn. As he did so the BMW pulled out of the gas station, turning south. The car was sleek as a shark and like sharks the two vehicles half-circled each other. The drivers looked at each other once and once again and simultaneously blared their horns.

It was Troy of course and Rud hit the brake pedal and craning his neck around blared the horn again. Troy's horn also blared. Rud shifted into reverse and cranked down his window and waved his arm. The BMW edged backward. Tsuruoka was gawking alternately at Rud and at Troy's car.

—How do you drive *after* drinking? he asked.

—My stepbrother, Rud said.

In the BMW Troy was talking to someone.

—My ex? Rud asked softly.

Because he didn't button his jacket until after he'd heelkicked on the emergency brake and climbed out and slammed the door, his hands were trembling as he fought with the steel buttons and turned his collar up. The snow was still vanishing into the pavement. He crossed as Troy's window powered halfway down then immediately back up. The interior light burst on the same time the door-ajar chime sounded as Troy pommeled out and threw shut the door behind him. He was boxy. Tired looking.

—Hey hey, he said, shit.

Rud watched him from a few feet away. Troy ran both his hands through his hair.

—Fucking speechless you are. Well that's a change, ha?

Under his flowing Aquascutum he was suited up, though his tieknot

had jet lag. From his inside breast pocket he pulled a softpack of cigarettes and wristflicked one partially out and with his teeth unsheathed it.

–Kleeshna kleeshna, he said, grinning and slapping his coat and
jacket pockets.

–I got your letter, Rud said.

–Sure – great.

–I was a while reading it.

–Of course, Troy said. Anyway – he gave up searching for a light – we,
we were just on our way up. To see you.

–We?

Troy's face became as stone. Behind his back he rapped on the car
window.

–You *did* get my letter.

–Yes.

–And you *did* read it.

–I've read more detailed license plates.

–Yeah – well when you've the gift.

The window slid half down. Snow swirled inside. Troy took the unlit
cigarette from his teeth and stepped out of the way. She was stretched
across the console leaning on one elbow, looking up at Rud from the
bluish glow of the instrumentation. In the sidereal light her hair was violet as thistles and so were her eyes, tired and raw. A flake of snow
lighted on one of her eyelashes. She blinked.

–Hi, she said.

Rud stepped closer to the window and leaned forward.

–Hi, he said back.

–There, Troy said, embracing Rud by the shoulder. Let's get outta this
weather. When we get up to the compound you two can – you know.

–You were headed the wrong way, Rud said.

–We had an errand first, right, Elay?

She nodded. Troy let go of Rud.

—Better roll up the window, Troy told her, it's real leather.

—Bye, Amaranta said.

The window slid up. Troy had his money clip out and peeled off two bills and brandled them at Rud.

—Get some supplies.

—Of all the unmitigated fucking gall, Rud began.

—Whoa, Troy said.

—Barging in here

—Hey, Gale phoned *me*.

—Waving your money.

—Here, Troy said, trying to take Rud's hand to give him the money, but failing. For fuck's sake.

—Not even for his.

—Come on – I'm throwing in the towel. It just happens to be green. He folded the bills into Rud's hand.

—*What* are you doing here? Rud demanded.

—Pick up some food, maybe some pasta. Lotsa vino. Brewskies. Some Newman's Own.

—What the fuck is this? Rud asked firmly.

—We're married.

By the time Rud and Tsuruoka shopped and made it back home the snow was launching a full-scale invasion. The BMW waited for them at the gate and followed them up the switchbacks. In the headlamp cones the snowflakes were green sparks. The hills porcupine gray. At the garage Rud parked. Troy stayed on Rud's bumper, three-pointed, then parked the BMW by the white front lawn.

—In case we need a fast getaway, Troy said, getting out and slamming the door and grinning and walking around the elegant rear fender.

—Welcome, Tsuruoka said to Troy, bowing.

—So, this is all yours?

—All but the snow.

Amaranta remained in the car. Rud had wrestled in either arm a brown paper grocery bag and he closed the truck door with his shoulder. From out of the garage-house corridor, his paws coigning lovely divots in the snow, pattered Cletis.

—The size of that dog, Troy said.

Amaranta's door opened. One leg at a time she got out and stood. She was pregnant. Her long coat was unbuttoned and when she arched her back to unstiffen, the coat's front panels spread open. She wore with its tails untucked above stretch jeans a silk blouse light blue as her eyes. Just starting to show, she was. But there was no mistaking.

—And who is this beautiful woman? Tsuruoka asked.

Rud was staring at Amaranta and Troy was watching Rud.

—Amaranta Elena Versalles, she said.

She and Tsuruoka shook hands. Rud was trying not to stare. Snowflakes poised on her hair. Cletis barked.

—That's only Penny, Tsuruoka said, my horse.

—No, Troy said, pointing down the mountain.

At the mountain's base and through the snow yet another set of headlamps dodged and hid from tree to tree.

—Hunters? Rud suggested.

—More visitors, Tsuruoka said suspiciously. The snow cascaded down. Show our guests inside, he told Rud.

He did and in the kitchen set the two grocery bags on the counter. They'd shed their shoes at the front door but retained their coats and, with the floor so ice cold, their socks.

—I should get you some slippers, Rud said to Amaranta.

—These are fine, she said, wriggling her toes inside her thick woolen socks.

Troy came into the kitchen.

—Turn down the effing heat, he teased.

—The woodstove cooks fast, Rud said.

—That is what you cook on? Amaranta asked.

—No. He pointed to the plug-in hotplate. Is two enough? Burners?

–For spaghetti.

They unpacked the bags. Four six-packs of beer. Four black bottles of Valpolicella. And to fortify the Newman jar sauce, mushrooms and bacon and olives and garlic.

–Where's the dojo? Troy asked.

–The zendo.

–Hey – kidding, just kidding. But the boys' room?

Rud pointed to the back door.

–You have enough plates? Amaranta asked.

Rud peered into either sack. Troy opened the back door.

–This isn't funny, he said, facing darkness and snow.

–Take the torch, Rud told him.

–You're serious?

–The flashlight. On the floor there.

–An outhouse? I'm gonna need a roadie.

Amaranta plucked a beer out of a six-pack and Troy popped it and took a long guzzle and went out.

–Mr Newman will not be pleased, Rud said, nodding at all the sauce's reinforcements.

He opened a beer for himself and crossed the kitchen to the wood-stove. He'd already that morning prepped it with paper and kindling and logs.

–Rud, Amaranta began.

–Of course he won't know, old Paul.

–Rud.

–Unless he's coming too, Rud said, getting to one knee.

–We have to talk.

–No, he said turning and smiling up at her. Not just yet – please? It's my fault – was my fault – and now

He lit a match and touched the flame to the paper and blew gently. The flame washed into the iron depth of the stove like brass and mercury. Satisfied, he shut the gate, stood, and stropped the ash from his hands.

—So – so what happened with Dedos?

—He – *they* – went to Seattle.

—Ahh. His wife hadn't heard of it.

—Del divorcio? She laughed sadly, lifting her shoulders. He hadn't.

She brushed her hair back one-handed behind her ear, but it didn't stay and with a finger she pinioned it back and looked down at herself.

—I'm sorry, he said. Really.

—First you left. Then Gio.

—You don't need to explain, he said. Honest.

She waved her hand at him.

—And so I went to find you – and there was Troy – and we

—Shush, he said.

—I won't shush, she said. You listen. And *look* at me, she said.

—I am.

—Look at me! She turned her back to him and gripped with both hands the counter's edge.

After a moment he stepped close.

—Hey, he said. He touched softly her hair.

She edged away. Picked up one of the small cans of olives.

—Rud, listen. It is not Troy's.

—I know.

—The baby. We will need a can opener, she said.

She pulled open the knife and fork drawer. He waited. She looked inside.

—Rud – help me with this?

He slid shut the drawer and pulled open the one to her left. She reached in and swished aside the potato masher. By their handles some carving knives.

—Don't you know? she said.

He took a breath.

—It's mine, he said.

—Who else?

—Not his.

—No.

—You're sure.

With two fingers she made a scissors and clipped twice.

—A vasectomy?

She nodded. He looked into the drawer.

—Mine, he said. Jesus – jesus christ.

He found the can opener. Put it on the countertop.

—When did he tell you? he asked.

—When I told him.

—What? I don't believe this.

—Why?

—Why? Jesus – what the hell else is he gonna say?

—No, she said, interrupting him. No – he would tell the truth.

The backdoor screen clumpfed open. Then the door.

—You two caught up? Troy asked, coming in and stamping his feet and batting the snow off his suit jacket harder than he had to.

An engine outside backfired with a crack. Everyone jumped.

—God! Amaranta said.

—Maybe the rushy's been shot, Troy laughed.

Rud drained his beer without tasting it.

—It was a joke, Troy said.

—He's an endangered species, Rud said. I'll go see.

The truck was an old International, orange in color. The snow had let up, falling slowly now as though each flake anticipated its journey's end. Vacantly Rud walked down the path while the driver three-pointed in front of the garage. Tsuruoka was not around but the garage door was open and the light was on in its bay. Shuddering, the International – a black motorcycle piggybacked and cinched to its bed – pulled up behind the BMW. The near side door opened, and Gale climbed out.

–You're back, Rud said.

She wore a Tibetan parka and her cotton monk's pants and over-the-shin mukluks. Rud pushed her door closed.

–You're angry, she said.

–Just preoccupied. So – how was it?

–Not angry then? she asked. For calling Troy.

–No. Maybe at first, but not now.

–He's still – she widened her eyes and shrugged – What's the saying? Handsome is, handsome *doesn't*.

–He has his moments, Rud said.

–Yes, she said, grinning. All in the eighth grade.

Rud laughed for a moment. In the garage the light clicked off and they turned. Tsuruoka walked out into the white grace of the night. At first Rud thought he toted a rifle. But it was a baseball bat. The driver's side of the International opened as if in response and a tall man, lank as a spring, climbed out.

–Kisa, Tsuruoka said.

–Roshi.

She bowed. The tall man walked out from around the rear of his truck. The only light was from the ranch-house front door but it was enough. The man wore dungarees and an army surplus coat. He and Tsuruoka eyed each other. Each took a step closer to the other, Tsuruoka using the blond bat handle to jab the snow like a cane. Slowly and deeply Tsuruoka bowed to the man. The man bowed back even deeper.

–Bernard-sensei? Rud whispered to Gale.

She nodded. Tsuruoka and the man then hugged each other like tribunes – though Tsuruoka's skull barely reached the other's shoulders. There was no patting on the back. Rud looked at the motorcycle, coiled and ebony, sweating snow.

–Is this just a visit? Rud asked Gale.

–Depends on Sensei, she said. And the roshi.

An hour and a half later they were all doing warmly, fed with spaghetti, fueled with wine. Even Amaranta and Gale. They had dragged down from Tsuruoka's bedroom his steamer trunk and draped a white cloth across it, now embossed with blood-red bracelets from the bottoms of their wine tumblers. They were in the kitchen, seated around the trunk on zafus. Two white candles oozed ivory wax. Tsuruoka had not relinquished the baseball bat, keeping it by the table as though it were some ceremonial mace. Troy and Amaranta on one side. Rud and Gale on the other. Roshi and Sensei at either end. They talked bricks. They talked babies:

–In January, Amaranta revealed.

Rud tried silently to calculate nine months backward but Amaranta was staring right at him. They talked golf. Bernard-sensei had been on the PGA tour.

–That is how I heard of Roshi, he said.

He was a graceful man, somewhere between Rud's age and Tsuruoka's. He had a thinning brillo of hair and a beatnik goatee.

–At the Montana Open, he explained.

–Makes sense to me, Troy quipped. He was fidgety.

–On the way here, Roshi, Gale said, I was talking about the *Heart Sutra* and Bernard-sensei mentioned the Sau – Sau

–Sautrantika, Bernard-sensei said.

–Sautrantika School of Buddhism.

–There is more wine? Tsuruoka asked.

Rud passed him the bottle.

–The Sautrantikas, Gale continued.

–Excuse me please, Kisa. This all? Tsuruoka asked Rud.

–There's one more, Rud answered.

Gale cleared her throat.

–The Buddha, they believed, preached that all things, including any state of individual personality, are only momentary.

–Please talk about something else, Tsuruoka asked with a bow of his head.

–Besuboru? Bernard-sensei suggested.

–In which case the Sautrantikas, like the *Heart Sutra,* render Julian Jaynes

–Please, Kisa, Tsuruoka repeated, no Sau – Sau-sect, no *Heart Sutra.* Even Sensei wants to change the topic.

Gale looked at Bernard-sensei. He put his finger to his lips like a librarian, his eyes sparkling.

–To the *Diamond Sutra,* he said.

–Unfair, Tsuruoka moaned.

Bernard-sensei turned to Rud and asked:

–Did Roshi tell you about how he came to Zen?

–His first night, Tsuruoka grumbled.

–Anyone want to go for a smoke? Troy asked.

–The Emperor's game? Did he?

–Yes, Tsuruoka said quietly.

–No, Rud answered. Well, not quite, actually.

Tsuruoka drank off his glass of wine. Troy, with exaggerated groans, stood.

–Hirohito, Bernard began, had never attended a baseball game before – this was 1958 remember

–Fifty-nine, Tsuruoka said.

–Rud? Troy mimed.

Rud shook his head no. Troy sidled behind Bernard.

–And, Bernard continued, watch the woodstove – and he, the Emperor, chose that night in May for he and the Empress to attend a game between Tokyo's Giants and Hanshin Tigers. Roshi was third base. For Hanshin.

—A sad rookie, Tsuruoka said.

—And after batting practice, while you were in the clubhouse?

—It is your story, Bernard.

—The crowd, it was in Tokyo, began to cheer wildly. Their majesties had arrived.

Troy poked at Rud's back with his toe. Rud slapped it.

—Thing was, Bernard continued, Emperor and Empress were scheduled to leave at nine-thirty – precisely. Precisely. Yet by the final inning the score was tied. Hanshin had tried to win before nine-thirty arrived but

—I struck out, Tsuruoka said.

—So, it was nine-thirty. The bottom of the inning yet to start. Roshi crouched fielding third base. Would the Emperor leave? Everyone held their breath. Hanshin had their best pitcher, Murayama. He threw fire.

At this Tsuruoka nodded and refilled his wine tumbler.

—The Emperor decided to stay for one last batter.

—Shigeo Nagashima, Tsuruoka said.

—A shobu – a great duel – between pitcher and batter. And this Nagashima, like Roshi

—Please, Tsuruoka interrupted. He was not like me – not.

—Third base? Young? A rookie?

—Yes, Tsuruoka said. But no. He shook his head. Finish – please?

Bernard stretched a long arm and brought the wine bottle to his own tumbler, poured, then drank. And resumed:

—Everyone hushed. Totally silent. The day before Murayama had thrown his fire past Nagashima, striking him out. And this time – this time the two fought like samurai until the count was two and two.

—Tsu e tsu, Tsuruoka said, slumped now, his face almost pained, the candles burning in his eyes. I could see catcher sign to Murayama, Tsuruoka said hypnotically. Two fingers sideways. I could feel the eyes of the Emperor. Of the Empress. The quiet. The breeze. The Giants' many championship flags moving. Inside fastball. Murayama winds up. Nagashima deep breath.

–Pok! Bernard said.

Tsuruoka looked at him. As did everyone else.

–No, Tsuruoka said softly, I was tricked.

–No Roshi, Bernard-sensei said. For as Nagashima circled the bases, ichi, ni, san – third base, your base, Roshi – hate wa.

–Tricked, Tsuruoka said to him.

–No, Roshi.

–Yes, Bernard – like tonight.

Troy bent and shook Rud by the shoulder.

–Rudyard, you have heard this, Tsuruoka said.

–Hate wa, Bernard repeated. The outcome.

–Outcome? Tsuruoka said. My mother, that day, was committed to an asylum. Tsuruoka examined each of the faces. Because of her voices. In her head. Voices of tricks? Or eternity?

No one said anything.

–And when she died, Tsuruoka said, when my mother died, she did not die nyūmetsu no gi.

He looked down at his wine. No one spoke.

–One's death posture, Bernard-sensei explained quietly.

Amaranta, as if by reflex, folded her hands across her abdomen.

–The one we choose at our death. Bernard waited. Nyūmetsu? A posture like the Buddha's – when he crossed over and entered Nirvana.

–Nirvana, Tsuruoka repeated softly. No, he said, looking up at Bernard, then at Gale. No Buddhism. No Zen. No roshis.

The candleflames flourished and shrank. Troy gently kneed Rud's shoulder.

–Rud-san, Tsuruoka said. If you do not go, I will.

Outside snow muffled the earth and the cars and trucks like white volcanic ash. Troy had one of the long wooden matches from the zendo and he popped with his thumbnail its sulfurous head.

—Weird fucking story, Troy said, wagging the match out.

—Mazeroski-ish, Rud said.

—That Japanese? Troy asked with a laugh.

Neither wore coats. They carried beers.

—Anyway, you're taking this real well, Troy said.

—All my time in the dojo.

—Nice. Well, the Poob – very impressed with you, re Gale's manuscript.

—You showed it to him?

—Rina did. When Gale's drawings came. And the Poob suggests we start a new imprint, specializing in books that show us boomers – we're at that age now – how to die.

—Since when has anyone needed help? Rud pointed out.

—Our books'll change that, Troy laughed. He sauntered down the path, his cigarette between his fingers. With a tasseled loafer he kicked up a furl of snow.

—It's like baby's breath, snow is, he said, that you can hold in your hand.

—And since when have you waxed fucking poetic? Rud asked, following.

Troy threaded himself between the BMW and Bernard-sensei's International.

—Anyway, Troy said, Rud's days of lugging a bookbag are finito. I suggested you to run the imprint.

—Me?

—There's only the two of us goddamn standing here.

They'd reached the brow of the hill. The night sky was interrupted with clouds and far away the valley, faintly glowing, tusked up to meet it. A freight train rumbled even farther west.

—Mustard Seed Books, Troy said.

—The imprint name?

—The Poob's brain wave – out of New York. Long Island actually. An office next to mine. Your own cellular. As for work authorization, though you're a fucking limey

—No, Rud said.

—You're not anymore?

—No to the job. I don't want it.

—Of course you don't – *now,* Troy said, biting a cigarette out of his pack and lighting it with the first. He exhaled. As I was saying, authorization's no sweat cause we can get it through your stepmother.

—Etta?

—Yes and

—Your letter, Rud said suddenly.

—What?

—Your letter said she'd joined the *atrics.* Geri?

—And Geraldine, Troy said grinning.

—Where?

—Palm Beach? Or Springs maybe. Hell, what's the diff?

—Three thousand miles.

—Well – my old man'll know. Anyway –

—Wait a second – did she sell the house? Move on her own? What?

—Who'm I – Nostradamus?

Rud turned away. Across the valley the freight train bawled, its light spidering through the trees like some coal miner escaping the aftermath of a cave-in.

—Rud.

He didn't answer.

—Rud!

—What?

—Don't start TM-ing. We're talking shop here.

—I'm not fucking TM-ing. I'm thinking.

Troy rested a hand on Rud's shoulder.

—That, stepbro, is your problem. Here and now, right?

—Troy, Rud said, looking directly at him.

–What?

–D'you ever get the what-ifs?

–Never.

Rud faced again the dark maw of the valley.

–You'll come around – on this job thing, Troy said.

–I mean, what if, all those years ago, I hadn't been minding the gate, at the hockey game, and your mom

–Forget it, Rud.

–No. I'm serious. You want me to consider the job. Well, consider this.

–Na da – no dice.

–Or at least if I'd been paying attention.

–No, Troy said. He dropped his cigarette butt and it seared a tiny caldera in the snow. It would not have made any difference, Rud.

–You don't know that.

–Shit! You know, it's awful fucking cold all of a sudden.

–But you don't know that.

–Yes, Troy said. He took a breath. Face it, Rud – she was a cunt – a walking cunt.

–Just a minute.

–A whore. Open all the gates you want, Troy snarled, but a whore

–Shut up! Rud shouted.

–Is a fucking whore.

Rud went to stiffarm Troy on the shoulder but Troy was fast even though his feet slid and he deked.

–Don't bother, Troy said.

–Fuck you, you prick!

–Aw, the biddy boy's offended. Well I'm goin in.

Troy turned and Rud shoved at him again.

–That is fucking it! Troy boomed.

They heard the front door open and when Rud turned, Troy – with a roundhouse – kicked him full force in the back of the knees. The blow

numbed him and he crumpled, reaching, grasping at the snowy
ground, and landed in a half roll.

–Rud! a voice called. Troy! yelled another.

–You wanted this shit, Troy said, you've got it.

Rud dove then. As he did so he could see Amaranta start down the
path toward them, saw Gale and Bernard-sensei try vainly to stop her
but she shook their graspings away as he crashed into Troy. It was like
hitting a bridge pylon. Amaranta squeezed between the vehicles and
Troy grabbed Rud's shoulder, wrenching at its socket as if shredding
his shirt.

–Troy! Amaranta called, running, her hair kiting.

Troy's fingers were spikes in Rud's flesh – it was the same side he'd
gashed that night at Amaranta's – and his boots dug for footing and
with one arm he embraced Troy's legs and, hammering Troy's fingers
free from his shoulder, he yanked.

Troy fell into the ground like a monument in an uprising. He might
even have bounced but Rud himself was shoved over. By Amaranta.

–Leave him alone, she told Rud.

–Shit! Troy cursed.

–Me? Rud snapped. He was sitting in the snow. His legs, still aching,
splayed out. Ask him. What he said.

–I don't care, Amaranta said.

–About Etta – you don't know

–Yes, she said cutting him off. Yes, I know.

–Don't feel sorry for me, Troy said.

–How could I not? Amaranta asked Rud.

–Either of you, Troy said. He rolled onto his side. Sat up. Gale and
Bernard-sensei had ventured as far as the edge of the lawn.

–You okay? Gale called. Amaranta?

–Troy, Amaranta began.

–Come on, you two, Bernard-sensei called. It's just the wine.

–Can we go? Amaranta demanded.

–She was a whore, Troy said to Rud.

–Troy, Amaranta repeated. Please?

–Sure. And that's why I own you, Rud.

–You don't own shit.

–A fucking

–Troy! Amaranta cried.

He looked at her. Then said to Rud:

–And you, Rud – the gate minder – feel all fucking guilty about it.

–Go fuck yourself.

–Stop it, Amaranta said.

–Whoo-hoo, Troy laughed at Rud.

–Both of you. You're childish – no better than my brothers.

–Why you can't turn me down, stepbro. Cause we're fucking joined – at the fucking hip.

Troy struggled to one knee and examined himself.

–Shit, he complained. I'm a mess. My suit. He winced. My ribs. He examined the back of his hands. Pointed a finger at Rud. It's a tad worse for you though, right?

–Troy, Amaranta said angrily. Enough

He waved her away.

–Is enough!

–Think about it, stepbro.

He stood, though still crouched over. Rud struggled to his knees.

–About what?

–You know damned well. He turned to Amaranta. You did – ?

She was striding toward the BMW.

–Wait a second, Troy said to her.

–Amaranta, Rud called.

–First you hurt the roshi, she said over her shoulder.

–No, Gale pleaded. Wait.

She stormed between Gale and Bernard-sensei. Tore open the driver's door.

—Then each other, she said. She got in. Who's next? she cried. Who? She slammed shut the door.

—Troy? Gale appealed.

—Don't worry, Troy said, I've got the keys.

The BMW door flew open. Out she lurched and half ran up the path. Tsuruoka now stood in the doorway and he made way and she plunged inside. Amaranta was back out in a minute. She had Troy's Aquascutum and, rifling its pockets and finding the keys, around the front fender of the BMW she came.

—In case you two stay the night out here, she said and, lariating the coat above her head, she flung it Rud and Troy's way. It soared through the air like a cast-off skin. Turning, she scissored her legs into the car. The tires seemed to roll even before the engine juiced and fired. The headlights shot on like burst hydrants spraying white diamonds and Amaranta was off.

—You can feel sorry for me now, Troy said, turning to Rud. He took the few steps to where his coat was corpsed atop the snow. Snatched it up with one hand. Chaffing the snow off it, he stood beside Rud. They watched as the car lights swept back and forth down the mountain, receding. Neither spoke.

—We were going to leave too, Gale called out.

She and Bernard stood by his International.

—Wait up, Troy responded. He turned to Rud and made the thumbs-up sign. Hey, he said, we finally came to blows. We did all right, huh?

—We were juvenile.

—Yeah, he said grinning. See ya at the office.

—Bee-eff and ee, Rud called.

—Lemme guess.

—Between forever and eternity, Rud said.

Troy laughed.

—I like this Zen stuff, he said to Bernard and Gale. Who's in first?

—Rud, Bernard-sensei said. You're welcome to follow.

—Coos Bay, Gale said.

—Thanks, Rud told them. But I've mortar to mix. By your water-first method.

—Not mine. I just followed the directions on the back of the sack. Well, perhaps we'll see you when you're done?

—Yes, Gale said. It's Sangaiji.

—Another different school.

—Yet the same, she said. More of us lucky ones.

Quiet for a moment, she looked down at the ground. At the tramped and punctured snow. She lifted her eyes, looking past Rud to the crest of the hill where the snow, undisturbed, lay settled on the grass in pleats — opening into the dark like some immaculate fan.

—Kisa? Bernard-sensei said.

She looked back at Rud and turned to the ranch house. In the doorway stood Tsuruoka, his shoulder resting against the jamb, one hand in his pocket, the other hand holding a wine bottle. Gale bowed. Bernard-sensei bowed.

—Roshi? Gale began.

—Tsuruoka, he corrected. He bowed at the waist, deeply and solemnly. Straightened. Masao Tsuruoka, he said.

◇

Two nights later Rud left Whitefish. The snow at the mansion had retreated up the hillside, leaving dribbles on the black rutted earth, and for those two days Rud cut with the bricksaw the bricks for the final courses. The saw clanged when it started up and he would pull by its handle the whirring blade down atop each brick. The deafening sound the blade made as its teeth ate through the brick was like some demented gunnery squad machinegunning a giant gong. The afternoon Tsuruoka laid the final brick the boss arrived. The BMW came sifting down the gravel drive to the hilltop and she descended the hill sideways on the toes of her high heels.

–Victoria, Tsuruoka said, bowing.

The woman from Peak Physique. She wore a navy skirt and collarless jacket, her hair gray but luxuriant, and her calves flexed as she walked a zigzag across the length of the red-bricked patio and at the far end turned to them.

–Beautiful, she said. Like walking on water.

When she left, Rud backed the truck down between the mansion and carriage house and they twisted the mixer off its cinderblocks in pegleg steps and hitched its tongue to the truck.

–I have a date, Tsuruoka told him with a grin.

At the crossroads two hours later Tsuruoka, spruced and relaxed, swung himself out by the curb of the Sinclair station into the crisp night. Rud had lent him his white-and-violet-striped shirt and a pair of jeans. He'd had to roll the cuffs up twice.

–You look good, Rud told him.

–A Kyoto cowboy.

–You okay to get back home?

–I was not planning to. But you are.

–Eventually.

–Well, my friend, Tsuruoka said, bowing. Hate wa. I will miss you, Rudyard-san. Your father too.

So he drifted west. Delaying at the Washington coast. South to Coos Bay? Early on a night when the Pacific sky fell in stage curtains of gray, he stood on the patio outside his Long Beach hotel room. Remembering the night after the ballgame back in April. It *is* mine, he told the dunes and the breaching sea. But when in mid December he'd recrossed the continent to Great Neck, New York, Amaranta was gone.

–Did she pull this shit with you? Troy asked as he showed Rud his office.

Rud thought for a moment.

—When I deserved it, he said.

—Which was all the time, right?

—We had our moments. Once, we even took a bath in a teacup.

—I can see why it was only once, Troy said. He pointed to Rud's desk piled with manuscripts. Anyway, good thing you like to read.

Rud looked out his office window. Northern Boulevard traffic poured by. Beyond that was a hanging garden of bridges past which Manhattan strained against the sky.

Came a knock at the open door.

—Troy?

An elegant young woman smiled at them. A print dress under an open navy blazer. Her blond hair drawn back.

—You remember Nash, don't you? Troy asked.

—Congratulations, she said to Rud.

—I've got her down here for a year, Troy said. As management consultant.

When Nash and Troy left, Rud poked through his mail. A soft lumpy parcel postmarked Whitefish 59937. His jeans and shirt. And a check for $1,560.52. *Your pay,* the note read, *less the pair of Wells Lamonts. Gale has left Bernard-sensei's. Any idea where she has gone, my friend?*

The woman copyediting Gale's manuscript was anxious to know too and Rud tore off from the parcelwrap Tsuruoka's return address and with a thumbtack ribboned it and the check to the wall by his desk. By January, editorial had acquired an address. *It's only a forwarding one, my friend,* Rud explained in his note to Tsuruoka. *M Michel's. She could be anywhere.* February, near his father's birthday, he received a pink envelope postmarked (5000) Córdoba. It was from Argentina and the little face on the card inside was brown as a sherpa's and blue-eyed as her mother. IT'S A GIRL, Rud announced in the Births columns of newspapers in New York and Toronto and London and at lunch hour a couple of days later clipped the notices from those papers and mailed the tiny bundle — first untacking from the wall and endorsing Tsuruoka's check – mailed it all to Amaranta's return address. And a replicate bundle to Etta, who was in neither Palm Beach nor Palm Springs but in De Bary, Florida, just north of Orlando.

Summer he put his property in Toronto on the market. It took a year to sell. By then his Mustard Seed imprint had, in addition to publishing Gale's suicide anthology, issued a selection from Montaigne. They titled it *To Learn How to Die*. It knew.

–Perhaps if we'd issued them as *little* books, Geoffrey Peale mused over the telephone one morning from London.

–Little stand-ups by bookstore cash registers?

–Yes, and have that remarkable woman illustrate them.

–Line drawings of Horace and Cicero?

–Right, point taken.

–Anyway, Rud told him, she's vanished again.

–You are not scheduling another search, are you?

–No, Mr Peale.

–Good, in a way. And, as always, it's Geoffrey.

Another year, other books. A reissue – reset so that all the *fuicides* became *suicides* – of John Donne's *Biathanatos* that Troy dubbed *John's Done*.

–Done it to us, Rud said, reading from it: *Homer is said to have hanged himselfe because he understood not the Fishermen's riddle.*

–Which is? Finally?

–Doesn't say, Rud told him.

–Fucking A! Troy exclaimed.

–Lice, Nash told them.

–Lice? they echoed in unison.

–I was a Rhodes Scholar. *What we caught we left behind, what we caught not we bear with us.* Lice.

–And he hanged himself?

–With an e, Nash quipped.

–Maybe the fems are right, Troy observed.

That December, Etta's letter said: *Dizzy from Christmas and this damned flu that I've had to miss my contra dancing. I'm writing to every-one. What is my granddaughter's address?* And Rud left the letter paper-weighted on his desk – hoping that Troy, the notorious reader of other people's mail, might read it – but when Troy did poke his head into Rud's office it was to say:

–Just heard from the Phoobulah. Incredible news.

–He's changing his name back to Geoffrey Peale?

–Retiring, Troy said. And – and this'll pull the fucking berber right from under those Brits – he's having the retirement party, a surprise one, from me.

And for the next weeks Troy paced the office floors with his hands thrust and jingling in his pockets. For the party he rented a Sag Har-bor yacht.

–Here's the kicker, Troy told Rud. It's in dry dock.

But on the party's eve Rud, returning from lunch, had a message from Troy's father: ETTA RUSH-SCHEDULED FOR BRAIN SURGERY.

He flew Delta out of Kennedy that night, trying to make the only last-minute connection available to Orlando. The flight left late and in Cincinnati the plane circled the airport while crews scraped ice and snow from the runways. Rud had an aisle seat and the captain put the plane down hard as a rollercoaster. Rud tucked his breath in his belly (–Not your stomach! Your belly) and folded his hands in his lap as, bounding along the blind black earth, the fuselage roared. But his flight out was cancelled anyway and in his Holiday Inn room later he phoned Central Florida Hospital.

–I have two contact numbers, sir, the duty nurse told him.

–Contact numbers?

–The surgeon's and a Professor Coltrane. She died, I'm afraid. Are you family?

–Her son.

He arrived late the next afternoon. The professor was staying at the

Deltona and in its parking lot wavered bethels of palm trees and in the brilliant sky clouds sat like white thrones. Rud's check-in message told him Professor Coltrane was out: *seeing to things.*

–The funeral, he told Rud that evening. It's going to be up in Amherst.

They'd had a quiet dinner in the hotel. And now they were anticipating a nightcap. Professor Coltrane looked a little like Bernard-sensei, only sadder and with white bulrush eyebrows.

–I ended up back at UB, he told Rud. He swung his legs out from under the table and crossed one over his other knee. The waitress came. Don't laugh, he appealed to Rud and ordered: Dry toast, warm milk, please.

–Did they remember you? Rud asked. He ordered sherry.

–There were none left, the professor said. First they thought it was the flu – Etta's, I mean. Then some sort of inner ear thing.

–Her dizziness?

–When she stepped backward, the professor said. During her dancing.

Their drinks arrived. They sipped them, then sat quietly.

–I was wondering, Professor Coltrane said after a bit, if you'd write the obituary?

The service was at Saints Peter and Paul. The Falls were a glacier fjord and the wide January sky was as blue as the frozen earth of Etta's newly dug grave. And as cold. When the procession reached Wehrle Road a firetruck hammered by, its siren pure and ringing. The hearses started up again and when they curbed between the cemetery gates Rud thought he saw Troy. But no. Caroline was there with her children dressed darkly, their ears reddening. Professor Coltrane, dressed in a heavy brown overcoat, stood like a tree from another forest. Though Rud and Caroline had hugged at the church, as they climbed the gentle rise where the wreaths stood black-green and sashed like ambassadors, they hugged again.

–Here, she said, sliding inside Rud's overcoat something flat and stiffedged: the postcard of the sea.

–Merci, Rud said.

After the Lord's Prayer Caroline's oldest boy, about ten, released his raw handful of cold and sacred dirt in tiny increments as if – the not-so-simple might assume – delaying the inevitable, though Rud now knew the lad was merely listening to its unique and peculiar rain.

epilogue

The tiniest insights spawn the greatest fools. Rud was no fool but still daft enough to believe there remained only one thing to do. And thus two months later, after resigning (–No hard feelings: I knew once the Poob was gone, the Rood wouldn't be long after) and writing to Bev in England, he was taxiing in from Heathrow through London's bazaar and zebra-crossing streets to the Cumberland Hotel. Though the sun streamed and rioted off the wrong-sided windows of the buses he wore the new raincoat he'd bought. And he had the urn.

–Is that him? Bev asked as they sat in the Duke's Bar.

–It better be, Rud said.

Bev looked so much like their father. Her dark hair that she kept short. They way she drank from her wine glass of brandy and ginger ale without her upper lip touching the glass rim. She told Rud how easy it all had been to arrange.

–It's a Royal Navy lifeboat, she told him, down beyond Southampton on the Solent. The skipper said he'd done this kind of thing quite often in the past. But it'll have to be at six o'clock I'm afraid, evening the next.

–And you're firm about not coming? he asked.

She nodded. She ordered them fresh drinks.

–You know, Rud began, we've had barely a greeting-card relationship, you and I.

–We've shared the important things, she noted.

He took a moment.

–Well – not quite, he said. You see, the letter I sent you, back when Dad died.

–The telegram?

–The reason it wasn't a letter, he said, was, frankly, that he

–Committed suicide, she said.

–You know?

She nodded.

–How?

–*She* wrote me.

–Etta, Rud said soundlessly.

–At Christmas of all bloody awful things.

–Perhaps she'd had presentiments, Rud tried to explain.

Bev just shook her head. Rud waited a moment.

–Did she tell you how he died? Rud asked.

–Did she ever, Bev countered, in all her years, tell you how our mother died?

He shook his head no and shrugged: Not really. And Bev told him. And when she was done she stood. He stood.

–I've a constituency meeting, she explained.

–Did anyone write an obituary, for her? he asked.

–Why wouldn't they have?

–Of course.

–One last thing, she said. When you scatter his ashes, please *don't* say goodbye from me.

He nodded. She held out her hand.

–Should we embrace? he asked and, thank heavens, she smiled.

The manner of his mother's death marauded his dreams and in the

morning he picked up the telephone in his suite to cancel his car. But
Etta had wanted this too and so, noonish, he drove south in his rented
Renault, passing patiently through the roundabout villages and towns
of Surrey and Sussex and Hants, swinging south at New Forest down the
western bank of the Solent to the overcast sea. A Phillips screwdriver
point up in the lapel pocket of his Harris tweed. The Navy lifeboat post
was amongst a concrete and prefab tundra but he parked and, carrying
the urn, walked by the hangars and a helicopter sitting on its pad like a
locust to the only prefab whose windows were steamed. It was warm inside and at one end were a desk and filing cabinets and at the other
bright orange slickers were hitched on wallpegs and hooded with pea
jackets. Two young sailors holding table-tennis paddles came out from
a rec room opposite the front doors where Rud still waited uncertainly.
When he told them he was here to see Captain Mills they shouted
Skipper!

He couldn't imagine where the boat was until, leaving the prefab and
marching across the concrete to its edge, they came to a wooden pier
moss-thickened by years of tides. A ladder was tentacled to the pier's
edge and Rud and the skipper and the two sailors rundled down and
boarded a lifeboat long as an ark. Three more crew members waited and
the diesel glottaled and with the day's light beginning to fade they
started out. The sea was a small hill and though flat it thumped the sides
of the boat like wet mortar. It was that color too. When the captain cut
the engines and said a short and common prayer he and his men left
Rud alone. Rud had already unscrewed the urn's base and he lifted with
care the sealed plastic bag containing the white particulate. Containing
all that remained. Our outcome. Ha-te wa. He could make out bone-
shapes the way on clear nights he could see dark faces in the white
moon. He slit open the bag and the first motes of ash floated down and
splashed the gray-green water unlike any rain he'd ever heard.

  —Like seeds, he said. Like seeds, he repeated to himself hours later in
the bathroom of his small suite in the Cumberland as he wrote with
fountain pen on hotel stationery:

Dear Mr Mazeroski,

Is there medicine for the dead? Wait, don't rip up the letter at least just yet. I'm here in the Cumberland Hotel in London as you probably figured out what with the letterhead and all sitting here in the bathroom of my suite sitting on the floor yes the floor with my back braced against the tub. I'm using my deceased father's cinerary urn, his bone urn, for something to press on. His ashes are still inside.

Still inside. We used to eat our dead and I'm certain in some parts of the world people still do. Even in the third world perhaps. I was to scatter his ashes on the sea near where he was stationed during the war but when the first white bits landed on the water floating with that almost out-of-breath motion a calm sea has. Arr, have you ever been to sea, Billy? No disrespect intended, Mr Mazeroski. When we emigrated to the States from England my mother and my sister Bev and I (my name is Rudyard Stirling Gillette) took the *Homeric.* My father flew ahead. When he landed at Idlewild – this was '57 or '58 – he found a bar. The bartender was listening to a broadcast of a hockey game, the Rangers and the Canadiens. The announcer's voice rushing in Dad's ears like the players themselves hooked him and though he couldn't skate he became a peewee hockey coach in Amherst where he cleaned toilets at UB dorms and took me to the games I couldn't skate I hated it but I was stick boy and minded the gate and at one game I was goofing off no that's a lie I was staring at a woman as her sweater erupted when she inhaled a cigarette and my father and she I know at that exact moment fell in love for what should have been forever.

It killed my mother. I stopped going to the games because that woman who was the mother of my father's best player was always there and always beside my father but one December night, it was a real wicked Niagara night, I somehow knew I don't know maybe a voice or something told me but I somehow knew that if I didn't go to the game this night my dad wouldn't come home he wouldn't but when I asked my dad said no and that started a row (rhymes with how) between my dad and mum.

It killed her. She knew. She slapped him and he threatened her and she sobbed and dressed my sister and me and out we went into a storm of fucking polar dimensions to struggle across Amherst town to a friend's.

Why is he telling me this, you are asking, right? Okay, I'll make it short. She died, I now know how and my dad and the woman married (jesus how I wish she was rotten and mean but she wasn't my stepmother wasn't) and the years shot past and my father had the latest in a string of industrial accidents if you can call a drunken accident at a brewery industrial and a letter came from workmen's comp that he was convinced was cutting off his entitlements and on a wretchedly hot August Monday almost seven years ago he bought a carving knife from Pascuale Bros hardware and dressed only in trousers stabbed himself six times. I found him. I was looking for him. I'd just made love or been fucking or whatever you want to call it and for the longest time I thought there was I getting my ashes hauled by this indescribable woman who I still still love and will forever and. But I was wrong. He'd done it earlier. You see I never until just now read the entire autopsy report. But knowing the when doesn't help me to fathom the why – why he chose that way why that way. Because I found him in the bathtub. He wasn't in his bedroom and the only room left was the bathroom and I pushed open the door and the shower curtain was tied up on the chrome rod (imagine the care it took him!) and the tile walls were bucketed with blood and he was on his side facing away and I said Dad Dad though I couldn't hear anything anything I was nine again and I took another step and his shoulder so white he was facing away from me his shoulder when I touched it

the coldest thing I've ever touched his body rolled as though sur-
facing out of the sea rolling toward me and I saw the red wounds
like red mouths tracking across his belly and chest ending where
the black handle of the carving knife was hilted through his heart.

Is there a God? My father never opened the letter. It was nothing, nothing, just a reminder of a date to meet with one of the
counselors. I moments ago opened it up. I hadn't because it was
addressed to my father and it was lovely all these years having it
unopened just in case he ever came back. Comes back. But there is
no life after death proves Julian Jaynes. As for God? Enlightenment? Satori? No. It gets worse. For not only is God dead ac-
cording to Jaynes, he was never alive. I wonder where my ex-Zen
master is. I went to pour my father's ashes into the sea and I saw.
But all the above is not why I am writing to you.

Mr Mazeroski, we are almost home. Twenty-five hundred years
ago there was a woman called Kisa-gotami (frail Kisa) and her
only child her baby son died and she carried the baby on her hip
and wouldn't let go seeking through the city of Benares medicine
for the dead. She went to see the Buddha and he told her to canvass
from house to house and from each house collect a mustard seed
and from those seeds he would prepare a medicine for her dead
baby but only from seeds she collected from houses where no one
had ever died ever. Where no one had ever died? Of course she
soon realized and walking out of the city cast her baby into the
burning ground.

In the middle of that Niagara night during that storm so long
ago my mother walked out of the warm basement apartment
where my sister and I slept and attempted to walk home. To con-
front my father? To find out if he really was betraying her? To forgive him? What does it matter. They found her collapsed in a park
she'd shortcut through so near to death it only remained at the
hospital to close her eyelids. She tried to make it home and she did

not. I cannot remember her this way. Will not. I demand some-thing else. I received it when the first grains of my father's ash touched and bobbed on the sea.

The October before she died our fifth-grade teacher Mr Wolfe who every day until then had let us listen to the World Series you were playing against the Yankees who I adored but on the day of the seventh and deciding game Wolfey wouldn't let us listen. Yes-terday de game, he said, today da Gama. Very funny. And after school was out I asked some bigger boys who'd won and they only laughed at my English accent teasing, Oo wonz ta naw? So I trudged home and the front door to our walk-up was locked as it always was and I sat on the step as I always did. The sky was cloudy. The neighborhood quiet. I loved to sit there. Waiting for my mum. And that day I can hear her even before I usually do hear her high heels on the sidewalk bone. I know it's her because I can tell by the rhythm the sound she makes. But I don't move. I don't run out to her. I just sit on the cold step and wait until I can see her hair it was reddish and very curly and forties long and it luffs won-derfully as she comes around the green corner of the cedar hedge. She looks like she's been crying but she always looks like that and she smiles and I look between my runners as I always do until she speaks and I ask her who won Mummy did my Yankees win and she says no no son I'm sorry but they had the game on at the bank someone had brought in a portable telly and in the bottom of the last inning this handsome young Pirate hit the ball over the hedgy fence and ran leaping around the bases and when he circled third base she thought of me and wished it wasn't so and perhaps I didn't know and would never know. Sometimes you win and sometimes you lose she comforts me and God doesn't mind he loves you either way right? And I know you loved them but it's okay to be sad in your heart because that's what love is, right? she asks again. And that's what keeps us alive, right? Right?

What keeps us alive.

Dear Mr Mazeroski, there *is* a mustard seed and it's the turn you took touching third base jumping with the crowd bursting out to mob you the turn we all take for home but my mother never got to or my father. The only turn we take. So tomorrow I will taxi across the world of this city to Saint Mary's Cathedral where my mother's grave awaits me and I will cover it with my father's ash and when it rains they'll

Rud sat back against the tub. He was done. Standing and unpacking his spine, he folded the letter, fearing if he reread it he would shred it and flush it down the white oval roar of the toilet. He rubbed life back into his face with a bathtowel. It was soft and warm. The towel bars were heated. Ah, for a cup of tea. He'd make one. But first: he took an envelope from the stationery packet and addressed it and tucked the letter in. He licked the envelope closed and went down to the lobby and asked the clerk, who wore a rose pinned to his lapel under his nameplate, if he had postage stamps and then asked how much first-class postage was to Córdoba, Argentina.

—I haven't the faintest, the clerk answered.